Beat

Keith R. Rees

Published in the USA
Amazon Kindle Direct Publishing
P.O. Box 81226
Seattle, WA 98108-1226
http://www.kdp.amazon.com

Printed in the USA

Edited by Keith R. Rees and Sherrie Keenan
Cover Design by Keith R. Rees
Cover Image (with permission)
Ravens by Jacob Mejicanos, Unsplash.com
Back cover logo courtesy of Keith R. Rees Books
Inside photo of Casper Rees courtesy of Richard and Claudia Rees
Ravens image courtesy of Christopher Rees, Reesnet.com

13-digit ISBN: 9798666806876

All names, characters, places and incidents are fictitious or used fictitiously. However, this is a historical fiction piece of work and the names of some historical figures have been used, but purely in a fictitious context. Any resemblance to actual persons, living or dead, and places or events is purely coincidental.

First Edition: January 2021

Other Titles by Keith R. Rees

Legend at Lanana Creek (KDP 2020)
Specter in the Glass (KDP 2019)
One Night in Bangkok (Savant 2018)
The Lunas (Lulu 2016)
The Hana Sun Does Shine (Lulu 2012)
Take the Water to the Mountain (Lulu 2012)
Shaking the Tree (Lulu 2009)
The Brazilian (Lulu 2008)
Legend upon the Cane (Lulu 2008)
Quill and Ink (KDP 2007)

For the entire Rees Family

Prologue

Saints are among us. Everywhere we go there is a possibility that someone we know or just a stranger passing by could be a saint in the making. In this day, it's hard to fathom such an idea. When people think of the saints, they think of the ancient world where the holiest of the holy walked among the people doing Godly things, living Godly lives every day. People read about them in the Holy Bible or some other historical context or see churches throughout the world bearing their names. It seems beyond belief that a saint could be living amongst us in modern times.

We do have them around us though, helping us in ways we cannot imagine. A few modern examples include Saint John Paul II, or Saint Teresa of Calcutta, or Saint Damian of Molokai, just to name a few, but all who are from very recent history.

We place these wonderful people upon metaphoric pedestals, viewing them in the highest regard for the extraordinary deeds attributed to them. It begs to wonder if the people who had the privilege of knowing them and working with them, who at the time were just ordinary men and women like they were, really knew how special and divine that person was. That that person was pre-ordained by God to live the life they would. That one day that saintly, or *beatific*, person would be named by a Pope to be one of God's select few in history.

This is the basic purpose for these stories. To show that throughout history, there were ordinary people among us doing extraordinary things and guiding us in ways we couldn't comprehend. Yet by the divinity of God's grace, our lives were made more abundant in peace, joy and love by these strangers in our midst. They could have been people that ascended to lofty positions of importance like a king or queen, or a bishop. Or the meekest among us such as a clergyman or a nun, or a mere peasant or slave, but touching our lives in the simplest, yet most powerful ways.

Although the list of saints from history appears to be lengthy, yet wonderous, it is still important to remember that they are in rare company in the Heavens. It is akin to a small ring of planets amongst a sea of stars. Choosing among them to tell these stories wasn't an easy task, but perhaps it was a gentle nudge from God that helped in deciding which saints to include here.

Among these stories will be people who are well known and some who may seem obscure, but the gravity of their wonderful lives are equal in every way. It is from these beatific people throughout history that these stories were conceived. Each chapter follows the story of one family, or clan, across many centuries and countless generations that were part of an ancient culture that stretched far and wide.

In the centuries that preceded the Resurrection of Our Lord Jesus Christ, there dwelled a culture of innovative and devoted peoples of mystery and grace. Their influences ranged from present-day Europe with roots that spread as far as Asia Minor, or the Anatolian peninsula. From Eastern Europe, they spread westward by way of trans-cultural diffusion, or migration, to areas of France, the Low Countries (Belgium and the Netherlands), the Iberian Peninsula (Spain), Bohemia (Czech Republic), Germany, Austria, and Poland. These areas were considered the homeland of this vibrant and distinct culture. However, the influence and range of this culture did not stop with mainland Europe. The most prevalent and modern presence of these peoples resides on the islands of Ireland and Britain, which include Wales, the Scottish Highlands and the Isle of Man. From a mixture of Gaels, Celtiberians, Lusitanians and Galatians, came the more commonly known culture of the *Celtici*, or Celtics.

From this Celtic culture came many close-knit clans that migrated very much like we do today. The movement of these peoples was due to their own free will or for reasons beyond their control. Some were forced to flee war or famine or even to escape bondage from slavery. Throughout the centuries, the clans were faced with many hardships or reasons to migrate from one place to another, thus taking their Celtic heritage with them and leaving their influences wherever they roamed.

One such clan from this remarkable culture found its roots in the Irish and Welsh regions in the early centuries after Christ. Their surname was *Ris*, or *Rhys*, meaning *ardour* or *fiery warrior*. Other variations recorded over time were *Rice*, *Ryce*, or *Reasce*. The modern annotation as it is today is simply, *Rees*.

This is my family's story. Albeit fictional, it is told as seen from the eyes of a curious, yet eager storyteller. The story unfolds with a handful of historic figures from different time periods intricately woven into each passage. These known historical saints date from the early fifth century to the mid nineteenth century.

Part of the research done for this collection of short stories was done with the aid of my father, Richard L. Rees', own diligent genealogical research. In my parent's travels and three-year residency in Europe, they were able to uncover the lineage of our family dating as far back as the seventeenth century. A major portion of my father's work was done at the church of Saint Alexius in Herbolzheim, Baden-Württemberg in the southern region of Germany. Therefore, the latter stages of this story will include actual Rees family member names, but in a fictional context, concluding with the first of our family to arrive on the shores of America.

Part I

The Year of Our Lord, 420

In the year our Lord, 420, the Roman rule of Britain had come to a merciless end. With its borders now unprotected, this gave rise to the Irish dynasties of the *Uí Néill* of which Gaelic kings such as *Niall Noígíallach* sprang forth. In the years and decades that followed, raiders from Ireland such as the *Laigin* routinely came across the sea to ransack and pillage the British coasts, plundering towns and capturing unsuspecting Christians and forcing them into slavery.

In the days since Jesus Christ walked the Earth, the Christian Word had spread far and wide, but not without scorn and persecution wherever it took root. Britain and Ireland were no exception to this persecution but no more so than on the Emerald Isle. Christians practiced their religion in Ireland but in secret in fear of the pagans and their long, dastardly reach into ordinary life. Properties and possessions were stolen and snatched away from local villagers if they were unable to pay the requisite taxes imposed by the ruthless kings. It was a time when only the harsh and tyrannical could be the master and those who wanted to live a life of God were made to suffer in bondage and slavery.

As like Moses, whom God lead from the lavish halls of Pharaoh to the mud-pits of Egyptian misery, another man came forth to the shores of Ireland, not as a savior, but as a humbled boy forced into his own life of slavery. Once again, history was repeating itself but in God's own way; that if the Irish were to become a free nation under God, the Irish would first need to be free of themselves…

Pádraig

The odist sat in a flowing field of emerald green, looking oft to the radiant shore. In the distance was the ancient channel of Saint George and the Irish Sea. He watched with a keen eye as the white caps appeared for mere moments and then quickly disappeared in the choppy winds. Standing not far from the old man were ravens, ducking from the winds as they skipped about the grassy hillside.

The old Irishman watched them with a gleam in his eye and a hint of a smile. The wind slapped against his leathery skin and the parchment before him fluttered madly on a rickety easel. He held it steady with one hand and another to his chin as he contemplated what thoughts he would put down for the day.

Beside him on the ground was freshly prepared, blackened mud with which to dip his scribe's tool. He guarded it closely from the wind as he prepared to journal his thoughts. Nothing was coming to mind as he watched the ravens dance to and fro in the lapping breeze. As an idea came to him, he quickly dabbed his writing tool in the black mixture and splayed out the parchment as flat as he could with his other hand. He grinned with satisfaction with each mark he made that brought his inspiration to life. After mere moments, he completed his task, grinning from ear to ear and even chuckling a bit to himself.

"This is the mark of a man," he said to himself. "This is what God wanted me to see today."

A young girl came skipping up the hill and plopped down beside him. "Grandfather," the cheerful young lady began, "are you finished with your writing for today? I am getting hungry."

"I am almost finished," he told his ten-year-old granddaughter. "Here, come sit with me." She inched closer to him and squinted her freckled face at what he had done. "What do you think?"

"But Grandfather," she protested, "you have just drawn pictures of birds; you have not written anything. Are you not going to write today?"

He chuckled at her and answered, "This is my writing today. I did not need words to say what I wanted."

"They are just birds though," she argued once more.

He smiled at his creation broadly and hugged her gently. "Yes. Yes, indeed, little Shea. Are not the birds just lovely?" He pointed

11

out into the tall grass toward the ravens that continued their hopping around in the blustery wind.

"Ravens, Grandfather?" she asked. "Why did you draw them?"

"It just came to me," he replied. "The Lord was retaining his Words from me this day. Nothing would come to my mind until I saw the ravens. He wants me to enjoy his feathered creations and wanted me to record this fine afternoon I am having with them."

Shea wrinkled her nose and answered, "Ravens are just loud and noisy."

"Oh, no," he corrected her. "Ravens are a sign of strength, yet a symbol of solitude. They tended to the prophets and the saints when they needed food. And do not forget what the Psalms say about the prophets who suffered; 'The Lord provides for them when they call.'"

Shea did not know what that meant but one aspect caught her attention. "The ravens brought food to the prophets and saints?" she asked curiously.

"Oh, yes," he continued. "Remember the great Saint Anthony? The raven kept him alive by bringing him bread." She pouted her lips and nodded acceptingly at hearing this. She knew all about the stories her father and grandfather would tell her and her brother, Liam, at bedtime. "That is why God called me to draw today instead of write." He picked up his writing tool and dipped it in what was left of the darkened mud. There was just a small bit left that had not dried in the wind. "I will write one thing to finish this creation."

On the parchment, Shea observed the distinct figures of three perfectly drawn ravens; two in the top corners and one centered below. In between the ravens at the top, he carefully wrote in delicate script, *RHYS.*

"Can you read what it says?" he asked with a smile.

"That is our name!" she answered excitedly.

"That is right," he replied as he pulled her onto his lap, hugging her little neck. "Strength under the watchful eyes of God's divinity."

"But there are only three, Grandfather. We are more than three in our family."

"Yes, that is true," he said. "But the three ravens do not represent how many we are, but the Holy Trinity. God the Father, the Son, and the Holy Ghost."

"Is the Holy Ghost scary?" she asked looking up at him.

He laughed out loud and answered, "Of course not."

Just then, a man came running up the hill and announced nearly out of breath, "Shea, come along. Father, you had better hurry. Moriarty is coming and it looks like trouble."

Shea immediately scrambled to her feet and nodded to her father obediently. She helped her grandfather to his feet, stumbling as he did. He quickly pulled the parchment from the easel and folded it neatly. "Here, child. Keep this for me and I will go see what the old boy wants." She tucked the parchment away inside her cloak.

"Are you coming?" the son called to his father once more.

"Yes, yes," he answered.

The 'old boy' was not his son, but the notorious Aldus Moriarty. He had only recently become notorious, however. He had at one time been just a local farmer like everyone else, but he was known for his cunningness and a penchant for brutality when it served his purpose. The king saw this and chose him as a trustworthy disciple to carry out his evil deeds. Moriarty was named overseer of the land south and east of the River Shannon. Lands that had been owned by families for generations were now being claimed in the name of the king if large sums of taxes were not collected. Moriarty was the enforcer and was given total authority over the region and was also given the power to obtain back-taxes by any means necessary. With the Romans now gone in Britain, the king and his henchmen, like Moriarty, did just that with little to no opposition.

Shea ran ahead to their home down the gradual slope. Smoke was rising from the stack on top of the stone cottage as she knew her mother was cooking the evening meal. She met her father at the door who was anxiously waiting for his own father to arrive, hopefully before Moriarty.

Finally, the grandfather came limping toward the cottage and acknowledged his son's anxiety. "What is the alarm today?" he asked, as if he didn't know.

"What do you think?" his son answered with obvious chagrin.

"Money, is it? We will talk with him, Seamus. You and me together."

A red-haired boy came striding up next to his father and announced, "I want to listen too."

"No, Liam. Mind your mother and older sister," Seamus told him firmly. "Help her get supper ready. We will talk to the men outside."

Just then, Moriarty came striding up with his staff in one hand, smiling like a jackal. Walking only a few steps behind him was his partner in crime, Finnegan. He was nothing more than a lackey, a yes-man, who would do any and all of Moriarty's dastardly deeds just so he wouldn't come under the same fate as the rest of the clans.

"What is it you want, Moriarty?" Seamus' father asked in a tired voice.

"You know what I am here for, Rhys," Moriarty answered with his slimy tongue. "Your three weeks have come and gone. What say you?"

"The same as before, old boy. The crops are not in yet, but the flocks are bringing in a small price. Nothing more."

"I will not have you call me that, old man. Remember who you are talking to," Moriarty fumed.

"I know who I am talking to and I do not like you coming to our home and pushing us about. You can take your little friend there and be gone with you."

"Now, listen here, Rhys," Moriarty said, raising his voice and shaking his fist at him, "I aim to bring back the king's taxes today and that is what I am going to do. If you will not pay, maybe we will take it from what you have inside." He tried to muscle his way past Seamus and his father to get to the door, but they both stood their ground.

"You are not invited inside, you hear?" Seamus snarled back at him.

"Oh, he has a voice now, does he?" Moriarty fired back, his lips dripping with sarcasm. "Keep your wimpy son out of my way, Rhys. We are coming inside."

"No, you are *not*," Seamus exclaimed, shoving the burly man back. "I do have a voice, and you are going to hear it. You are *not* coming into our home."

Moriarty stared him down and smiled connivingly and said, "Such bravery, Seamus. Full marks to you, but I have news for you, boy. It is *my* home now." He motioned for his lackey to intervene, ordering, "Fin, ask these men to stand aside."

Finnegan approached, abruptly drawing a wide sword and pointed it at their throats. "We *are* coming in. Let us see what we are having for supper, shall we?"

Finnegan and Moriarty barged in at once leaving Seamus and his father outside. A short, stout woman, wearing a scarf about her hair, whirled about from the pot of stew she was standing over. "What is all the fussin' I am hearing?" she asked. Her expression changed little when she realized it wasn't her husband over father-in-law coming inside.

"Hello, Miss Lovely," Moriarty drawled.

She rolled her eyes at his disregard for common decency and said, "Eh, Aldus, what brings you and Fin here this evening?"

"The king brings us here, lovely," he answered suavely.

"I will not have you call me that." Just then Seamus and his father came in behind them. "You will address me proper in my house, thank you."

Moriarty's tone changed abruptly though, and his grin changed to a wrinkled snarl and announced, "I will address you as I please, Clodagh." He sauntered over to where she stood and reached around her waist. She quickly stepped aside to avoid his grasp when suddenly he grabbed the cauldron and gave a swift yank to the floor. "And supper is going to be late."

She watched with her eyes agape and gasped, "Are you daft, man? That was food enough for days." She pressed her hands to her cheeks in dismay, watching the stew run all over the dirt floor. "I had been slavin' on it all afternoon."

"Funny you should use such a word, old woman," Moriarty answered.

"What do you mean?" Seamus said as he stepped closer, his fists clenched. "How dare you ruin the fine meal Clodagh was preparing."

"Like I say, Rhys, this house is mine." He let his words sink to all who were listening in the room. The children looked on quietly, struck in horror. Liam looked bewildered as his supper seeped into the dirt floor, carrots and potatoes covered in dirt and grime. "All of you are to leave immediately."

Seamus shook his fist in Moriarty's face and declared, "No one is forcing my family from here, you understand? You think you and Fin can handle that on your own? You will need an army to make us leave. I will not stand for it."

Moriarty looked at him smartly and smiled fiendishly. "If that is what you say, boyo, you had better take a look outside."

Immediately, Seamus and his wife ran to the front window and peered out into the early night. Clodagh gasped with her hand to her mouth and Seamus' heart sank in his chest. Seamus' father stared at Moriarty with a disgusted look as he passed by to open the front door. Moriarty stood proud as he saw his previously arranged garrison of fifteen men situated in a blockade just outside the cottage. The soldiers stood with swords and torches in perfectly aligned detail. The leader of the troop stood off to the side of the front door, awaiting instructions.

Moriarty sneered at the soldier, "Burn it."

The Rhys family stood helplessly under the drooping branches of the willow trees as they watched their cottage go up in flames. The stone walls crumbled all around the incinerated wooden supports and window arches. The glow of the fire cast a flickering light down the slope and into the barren abyss below. The children watched wide-eyed and shocked and the adults watched in horror and sadness.

Seamus didn't know what to say to them. He didn't know what to think as Moriarty had finally made true on his threats. He didn't think it was possible for someone to be so evil, but it was there right in front of them. Their family home passed down from generation to generation for decades, even more than a century, had gone up in flames in mere seconds. He thought of their lands and their few possessions. *Would it all be lost at the hands of these madmen? How would they eat and where would they sleep?* His mind ached too much to even try and come up with the answers.

Before they knew it, they were being shoved downhill into the darkness. Seamus took extra care to look after his stricken, elderly father as he could see the expression on his face was beyond consternation. As he guided him down the hill amongst the shoves and curses from the soldiers, he gave a reassuring look to Clodagh and made certain she held onto their children's hands.

Soon, they saw the glow of light in windows of old shanty mud homes down below. The ground changed from wet dewy grass to thick, sloshing mud. The shoes and hems of their garments were caked in it in a manner of seconds. The children began to weep as they trekked onward toward the desolate barracks.

"Open up!" one of the soldiers barked from the near darkness. A door flung open at the entrance and instantly they shoved the new captives inside. The door slammed behind the stricken family before they could even turn around. "And keep it quiet in there."

The five of them stood shaking, trying to catch their breaths. The firelight from the soldier's torches began to grow dimmer as they marched away in silence. Soon, it was near darkness inside, and the children wept harder.

"What is this place?" Clodagh cried to herself.

Suddenly a fire was struck several feet from them in the corner of the room and a torch was lit immediately revealing the inhabitants of the desolate place. Little by little, as they scanned around the room, the light revealed children, women and men lying about in various positions. Some were sitting against walls, others were lying still, and some men were even standing in the darkness, having a quiet smoke. The room was easily filled with twenty or more people. Some coughs were heard in the dim light, but no one said a word.

Clodagh, always the one to try and make the best of things, curled her lip and tried to reassure her little ones, and her shocked husband and father-in-law by saying, "It could be worse. We can manage this for now."

Seamus shook his head and fretted, "How could it possibly be worse?"

A man leaning against the wall, puffing on his pipe, spoke up and answered him, "There are at least thirty more through that doorway behind you. That is how much worse."

Seamus slumped his shoulders and he turned to see the shadowy doorway just behind him. The man with the pipe handed him a torch and said, "Look for yourself."

Seamus took the torch and slowly walked just inside the doorway and lifting it to reveal the contents therein. He was even more taken aback by all the eyes of people staring at him. The larger room was filled wall to wall with broken and bruised bodies. People of all ages, faces streaked with mud and cuts all staring at him in desperation. They looked at him for a brief moment with hope in their eyes, but soon that hope vanished into misery once more when they realized he was just another slave like they were.

He stepped back into the room with his weary family and said to them, "It is best if we find room to sit in here. Let the children rest and I will think of something by morning."

Clodagh couldn't help but cry as she tried her best to squeeze in on the muddy ground in which to sit. Immediately Shea and Liam both sat on her lap to keep from sitting in the mud. Tears streaked down their clean, rosy cheeks and Seamus, filled with pity for them, found a place next to his wife. He guided his father to the floor and gave him a simple look, saying, "I am sorry, Father."

His father shook his head and answered, "This too shall pass, my Son."

The darkened gray and white clouds blew in from the sea and the chill of the early morning air was crisp. Showers had come and gone on the rocky, moss-ridden shores and the smell of rain was fresh in the air. Two weather-beaten peasants trampled down the treacherous slopes toward the sea, as ordered by their taskmaster. They stood side-by-side, their heads covered in cloaks, as they waited for the ships to arrive.

Seamus, thick-bearded, sprinkled with amber and gray, stood near his exhausted wife. Her hands were gnarled with years of toil in the fields and kitchens of the local peasantry. Her face was wrinkled and leathery from the ravages of the wind and cold, yet she stood like a rock next to her husband.

They had barely slept a wink the night before in the overcrowded mud-covered shanty, yet they were pushed from their slumber before the crack of dawn to face their new hardship. They had left their two children behind frightened and hungry and knew not how long this captivity would last.

"What do you think we are waiting on?" Clodagh asked wearily.

"I do not know," Seamus answered, "but I get the feeling most of our new friends in the barn are not from around here. I barely recognized a one of them from these parts when I got a glimpse last night. It is clear though, they are rounding up all the clans and sending them here. Those of us who are the lowest in their eyes at least."

"No talking," a gruff voice snarled behind them. A soldier carrying a blade at his side came brushing past and bounded down the rocky shore. Seamus stared at him wild-eyed, shaking his head with ever-more confusion.

Just then, Moriarty himself came striding up behind them as well. "You will be helpin' with the boats as they come in. And I want you to move quickly. No lazin' about! A long walk is ahead of them." He immediately strode off and waited with the other men down the shore.

"Who?" Seamus whispered.

"Shush," Clodagh snitched back at him. It was then they both realized who was coming. With the Romans gone, there was no one left in Britain to oppose the pirate pagans from Ireland. They knew it to be only one answer: more captives.

The sun never crested over the horizon and the sky stayed just as gray as it was when they left in the early light. A rumble was heard far off in the distance.

"Rain is coming," Seamus stated bluntly, as if she hadn't noticed it herself.

"Keep quiet," she scolded again. "The overseer will hear you." He rumpled his lower lip as she motioned toward the open sea and said, "Here, the boats are coming." They both could make out the faces of the British captives who would become Moriarty's newest prize. All of them had the same look of confusion and dismay as Seamus and Clodagh did the night before. They knew right away that more misery was arriving on shore.

"Man the boats!" a soldier shouted. "Move quickly!"

One by one, a half dozen ships came sliding onto the rocks and Seamus and Clodagh joined the other slave men and women sloshing out into the water to haul the boats closer inland.

Clodagh watched in horror as men and boys of all ages, some as young as ten, were thrown over the side and dragged onto the rocks. They were all bound with their hands behind their backs and barely could stand as their feet were bound as well. They coughed up water as they fought to stand in the crashing waves. Seamus immediately let go of his side of the ship and began to help as many to their feet as possible.

"Back away!" a man shouted and walloped Seamus upside his head, throwing him backward into the waves. "They can stand on their own. So, can you."

"Seamus!" Clodagh cried and quickly left her place to come to his aid.

Before she could reach him though, the soldier smacked her with the back of his hand, sending her thumping into the side of the boat. "*Back* away, I say. Or you will be put into those shackles yourselves. Secure these boats now, all of you."

Seamus stumbled to his feet, coughing up seawater. Blood trickled down the side of his head and he stood dazed, locking eyes with his stricken wife. She rubbed the side of her head but motioned to him that she was alright.

"God, help us," Seamus muttered under his breath. "They are all truly madmen."

The new captives marched for hours in their chains and bound hands. The parade of the weary came to rest in the muddy confines just in front of Moriarty's quarters. His was a fine house of wood and stone that he saved just for himself after one of their many raids. No one dared to set foot inside or even on the porch, lest they be beaten away or worse. Finnegan was never far away from his guard-post in front of Moriarty's lair. Like a faithful dog to his master, he was always nearby.

Finnegan smiled with a toothless grin as the captain of the ships lined up his prisoners, awaiting his sales to the taskmaster. Moriarty marched up down the line with Finnegan lagging not far behind at his heels. He stopped at one man, no more than thirty years of age and burly as an ox, staring down Moriarty with contempt.

"How much for this one?" Moriarty asked.

"He is a feisty one," the captain answered. "Gave a lot of trouble the entire way. Five gold pieces."

"Ha! He must be a feisty one for that steep a price." Moriarty looked him over thoroughly. The grisly man became more and more agitated as each second passed. "Strong arms. Stout legs." He bent down to examine the captive's feet when suddenly the man spat on the ground near Moriarty's face. Enraged, Moriarty socked him right in the jaw. "Try that again, slave, and you will get worse than that the next time. Four gold pieces. No more than that."

"But you cannot damage the merchandise before I even agree," the captain complained. "What you do with them after you pay is your business, but not before."

"Are you saying I am being unfair?" Moriarty fired back. "Hold your tongue, or I will lower my offer even more."

"Four gold pieces then. Done." The captain motioned for his aid to unshackle the large man.

"Put him with the pigs," Moriarty ordered. "If he gives you any more trouble, see to it that he learns. And learn him well." They continued their shameless folly until all the slaves were sold and the captain and his men made their way back to the ships.

Clodagh and Seamus eventually found their children and their grandfather. They all had been gathering vegetables in fields that were once worked and owned by them.

"Have you eaten anything, children?" she asked them.

Liam, putting the bravest face he could muster, answered, "Yes, Mother. Do not worry. We boiled some cabbage at noon and Grandfather ate as well. I hid some away for you and Father, so I hope it is still there in our new home."

"That is a good lad," Seamus said, patting him on the head. "It is not our home, though, I promise you. My heart will not be at rest until we have our home again." He looked over at his father concerned and could tell he was exhausted after being forced to toil in the fields doing manual labor for the first time in years.

"It is alright, boy," he assured him. "The work is good exercise for an old man like me. The mud floor will be a welcome sight tonight."

"Curse the mud floor and these bloody savages," Seamus swore in anger.

His father shook his head though and corrected him, saying, "That is not the attitude a Christian should have, Son. The Good Lord says to love your enemies and to show mercy and forgive." Seamus began to turn away as he was too angry to even respond. His father grabbed him though and said, "I do have some good news. I found an old friend of ours."

It was Mr. O'Day, who came striding up happily next to them out in the field. He was a tall, thin man who was well past middle age with wispy, red hair that sparsely covered his balding head.

"Hello, old chaps," he said cheerfully. "Fancy seeing you again, Mrs. Clodagh." She smiled at him gratefully. He was a sight for sore eyes to all of them. "I would keep the Christian talk down if I were you, though. If there is one thing that enrages them most, it is the comforting words of the Good Book."

Clodagh was curious and asked, "You mean hide our faith? As if we had just run away from the crucifixion?"

"Aye, I do. That is a bit extreme, but since you put it that way, yes." He leaned in closer to them and whispered, "How do you think I am still alive?"

"You mean they do not know," Seamus whispered back, "that you are a man of the cloth?" Mr. O'Day nodded affirmatively. "Geez, man. I thought everyone in the countryside knew that." Then it struck him on the other point Mr. O'Day made. "They would actually murder us if we are found to be Christian? The king would want this?"

Mr. O'Day shook his head as he looked over his shoulder to make sure no one was watching them. "Who can tell what the king really wants. But I have seen it in the eyes of Moriarty and his devilish son. They are putting it into the minds of their soldiers too. The pagans despise us and being poor is not the only reason we are here." Then he paused for a moment to let his words sink into his weary friends. "It will not stop me from being a priest, though. We will carry on in secret if we must. We will even read the Gospel when we can, and God willing, celebrate a Mass or two."

Grandfather smiled and tapped him on the shoulder appreciatively and said, "A good man, you are." He began to lead his family back toward the shanty, and said, "Come on. Let us get some food in the lot of you." He nodded to his old friend, saying, "Evening, Mr. O'Day."

"God be with you, Rhys clan," Mr. O'Day replied.

As the weeks passed, more and more captured British were brought across the sea and forced into slavery. Soon dozens became hundreds, and all were forced to toil in the fields and pig pens. It was not long before Moriarty realized his decision made in angst of burning the cottages that dotted the countryside was a blundering misstep. The shanties overflowed and people were forced outside to sleep on the cold, damp ground. Soon, illness began to spread around the camp with some even dying. It was plain to see for Moriarty, even in his stubbornness, if he were to keep his laborers alive, they would need roofs over their heads.

So, he put them to work building their own huts made of mud bricks and straw. They formed a mud-pit alongside the stream and made them gather straw in the fields. The soldiers assigned the strongest men to form the bricks into molds and carry them on their backs to the bricklayers who built small, eight by eight structures, one after the other. Everywhere in their daily toil was the lash. If any were to slow down in their duties or dare to even rest, they felt the whip across their backs.

However, when Moriarty saw them building only living quarters, he stopped the masses from doing their hard labor and announced loudly, "No! You will not build the huts first. Carry the bricks to the main camp to build a new prison. It will be a reminder to all who are insubordinate."

So, they built the prison first, carrying the bricks hundreds of yards from the mud-pits on their backs. When the prison was finally completed, only then could they resume building their own shanty homes.

Everywhere was misery with the old lay dying on the ground and children crying at their mother's feet while they slaved in the fields. They worked in the heat of the summer and the blistering cold of winter. The only escape from the daily nightmare was when they slept from sheer exhaustion.

No one knew of Moriarty's wife nor was he ever seen with her at his side. She disappeared mysteriously years before and rumors swirled that she met her fate by his own hand when she refused to abide or condone his harsh treatment of the lower clans. No one dared to speak of the rumor, however. Even to mention it would mean certain death.

The captives were only to drink from the rivers and streams, but never from the well of O'Sullivan that stood prominently in the center of the main camp. Moriarty, his son Aldus the Younger, and his men were the only people allowed to drink from the well. Anyone else who dared to draw from it were met with the lash or even worse, the sword.

One day, an elderly man, too tired to barely even walk to the nearest stream to drink, decided the well was his only option. He begged soldiers for a drink from any bucket, but his requests were only met with anger and contempt. They pushed him away and told him to find his own water. Dying of thirst, he made one last effort on his hands and knees and began crawling toward O'Sullivan's well. He pulled himself up and sat on the stones next to the wall and with shaking hands, he lifted the bucket fastened to the rope and tossed it over the side. He listened for the familiar splash from down below, then struggled with all his might to raise the bucket. Each pull was agonizing, but he prayed and summoned God for strength and soon, slowly but surely, the bucket raised, and he was overwhelmed with joy as it finally cleared the wall and rested next to him.

He smiled triumphantly and dipped his hands eagerly into the bucket to take his first drink in days, when suddenly a voice shouted, "You there! How *dare* you drink from Master Moriarty's well!"

Startled, the man flipped his wet hands away, sending his life-giving water sailing to the ground. He tried to stand but he couldn't. Instead, he fell to his knees, pleading with the soldier. "It is not his well, and I am dying of thirst."

"You will get water from the streams just like everyone else, you swine," the soldier barked at him.

Soon, a small gathering formed, including Shea and her mother as the old man continued to plead with the soldier. "Only one drink is all that I ask, and I will be on my way."

"You and then a hundred more if I allowed that. Be gone with all of you!"

"What is going on here?" Moriarty shouted as he pushed his way through the small crowd at the well. Finnegan was right behind him like an obedient mutt. "What is this old fool doing at my well? Why are you not driving these animals back?"

Before the soldier could answer, the old man on his knees spoke up, saying, "I am in need of a drink and here is where I will quench my thirst, against your wishes or not."

"Would you listen to this silly old fool?" Moriarty laughed. "I admire your courage, old man. But give me one good reason to not run you through for stealing from my well."

"It is my well," the old man said proudly. "I am O'Sullivan. I drank from this well since I was a boy, and my father before me and his father before him. It was dug by my grandfather four generations ago. His mark is on the side, plain to see. Read it for yourself. Everyone knows who this well belongs to. My family shared it with all who thirsted. Now, you say I cannot drink from my own well."

Moriarty pulled a dagger from his side and leaned close to the man and whispered in a nasty tone, "I do not have the time, nor do I care about your family tree, old man. Nor can I read." Before the man could answer, Moriarty thrust the dagger into the man's belly. The crowd was aghast at the sudden and shocking carnage before them. The old man convulsed, gasping for air. Blood spilled from his lips before he keeled over choking on his last gulp of air. "And now you are not thirsty anymore either, you old fool."

Moriarty quickly withdrew his dagger from the dead old man, Finnegan smiling like a jackal behind him. "Let that be a lesson to all you. Now get back to work!"

Later that night, the family gathered on the floor of their hut eating silently the small bit of vegetable stew Clodagh had prepared. Shea was waiting for her mother to speak about the horror they witnessed by the well, but she remained silent. She was desperate for any type of conversation to help relieve the tension. She felt like the four mud walls were closing in on the entire family. Shea was relieved when her father finally broke the dreadful quiet.

"We started work on the kiln today," Seamus said as he scooped some stew into his mouth. "We will have bread before we know it." He looked around the room waiting for the expected response of joy but heard none. He hesitated before he added, "It…will be for all to enjoy. The fresh smell will lift everyone's spirits, yes?" Still no one said anything. "What is this? Why is everyone so deathly quiet? Speak up." He was becoming quite frustrated.

"Poor ol' Martin," Clodagh finally answered.

"Martin?" he asked. "You mean O'Sullivan?"

"Aye."

Seamus took another bite of stew and nodded as if he knew what she was going to say but he asked anyway. "What about him?"

His father answered before Clodagh could, however. "He is gone. My dear old friend of forty years. Gone for the price of a drink."

"What do you mean gone?" Seamus asked in disbelief.

"Moriarty murdered him," Clodagh answered frankly. "Right in front of Martin's own well in full view of everyone, even our little girl. Just because he dared to draw from the well. The man was dyin' of thirst." Her voice began to crack as the pressure of the ordeal began to mount. A tear rolled down Shea's cheek as she tried desperately to contain her emotions. "I do not want to go on like this. Our children witnessing these horrors, getting threatened with the lash at every turn. I do not want to stand for it any longer."

"No one wants to stand for it any longer, my love," Seamus pleaded with her. "But what are we to do about it? We have no means with which to fight them. All we can do is watch over our little ones as best we can. It saddens me what happened to poor Martin. He was my friend too. To all of us. But what am I to do?"

"Pray," his father answered. "And pray for poor Martin, God rest his soul. Pray that these wicked ways will be put into the Lord's hands to be done away with. I will say no more on it."

Seamus reached over and wiped away Shea's tears. He brushed her hair back and smiled at her lovingly. "Worry not, my child," he said. "Though you have witnessed this evil, pray that God will deliver us away from it. Though we may see even more evil before this ordeal has passed, pray that God will always watch over us with Heavenly angels." She breathed out a heavy sigh of relief in hearing his comforting words. He put his arm around his son Liam and tried his best to reassure him. "You must never lose faith in our Lord." He nodded in satisfaction and smiled at his family and said, "Tonight, we will all pray together for poor Martin."

The next morning, Seamus and Clodagh were ordered out before the crack of dawn. "Today, we will go down to the sea and wait for the ships," the taskmaster instructed.

They both now knew the routine. They marched in silence with a line of other slaves through the tall reeds and dew-covered marshes, across the rocky shoals and down the treacherous slopes toward the sea. The wind blew cold as the winter approached, and high waves lashed the coastline in the early morning light.

It seemed like hours as they stood silently staring out to sea, waiting for the ships to arrive. Waiting for more of the unlucky to be delivered to a life of hard bondage. The dark gray clouds grew thick as they moved fast overhead in the howling wind. Although it was well past sunrise, it still seemed eerily dark along the coastline.

Soon, a call rang out from the sandy shore. "Ahoy! Ships approaching!" Seamus and Clodagh, as well as the other captive statues standing next to them, quickly darted their eyes out to the horizon. A half-dozen boats approached in the choppy waves. "Quickly now. Quickly! Prepare to man the boats!"

As the men paddled hard in the small crafts, those on shore waded to waist-deep waters to assist. Lines were tossed to the strongest men to heave the boats inland. The new captives were thrown or forced to jump one by one into the cold thrashing waves. Men and women lined both sides of each vessel to help guide the boats in and dragging the new arrivals ashore.

Out of the corner of his eye, Seamus spotted one captive who stood out amongst all the others. He found it curious that a young man, looking terribly gaunt, his eyes full of fear, was dressed in a bright blue tunic. He was not dressed like the other prisoners who had on drab, torn brown and black or beige garments. No. This lad was dressed like the son of a rich man. He had a head full of dark curls that was neatly trimmed and if not for the utter fear and exhaustion displayed on his face, Seamus would have sworn he was seeing a member of royalty.

Immediately the bright blue clad young man was forced overboard into the cold sea. He splashed right in front of Seamus who helped him stand.

"What's happening?" the young man coughed as he staggered to his feet. He looked to be no more than fifteen years old. "Who are you? Where am I?"

"*Quiet,* boy," Seamus hissed at him.

"Please. You must help me."

"Quiet, I say," he shushed him again. The boy straightened himself in the shallows and stared at Seamus for what seemed an eternity. He saw how the others were being unloaded and lined up on the shore, all of them deathly silent. It was then he realized that the helpers were also captives. "Join the line on the sand and say nothing or we will all pay the price."

The young man finally understood and took his place in the line. Soldiers surrounded them and quickly shackled them all together at their feet. There were no more than a few paces in between each person and when the front of the line moved, they all moved. If one were to fall, they were whipped until they got to their feet again. The seasoned captives were not shackled but they knew to walk single file along with the new arrivals and dared not to fall behind on the long journey back to camp.

Clodagh and Seamus, along with the other curious onlookers, couldn't help but stare at the young man in blue. He clearly stood out from all the rest being forced up the hill. It was obvious that the pagans had struck at the heart of the British elites on this raid, an act that would surely draw a quick response. At least that was Seamus and Clodagh's hope for they knew that this boy came from money.

Seamus wondered to himself as the shackled troupe struggled their way onward, *Could this be the sign we have been waiting for? A slip-up in Moriarty's hasty raids? Did they finally kidnap the wrong man? How long would it be before the Brits would send help from afar?* He could only hope their prayers had been finally answered.

They arrived at camp hours later, everyone thoroughly exhausted. People stopped what they were doing to watch the new arrivals being dragged to the center in front of Moriarty's hut. All eyes were fixed on the young man dressed in bright blue and people murmured to themselves as he passed in front of them. He was easily the center of attention and he caught Moriarty's steely gaze right away.

"Well, captain," he boasted with a smile on his face. "What have we here? A bit of royalty, have we?" He laughed out loud at his own wit and the men gathered laughed with him. "We should give the lad a royal welcome now, should we not?" The gathering laughed even louder. "How much for the brightly colored centerpiece here, captain?"

"Five gold pieces," the captain answered.

Before Moriarty could counter his demand, surprisingly the young man in blue spoke up, saying, "I will pay you twice that for my release."

The captain immediately rebuked him and slapped him away, saying, "Hold your tongue, boy! You will speak when you are told to."

But the disheveled and weak boy pleaded with them. "I tell you there has been a mistake. I am Pádraig of Bonaven Tabernia. I should not be here. My father will pay you twice that for my safe return."

The captain heaved back his whip to strike Pádraig once more, but Moriarty stopped him. "The boy has spirit. I like that. But you are the one who has made the mistake, lad. You must pay for the sins of your father. The Brits are a weak race with weak minds. Your father will not be able to buy you out of this in any way shape or form. Here is where you will stay." He stepped closer and shook his finger in Pádraig's face, saying, "And you will *do* as you are told." He looked at the captain and said, "Four gold pieces."

"Done," the captain answered. He quickly unshackled Pádraig and shoved him off the stage into the waiting arms of Finnegan.

"I beg you," Pádraig continued to plead, "this is all a terrible mistake!"

Moriarty swatted him with the back of his hand, smacking him to the ground. Pádraig rolled in the dirt stunned and in pain. "Lock him up until he has learned to keep his mouth shut," Moriarty snarled. "I will deal with him later. Now get him out of here. I have more business to tend to."

Pádraig sat in the tiny cell in the dark and damp prison. The only light was from a single candle affixed to the wall in the corridor. He trembled and his cold body ached from the arduous journey and he was starving for food. He heard the main door to the prison slowly creak open and a low shuffle of footsteps coming toward his cell door. Pádraig sat chained to the wall with a single leg iron when he saw the shadow of a face appear in the barred window of his cell door.

"Brought you food, boy," the voice whispered.

Pádraig immediately scrambled to his knees, eagerly anticipating food of any kind. The door opened and Seamus' father shuffled in and placed a bowl of soup before Pádraig who quickly began to scarf it down. Within a minute he had devoured every drop in the bowl, and he fell back against the wall with his hunger briefly satisfied.

"I was desperate, old man," he panted. "I thank you." He wiped his parched lips with his sleeve and studied the man still standing before him. "Might I ask your name? If I am permitted to, that is."

"I am not your master," the old man answered. "I am the same fate as you. They ordered Nuala to bring you food, but I volunteered. My name is Rhys, and I will be the last of my clan to die here."

"Nuala?" Pádraig asked curiously.

"The taskmaster's mistress. But a slave like the rest of us."

Pádraig was also curious about the other statement the man made. "Why do you say you will be last to die here?"

"Escape is the only way for our freedom," he said bluntly. "My son has hopes that your family will send soldiers to come for your rescue and wipe out these pagan overlords, but I know that will not come to be."

"You are right, Rhys. No one will come for me, for they do not know where I am or what happened to me. But if you know of way to escape, I am with you."

The old man chuckled and said, "I have no way, my son. This is my home, and this is where I will stay. But that does not need to be my family's fate. I see God is with you as I saw it the moment I set eyes on you. I see hope in your face."

Pádraig scoffed and stared dejectedly at the mud wall. "I am sorry, sir, you are mistaken. I am just a foolish boy paying the price for my awful decisions. I was tempted and fell right into the trap. Had I not been lured by my friends to witness the pagan ritual by the fire that night, I would not be sitting here now. But the fire hypnotized me, and I could not turn away. I took part in the ritual drink which turned my mind into a drunken haze. Everything went into disarray when the marauders came, and everyone scattered. I was lost in the fray until I felt a club knock me unconscious. When I awoke, I was at sea in shackles." He looked up at the old man contritely, tears welling up in his eyes. "I am here because of my own foolish pride. God wants nothing to do with a pitiful sinner like myself. No, there is no hope in me, only shame."

"We all make mistakes, lad," the old man assured him. "But God gathers the lost sheep of the flock. Even if one in a hundred is lost, He will never stop looking until the one is found. Admitting your mistake is the first step, young Pádraig. God will not abandon you." He made for the door when he heard the guard coming. "I must go. Rest now. You will not be here long as we are all required to work."

"What am I to do? I need to get out of here," Pádraig pleaded in desperate panic.

"Fear not, for the time has not yet come for you. First, you must focus on your duty here." He shut the door and gave Pádraig one last warming gaze from the barred window and said, "Rest now."

Just as he expected, the following morning Pádraig found himself free of the prison but his hands still shackled behind his back. He stood motionless with Finnegan grasping his arm tightly. He could smell the garlic emanating from Finnegan's putrid breath.

"Where to go with this one?" Finnegan asked Moriarty who finally emerged from his hut.

Moriarty, who had also partaken in the same garlicky breakfast, wiped his mouth with his sleeve. "A night in the cell helped shut that royal mouth of yours, did it?"

Pádraig stayed silent as he learned to take their abuse, lest he get into more trouble. From the corner of his eye he noticed a beautiful young woman carrying a water jug to Moriarty.

"Hurry up with that water, Nuala," Moriarty snapped. "Then get to cleaning those floors. It's becomin' a pigsty in there." He yanked the jug from her and quickly poured some fresh water down his gullet. "Take this one out to the flocks on the southside. Let him plead for his freedom with the sheep if he likes."

"Aye, sir. Come on you," Finnegan drawled, yanking Pádraig by the arm.

Before Pádraig left, he made eye contact with Nuala who gave him a quick smile and a seemingly assuring gesture. He could almost read her mind in telling him working with the flocks will not be such a bad thing. To Pádraig, it didn't seem that bad of an idea at all.

Finnegan made sure any notion of an easy time would quickly be forgotten. He made Pádraig's journey to the southside a living nightmare. He dragged him by a rope that was tied at Pádraig's neck and if he fell behind, Finnegan only jerked on the rope harder. Pádraig stumbled and gasped with every step through the rocks and tall reeds and thick tree cover. If he fell to his knees, Finnegan grew angry and whipped him with the lash until Pádraig would stagger to his feet once more. It was the same response with every fall and every miserable step of the way.

It would be hours before they finally reached the flock of sheep grazing on a hillside that overlooked the sea. Finnegan had purposely taken him the long way to get there. He removed the shackles from Pádraig's hands and yanked the loosened rope from his neck, giving him an awful final sting.

"Tend the sheep, rich boy," Finnegan mocked. He leaned in closer with his garlic breath and snarled, "And not *one* will be lost." Pádraig recoiled at the stench, blood dripping from his scarred face from all the thrashings. "If I find out any are missing, I will not be as nice with this the next time." He shook the whip in Pádraig's face, taunting him.

Pádraig looked around his new surroundings and found only a weather-beaten lean-to and shepherd's staff leaning against a boulder. "Where am I to sleep? And what am I to eat?"

"That is not my problem, rich boy," Finnegan laughed as he started on his way back to the camp. "You will have to learn that on your own."

Pádraig stared in horror as he watched the man disappear around the bend. He was left alone with just a staff and the sheep, and no food to eat nor any water to drink.

Shivering in the early morning wind, a thoroughly spent Pádraig hugged his knees in the faint light, trying to stay warm. The lean-to was nothing more than a pile of rotted sticks stacked together that had mostly fallen away and in desperate need of repair. He felt if only he had fire, he could burn it to keep his hands warm at least for a little while.

"Why have you left me here, oh Lord?" he whispered to himself. Just then he heard someone coming in the delicate light of morning. His heart pounded in his hollow chest, expecting the worst to come again with the lash. "Who is there?" he shrieked. His voice cracked through his numb lips.

"I have brought some food," a young woman's voice answered. He was incredibly grateful it was not Finnegan or worse, Moriarty. "And water too."

He got to his feet on his wobbly knees. When he saw that it was Nuala, he smiled at her warmly even though he hardly had any strength left. "Hello," he said. "I have seen you before."

"I am Nuala," she answered. She quickly produced a loaf of bread and handed it to him. He immediately began to tear pieces off and shove them into his mouth. "I noticed you at the prison yesterday. Well, everyone did once you arrived."

He sat in the grass and continued scarfing down the bread. He spoke in between bites, trying not to be rude to her. "What a horrible spectacle I must have been." He eyed the water skin she was carrying and knew if he didn't drink something soon, he might cough up everything. "May I please?" he asked as he reached for the water.

"Yes, yes. How silly of me," she said as she fumbled with it and handed it to him.

He doused his thirst with the water and couldn't remember the last drink of water he had had. The food and water immediately revived his entire body. It was if he had come back to life again.

"I am so thankful to you," he said in between gulps. "I do not think I would have made it through another night without food or water." He glanced at her as she watched him with a smile as he satisfied his hunger and thirst. She was pleased to see how it had helped him. "You must have walked for hours to get here," he commented, recalling his horrendous journey the day before.

"No more than half an hour's walk from the village," she replied. He stopped eating for a moment, looking at her with a blank expression. "I am afraid Finnegan took you well out of the way to get you here for his own devilish amusement, I am certain."

Pádraig's face was pained, knowing that he was tormented for hours needlessly. He felt like he wanted to sob, but he held back his tears in front of her. "Why has God delivered us into this slavery? Why are we in this wretched place? Why have I been forced on this desolate hillside, battered and bruised? Yesterday, I was young lad full of promise with aims to follow my father to study law. Today I am a prisoner in a foreign land." The sheep began to bleat at the sound of his voice. As the sun began to rise, the flock hurried over to where they heard him. He was alarmed at first at seeing so many gather around him, then he smiled at their curious faces as they continued their early morning greeting. "Why are they gathering?" he asked.

"They are drawn to your voice. They respond best to a soft and soothing one and seems you are a natural." She reached to pat one of the sheep on the head, but it scampered away. "You should lead them down the hill a ways to let them graze. There is better grass down there." She sat next to him and rebuked him though, saying, "But this is not a wretched place. This is Ireland and it is my home. I will do whatever I can to see the day when we will live free again. And God did not lead us into slavery, men seduced by evil forced us into slavery. We are all led by God, Pádraig, but not into bondage. This is only a stop along the way to God Himself. God has led you here for a reason, Pádraig. It may be hidden from you now, but one day you will know."

"Why would God lead me to such ruin and despair?" he fretted. "Why would God want anything to do with this hopeless hillside or the vile people who forced me here? My mind is a pitiful mess, and I am ashamed. What am I supposed to do?"

She got to her feet with a disgusted expression. It was the kind of bellyaching she had heard too much already. "Right now, Pádraig, the sheep are your charge. Take this time to come to terms with your current situation like all of us have had to do."

"I am sorry," he said as he stood. "I do not know what hardships you have faced. Yet you bring me bread and water. Please know I am grateful to you."

"It is alright," she assured him. "Listen, you are not far from the village. Just follow in the direction that I return and go straight over the ridge. The best comfort we have right now is Father O'Day but do not address him that way in full view though. We must hide our faith and our priests. But now that we can bake bread in the kiln, he secretly offers the Mass in small groups whenever possible. We are having one tonight if you would like to come. Just look for me standing outside one of the doors where the huts are located. That is where I will be tonight."

"I thought I was to tend the sheep?" he asked.

"During the day, yes. But where can they go at night?" she laughed. "We might be captives, but at least we can seek out our friends when the day has ended." She walked over to the boulder and picked up the staff and handed it to him. "Now you must work as the sheep are hungry." With that, she left him standing alone with the shepherd staff.

"Thank you for your kindness," he called out to her.

Without turning around, she called back, "Good day, Pádraig of Bonaven Tabernia!"

That night, it didn't take him long to find his way back to the village. He constantly looked over his shoulder in fear of being caught and flogged again, but he was able to walk alone unnoticed. It was the first time he had seen the row of mud huts where the other captives lived. Dogs ran around but very few people were out in the early dusk. He got the feeling that they were made to stay indoors after the sun had set, yet he was curious that he didn't see any soldiers.

Soon, he saw a familiar face standing outside an open doorway to one of the huts. He slowed his pace as he didn't want to alert his presence to anyone but Nuala.

Out of the corner of her eye, she saw Pádraig approaching in the darkness, still carrying his staff. She quickly turned away again to listen to what was being said inside.

Pádraig stopped opposite of her at the doorway but kept out of sight of those in the room. He could hear a man preaching from the tiny confines of the hut in the dim firelight.

"Even on the cross, Christ prayed for the forgiveness of those who were putting him to death. We must do the same for those who persecute us."

As Father O'Day prepared the bread for the Eucharist, Pádraig peered inside to see the gathering. On the mud floor sat the preacher with Seamus and his family and noticed right away a familiar face.

"I know that man," Pádraig whispered to Nuala. "This is the Rhys clan?"

As she watched Father O'Day raise the bread and pray silently, she leaned over and whispered back, "How did you know that?"

"The old man," he replied. "He brought me food while in prison and was kind to me."

"Yes, they are all kind. But battered and bruised, just as you. Just as everyone here."

Father O'Day continued, "And the Lord said, 'Take this bread and eat it. This is my body given up for you.'" He tore off a small piece from the loaf and ate it. Then he handed it to Seamus and told him to do likewise. "Pass it around." Nuala came in and sat next to Shea who handed her the bread. It was then Father O'Day noticed Pádraig in the doorway. "You must be Pádraig. Come in, my son. Join us."

Pádraig felt embarrassed, however. He felt ashamed for all the second guessing he had done regarding God and his faith and he shied away from the priest's invitation. "No, I do not wish to intrude. Only to say hello. I should be on my way."

"Pádraig, please," Nuala persisted.

Father O'Day smiled with a wave of his hand. "Let him go in peace. Let him search his heart on his own time." He went back to the Mass as Pádraig slinked away into the darkness. He slowly walked away feeling ashamed once more as he heard the faint words of the priest, "Then the Lord took the cup filled with wine, saying, 'This is the blood of the new covenant poured out for many...'" He walked alone in sadness in the dark all the way back to his flock.

The next morning, he was awakened by yet another visitor coming down the hillside. This time, to his surprise, it was Father O'Day carrying more bread and another skin filled with water. He was also carrying a bundle of sticks and chopped wood. The sheep bleated and scattered and Pádraig calmed them with his soothing voice.

"Good morning," he said to the priest.

Father O'Day approached with a cheerful smile on his face and dropped the bundle on the ground. "Ah, good morning to you too, lad. I hear you are in need of a better lean-to and a little firewood to keep you warm."

Pádraig was astonished at how friendly his fellow captives were to him even after his shameful disappearance the night before. "Everyone is so kind to me. I do not know what to say."

"Well, it can get lonely on this hillside. And Moriarty certainly will not be bringing you provisions. Besides, you missed out on a nice bit of bread last night." He handed him a fresh loaf and the skin of water with a wink of his eye. "This one is not quite so holy but still tastes good."

"I apologize for my rudeness last night," Pádraig offered. He meant it too.

"Ah, do not worry," Father O'Day assured him. "Everything has been a bit traumatic for you. It will subside over time." He pointed his finger farther down the slope, saying, "There is a fresh stream not far in that direction where you can refill these skins. Keep you from drying out in the blustery wind."

"Oh, thank you. I shall make use of that." He shook his head as he knew he was red-faced. "I am embarrassed by my actions. I guess I have been a bit traumatized. You are very kind, Father. Thank you."

"Please, even out here, just call me Colin," he insisted. "Moriarty has eyes and ears everywhere."

"I understand. It is nice to meet you, Colin."

"Likewise. I will help you get started on the repairs, then I must be on my way. Working in the fields today."

Pádraig waved him off though, and said, "I think I can manage. You helped me far too much already. I should get to work with the sheep myself."

Father O'Day smiled and said, "Very well, then. I will leave you to it." He stared out to sea and took in a deep breath of fresh air. "Not too bad on the 'ol hillside. Good place to get in some good deep thought. Maybe even talk to God," he hinted.

"Sometimes I do wish God would talk to me," Pádraig responded. "I think it would make things a lot easier and clearer."

"That is the mystery of the Good Lord," Father O'Day laughed. "He gives us freewill to make things clear on our own. And not always His way is the easy way." Before he turned to leave, he smiled and said to Pádraig, "But be careful what you wish for, lad. You might get it."

Weeks later, Seamus, Liam and Father O'Day were working out in the wheat fields. Men were spaced far apart in the vast field, gathering up the harvest. From the corner of his eye, Liam saw someone running from the hillside. "Father," he asked, "who could that be running so fast?"

Seamus removed his cap and looked out to the horizon and saw the person running at top speed. "Well, look at that," he blurted out. "He is running like the wind."

They soon realized it was Pádraig looking like he was running for his life. "Goodness!" Father O'Day exclaimed. "What has gotten into him?"

They thought he was in distress, but soon it was obvious Pádraig was waving his arms and shouting with joy. "Father! Um, sorry. I mean, Colin!" Father O'Day looked about but there were no taskmasters or soldiers around. "Colin, may I speak with you? Hello, Seamus. Hi, Liam!" He skidded to a stop next to the surprised Father O'Day, panting and wheezing. "May I speak to you?" he asked again.

"Of course, you can. Here, help me gather while we talk." Father O'Day glanced and asked curiously, "And who is minding the flocks?"

"I let them be for a while, they were all napping anyway," he happily responded.

"If you say so," Father O'Day laughed. "So, what has got you so riled up?"

"You are a confessor to the people, are you not? May I confide in you?"

Father O'Day nodded and said, "Keep working. Yes, I will hear your confession."

Pádraig continued as he helped gather the wheat. "Well, it is not really a confession, but if I do not tell anyone soon, I think I might burst."

"Well, go on. Out with it."

"Father, God spoke to me," Pádraig finally said in a whisper. Father O'Day stopped for a moment and tried to understand what he was saying. "For weeks I have been praying for God to show mercy on my sinful ways. I pleaded and begged for mercy. And He did! I heard His voice! He told me not to be anxious anymore and to heed His Words."

"And what were these words?" Father O'Day asked curiously.

Pádraig shook his head worriedly, as if he had missed something in God's message to him. "I do not know. Those were the only words He revealed to me. But my mind has been freed, Father. I am no longer anxious. In fact, I am overjoyed. I rejoice in this day!" He looked at his staff as if it had become a cherished part of his own hand. "And I rejoice in the task of being a shepherd of His flocks."

"And a good shepherd, you are, Pádraig," Father O'Day answered. "The call from God is a blessed event and I share in your joy. I will never forget when He called me to the priesthood."

Pádraig shook his head, knowing his friend was not understanding him. "I know what you are saying, Colin. My closest friend had the same calling before he entered the monastery. But of the spiritual calling. What I am saying is that God *spoke* to me. I actually *heard* Him." He threw down a stack of wheat onto the pile and leapt for joy. "I heard Him! Ha ha!"

"Alright, calm down," Father O'Day said, looking around worried others may see. "We do not want the whole countryside to hear." Pádraig did as he said and waited patiently for his response. "You must get back to your flocks. You have been away too long already. But think on this as you make your way back, Pádraig. Just remember to be ready with your ears and your mind and your heart open to God. If God has called on you once, He will surely call again."

Pádraig did just that. His heart welled up inside him and he fully embraced the call of the Lord. He no longer dreaded his position as a shepherd, and he took pride in it and gave the best of care to the animals. Even in the harsh rain and cold wind he would shelter the lambs as many as he could gather to keep them from being afraid. He prayed tirelessly day and night. He prayed as he worked, and he prayed as he lay in bed until he would finally drift off to sleep. He had become entirely devoted to the Lord in every way, mind, body and soul.

Whenever he could, he would preach the words of the Bible to whoever would listen. He helped his neighbors in their daily tasks whenever he could spare a moment. His renewed faith had spread far and wide and worried not if Moriarty and his men caught word of his preaching.

His concern grew for his fellow captives with each day, though. Not only did he yearn for his own freedom, but freedom for all the Irish. At night, he would seek out those would listen and to those who had fresh ideas on how they could better themselves.

One night, he heard a gathering of men speaking and plotting against their oppressors. Seamus and Liam were among them.

"We should rise up in secret," one young man said. "Send spies out to the countryside to the other encampments until we have gathered a hundred men with clubs and swords. Then, we will rise up!"

"Yes, and bring death to five hundred more," Seamus rebuked him. "Including our women and children. Think of what you are saying. Have you gone mad?"

Pádraig was listening to what was said and could not stay silent any longer. "We are Christians, are we not? Have we not been taught the words of the prophets? That it is not by force that God will fashion His kingdom here on Earth, but by the staff of a shepherd. And it was Jesus himself who once said, 'Live by the sword and you will die from it.' That is all I have to say."

The father of the angry young man grabbed him by the arm and scolded him, saying, "Now, come along with me until you have learned to respect your elders."

"But I am more eld than he is," the son complained.

His father quickly admonished him though, saying, "It is not his age you observe but his wisdom. That is what you should recognize. Come now."

As time went on, Pádraig continued to grow older and wiser. The people even came up with a name for his unbridled enthusiasm for the Lord. They called him the *Holy Youth* and soon, word did reach Moriarty about Pádraig.

Moriarty marched all the way out to the hillside to reprimand him. "I hear what the people are calling you, boy, and I do not like it. Preach to the sheep if you like. Yell it out to the wind and sea, but the people you will not preach to. If I hear of it again, I will come and do away with you myself."

As Pádraig grew older, so did Liam and Shea. After five years, Liam was a strong young man of fourteen and Shea was beautiful and striking at the age of seventeen. With her beauty though, came more attention least of which was from Aldus the Younger. His conniving and lustful stares at her did not go unnoticed by her mother or her attentive brother. Although younger, Liam was quite protective of his sister and made sure she received work far from the village and the glaring eyes of the master's son. Soon, even distance wasn't enough, and her mother could see that Shea was vulnerable anywhere she went.

One evening, as they prepared the meager meal of vegetables and soup, Clodagh pulled her daughter aside to speak with her.

40

"Come, girl. Let me show you something." She produced a small dagger she had rolled up in her tunic. Shea was surprised to see that her mother had kept it concealed all this time. "Hide this, just as I have. If any man tries to get wise with you, putting their hands where they should not, you give them one of these."

"*Mother*," Shea exclaimed, "you want me to kill them?"

"No, child. But you brandish it right where it counts if you get my meaning."

Just then, Seamus and Liam entered the hut and Shea quickly tucked the dagger away into her tunic. "We have bread for the soup tonight," Seamus announced happily.

Pádraig's love for the Lord drew the curious attention of another young man in the village named Palladius. He was younger than Pádraig but still fully capable to learn the ways of a shepherd. So, Pádraig took him on as an apprentice and protégé of the Gospel. As Palladius grew more confident with the sheep, Pádraig would have more time to go and retrieve provisions from the village.

One morning, Pádraig arrived just after dawn and Liam and Shea had found him far out in the field and decided to walk with him into the village. As they approached, they found Nuala drawing water from the well for the taskmasters.

"Pádraig," she asked, "what brings you three here this early morning?"

"Good morning, Nuala. Is it not a fine morning at that?" Pádraig asked with his typically happy and holy grin on his face. Shea and Liam loved his unquenching enthusiasm and always enjoyed being around him when he came.

As they were conversing, Moriarty stepped out on his porch. Young Aldus came out as well, wearing a sheepish grin when he saw Shea standing by. "What is going on out here?" Moriarty barked. "A social gathering? No standing around. Everyone back to work." Then he noticed the wide grin on Pádraig's face. "What are you smiling at? It is the *Holy Youth* himself, eh? Why are you not with the flocks? Am I being too soft on you? Goin' around smilin' everywhere. Do not forget, boy, who your master is."

Pádraig didn't hesitate in answering him, saying, "Aye, a master of men you are, but the master I answer to is far greater than yourself." Nuala, Liam and Shea's eyes all grew wide in disbelief. They knew for sure that he was in trouble.

Moriarty was incensed, and furiously responded, "Why, you good for nothin'. I will run you through myself right now." He snatched a blade from the ever-lingering Finnegan and drew it back to strike at Pádraig. When he saw Pádraig standing defiantly, showing no fear at all, he withdrew the sword. Pádraig's friends let out of huge sigh of relief. "You are an ornery cuss, you are, boy. But I need to protect my investment in you. From now on though, I would keep eyes on the back of your head. I may decide my investment is no longer worth it in you. Now get out of my sight."

After gathering his provisions, Pádraig bid farewell to his friends. As he made his way out, he came upon the pig pens where he saw the elder Rhys, looking frail and gaunt, sloshing about with the pigs in the mud. A soldier stood by with an angry expression hawking over the old man's every move.

Pádraig grew upset at the ghastly scene and asked, "Why do you have this man in that filth? Can you not see he is old and gray? Have you no mercy?"

The soldier snapped at him, saying, "He has been insolent all morning. In the fields, the barns, everywhere. Now I am teaching him a lesson."

Pádraig immediately threw down his provisions and climbed into the pit. He sloshed his way over to the old man to help him. "Teach me a lesson, will you? But not the old man. Let him go and I will do the work here in the mud."

"Get out of there," the soldier demanded. "It is his job to do and I will see to it."

"I will not!" Pádraig shouted defiantly.

Seamus' father stood proudly next to Pádraig and continued his verbal defiance of the soldier. "We are men, not animals. We are not made to suffer in hard labor and bondage. You call us slaves, but we are men made in the image of God. I will stand defiant for as long as I live!"

"Here, old man," the soldier angrily retorted, "you can live your life with this image!" The soldier flung a spear at the old man and struck him in the belly. The man winced in shocking pain, pulling the blade free as he fell backward.

"No!" Pádraig shouted. He quickly sloshed over to the elder Rhys who fell helplessly into the mud.

"Leave him be!" the crazed soldier shouted. "Or you will die alongside him. Take his place tending the swine."

Pádraig ignored the soldier though, saying, "Strike if you must, but I will not leave a man to die in the mud." He carefully lifted the old man and pulled him to safety on dry ground.

As the man lay dying, he said to Pádraig, "Do not worry over me. Death is but the beginning. I prayed that God would let me live long enough to see hope for the people of Ireland." He reached up and placed his hand on Pádraig's cheek and said, "I see that hope in you, Pádraig. You are the hope for my people. I can die happy knowing that now."

Tears rolled down Pádraig's face as the man gasped on his final breaths. "Please, sir. Might I know your given name, so I may remember it?"

The old man coughed as blood trickled from his mouth. "I am called Michael," he answered. With that he breathed his last.

Pádraig drew Michael's eyes closed and said softly to him, "God be with you, Michael Rhys."

The Rhys hut that night felt like a tomb. The four family members sat around a small makeshift table in silence. The loss of their patriarch was devastating, and they shared their sadness with Pádraig and Nuala who sat with them in sympathetic silence. Before long, Father O'Day had joined them in the tiny room as a single torch burned in the corner and was their only source of light.

Seamus finally broke the deathly silence, his voice shaking with anger. "He only wanted to be treated as an equal. He only wanted freedom." He kicked the dirt on the floor in frustration and sat trembling, barely able to control his emotions. "Maybe our friends are right. Maybe we should rise up."

"That is not the answer, Seamus," Father O'Day quickly countered.

Seamus slammed his fist on the wood, startling everyone in the room and exclaimed, "At least give it a chance!"

"Seamus, please calm down," Father O'Day continued. "We are far outnumbered, and with no weapons to speak of. You said so yourself an uprising would bring death to hundreds more." Seamus relented and stopped arguing for the moment. His heart ached too much for his murdered father. "I have heard rumors from the north that the king is pressuring the likes of Moriarty even more now to increase his wealth. The brutality is getting much worse. We must all watch over one another very closely. We must be careful. Fighting back verbally only brings more wrath. I am not blaming poor Michael, he spoke for truth and justice, but we must watch what we say."

Clodagh shook her head as she wept, "How did we ever get to this?"

Quietly, Shea produced a parchment she had tucked away in her tunic. She had carried it with her ever since their last day of freedom when her grandfather had created the drawing. She had never revealed it to her family until this moment. She carefully unfolded it and lay it flat on the wooden table for all to see.

"He drew this," Shea said softly, trying desperately to hold back her tears. Everyone in the room stared at the simple, yet powerful drawing of the three ravens with the family name inscribed at the top. "He said the ravens were a symbol of strength who tended the needs of the prophets."

"God's heavenly creatures," Father O'Day added.

Pádraig stood and went outside briefly and came back with a twig. "Does anyone have a carving tool?" he asked. Shea happily handed over the dagger she had hidden away.

"Where did you get that?" Seamus asked curiously.

Clodagh answered in an innocent tone, saying, "Never you mind."

Pádraig smiled at their playfulness even in a time of mourning. He knew they loved each other deeply and saw strength in them both. He admired Seamus and Clodagh very much. He quickly whittled down two tiny pieces of the twig into sharp nails. He then picked up the parchment gently from the table and without even asking for permission, fastened it to the wall. Those present sat silently, yet proudly, as they observed the family's crest in the firelight.

Father O'Day stood and saluted the parchment saying, "To Michael: May it be a symbol of his courage and the strength of the Rhys clan for all time."

A few days had passed, and everyone was back at their daily tasks. Pádraig and Palladius rotated their duties in watching over the flocks. While Palladius tended the sheep, Pádraig was constantly in a state of prayer and even when he watched the sheep, he continued his praying.

Shea and Clodagh worked around the huts, keeping the paths clear and feeding the chickens and swine. All the while Liam, Seamus and Father O'Day worked in the vegetable gardens close by.

As they all worked, they were under the watchful eye of the taskmaster's son, Aldus. He came around more and more often just so he could get a long stare at Shea. He had become obsessed with her and didn't care if she was a slave. He wanted her and he wanted her for his own.

Clodagh smiled as one of the young men brought in pile of potatoes from the fields. "Ah, that is a good lad. Everyone will have some nice, boiled potatoes tonight." She took the sack from the boy and called out to her daughter. "Shea, take these around and put a few in each hut. We want everyone fed tonight."

"Yes, Mother," Shea replied and hurried off to deliver the food to all the huts of their fellow workers. She popped in and out of each doorway, placing two potatoes in every home. She smiled at her new task and delighted that she was helping so many. She went from house to house until she came upon their own. She stepped inside and decided to tidy up a bit before continuing with her deliveries. After she had finished sweeping, she dusted off her hands on her apron and headed for the door. Before she could exit, she was startled to see Young Aldus appear out of nowhere, blocking her way.

"Good morning, young Rhys," he said suavely.

Flustered, she blurted out, "Aldus, what do you want?"

"Just wanted to say hello," he answered innocently. "I wanted to see how you were getting along."

"I am doing just fine, thank you," she stammered. "If you will excuse me, there is still much work to be done."

She tried to brush past him, but he side-stepped to block her once more. "The work can wait." He then grabbed her by the shoulders and whirled her gently against the wall. "Shea, do you not think it is time we got to know one another? I think you are the most beautiful girl I have ever seen."

45

She began to tremble as she tried to look around him, hoping someone would come in and intervene. But no one came. She answered nervously, saying, "Well, that is quite flattering, but I am just a poor peasant slave, and you are the taskmaster's son."

"That gives you all the more advantage," he answered connivingly. "I am sure there is some way you and I can come to an understanding." He forced his lips on hers and pressed her firmly against the wall. She moaned in desperation trying to wriggle free. Finally, she slipped from his grasp and ducked quickly under his arm to free herself. She scampered over to the other side of the room and stood under the family crest. She wanted to cry for help but knew if she did, he could easily slit her throat.

"Trying to play hard to get, are we?" he playfully laughed like a jackal. He sauntered around the table, observing the parchment above her head. "Interesting décor you have in here. I did not realize your clan was so proud of being captives." He once more tried to kiss her, but this time was much more forceful with her, groping her and trying desperately to get his hands under her cloak. He finally succeeded in finding her bare thigh and slowly inched his hand up when suddenly he froze. He felt a cool, yet razor-sharp edge of a blade firmly pressed against his own privates.

Shea smiled triumphantly and snarled in his face, "Move that hand one more inch and I will flick this blade one more as well." He quickly removed his hand, yet she pressed the blade even harder to his skin. "Are we understanding each other now?" With one swift move, she pulled the dagger away and shoved him backwards. "The *décor* is not for your filthy benefit. It is for *ours* and I am *proud* to be a Rhys. I love the Lord and I am happy to be called a child of God which is something you will never, ever understand. Now get out!"

Just then, Seamus and Clodagh came barging in. When they noticed that Shea had not been seen in a long while, they went racing around looking for her. They were stunned to see Aldus leaving in a rush with an embarrassed expression on his face.

They watched as he left, then looked over at their daughter with great concern. "What happened here?" her mother asked.

Shea answered proudly, "Nothing, thanks to your gift. He tried to take advantage of me."

"*What?*" Seamus was incensed. "I will tear the man apart!"

"No!" Clodagh pleaded. "That would be madness and death to us all. Do you not see she can defend herself?"

Seamus calmed down and nodded his head with approval at his daughter's courage. "You have done well, girl. I am proud of you. How did you manage to thwart him and have him leaving with such a red face?"

"I threatened to castrate him," Shea answered bluntly. Her mother's eyes widened in disbelief. "It nearly came to that too. The only problem was I did not find anything."

Her parents nearly burst into laughter. The two of them embraced their daughter as Seamus said under his chuckles, "Well done. Well done."

After that, Aldus was enraged. He stormed around the compound looking for anyone to abuse. He shoved people aside, he toppled over tables, chairs and even fences. Anyone who crossed his path was either verbally assaulted or beaten. "*Where is he?*" he rampaged shouting over and over.

Liam came running up from the field when he heard the shouting and quickly found his family and joined them inside. "Liam! Thank God you are here," his mother said. "The man has gone mad."

"Oh, my," Shea gasped. "What have I done?"

"I know where you are, preacher man!" Aldus shouted ever louder, his mouth frothing with rage. He ran toward the fields cursing and swearing. Before long, he found the target of his wrath. "I knew I would find you!" He drew his sword and charged directly at Father O'Day who was working in the gardens.

"Colin, run!" Seamus shouted.

Father O'Day was stunned to see the wild man charging at him with the blade. "No, master! What are you *doing*?" He tried to run but he was no match for the quick and nimble rampaging beast.

"Preaching to the children of *God*, are you?" Aldus lambasted as he drew closer, running at top speed. "Do not think I *know* who you are and what you have been doing!"

Father O'Day braced for the sudden impact, raising his outstretched arms in a futile effort to try and stop him. "Do not do this!" But it was too late. Aldus pounded into him like a bull, flailing him to the ground. The priest lay crushed with his face flattened in the dirt. Aldus sat on him and in an instant thrust his blade into his heart, killing him with one sharp, bloodthirsty strike.

Aldus stood defiantly over the dead priest and raised his bloody sword into the air and shouted, "There will be no more preachers in Ireland! There will be no more children of God!"

The people stood around speechless and stunned. Some began to weep at the sight of Father's O'Day's bloody corpse. Aldus panted with his face covered in sweat, drool running from his mouth, his hair in a crazed heap on his head. He was a madman and the people stared at him like one. "Now get back to work, you dogs," he bellowed in short breaths. "Or you will all meet the same fate as this devil."

Liam grew angrier and angrier with every second. The word 'devil' rang out in his mind and angered him even more. He couldn't stand the brutality any longer.

Aldus put away his sword and staggered back to the camp. As soon as his back was turned, Liam charged him. In a split second, he plowed into his back and tackled him to the ground. Stunned momentarily, Aldus bucked like a mule and sent Liam flailing off his back. He rolled to his knees to see who had attacked him when Liam seized on the opening and punched Aldus square in the jaw. Aldus, still filled with rage, reacted with a swift blow of his own to Liam's head. Liam was flat on his back, stunned by the sharp impact. Aldus began to kick him wildly and then pulled the boy up to strike him in the head once more when suddenly someone grabbed his arm.

Aldus was shocked to see Seamus holding him back. "Stop wailing on my son!" he demanded.

"Rhys!" Aldus hissed. "I curse your whole clan. You will all meet the point of this blade." He drew his sword and sliced at Seamus, sending him tumbling backward. Blood began to stain Seamus's clothes at his upper torso. "I'll start with the boy!" Aldus once again turned his wrath on Liam who lay helplessly on the ground. Aldus reared back his sword…

"Young Moriarty!" a deep voice bellowed. Aldus froze in mid-air. "That is enough bloodshed!" Aldus turned around to see his father. "That is enough, my Son. You kill all the slaves, then who will do the work?" He led his son away back to the village, leaving the people in stunned silence. The people looking on were even more stunned to see the taskmaster showing a slither of compassion.

Seamus helped Liam to his feet, who was still wincing in pain. "Are you alright, Son?"

"Yes, Father. I am alright. You are wounded."

He nodded at his cut and shook it off. "Mother will patch me up. I will be fine. Come, let us tend to the priest."

Shea was left crestfallen at what had happened. Tears ran down her cheeks as she ran off toward the hillside. She ran all the way until she found Pádraig tending the sheep. Palladius had fallen asleep in the lean-to and didn't even notice when she ran past.

Pádraig saw her coming and called out to her, "Shea, what brings you out here?" He could see how distraught she was. "What is the matter?"

"Pádraig," she began, "forgive me for disturbing you. But you are a Godly man and a pious man. Will you please be my confessor?"

He shook his head though and answered, "I am not a priest, Shea. Father O'Day is the one who would hear your confession."

"He is dead."

Pádraig looked at her confused and shocked. "What?"

She repeated it again. "He is dead at the hands of Young Aldus. He murdered him because of me."

Pádraig tried to hold back his tears for his fallen friend. "Why would he do this?"

"Aldus tried to take advantage of me and I foolishly thwarted him with a dagger. But all it did was make him angry and he turned that anger on Father O'Day." She fell to her knees and wept bitterly. "He is dead because of *me*. I should have let Aldus do as he wished."

Pádraig did his best to console her. "No, Shea. You did the right thing. You were right to defend yourself. No man should ever force himself on a woman. No, Young Aldus did not kill Father O'Day because of you. Young Aldus killed him because of Young Aldus. The darkness has overshadowed his God-given reason."

Shea, sullen and grief-stricken, looked wearily at Pádraig and said, "We will never be free."

Clodagh sat with Seamus alone in their hut and while she patched the wound on his chest, she fretted aloud. "What is to become of us? Any chance Young Aldus gets, he will come after us all. We need to get out of here."

Seamus threw his hands up and answered, "What would you have me do, woman? Where could we go?"

Clodagh pressed him though, ignoring his questions. "Are we not to have freedom ever again? Will this be our divine punishment?"

"Clodagh, we must not mock the Lord," Seamus answered.

"What about our children then?" she persisted. "Are they to live a life of slavery forever as well? We cannot stay here and let them chase us like dogs or have their way with an innocent girl."

"I have prayed on this, wife, constantly. In my heart I know our children will be the bearer of a new dawn away from all this."

"As *we* lie on our *deathbed*?" she asked bewildered. "Waiting for this new dawn to pass us by? Listen to me, Seamus." She placed her hands on his face lovingly and continued, "I want to face the new dawn too. All of us together. To grab that freedom, we must rise early and let the dawn wait for *us*. I want to be the bearer of that freedom too." She looked deeply into his eyes and kissed the top of his forehead. "Do you not?"

He looked at her nodding his head. He loved her dearly for her courage and conviction. "Yes," he said softly to her.

Pádraig sat on the hillside alone in the darkness under a blanket of stars. He held one lamb on his lap who bleated happily in his warm arms. The full moon shone brightly in the early night sky as he looked out over his flock and nodded with approval. He let the lamb scamper away as he got to his feet and walked over to the lean-to to find Palladius on his back staring at the stars.

"Palladius," he said, as the young man lifted his head, "I leave you to tend my sheep."

Palladius said nothing but looked at Pádraig quizzically. He knew what his duties were already and didn't know why Pádraig felt the need to remind him. Pádraig patted him on the knee and then departed.

Not long after, Pádraig was standing alone in the moonlight at the sight of Father O'Day's grave. "Father, you told me that God would call on me again. You were right. He did." With that, he ran like the wind toward the village.

He came to the hut of his friend, Nuala and her mother. He called out to her in a whisper. "Nuala?"

Nuala came to the door, surprised to see him. "Pádraig, what brings you here at this hour?"

"Nuala, I came to say goodbye."

"*Goodbye?*" She closed the door and stepped outside with him. "You are leaving?" She was stunned and perplexed. "How? And why?"

Pádraig was as frank as he could be. "God told me I must. He said my ship awaits."

"Your *ship*? How do you know of a ship?" Then it dawned on her what else he had said. "What do you mean God told you?"

"I do not know of any ship, but nevertheless, God said that it awaits. I must leave now, tonight, and heed His word. But speak to no one of this." He hurried off in another direction.

"This is madness," she answered. When she saw how serious he was and how quickly he left, she fretted, saying, "Wait! Where are you going?"

"I must get provisions. I will return shortly."

While he gathered what he needed for his journey, he decided to make one other stop at the Rhys' hut. He had to say goodbye to them as well. When he arrived, he saw that Nuala was there too.

"You are a mind-reader," he joked with Nuala. "Have you told them anything?" She wouldn't answer him though.

The door was already open, so he stepped just inside. "Seamus, I have come to…"

"Take us with you," Seamus stated flatly.

Nuala came in and stood behind the family with a guilty smile. "I am sorry, Pádraig. You do not hear news like that every day. I had to tell someone. I imagine if God were to speak to anyone it would be you. You are the most devoted person I have ever seen." She looked at him seriously and motioned to the Rhys' standing before them. "You know they are all targets. Young Aldus will stop at nothing until they are dead. Moriarty cannot watch him every minute and Aldus will be lying in wait for that chance. Take them, Pádraig, before it is too late."

He looked at all four of them, knowing that Nuala spoke the truth. He noticed that they had already gathered what few belongings they owned, including the family crest that was no longer on the wall. He nodded in acceptance and said, "Come. We will go together."

Nuala did not follow them, however. She stood motionless in the doorway, her face glowing in the moonlight.

"You must come with us, Nuala," Pádraig insisted.

She shook her head though, saying, "No. Here is my home and here is where I will stay. If God is to bring back His flock to Ireland, then I will wait here for His shepherd to return."

He embraced her warmly and smiled at her lovingly. He gave her one last look and then set out.

The five of them hurried out of the camp in the full moon light. Past O'Sullivan's well, past the shanty lane lined with mud huts and past the brick pits and pig pens. They hurried off in a direction where none of them had ever gone.

"How do you know which way to go?" Seamus asked him quietly.

"I do not, but God will lead us this night. Have no fear."

They walked for hours in the darkness, stopping only to quench their thirst at streams. As they drank and rested for a moment, Seamus smiled at the stars that canvassed the sky alongside the full moon. He looked over at his anxious wife and children and then at his friend, Pádraig.

"Though I may leave," he told them, "in my heart will always be the blood of an Irishman. Ireland will always be a part of me."

Two hours later, they arrived at the seashore and dawn was just beginning to break and Pádraig looked anxiously in every direction. At first, he saw nothing on the sand and rocky shore.

"Have no fear," he told his companions, "we will find it."

They walked for another half mile when finally, they saw something. Clodagh gasped when she saw it. "Oh, my goodness." To their amazement, there sat a large wooden boat, being prepared by two men about to set sail. They were traders waiting for the first light to set out. "My goodness, Pádraig," she said again. "You were right. God be praised."

Pádraig and the Rhys' walked toward the ship and then he motioned for them to wait behind while he talked to the men. The captain and his first mate were shocked to see someone else on the shore where no one else was around.

"Are either of you the captain of this vessel?" Pádraig asked with a wide grin.

"I am the captain of this ship," a short, thin man with a freshly trimmed beard answered. "What is it that you want from me?" He observed the small group of people not far behind the broadly smiling stranger.

"God has told me that your ship was waiting to take me across the sea to my homeland," Pádraig confidently announced.

"Is that so?" the captain laughed along with his first mate.

"But I have no money," Pádraig continued. "I am hoping that will not be an issue being this is a matter of great importance."

"Oh, but it is a problem. No matter the importance," the captain shot back. "I suggest you pray to your God to give you some money, or you will not be getting back home anytime soon, lad." He and his first mate laughed even harder at themselves.

"Very well," Pádraig answered. "I will do as you ask, but it is strange that God should will something just to have it refused. If it is your wish to ignore God's will, then so be it."

The captain observed him keenly as Pádraig moved several steps away to kneel and pray. As Pádraig fixed his gaze across the sea, holding his hands in prayer, the captain stated flatly, "The man's crazy."

The first mate was amazed, yet uneasy. "Look at how devoted he is to his god," he whispered. "Even now, as he is turned away without any money."

The captain frowned and argued, "It is not my fault the man has no money. Now, let us be gone." He angrily tossed one line of the boat inside. "Besides, I am not a Christian. I know nothing of his god, nor do I care."

"I am not a Christian either, cousin. That is why it bothers me. What do we know of God? We know nothing. It is a bad sign to set sail on terms like this."

"What *terms?*" the captain blasted. "Do not be daft in front of me, boy. We anger one god of land we anger another of the sea?" He swiped his cousin on the back of the head and said, "Stop your nonsense. Come on, we have work to do."

"But cousin," the first mate persisted, "just *look* at him."

Pádraig calmly took a deep breath, his hands still clasped in prayer and closed his eyes. Then after a few moments, he began to pray aloud, hoping the captain and his first mate would hear. "Oh Lord, help these men make just decisions and help them mend their wicked ways. Help them to give up this life of dealing people for profit, and..." He kept one eye on the captain who was watching him with a twisted expression. "And for the captain to give up the peasant woman he keeps on this side of the channel."

Immediately the captain's eyes flew open wide as saucers. He scampered over to Pádraig and whispered, "How did you know that? You cannot go around *sayin'* that, man."

"Does this mean you will let us come aboard?" Pádraig asked keenly.

"Who is *'us'?*"

Pádraig pointed to the Rhys clan standing nearby patiently. "The family there who is traveling with me."

"Forget it, boy," the captain scoffed. "I know slaves when I see them, including you."

"You are right in saying we are slaves," Pádraig answered. "But remember, men made slaves, but God made men first."

The captain was becoming clearly flustered at the stranger's profound wisdom. He shook his head and said, "The king will hear of it if I help slaves escape."

"Is the king here now?" Pádraig asked smartly.

The captain looked one way down the shore and then the other. No one was around except for them. "No," he answered sheepishly.

"Then it is settled," Pádraig said with a broad smile.

The captain looked at the Rhys clan wearily and then back at Pádraig. Still shaking his head, he said to them, "If it pleases your god, climb aboard."

Pádraig motioned for the family to come with him to board the ship. They eagerly followed him and sloshed through the shallow water. Shea and Liam were both smiling happily, splashing about as they climbed in. Clodagh gave Pádraig a huge hug before she climbed in as well.

"You have done well, Pádraig. God bless you," she said.

Seamus leaned into Pádraig and whispered in a curious tone, "How did you know about the woman?"

Pádraig shrugged his shoulders and answered with a grin, "I did not."

The last of them climbed aboard as did the captain and the first mate. The captain shouted, "Cast off!" and the ship set sail out to sea until it disappeared over the horizon.

Coda

After they reached Britain, the Rhys family set out on their new life together in a new land, free from the bondage of slavery. They traveled inland for days until settling in the picturesque Welsh hills west of the River Severn. There, they reestablished the life they once had in Ireland. They cultivated farms and raised animals on the pristine slopes of Wales. They were free at last to live as they chose.

Shea would marry as did Liam and the two new families would be blessed with eleven children in all to the proud delight of Seamus and Clodagh.

Pádraig continued onward to his parent's home after six long years of captivity. They knew not where he had been nor the hardship's he had faced but were overjoyed in his return.

God continued to reveal His word to Pádraig, and he obeyed them without question. His father tried to persuade him into going off to school and live the privileged life they had always intended for him, but the call to the holy life was too strong. His parents were reluctant, but they soon embraced Pádraig's decision to enter the monastic life.

Once at the monastery, he still had his work cut out for him in persuading the bishop to allow him to study the priesthood. God guided Pádraig in what he should say, and he learned the power of persuasion quite well. He did become a priest but then he had one more request of the bishop, and that was to return to Ireland.

It took all the gifts he had in his persuasion of the bishop to finally grant Pádraig's request. And thus, history was made in Pádraig's triumphant return to Ireland, where he was named bishop. God followed Pádraig and blessed his relentless and tireless mission to re-establish Christianity on the Emerald Isle. His efforts would soon lead to the freedom of the Irish people, and the freedom to serve the Lord as they so desired.

The people of the island, and the entire world, know this great man as *Naomh Pádraig* or *Saint Patrick*: *The Apostle of Ireland*.

Part II

The Year of Our Lord, 533

In the year of our Lord, 533, Christianity was more abound in England as it was in Ireland. The Roman Christians had left many converts before their departure from the island, and many men entered the monastic life. Monasteries for women, however, were still unheard of. Many young girls and women yearned to heed the calling of the Lord to the religious life but were not allowed to form convents as the priesthood was only for men.

It was the time of the Anglo-Saxons, and the Celtic Church had a more stable founding in England. The pagans remained strong however, and with the Romans no longer present on the island, they took advantage of their position. Christians were still persecuted, although they were not forced into slavery. Yet the two facets of peoples often clashed as the pagans resented newcomers or converts to the Catholic faith.

In an area of southeast Wales, in the county of Gloucestershire, there lived the descendants of the Irish clan named Rhys. For over a century, the children and grandchildren of Seamus and Clodagh flourished on the hillsides near a tiny hamlet called Kington.

It was the time of a great scholar and Catholic priest named Dubricius, or Dubric, as he was called by the locals. Dubric was known to have the healing power of laying of the hands. He was a priest and healer but throughout Wales, he was best known as a profound teacher of the Word of God. Many were eager to be his pupils, men and women alike and he taught freely to anyone who would come and listen to him. The pagans resented him greatly, but his influence towered over their petty insecurities.

One young woman in particular found Dubric to be most insightful and she yearned to be his student and especially wanted to live the monastic life as he did, dedicating her life to God. Her name was Arilda.

Arilda

She had the face of an angel. She was small and waifish, a thin frame and skin as pale as birch on a summer day. Her nose was narrow and sloped downward to a point no larger than a perfectly rounded pea. She possessed an enchanting beauty that was the envy of all the young maidens of Oldbury.

Mathilda was indeed beautiful and on this day her radiance glowed even more as it would be the great announcement of her betrothal to Pedr, the first-born son of Lewys and Efa Rhys.

All the inhabitants from the sprawling farmland county gathered near Oldbury parish, which stood prominently on the crest of a hill, overlooking the peaceful countryside and the majestic River Severn. They came to celebrate the upcoming nuptials of Pedr and Mathilda with a great feast as well as singing and dancing.

Among the festive crowd was Arilda, the younger sister of Mathilda. She was just as beautiful as her sister and her smile this day matched that of Mathilda's, as she was very happy for her. The beauty of the two girls never went unnoticed. Mathilda reveled in the attention, much to the chagrin of her betrothed, but Arilda did not. She was always keenly aware of the stares and flirtations of potential suitors, but it didn't matter to her. She never had the inclination as the other maidens did, to capture the attention of a young man to marry. Arilda's ambitions and aims were focused on a much higher level than Earthly love. Her love was of the Heavenly kind and all she wanted was to love and serve the Lord.

When she was younger at the age of nine, Arilda was like any other girl growing up on the rolling hillsides of Gloucestershire. She loved to run amongst the wildflowers in the springtime and to venture out into the snow in the winter when the sun would return to the skies. She obeyed her parents and did her chores around their cottage and tended the animals in the barn, but what she loved most was playing with her closest friend Mari Rhys, Pedr's younger sister.

Arilda and Mari were inseparable in the warmer months, making up games of hide and seek in the forests, counting tadpoles in the streams and jumping over mud puddles. They loved to laugh and giggle just as all young girls do, and of course they never minded if they became muddy after 'accidentally' falling into one of the puddles. As they grew older, their fondness for playing and spending time together never waned.

It was always a treat for Arilda and Mari when there was a great celebration as they were having today. They loved to dance to the music that was sung by a harmonious trio. Mari especially enjoyed it due to the fact that two-thirds of the trio was her father and mother, Lewys and Efa. Rounding out the popular singing group was Wynfre Bulward, the red-haired father of Municus.

Wynfre was known for his delightful singing voice but also had a penchant for having a constant runny nose and fits of sneezing in the springtime. This fine Sunday afternoon was no exception to his yearly ailment. During numbers or even in between them, poor Wynfre would plunge his irritated nose into his commonly known red handkerchief. Many of the villagers had linens or cloaks tinged with the same amber color due to the waters in nearby streams that sometimes ran red with *Hildenbrandia*. None were more prominent in color than Wynfre's handkerchief, though. Everyone knew when they saw the flash of red being pulled from his cloak, a litany of annoying sneezes was forthcoming.

"I am sorry, Lewys," Wynfre said, wiping his nose once more. "The wildflowers are wonderful this time of year, but I am afraid my nose does not appreciate them as much. We were doing so well just then."

"It is alright," Lewys assured him with a smile. "Efa and I can carry on if you want to sit this one out."

Wynfre nodded in agreement, saying, "Right so. I may sit down a bit and get some water. Maybe have a dash of rarebit."

"Cooked it fresh this morning," Efa added. "It will cure what ails you." She turned to her husband and said, "Come, let us do a few more as we have some dancers waiting for us."

As always in the middle of the festive atmosphere, there was Dubric, the local priest. He spent his days traveling the county and even places farther away, tending to the faithful, comforting the sick and saying Mass whenever possible. He was always ready to listen to a person in need or lend some helpful advice on any given matter. Or just simply be there for someone who needed some prayers. Sundays in Oldbury after Mass were always one of his favorite pastimes. Today it was even more special, as he was honored to be the priestly witness to the new betrothal and to bless it as well.

"Very tasty rarebit, today," Father Dubric said, licking his lips, sitting next to Wynfre. "Sniffles put you out of commission, did they?"

"I am afraid so," Wynfre said, still wiping his nose. "But it was time to sit for a spell anyway. They sound so much better than with me up there hacking all over."

"Nonsense, old boy. We need the three of you up there together." He looked at Wynfre sympathetically. "Maybe I will give your nose a special blessing this afternoon." Just then, two more people came, Cadoc and Bethan Glas, and sat with them to eat. "Ah, come join our meal. Good to see you, Cadoc and good afternoon to you, Mrs. Glas. Might I formally congratulate you on your daughter's betrothal."

"Dubric," Cadoc said cordially. "Thank you. Pedr is a fine lad."

"He is indeed," Father Dubric concurred. "And what a fine catch for young Pedr. Mathilda is as beautiful as her mother. Do you not agree Mr. Bulward?"

"Of course," Wynfre answered dolefully.

"Thank you, Father," Bethan added. "We are very happy for them."

Father Dubric nodded in approval, saying, "It will be a fine wedding day."

As the music began to wind down, children dispersed into the hillside to play while the adults sat together and ate. As usual, Arilda and Mari headed to the wildflowers to gather them so they could take them down to the stream and toss the petals in one at a time. Municus, who was close in age to Arilda, was never far behind. At thirteen, Mari was two years younger than Arilda and four years younger than Municus. Mari didn't mind though, she loved Arilda dearly and regarded her as a sister more than her best friend. She scoffed at the idea of boys following them around though. She knew it was because they liked to gawk and stare at Arilda, but never had the courage to speak to her properly.

Municus picked the bark off a tree, pretending not to be noticed by them at the stream. The girls tossed the flower petals into the water and laughed each time, ducking over their shoulder from time to time, to see if they were still being watched.

"Is he still there?" Arilda whispered.

"Yes," Mari answered sourly. She blew out her breath and finally turned all the way around and barked at Municus. "Stop following us around and go find my brother Pawl or something."

Municus tried to act like he wasn't paying attention to them and said, "He is busy with Angelika all the time now. I will go find him if I want. Let me be."

"You let us be," she retorted. "We want to throw flowers."

"Hmpf. I do not want to do those girl things," he said as he turned and ran back up the hill.

"Good," Mari said triumphantly. "So, Mathilda is finally going to marry Pedr. I think it is so romantic. We will be like sisters!"

Arilda smiled at her as she tossed more petals in the water. "I am happy for her, but I will never get married. It is not what God wants for me."

"How can you be so sure?" Mari asked curiously.

"I just am. I wish I could ride with Father Dubric and see what he sees and do what he does."

Mari wrinkled her nose and answered, "He sees a lot of sick people and dead people too. That does not sound too appealing to me."

Arilda took in a deep breath of fresh air and smiled toward the Heavens. "It does to me tending to the needy as Jesus said for us to do. I want to learn everything I possibly can about the Lord and serve those around me. I just…I just want to learn. I want to soak up everything there is to know. I want it so much sometimes I cannot even sleep. My mind is just full of curiosity, it never stops." She looked around the peaceful stream and the trees and the chirping birds. "There is beauty all around us and so much knowledge to gain." She stretched her arms high into the air as if she were reaching for the clouds. "I just love it!"

"You cannot sleep?" Mari asked befuddled. "After all my chores around the farm, I am asleep before my head hits the pillow." She heard her mother calling to them. "They want us to come eat now. Let us hurry so we can sit next to Pedr and Mathilda. Race you!"

The girls took off running up the hill, laughing and giggling all the way. They made it just in time and Arilda took her place next to Mathilda while Pedr, Pawl and Mari sat across from them.

"Father, will you say a blessing before the children eat?" asked Efa.

The priest bowed his head and prayed aloud, "Thank thee, oh Lord for this food and bless this bounty so it may nourish these young minds. And especially bless young Pedr and Mathilda this fine day of their betrothal so that in three months they may be joined in the holy sacrament of marriage."

The entire gathering answered in unison, "Amen!"

The table was crowded with over twenty children from the area. Pedr sat across from his fiancée and they couldn't stop smiling at one another while they ate. All the while Municus sat alone at the other end of the long table eating some fruit and occasionally staring at Arilda dispiritedly.

"I cannot believe you will be married in three months," beamed Mari.

"I am so envious," Angelika added.

"Will you build her a cottage?" Mari continued excitedly. "Will you build her a wagon just for two?"

Mathilda's face turned red and Pedr laughed at his curious little sister. "There is still plenty of time yet. Do not rush me."

Mari couldn't stop her gushing. "Oh, I bet you will do just like Father did for Mother. Then it will be your turn, Pawl."

"Hey, slow down there," Pawl laughed, his face turning red. Arilda couldn't help but laugh at her friend's exuberance.

"Then they will have children...," Mari sang in a delighted tone. "Oh, I cannot *wait* to be an aunt."

Pedr and Mathilda both became red-faced and he reached over playfully to cover Mari's mouth and said, "Alright, that is enough woolgathering out of you."

Later as the sun was setting and the festivities were concluding, Wynfre walked home with his son, Municus. "Why do you not talk with the other lads anymore? Are not you and Pawl getting along?" He sneezed into his red handkerchief as soon as he stopped talking.

Municus shrugged his shoulders and answered, "We get along fine but he is more interested in Angelika now."

His father nodded in understanding. "Children grow up. Their interests change."

"I guess so."

"Do you have any interest yourself in any of the young ladies?" he asked curiously.

"I do not know," he mumbled.

"I noticed you had your eye on Mathilda's sister," Wynfre remarked. Municus tilted his head with a guilty grin. "I thought that to be the case. She takes after her sister quite so, does she not?"

Municus shook his head though, saying, "Arilda does not want anything to do with me. All she talks about is God."

Wynfre scoffed at the notion though. "Well, she cannot marry God. She will need to marry a man like you if she wants to get on. A waste of time it all is, wanting to learn about God. Takes all that I have to sit at table with the preacher. I have nothing to do with God."

"Then why do we go to these things on Sundays?" Municus asked bewildered. "You sing with them and you eat with them. Nobody ever talks to me at all."

His father looked at him matter-of-factly and laughed, "To get a decent meal once a week. What do you think? You know I cannot cook for anything. Your mother did all that."

"Do you ever worry people will learn we are not Christian, and we are sidling up just to get a hot meal?" Municus shook his head as they walked along.

Wynfre sneezed again before saying, "Has not worried me yet, Son."

Mari walked with Arilda down the dirt path toward their homes. The Rhys and Glas families lived half a mile from one another in the vast countryside. As they skipped along, Mari asked, "Will you come inside with us before you go home tonight?" She had stolen her father's thunder who wanted to ask the same question.

"Yes," Lewys echoed his daughter. "We would like to invite Mathilda inside for a moment to show her something, if that is alright."

"Can Arilda come too?" Mari asked hopefully.

Bethan answered, "Yes, you may both go inside. But be right home after."

Pedr opened the door to let his mother and fiancée inside first. Lewys smiled proudly and elbowed his younger son, Pawl, playfully.

"He is such a gentleman," Mari cooed. She grabbed Arilda by the arm excitedly. "Come in and see this."

Lewys walked over to a small chest in the corner of the quaint cottage and opened it. He removed a piece of goat skin and carefully unfolded it on the dining table. "This is an heirloom that has been in the family now for over a century," he explained. Everyone gathered around to see what it was. "This is a parchment made by my ancestors in Ireland before they came here. Legend says they came on a ship with Bishop Patrick himself."

Arilda was fascinated at hearing this. "Bishop Patrick? How amazing! I have so wanted to study his writings."

Lewys continued, "No one really knows if *that* is true or not, but this is what I wanted you to see, Mathilda."

She stared at the old and tattered fabric that displayed three ravens. "It is *extraordinary*. And over a hundred years old."

Lewys continued, "Since you will be part of the family soon, we wanted to show you the family crest." He pointed near the top of the aged parchment. "You can see the three ravens and here, it is hard to read, is the family name."

"Yes!" Mathilda exclaimed. "I can still see the letters for Rhys. This is so wonderful. I am so happy you have shown it to me. Thank you. Thank you, all." She smiled at Pedr lovingly.

"It was your great-grandfather who kept it in the family, was it not? What was his name?" Efa recalled.

"Liam. No, his sister is the one that kept it, I believe," Lewys answered.

"What was her name?"

"Shea. My great-aunt. She always held onto this I was told."

Mathilda smiled and said, "Shea. What a pretty name."

Pedr couldn't resist and said, "Not as pretty as yours though."

"Oh, Pedr," Mathilda responded, her face turning red.

"I think we should be going now, sister," Arilda said, pulling her by the arm. "Thank you for sharing this with us."

"Yes, thank you," Mathilda echoed as she stumbled trying to keep up. "Goodnight, Pedr."

"Goodnight," Pedr called out to them.

Lewys nodded in approval as the girls left and said, "A fine choice, Son. A fine choice indeed."

Two months had passed and Pedr and Mathilda were now more eager than ever as their wedding day approached. Pedr had finished his work for the day and decided to call upon the Glas' so he could visit Mathilda as he had not seen her in nearly a week. As he walked down the path, he came upon his sister and Arilda.

"If you are looking for Mathilda, she is not at home," Arilda said plainly. She and Mari sat upon the rock wall that separated the fields. "She has been very quiet lately. She must be deep in thought with only a month to go. Are you as nervous as she?"

"No," he laughed. "What are you two doing?" he asked as he walked by swiftly.

"We cannot tell because it is just between us girls," his sister said smartly. "Now just move along. We will not be discussing your wedding day, rest assured."

Pedr laughed and said, "I will keep moving. Do not worry."

He came upon the Glas' cottage and as soon as he approached the door, Mathilda's father opened it. "Pedr," he said in a concerned tone, "we have been worried. Have you come to see Mathilda?"

"Yes, I have."

"We have not seen her since early this morning," Mrs. Glas said as she came to the door.

Pedr could see the worried look on their faces. "I will go and look for her. She cannot be far."

He headed off knowing all the places they had spent time together. The stream at the boulders, the barn with the milking cows, and the tree that overlooked the pond. He thought for a moment about the first place he would look and said to himself, "The tree."

His quick pace became a jog as he trotted through the high reeds and leapt over the rocks on his way to the large sweet chestnut tree. It was the same tree where he proposed to her under its broad, majestic branches that sprawled into the sky from its massive trunk. It was the same tree he and Pawl had played and climbed in as boys. It was a very tranquil place that the children loved to go and play, with its inviting leaves and branches overlooking the sheep pond.

Soon, he caught sight of the tree and his pace slowed. He could sense that she was there, somewhere in the protective shade of the guardian tree. He came to the trunk, almost to the very spot where he had proposed only two months before, but she was not there.

It was then he heard someone sobbing over by the pond. He saw her sitting on a boulder only a few feet from the water. "Mathilda," he called out. "I found you." She didn't turn around though, and she just sat with her shoulders slumped, staring at the brown, placid water. "Why have you been gone all day? Your mother and father are worried." He walked over to her gently, sensing that something was the matter. He placed his hand on her shoulder when she finally turned, but couldn't bring herself to face him, however. Kneeling beside her, he asked, "What is troubling you, my beloved?"

"I have been here all day," she spoke in a weak and raspy voice. "I have been trying to find the words and the strength."

"Strength for what, Mathilda?" He grew evermore worried about her as he had never seen her this distraught before. He took her hand in his and said, "Please tell me."

She shook her head, fresh tears streamed down from her puffy red eyes. He could see now that she had been crying most of the day. "I am no longer worthy of you. I am full of shame."

He was confused and shaking his head. "Do not be nonsensical. We are *both* worthy of each other. Wh…why would you feel shame in this?"

"I do not feel shame in that, Pedr," she said continuously shaking her head in sorrow. "I am ashamed for what I have done. I have dishonored my mother and father and I have dishonored you. You must flee from me. Free yourself from my wickedness."

"Mathilda!" he pleaded. "There is no reason for you to say this. Please tell me the matter." She went silent, her hands trembling. She didn't know how to get the words out. "My love, you can tell me. You know that I love you."

She finally looked at him and her eyes pierced through him as if they were daggers. "I am lower than the dirt," she confessed. "I have allowed a man to touch me. I am with child, Pedr."

Pedr felt as if a sword had pierced his very soul. He fell backward in a trance, releasing her hand and sat on the ground beside her feeling dumbstruck. He opened his mouth, but no words could escape.

"I am unclean," she continued. "Cursed by the forced hand of a man."

Pedr came to from his trance. "*Forced?*" he asked, his voice rising in anger. "*What* man forced his hand on you?"

"I cannot say," she cried. She whirled away from him and buried her face in her hands.

"You *must* say," he wailed.

She wept ever harder though. "I cannot," she repeated over and over in between her cries. "I am unworthy of you and your family. I am a wretch."

He got to his feet, his fist shaking with fury. He pleaded with her once more. "You must tell me what man did this to you. Who forced himself upon you? Please, you *must* tell me."

"I cannot," was her only response once more. She fell over, tumbling off the rock to the ground, filled with shame and self-pity.

He felt himself running backward. The boulder from which she sat drew further and further away. "This will not stand!" he shouted. "This will *not stand.*" He ran all the way back to his home as fast as he could.

"Are you *sure?*" his father asked, dumbfounded, sitting at the family table with his wife.

"She told me herself," Pedr said, panting in distress. His hands trembled and his whole body shook. "I have never felt so betrayed in all my life. What am I to do? What am I to *do*? What shame this will bring upon us."

"She has not betrayed you, my Son," Efa exclaimed. "You must not think that way. She was assaulted against her will."

"He is right, though," Lewys countered. "What will the people say?"

"Do you not believe a woman's word to be the truth?" Efa asked, aiming her ire at her husband.

"Calm yourself, wife," Lewys assured her. "Of course, I believe her word. But others may not see it as we do. We know Mathilda to be an upstanding child of God."

"The vow must be broken," Pedr said through tears. "I shall end the betrothal in secret. Send me away if you must. I will take the village's scorn for leaving her. Just please, do not expose her shame." He headed for the door, sobbing in his hands, "I cannot let you see me like this."

His father stepped in his way though. "Please stay here, Son. You must search your heart in this matter. There is nothing out there tonight but darkness. Stay here and let us pray together. Pray for Mathilda and her parents. And we must pray for the wretch who has caused this abomination."

All the while, Pawl and Mari pulled their blankets closer to them as they listened to all that was happening in the next room, their eyes widened in disbelief.

The next morning, Pedr would not eat anything. He hadn't slept the night before either. He just sat next to his mother while she stirred the fire, getting it prepared to warm their breakfast.

"You must eat something, Pedr," she whispered, trying not to awaken the others. "If anything, you should seek out Dubric." Pedr looked even more distraught at the idea. She sensed what his thoughts may be before he could answer. "You can trust revealing things to him in confidence. He can advise you, help you keep your heart on the righteous path." He relented and decided to make his way to the chapel to seek out Father Dubric.

Dubric was having an unusually busy morning. He had plans to set out for Kington to celebrate Mass with the faithful there, but his plans were delayed with one expected visit and another quite unexpected.

It was routine to find Arilda at the chapel, either to pray or to assist Dubric in anything he needed. She would offer to clean, straighten out journals, anything she could find as long as she could be near the holy place. He saw her coming into the chapel and pretended to be in a rush.

"Good morning, Arilda," he said cheerfully. "I am sorry I do not have any work for you today. I am just on my way to Kington for a few days." She looked terribly distraught and seemed to ignore everything he had told her. She paced around the sacristy of the chapel liked a caged animal. "What is it, my child? I have never seen you this way."

"Please, Father. Please just let me stay here. I can look after things while you are away. Just please let me be here, close to God. I only want to live in His house. I am certain I am meant for the religious life, just as yourself."

Dubric smiled and tried to calm her. "I know this, young Arilda. You have told me time and again. God knows the profound love you have for Him. But I have told you, you cannot stay here. It is forbidden for women to cloister at the monastery or here for that matter. As always you are welcome to come and pray and the cleaning you do is very much appreciated. Your dedication is exemplary, but the monks can come from the monastery to tend to the chapel in my stead." He could see that she was worried in a way that he had never seen. "Tell me why you are so anxious." He tried to think of a simple chore for her while she composed her thoughts. "Come with me. Maybe you can help me with a small task. I am needing to draw from the well for my long journey."

They walked together carrying two water pouches to fill at the well that was situated in the center of the tiny hamlet. Her hands trembled as she drew up the pail from the depths. As she raised it, she finally broke her silence. "My sister has come home and given my parents horrifying news. She is inconsolable and Mother and Father have gone silent to anyone. It is like a tomb there. A dark cloud has fallen over our home and all I can think to do is to pray for her and get away. The House of God is the only place for me now. Please do not make me go back."

Dubric finally understood her trepidation and knew that time was of the essence, no matter what may have occurred in her home. "It matters not what has happened," he began. "What is most important right now is for you to be with your family. Mathilda needs you, and so do your parents. You must not hide away and hope the dark times will pass you by. Remember the Lord's commandment to honor thy father and mother and love your sister as I know you do. Please, you must go. I will come to the cottage as soon as I am able. I will delay the wagon to Kington."

Reluctantly, Arilda agreed to go back home. She knew he was right that she must honor her family and not hide from them. Dubric retreated to the chapel, leaving her standing alone at the well.

Unbeknownst to her, Municus had been watching her and Dubric. It was always his wish to speak with Arilda privately but never had the courage when the chance came. He cautiously approached her from behind, asking, "Why are you always with that old man?"

"Municus, I did not see you there. You startled me."

"I did not mean to," he said. "Are you wanting to marry him? You are always here at the chapel."

She laughed nervously at him. "That is absurd. He is old but he is a wise man of the cloth. I only wish to learn from him."

Municus shook his head, saying, "Such a waste of time. Who would want to learn those things?"

"I do not understand how you can say this when you attend Sunday Mass as everyone does," she protested. "*I* want to learn those things if you must ask. Now, if you will excuse me. I should be getting home." She quickly left leaving him alone by the well.

Pedr scurried up the hillside and made his way to the chapel. He quickly entered the sacristy to find Dubric preparing to leave. "Father, may I speak with you? It is quite urgent."

"Pedr," he exclaimed, "I am surprised to see you here." When he saw Pedr had come to speak with him privately, he knew then that the matter with Mathilda must be much more dire than he had suspected. "You look pale. Let me get you some water."

"It will not be necessary, Father. May I speak with you?" he asked again.

"Yes. Yes, of course. Sit down, young Rhys."

"Father," Pedr began. He didn't know how to get the words out. "I am in a terrible way. Mathilda…"

"Yes. Go on."

"She has confided to me that…that she is with child." Dubric's eyebrows raised slightly at hearing the unexpected news. "She has told me that it is due to some unknown man that accosted her. Forced himself on her." Pedr began to cry profusely as his emotions overwhelmed him. "She will not speak of how this happened to her."

Dubric now knew the full extent of the haunting shadow that was engulfing both houses, and why Arilda was so distraught. "I am to travel to their home as soon as I can. Prayers is what Mathilda and her family need most right now. But Pedr, as your confessor, I beseech you to tell me what you know of this. Are you the man she is hiding from the light of truth?"

"*No*, Father. I promise that I am *not*," Pedr answered, his voice rising in panic. "But I am her husband to be. I am so filled with shame, but I am deeply worried what people will think of her or what they might do to her. Please help me, Father. What must I do?"

"Even though you are not formally wed to one another, the vows between you have already been declared. You must stand by her and protect her. Now is the time she needs you the most." Dubric took him by both hands and looked him seriously in the eye, saying, "Forgiveness is what Jesus has taught us. Let your heart be your guide. Justice will be served to this assailant but by God's way, not by ours. Now is the time for clear thinking and many prayers. Your place is with her no matter the circumstances."

Later that afternoon, dark clouds began rolling in from the horizon and thunder could be heard in the distance and a cold wind began to swirl. Pedr stumbled on his way down the rocky path in the punishing wind. He had wandered the hillsides all day trying to make sense of all the madness in his thoughts. It was the hardest day of his life, but he knew he must return soon to face it all. He had to show Mathilda that he still loved her, and that he would stand by her no matter the cost.

It was nearly dark when he arrived home and the storm rolled in with the rain coming down in a torrent. His family jolted to the sound of the door slamming shut.

"Pedr!" his mother cried. "Thank the Heavens you are home."

"Where have you been?" his father asked.

Pedr knelt by the fire, his hair matted and dripping. "I needed time to think. I must go to her at once. My place is with her now."

"The weather is too harsh, Pedr," his father told him. "Let the rains die down, then we will go together. We must show her clan that we stand together. She is still a part of *this* family too."

Just then, the door flung open again. To their surprise, it was Cadoc, Bethan and Arilda. Dubric stumbled in behind them as well. They were all soaked to the bone and out of breath.

"*Cadoc*," Lewys said in surprise. "Please, all of you, come by the fire."

"There is no time," Cadoc said frankly. "We demand to know what Pedr's role is in this travesty."

Bethan grabbed Cadoc by his cloak and pleaded with him, "Husband, you said you would not."

"Quiet!" Cadoc looked Pedr directly and said, "Tell the truth, boy. Is it because of you our daughter is so tormented with guilt and filled with shame?"

"We must not judge, brother Cadoc," Dubric interrupted. "We spoke of this, I tell you."

"What are you saying?" Lewys asked sternly. "That my son is dishonest? That he would shame himself and both our families? He has never told a lie his entire life."

Efa pleaded with Cadoc as well. "You know Pedr just as well as we know Mathilda. We have known each other's children since they were born. You must not ask such things."

Pedr got to his feet. The turn of events was too sobering for him to stay silent any longer. "You must *believe* me. I have never been with her. I swear!"

"Pedr, do not swear," Dubric said, reprimanding him. He turned to Cadoc and said, "I know the boy to be truthful. Now out with the reason we are really here."

Mari got up and stood next to Pedr, her face had gone ashen with fear. Her intuition made her feel something was terribly wrong. "Where is Mathilda?"

"She has gone away," Cadoc answered sadly. "It is why we have come. She left before the storm came."

"She never ate a morsel the entire day," Bethan added. The look of worry on her face was palpable. "She hardly spoke. I know she was waiting for you, Pedr."

Cadoc continued, "Now the rain is a downpour and darkness has set in. We know not where she could be. We need help."

Pedr immediately spoke up. "I will go."

"As will I," Lewys said.

Pawl stood and said, "I am coming too."

"Arilda and Bethan, please stay here with us," Efa instructed. "The men will find her."

Lewys turned quickly to Dubric and said, "Stay with them, Father. No sense in you going out in this again. Lead them in prayers as we need them more than ever."

Pedr was almost out the door when Cadoc grabbed him and hugged him tight. "Forgive me, Pedr. I was wrong to accuse you."

"I will find her," Pedr assured him. "You have my word."

The four men dashed out into the fury. The pounding rain soaked them immediately and they shielded their eyes from the driving wind. "We will split up!" Lewys shouted. "That way we can look in four places at once." They all agreed and ran off in opposite directions.

Arilda paced before the fire while Dubric led them in praying the rosary. She was too worried to even say the prayers though. She paced in silence while the thunder clapped overhead. Finally, it was more than she could bear.

"I must go after her," she said, interrupting their praying.

"Child, it is much too treacherous out there," Dubric pleaded.

Tears rolled down her cheeks and she said, "She is my sister."

Mari ran over and hugged Arilda tightly. "I will go with you."

"No." she answered. "Stay here with your mother."

Bethan stood and looked upon her daughter proudly. She could see she was no longer a little girl anymore. Right before her eyes, Arilda was becoming an adult. She quickly walked over and put an extra cloak around her. "Go, Arilda. Help Pedr find her." With that, Arilda set out in the torrential rain and thunder.

Pedr knew exactly where to go. In the driving wind and rain, he made his way down the sloshing hillside in near darkness. It was useless to carry torches in such rain, so he urgently carried on by sense and touch. He ran into branches as they swayed in front of him, scraping his face. The wounds ran red with the water down his cheeks. He knew he was nearing the giant chestnut tree where he had proposed to her and where she had shared her dreadful secret.

He reached the base of the low hanging branches that swirled in the wind. "Mathilda!" he called out over the thunder. There was no answer. He walked over to the rock she always liked to sit upon and stare at the water. The wind was so harsh he could barely make out the white face of the large boulder. The water had risen very high and spilled out of its banks and his feet sloshed in the mud and water, still trying to search blindly in the darkness. "Mathilda," he said again. He stepped from side to side retreating from the rising water. As he backed away a branch brushed against his head frightening him. It brushed against him once again and he flung his arm to swat it away.

It was then he knew it was not a branch at all and turned to see what was batting against him in the wind. He was shocked to see two bare feet dangling before his face. He put his hand to his mouth and gasped and stumbled backward and fell off his feet, landing in the muddy water with a thud. "*No!*" he shouted in horror, staring petrified at Mathilda's lifeless body swaying from one of the branches. A noose fashioned from tree vines was wound tightly around her neck with her head lying flat against her shoulder. Her arms dangled at her side, her clothes drenched, as the wind blew her gently back and forth.

"My God!" he shouted again in disbelief. He thrashed his feet in the mud, trying to get away from the horrific sight until finally he gained some traction, getting to his feet. He spun around to dart away and ran right into Arilda. He grabbed her by the shoulder and wept, "Arilda...Arilda." He let go and ran as fast as he could back up the hill.

Arilda slowly approached the haunting sight of her dead sister hanging from the tree. No words would come as her head shook and her body trembled as she looked in horror at Mathilda's bloated face. The wind had subsided, yet the rain kept falling in a steady downpour. The body twisted in the breeze soaked through and through. It was then Arilda saw something even more disturbing. Sewn to the hem of Mathilda's cloak just above her bare ankles, was a square of red fabric. The red color stood out prominently in the darkness against the drab brown of her garments. Arilda's eyes widened in incredulity and stared at the red square, wanting to scream out loudly, but no sound could come from her shocked expression. Suddenly, she heard voices coming and feet sloshing not far away.

"We heard shouts!" she heard her father say.

Immediately she reached up and ripped the red fabric from Mathilda's dress and hid it away in her cloak and ran toward the others and shouted, "Father! Dear God in Heaven. She is here!"

Pedr was sobbing uncontrollably as he stumbled back with the other three men. When Cadoc saw the ghastly sight, he fell to his knees in shock. Pawl and his father couldn't believe what they were seeing and Arilda just stood and sobbed, clutching to Pedr's shaken and sodden frame.

When word reached those at the Rhys cottage, everyone hurried into the night to the Glas' home. The one-room cottage was filled with firelight and sorrow. The women wept and the men sat stunned, staring at Mathilda's still soaking corpse. She lay in her mother's arms who couldn't stop wailing. She swayed Mathilda from side to side as if she were an infant again, shaking and sobbing as she did.

"Tormented so that she would take her own life," Dubric said mournfully. "We knew not how long she suffered this way in silence. Now she has taken not one but two lives. And we will never know who brought her to this act."

"The child will die with her in secret," Cadoc said, looking like a ghost himself.

"I can stay silent no longer," Arilda said, her voice cracking, her face swollen from hours of tears. "She left us a clue as to who her assailant was. I would know her stitching from anywhere and I know it was her hand who sewed this to her garments."

The room fell dreadfully silent as she produced the torn red handkerchief and laid it on the table. A roll of thunder boomed in the distance as Pedr stared at the red square in shock. His blood ran cold in his veins, his anger welling up inside.

"Where did you find this?" her mother gasped. She knew the answer already as she rolled Mathilda's body to one side to see the tear at the base of her dress. Her eyes widened in horror.

Mari spotted it too. "There is still part of it attached to her clothes. It matches what was torn from the handkerchief."

"She did sew it on herself," Efa exclaimed. "Dear God in Heaven."

Dubric stood against the wall, fuming. "The foolish man must have unknowingly dropped it after committing his dastardly deed. It would be God's will that poor Mathilda would find this. She is clever now even unto death."

"I will tear the man apart!" Cadoc cried.

Dubric grabbed him by the arm and shook him. "We shall *not* spill his blood in revenge! To kill even then would be unforgiveable."

"What *Bulward* has done is unforgiveable," Pedr countered angrily. "I will kill the man *myself*. I care *not* what happens to me."

Lewys jumped across the room to stop Pedr from leaving. "You cannot think this way, Pedr. Listen to what the Father is saying. Taking revenge is not the answer. Please, we need calm at this moment. Let us think of poor Mathilda now. We must give her a proper burial and let her rest in peace."

"Pedr," Dubric said as he crossed the room to speak to him directly, "we must remember. Blessed are the merciful, for they shall obtain mercy."

"Yes, Father," Arilda agreed. "Please listen to him, Pedr."

"You must erase these vengeful thoughts from your mind," Dubric added. "Now let us tend to Mathilda."

She was buried in a plot next to their cottage under a willow tree. They mourned her for days with constant prayer. Pedr never spoke nor did he do much of anything. His brother kept a close watch over him as he knew that his heart was aching more than he could imagine. Early one morning, Pawl went looking for him when he saw Pedr was not in his bed. He heard the thump of what sounded like an axe-hammer just outside the cottage. He found Pedr outside in the early morning light chopping wood.

"Hello, brother," Pawl said.

Pedr threw the axe down chopping a piece of wood cleanly down the middle. "It makes me feel better," he answered Pawl, as if he could read his brother's mind.

"It is good work," Pawl concurred. "How are you?" He looked around to see the work he had done. Pawl concluded he had been there for quite a long time, judging from the large pile of chopped wood.

Pedr took in a deep breath and rested his axe. "I will be fine, Pawl. It is good work." He stopped and looked out across the horizon, gazing at the dawn sky. "I hear there are forests so vast in the north. I would like to see that someday. A man could get a lot of hard work done in a place like that. Good, hard work."

Pawl nodded in agreement. "The wilderness is a fine thing. Have you let your anger subside?" he asked, getting to the point.

Pedr thumped the axe one more time into a fresh log. "I feel nothing now. I will carry on, but I just do not know in what way. All I know is God will judge us all in the end including…that man."

"Yes, He will," Pawl answered. "He will also keep you on the right path, Pedr. You must remember that too."

Weeks later, in the early morning before the dawn, Wynfre hobbled slowly toward the milking barn carrying a wooden pail with him. Inside he found the shaggy Highland cow patiently waiting for fresh straw. He used a narrow pitching fork to throw a few heaps of straw in front of her to let her eat while he drew some milk. The straw made him sneeze loudly and the cow let out a gentle moo. He wiped his nose with a plain brown handkerchief, then tossing the pitching fork aside he plopped down beside the cow on an old wooden stool.

"There you go, girl," he said, patting her gently on the side.

He sat beside the cow while she ate and squeezed one hand after the other, quickly filling the shallow pail. When he finished, he made sure to put more straw in front of her as a reward. When he reached for the pitching fork, it wasn't there.

He looked around saying to himself, "Now, where did I put it?" It was then he noticed a shadowy figure in the doorway. "What are you doing here? Is that you, boy? Come help me find the…"

The shadow lunged forward with the pitching fork, impaling Wynfre to the wooden barn wall. Wynfre gasped in shock, grunting and writhing in pain trying to free himself, but the person was too strong. The assailant dug the fork ever deeper and with brutal force, not allowing the dying Wynfre any chance of escape. Suddenly his body fell limp, blood tricking from his mouth. The shadowy figure let the handle go, leaving it dangling from Wynfre's chest. Wynfre was left impaled to the wall, his body slumped over the handle and his glassy eyes bulging from their sockets. The shadowy figure darted out of the barn, unknowing that Municus had witnessed his escape from cover of the reeds.

Municus stood before his dead father in stunned silence. He immediately pulled the pitching fork from his father's chest, letting his body slump to the floor in a bloody heap.

Later that day, Arilda stood at the well, slowly drawing up some water while keeping one eye on the chapel door. She was eagerly waiting for Dubric to emerge. In her days of mourning her sister, she had less courage to seek him out personally though. She felt her constant badgering about her monastic desires was wearing him down. Through her sorrow, she didn't want to bother the priest any longer, yet she still yearned to learn from him.

Soon, he did emerge from the chapel and spotted Arilda immediately. She stared at the ground shyly, knowing he already knew what she wanted to talk about. She hadn't the courage any longer though, so she quietly continued pulling up the pail of water from the well.

"You need not avoid me, my child," he said warmly. "You act as if I will be cross with you. Now why would I do that? I am most concerned about your family still. Please, tell me how your mother and father are getting along?" She finished filing her water skins and stood silently staring at her feet. "Will you tell me how your family is doing?"

"They are very quiet," she finally admitted. "Pedr never comes by any longer. Mari has but I have not much motivation to spend time with her now. I know I have neglected her."

"It is perfectly understandable, my child. Grieving can only be healed by time. This too shall pass." He tried to get her to smile at him, or at least look him in the eye. "I will be traveling soon to Herefordshire to check on the monks at Hentland. I promise to keep making known your wishes to the bishop." Arilda perked up when he said this and finally smiled at him. "Does this please you?"

"Oh, yes, Father Dubric!" she exclaimed. "Thank you, kind sir. My spirits have been lifted immediately."

"You are most welcome, Arilda," he said, chuckling at her. "I wish all men and women shared your love and passion for our Lord."

As she walked back through the swaying grasses and rows of walled fields, sheep bayed in the distance and the sun shone high in the afternoon sky. She became increasingly aware that she was being followed. It came as no surprise to her that Municus was not far behind. She noticed him walking along the top of the wall, hopping down for a few steps and then leaping back up again.

"You seem quite jovial this afternoon," she said to him. "Have you not any work to be done?"

"My work is done, fair maiden," he said. "I have nothing more to do ever if I wish."

"That seems a bit audacious if I may say," she added. She found his carefree attitude puzzling. "What has gotten into you? Everyone has work to be done."

"I do not wish to work," he answered plainly. "But I do wish to speak with you privately." He stopped under the shade of a large tree. "May I?"

She stopped abruptly and let out a deep sigh. "What is it that you want, Municus? I must get home."

"You are always needing to get home. I only wish to speak with you here if you will allow me." He motioned for her to come closer under the tree with him. "I think it is time that I proclaim my intentions for you."

"Your intentions?" she asked as she stepped under the shade of the tree.

"I wish for us to be married. My father would be quite pleased and as I would be."

"Married?" she asked befuddled. "But the way you chastised me about how I enjoy speaking to Father Dubric. And how you said Sunday Mass was all a waste of time. I cannot marry a man like that. And besides, I will never marry. That has never been a secret. My life is for God."

"But if you knew how I truly felt about you, Arilda," he pleaded with her.

"It matters not," she snapped. "What I do know is how you feel toward God. This I cannot accept. If I were to marry a man, and I never will, he would be a God-fearing man, and upright in the eyes of the Lord." She began to tremble as the thought of what his father had done to Mathilda filled her mind. She saw a vision of her hanging from the tree and she recoiled in disgust as the harsh wounds in her heart began to tear open again. "And knowing the things that I know, there is never a lifetime where I would marry you."

"What things do you know?" He lunged forward and grabbed her by the arm, knocking the water skin from her and spilling on the ground. "Please," he said in panic, "if you can stay just for a little while."

"But why?" she asked, her voice beginning to crack. She wanted to run but his hands were too strong.

"I just want to spend *time* with you. For *once*." He pulled her closer to the trunk of the tree, looking around to see if anyone was nearby. "Come sit with me here by the tree on the smooth, soft grass. Let me show you how I feel about you."

"I...I...I cannot," she sobbed. "Let me go."

He pulled her closer to him, grasping her by the shoulders, forcing her to face him. "We are not children any longer. We are man and woman now and I want to be your man, your husband. Lie with me, and you will know it to be true."

"*What?*" she gasped in shock. She struggled to break free but couldn't. "I will do no such thing!" She wrenched one arm free of him and slapped his face as hard as she could.

He became enraged and threw her to the ground, tearing her dress from one shoulder. She lay bare-shouldered, stunned and breathless. She tried to get up, but he pushed her down again. "I will have you," he groaned like a madman.

Before he could lay on top of her, she swiftly kicked him as hard as she could in the groin. He rolled over in agony on the ground and she quickly seized upon the moment and scrambled to her feet. "You stay on the ground, young Municus!" she fumed. "No man will ever touch this body as long as I live." She backed away, tripping over the empty water skin. He crawled to his knees and finally stood, doubled over in pain.

He tried to reach for her, saying, "As long as you live, you say?"

"Yes, I do say," she countered fiercely. "And I will tell you the things that I know. I *know* what your father did. I know what he did to my sister. Just the same as you are trying to do to me. *He* is the reason she hung herself from that tree."

Municus smiled at her connivingly. "And I know what *your* father has done."

She stood holding her dress to her shoulder, staring at him beleaguered and inquisitive. "What are you talking about?"

"Hey!" a voice called out.

Arilda and Municus were both stunned to see Pedr leaping over the wall and running at top speed directly at Municus. Before he knew what happened, Pedr struck him on the face, sending him tumbling to the ground. Holding his eye, and panting like a wild boar, Municus got to his feet and scampered away.

"Thank the Heavens, Pedr," Arilda sighed with tremendous relief.

"Are you hurt?" he asked.

"No," she answered, catching her breath. The whole moment was a blur to her, and she was dazed and confused. "He lured me in with talk of marriage, but all he wanted was to lie with me. I refused and fought him off." She stumbled around with her shoulder still exposed. "I…I must get home to mother. She will worry about me."

Pedr held her steady and pulled up her sleeve to cover her shoulder. "You are brave, Arilda. Worry not," he said. "I will get you home."

"No," she panicked. "The water. We must get more water. Please come with me, Pedr."

"Are you certain?" he asked concerned. "I will run and draw some for you."

"No, please. Walk with me," she insisted. "I know I will be safe with you."

He relented and walked with her back to the village to draw more water from the well. No one was there so they walked over to it and he immediately began to draw up the pail for her.

"I will fill it, thank you," she said. "Rest if you like."

"I will go into the chapel for a moment," he told her.

She nodded with a smile to his idea and replied, "Yes. Prayers are good. Say one for me." Pedr removed his cap and went inside the chapel to pray.

Arilda sat on the edge of the well, refilling her water skin. She had calmed herself with walking with Pedr, but she had a strong desire to get back home to her grieving parents after such a horrific encounter.

She finished filling the skin and then placed the pail to the side and secured the rope when an eerily raspy voice was heard behind her, saying, "As long as you live."

Before she could turn, she felt the cool sensation of an icy blade pressed firmly against her throat. In a flash, it was yanked away slicing through her delicate flesh. She gasped at the sudden shock, clutching her throat, coughing and gurgling for air. Blood flowed forth from her like water. She rolled over with a moan and a wheeze and hung over the edge of the wall. She lay catatonic, her eyes wide open, with one hand clutched to her blood-ravaged throat and the other hanging lifelessly over the edge. Blood trickled down her arms and her placid-pale fingertips, dripping steadily into the well. All the while Municus stood over her clutching the dagger in his fist.

The door opened to the chapel and Pedr screamed out frantically, "*Arilda!*" His voice echoed across the countryside, scattering the birds in the trees. He dashed across the courtyard to catch her body as it slid from the edge of the well. He fell to his knees clutching her lifeless body and cried in horror as Municus dropped the dagger and ran away wailing and screaming.

Coda

Pedr would never be the same after the loss of Mathilda and the shocking murder of Arilda. He was forever wracked with guilt over leaving her alone for only a few moments at the well.

His memories from the past haunted like him like ghosts. So, in the spring of the following year, he set out to free himself of his demons. He headed north to the forests of Yorkshire and Kielder in an area that would one day be called Northumbria. He would never marry nor return to the county of Gloucestershire or Oldbury-on-Severn.

Mari, the ever dedicated and closest friend to Arilda, courageously picked up Arilda's pursuits and continued the crusade for women to be free to join the monastic life. Her efforts were noteworthy as she made great strides in her cause. She vowed never to marry, as many women had done after the horrific death of Arilda. Her love for God was strong and was the same as it had been for her tragically lost friend. She never lived to see the success of her crusade, but nearly a century later, Eanswith, the Christian daughter of the king of Kent, established the first nunnery in England in 630. It was called Folkestone Priory.

Dubric would soon be known throughout all southeast Wales as the Bishop of Ergyng. His work with the poor and the sick were widely known as was his work as a teacher. Later in life, he was named Archbishop of Llandaff, and legend says he crowned King Arthur. He is known today as Saint Dubricius.

Pawl and Angelika were married a year later and resided in Oldbury the rest of their lives, raising nine children. From their children came thirty-one grandchildren.

One grandson, named for his grandfather Pawl, and after hearing of his great-uncle Pedr's flight to the northern forests, decided to seek him out in the wilderness and work as a woodsman.

Little else is known about the virgin martyr Saint Arilda, other than her steadfast devotion to God and her tragic slaying at the hands of Municus. A few churches in the area, including Saint Arild's Church in Oldbury, are dedicated to her, as is the well that bears her name. Legend has it that the water still runs red with her saintly blood. The actual well is said to be located in the countryside near Kington.

Part III

The Year of Our Lord, 677

In the year of our Lord, 677, Christianity in England was decades into a new era that was ushered in by Pope Gregory I in the waning days of the 6th century. The centuries that followed the Roman departure of England left a void between the small pockets of Roman and Celtic Christians and the incoming Anglo-Saxon pagans. When it was learned the pagan king of Kent had married a Christian princess, the Pope sent missionaries led by Augustine to establish a new dawning of Christianity on the island. It would come to be known as the Gregorian Mission and its main purpose was to convert as many of the newcomer pagans as possible. Having befriended the king, Augustine was named the first Archbishop of Canterbury. The new era of Christianity swept across England and reached as far north as Scotland, with new monasteries and convents being established in many places.

Among these Anglo-Saxons was a man born thirty years later in the northern kingdom of Northumbria. He was solely dedicated to God in all his works and practiced his faith in the Celtic tradition, which often collided with his contemporaries who promoted the Roman tradition.

Entering the monastic life at Ripon, he quickly ascended the ranks of importance amongst his peers. His dedication to the poor and to the needy was commendable and there were even miraculous cures attributed to him. He lived a strict life of piety and obedience even though his fame had spread throughout the area. After being made prior at various monasteries and after decades of service to the people, he decided to go into seclusion at his hermitage to focus solely on his devotion to God. He lived as a hermit in the caves near Holburn rarely venturing out to meet visitors.

It was not until an unexpected visitor would he consider going back to his life as a monk and prior. The encounter would change the old man's life and the history of Northumbria forever. After his wondrous and mysterious visitation, the hermit made a vow that said: *Show kindness to strangers, for you were once a stranger too.* The old man's name was Cuthbert.

Cuthbert

Flames raced through the dry, brittle forest and trees that stood like cloistered towers were being pulverized by a maddening storm of fire. The entire forest was engulfed in the driving maelstrom.

Paulus had no time to even catch his breath it had come upon him so suddenly. He dropped his axe and stumbled over fallen trees that were victims of his own work. The flames were nearly on top of him as he scrambled to his feet once more. His stumbling turned into an all-out sprint over the nearest ridge and down a gradual slope. He dodged thick brush and low-hanging limbs trying to escape the inferno that was chasing him relentlessly. He could hear the raging crackle of limbs and branches fall behind him like stones dropping from a cloudless sky. He ran as hard as he could with the flames barreling down and could feel the scorching heat on his back and heels of his feet. Paulus stumbled and rolled over some thickets lacerating his face. He didn't feel the sting as the fire lapped at his feet. Regaining his traction, he headed for the spring pond where he washed his face time and again after a long day's work. He could see the placid pool shimmering in the firelight just paces away. Lunging with all his might, he threw himself into the water at full sprint, splashing face first into the pond's welcoming arms just as the flames soared overhead, reaching out like the tips of devilish fingers.

Paulus sank straight to the shallow bottom, his eyes still widened in terror underwater watching the flames darting overhead. It was like the fire shrieked in frustration that it could not penetrate the protective waters. He held his breath for what seemed like hours when in fact it was merely seconds. The flames subsided directly overhead, and he decided it was safe to come up for air. Taking a deep breath, his lungs rasped as they grappled for the scorched air. The entire pond was encircled with maddening, hellish fire and the dry wood crackled and splintered into ash in seconds. He scratched and clawed in the muddy bottom to steady himself in the water as his feet were numb from the punishing heat. It took all his might and steely nerves to cling to the muddy bottom and keep air flowing into his nostrils that hovered just above the surface.

A roar of thunder and the shrill cry of beasts was heard high upon the slopes. He scanned the smoky horizon of fire and black ash until he saw it. Opposite from where he made his lifesaving leap, he saw the animals of the forest, birds, insects, and all manner of creatures flying and stampeding southward to safety. Deer, fox, rabbits, bears, squirrels, every living thing was making a mad dash through the flames in pure anarchy.

He found a charred log floating nearby on which to rest. Splashing water all over it, the wood was finally cool enough to grasp onto. Paulus wrapped his arms around the ashen wood and tried to catch his breath. He let in and out deep breaths of precious air and his teeth chattered as he lay in the murky water. Or was it the wrath of horror that made him tremble? No matter. He closed his eyes and passed out from sheer exhaustion.

He never knew how long he was out. His grip had loosened on the log and his face fell to the water. Water rushed into his mouth and lungs and immediately he startled awake, coughing and spewing up the muddy water. He tried desperately to get his bearings in the bowels of the dimly lit cauldron. The flames had raced on to engulf more fresh timber and all that remained around the desolate pond was blackened, scorched Earth. In the middle of the hellish landscape was Paulus, soaked to the bone and clinging to a charred piece of fallen pine.

Crawling on his hands and knees, he emerged from the murky pond. Nothing had been left untouched and everything around him was charred black; smoke still emanating from the remains. Tears welled up in his eyes as he looked on in horror. He had to get back to the village to what, if anything, that was left.

He clambered through the ashen terrain in the twilight of sunset. Through the haze and smoke, he could see the sky dotted with sporadic stars as he continued onward, thrashing through blackened trees and scorched ground.

After what seemed like hours, he reached his home or what was left of it. He staggered around, his hands grasping his head in disbelief. Where was his cottage? Where were his neighbor's cottages?

He cried out in a raspy voice with lungs filled with airborne ash, "*Keira*," but his voice only echoed across the barren landscape. In the last faint of light, he could see the outlines of each home until he knew he had come across his own. Two small piles of ash lay side by side in what was his bed chamber. He fell to his knees and crawled toward them, his eyes raining down tears. He brushed away the ash until his fingers came upon the solid remnants of their bodies. Side by side lay the charred remains of his wife and five-year-old son.

He couldn't even make out their faces as they were just blackened human forms. He delicately lifted his son's body and cradled him in one arm, then cradled the body of his wife in the other and sobbed as if his own life had ended. He cried holding them the rest of the night.

The first morning light cascaded through the smoldering, splintered twigs that were once an abundant forest. The beam of first light warmed Paulus' weary body as he stood over two freshly covered graves. A charred wooden cross was placed at the head of each grave as he stood emotionless staring at his family's final resting place. His face was still scarred and covered in ash as was his dark beard.

Paulus didn't know where to go from there. As the night turned into day there was still no one around but himself. None of his fellow woodsmen had emerged from the destroyed forest, nor did any of the other villagers appear to have survived. He was alone.

He hung his head and departed from the graves and wandered for days through an endless sea of destruction. Rain fell, adding to his muddy and ash-covered misery. It wasn't until the third day did the landscape transform from hell on Earth to a forest of lush and vibrant-green vegetation. He was immensely relieved as it was like he had stepped into another world.

He heard the sound of trickling water not far away, so his pace quickened, dashing madly forward until he found it. Falling to his knees, he sank his hands into the clear running brook, lapping up the life-giving water until he fully quenched his parched thirst. Near the brook was a tree with ripened berries and he splashed across the shallow stream, beholden and breathless. He picked as many as he could find and devoured them all. After satisfying his thirst once more, he collapsed on the ground of the valley floor and fell into a deep sleep.

When he awoke, it wasn't hunger but another downpour of rain that aroused him. He walked all around the area searching for cover but found none. He had no tools with which to cut wood to make a lean-to, so he just sat by the brook and waited for the rain to stop.

Later that day, after the rain had subsided, he managed to fashion a spear using nearby stones to sharpen the point so he could catch fish. His invention proved successful and he was able to spear two fish in the stream. His hunger was ravenous but not enough to eat the meal raw, so he began to search high and low for a particular kind of stone on the wet, soggy ground. Carrying the fish with him, still stuck to his spear, he searched for the familiar grayish, black-tinted flint stones. He brushed leaves aside and tossed rocks away feverishly. Finally, to his surprise, he found what he was looking for.

Clearing more leaves away and pulling away the muddy topsoil, he dug a few inches down to fresh, dry dirt. He fashioned the hole into a firepit and then threw in some leaves and moss. Smacking the flint against another stone, the sparks immediately ignited the moss. Before long, he had a suitable fire with which to cook his meal.

Nightfall came, and the sounds of the creatures of the night began to chirp and sing. He sat by the smoldering fire, eating the last of the fish that he had prepared. Leaning against the tree, he fell asleep.

The next morning, he was awakened by a persistent rain once more. Rejuvenated by his first hot meal in nearly a week, he set out to find better shelter. He walked with the staff through the dense forest along the sides of the inclined valley walls. He soon came upon a clearing away from the trees with an out-cropping of rocks. As he drew closer, he realized the rocks surrounded a crevice in the ground. The cave opening was nearly twenty feet wide but only a few feet from top to bottom. Ducking underneath the opening, he examined the interior of the cave as best he could in the unsubstantial daylight. He heard water droplets echoing from inside the chamber and was tempted to go inside but something in his mind was holding him back. The find was suitable however and he nodded with satisfaction.

This will do, he thought. He decided to go fetch more fresh leaves, moss and twigs in which to start a fire. He wanted to gather as much as he could store inside the cave for the night.

As soon as he turned to descend the embankment, he was stopped cold in his tracks by a silvery blade of a machete pointed directly at his head.

"Are you an assassin?" an old man's voice boomed. Paulus was stunned. It had been nearly a week since he had seen or spoken to anyone and his heart raced in his chest, not knowing how to respond. "What are you doing at my cave?"

Paulus raised his hands in surrender, his arms trembling like twigs. Filled with fright, he opened his mouth and uttered in a raspy voice, "Shelter."

"Are you sure you are not an assassin?" the man repeated, pressing the point of the blade against Paulus' head.

"You may kill me," Paulus fumbled as he spoke. "I am prepared. Free me from my misery."

Immediately the man withdrew the blade and looked at him curiously. "Misery, you say?" He looked even more perplexed as he thought about the request. "Why, being alive is the best remedy for misery." The old man walked over and sat on a tree stump, his favorite and daily place to sit. He was dressed in a gray cloak and his beard was long and white but neatly groomed and matched the color of his thinning hair. He chuckled to himself and said, "Living the life God intended is the best cure for misery."

Paulus lowered his arms when he saw the man retreat and sit, as his heart slowed the pounding in his chest. "You are not going to kill me?" he asked. The old man laughed again and chucked the machete to the ground. "I did not know it was your cave."

"It is my dwelling place," he answered. "Please tell me your name."

Paulus fell to his knees, exhausted from fright and sat on the ground facing the man. He had been alone for so long, he felt relieved to be speaking to someone. "I am called Rhys. I am a woodsman."

"What is your Christian name, woodsman?"

"Paulus," he answered. "What is your name?"

The old man took in a deep breath of air and exhaled satisfyingly. "In the wilderness, I have no name. With God and the birds in the trees, I am just a man." The man noticed Paulus' staff and how sharp the point was on it. "Are you skilled at catching fish? If you are, then I will allow you take shelter from the rains. I miss the taste of fish, but I am too old. They are too fast for me."

Paulus looked at his staff and instinctively grabbed it and jumped to his feet as if new life had coursed through him like lightning. "The stream nearby," he said breathlessly, "I will get you fish." He quickly jogged down the slopes toward the creek with the old man watching him with a broad smile.

It wasn't long before Paulus returned with four fresh fish all stuck on the end of another staff he had made by the water. Within no time, he used his flint rock to start a fire and had the fish roasting soon after.

"You are skilled indeed, young Paulus," the man commended. "I see you washed your face in the water. You should bathe completely to rid yourself of the ash after we have eaten. You will feel better."

Paulus looked at him crazily. The man spoke to him as if he were his father. When the fish were fully cooked, he handed some to the man.

The old man smiled with a satisfied grin, saying, "You have made me content once more. A tasty meal indeed. I thank you." After they were done eating, they both rested on the ground near the fire. The sun was setting, and the cooler air was ushering in the coming night. "Tell me, Paulus. How is it that you are here and all alone? What happened to you?"

Paulus stared into the fire, poking it around with a stick and thought of the events that transpired nearly a week before. He thought of the morning he left for work in the woods, seeing his wife Keira and his son for the last time, not knowing it would be. The old man waited patiently for him to respond. Finally, Paulus found the words to describe it.

"We never knew who they were," he began. "They had tried before to ransack and burn our village, but each time we had thwarted the marauders. We were close to the highlands on the edges of the forest. I could only guess that is where they were coming from, high in the mountains. The dry winds had blown in for months and the wood was easy prey for fire."

"There was a fire?" the man inquired curiously.

Paulus nodded with a solemn expression. "Like none I had ever seen. It moved as if it were alive. Strong, towering and swift." He shook his head as he recalled the raging inferno he narrowly escaped. "I never saw it coming." He took in a deep breath, holding back his emotions. "Those at the village never did either. I was fortunate as I had been working deep in the forest all day."

"And the village?" the man asked curiously. "Was anything left?"

"Nothing," Paulus answered somberly. "Nothing and no one."

The man contemplated carefully what Paulus was saying and he understood the gravity of his situation. He knew he had lost everything. "You had a family, yes?" Paulus nodded, fighting back the tears. "A wife? Perhaps children?"

"A son." He couldn't contain himself any longer and Paulus buried his head in his chest and sobbed.

The man gazed upon him sympathetically, letting him expel his emotions. "I am sorry, my son."

Paulus wiped his eyes and his nose with his sleeve, trying to regain his composure. "I buried them side by side. Afterward, I walked and wandered for days, not knowing where to go. I have felt nothing ever since. My body, my mind, have just been numb. I died with them."

As the sun set, they retreated into the cave when they heard thunder in the distance. "We should light a fire," the man said as he stooped awkwardly into the cave, carrying a torch. He pointed to a spot on the rocky surface that was covered in ash. "I have a small pit there in which to start one. It will keep us warm and the critters out."

"I will work on it," Paulus obliged.

"There are some good flat rocks over there. Find a good one to rest your head."

Paulus winced as his knees knocked on the hard floor of the cave. After he lit a small fire, he found a decent place to lie down. He tried his best to get comfortable, but it was fruitless. He much preferred the soft ground outside.

The crash of thunder boomed overhead, and the rain began to pour right on cue. Drops of rain fell sporadically inside and water trickled down the cave walls, but they were mostly dry inside.

"Yes," the man's voice echoed in the near darkness. "I imagine you are glad to be dry for once. Rain is here again. And hard I hear."

"I am dry, yes," Paulus answered, his body aching. "I could use some straw to settle my back though."

"Should have thought of that before," the man replied wryly, sounding like a parent again. Paulus glanced over at him through the firelight, frowning as he saw the man resting comfortably on a big pile of straw.

Trying to forget the pain in his back, Paulus thought of other things. One curiosity had been in the back of his mind ever since he had met the old man and finally decided to ask.

"How is it that you are out in the wilderness living alone in a cave?" Paulus asked. He didn't receive an answer right away though. "Why are you here?"

"To be," came the response.

"To be?"

The old man let out another deep sigh as if he were too tired to explain. "I came to cleanse my spirit," he finally admitted. "It is my wish to be one again with God. To be in nature, to be in the wild away from the distractions. Away from everything. Only to be." He stared at Paulus through the firelight and stated plainly. "I came here to die."

Paulus did not know what to say after that. Then it occurred to him that he himself felt as if he were already dead. Perhaps the old man was dead too and was a ghost visiting him. He laid his head back down on the flat rock once more and stared at the blackened, wet ceiling.

"Now, sleep," the man's voice echoed across the cave as the thunder rolled far off in the distance.

As the days and weeks passed, Paulus' skills in the forest returned to his senses. He became more acclimated to the surroundings and he re-honed his skills as a hunter. He set snares using vines stripped of their leaves to catch squirrels and other small animals.

One afternoon, the two of them returned to the site of his trap and found a squirrel caught in the snare. "You do well, woodsman," the man complimented. "We have had enough fish for now, I must agree."

As they sat by the fire, eating the freshly cooked squirrel, Paulus stared at the sky that was blanketed with bright, twinkling stars.

"We will not be blessed with the rain tonight," the man said. "Is it not amazing? The Lord's universe spread so far and vast. It is humbling to see how small and insignificant we are against such a multitude."

"You find that troubling?" Paulus asked curiously.

The man shook his head, saying, "No, I find it extraordinary."

Paulus retreated to the cave with a torch and stared at the wall above his bed of straw. Observing the small puddles of water and the blackened ash from the firepit, he sat down and began to mix the two together. Holding the light in one hand, he dipped his finger into the dark paste and began to draw on the cave wall.

The old man hobbled into the cave to retire for the night when he saw Paulus drawing. Curiously, he stumbled over to see what he was doing.

"What are you drawing?" He raised the torch to see the wall better. "A bird?"

Paulus kept drawing with his finger very delicately. He cleared his throat and answered, "Raven."

"A raven?"

"The symbol of my ancestors," Paulus added. "It was once shown to me by my grandfather who had learned it from his."

"Ah yes, the Lord's provider and man's symbol of renewal and strength," the man said smiling. Paulus stopped his drawing and glanced at him strangely. The man began to quote from scripture, saying, "And the Lord said, 'It shall be that you will drink from the brook. And I have commanded the ravens to provide for you there.'" He hobbled over to his side of the cave and sat against the wall and rested while Paulus stared at him quizzically.

"Who did the ravens provide to?"

"God was speaking to the prophet Elijah. The ravens saved him from starvation." Paulus looked on blankly as it was a story he had never heard. "The book of Kings," the man said smiling. He let out a deep sigh and then said, "Tell me of your forefathers."

Paulus turned back to his drawing and answered, "They were woodsmen, the same as I, four generations past. I was told I was named after the first."

"He was called Paulus?" the old man inquired.

"Pawl."

"And it was the same name you had given your son."

Paulus stopped his drawing as he had finished it anyway. He stared at the three ravens of his family crest and answered, "How did you know that?"

"I did not know," the old man admitted.

"Yes," Paulus answered. "His name was Pawl." He traced his finger from one raven to the other and then to the third. "We were three made into one. We were strong and we were happy."

"Perhaps you will find happiness again, young Paulus."

He shook his head though and stated, "It is not for me. The barbarians made sure of it. They chased me away and killed everything that I was. I am a man without a home, a family or a country."

The man sympathized but tried to encourage him. "A man who is lost in his homeland, perhaps. Or maybe you just need to find another one." The man then lay his head down. "Would it trouble you to tell me of your wife?" Paulus thought for a moment as he didn't know how to answer. "It is alright if you do not wish to speak of her."

"No," Paulus replied. "It is alright." He composed himself as he remembered Keira. The very thought of her instantly brought a smile to his face. "She was Scandinavian, of Norwegian descent. Brought with travelers searching for a way to a new world but they were marooned on our shores. She was but a young maiden when I came upon her clan. You never forget a face like hers. Her eyes were those that could make a man melt. She was small, petite, with a demure smile and her hair was as black as coal and her eyes as green as emeralds. I was hers for eternity from the moment I saw her."

"Ah! Young love," the man cooed in the darkness. "How wonderful that must have been for you."

Paulus continued, "I had never known love in such a way until I knew her. We were married soon after, and then she gave me a son. It was then that true happiness had found me. I thought it was forever. She consumed my very soul, and I was happy to let her." He went silent though and couldn't speak any longer.

The old man glanced over at him with concern, waiting for him to say more but he only watched as Paulus lay his head down, saying nothing.

"Time to douse the torch," the man said. "Let the fire burn though." Paulus heard him yawn across the room and he smiled at how carefree he was. Then the man said one last thing to him. "Tomorrow I will show you something wondrous."

The next morning, they hiked together through the dense trees. The ground was wet from dew but still firm underfoot.

"Where are we going?" Paulus asked, full of curiosity.

They continued up an escarpment, past the tall pines and spruce and burrowed through thick brush. The old man cleared the way with his machete, but when he grew tired, Paulus took hold of the blade and continued hacking through the brush. Soon, they reached a clearing and Paulus dropped to one knee to catch his breath.

"The underbrush has grown thicker than I remembered," the man commented. "You never know what you are going to see out in these woods. That is why I find it so breathtaking. When I took my leave from the outside world, I remember being nervous as I set out alone." Paulus listened intently as it was the first time the old man had mentioned his previous life. "But while I walked along, I suddenly came upon a magnificent stag. He had a full rack on his head and looked mighty. He ran straight up to me and halted less than twenty paces away. I was astounded! It was if he was there just for me to look upon him. It was then I was no longer fearful of the wilderness. I knew that God would be with me in my solitude."

"That is quite a story," Paulus admitted.

"I never saw him again after that," he said, sounding disappointed. The two walked farther until they came to their destination. The old man smiled and said, "You ask where we are going. I am here to prove to you that you have not died, as you say." He grabbed Paulus by the arm and guided him another twenty yards to the edge of a cliff. Before them was a majestic view of the sea and the jagged, grandiose cliffs of the island. They went on as far as the eye could see, splendor in green and marvelous and noble. "Tell me, my dear Paulus, would this be a gift to the dead?"

"Splendid!" Paulus exclaimed. "Never have I seen such a sight." He thought carefully though at what the old man had said. "Would not Heaven be an even more inviting sight to the dead though?"

"Ah!" the old man marveled. "So, you do believe there is a Heaven. There is hope for you yet, woodsman." As they stood taking in the awesome spectacle of nature, the man placed his hand on Paulus' shoulder and said, "You have suffered a great loss, my son. Let God comfort you and renew your spirit."

Paulus grew dour once more though and tears filled his eyes. "If only I could have shared such a magnificent sight with them," he said, his body trembling with sadness. He regained his composure and took in a deep breath of the fresh, sea air. "I once heard of a man who could work miracles. His name escapes my weary mind, but if I heard it spoken again, I would remember. He cured the sick and even saved people from death. If only I knew this man before."

The man chuckled softly and replied, "Miracles can only come from God, not from man. That is why you must submit to Him, for He is the wealth of understanding."

"How can God understand the pain that suffers my heart?" Paulus cried.

"God witnessed His only Son die just as you have. Do you not think that He understands?" The old man turned to Paulus and looked at him directly. "Now is not the time to turn away from God. Now is the time to embrace Him."

They stayed until mid-afternoon taking in the extraordinary view and Paulus prepared a meal by a fire and they ate together. After their meal, he stretched out on the ground with his hands behind his head, still marveling at the awesome display.

The man gazed at him, wondering what he must be thinking about the place he'd brought him to. "Your mind is wandering," he said. "What do you see when you look out across the ocean?"

Paulus sat up and leaned his back against a large boulder that rested behind him. "I do not know," he answered. "Waves, endless miles of water."

"There is life out there, Paulus," the man said confidently. "Not just the fish under the waves, but out over the sea to new and exotic lands. Life awaits elsewhere. If you have lost your home and your life in one place, the path to God can lead through wondrous new places. Your life is not at an end, as I have shown you from this mount. If you choose new life, then new life awaits you."

Paulus took in his words silently, just staring at the view below. With only hours before sundown, they started on their way back to the cave. It was near dusk and the light of the sun had disappeared from the tops of the trees that guarded the western slopes overlooking the cave. They had just enough time to make a fire before retiring for the evening.

As Paulus gathered wood and dry leaves at the cave entrance, the old man reached over to grab his torch. "Get a good flame going," he said tiredly. "I will light our torch."

Just then, they were startled to hear a deep-throated growl come from the depths of the cave. Paulus jumped back from his freshly lit fire, scrambling away from the cave on his behind.

"Oh, my," the man mumbled. "We were gone too long today, I am afraid. Our visitor needs to be put out. Take my torch."

He stood offering the lighted torch to the frightened Paulus. He looked at the old man as if he were crazy. "Needs to be put *out*?" he asked in a crazed tone. "What is in there?"

"Brown bear most likely. They are too nimble for me. You had best go in there and flush him out."

"*Me?*" Paulus yelped, still scared out of his wits.

The old man looked at him disgusted and asked, "Well who else? The rains will be coming soon, and I want to rest my head on dry straw, not soggy mud. Come on, get to your feet, woodsman. Get that bear out of there!"

With a demented expression on his face, Paulus stumbled to his feet and grabbed the torch. "Stand aside from the entrance."

"Now that is the spirit," the old man laughed and did as he was instructed. He watched patiently as Paulus entered the cave slowly with the torch. For a moment, he heard nothing. He stepped closer and put his hand to his ear, leaning ever closer to the entryway. From the bowels of the depths, he heard another deep-throated roar. Next, he heard a tyrannical scream that could only have come from Paulus. Then another growl and another yell and a curse. The last thing he heard was a deathly, snarling, screeching howl. Without warning a flash of brown, singed fur came lumbering madly from the cave, sending the old man tumbling backward. He caught himself on the rock wall just in time to watch the bear scramble away leaving a trail of thin smoke emanating from its hide.

Paulus came stumbling out of the cave, still carrying the torch. His face was pale as a ghost, his eyes glassy and emblazoned with fear.

The old man watched astonished as the brown bear bounded quickly into the forest, still yelping and snarling. "What did you *do?*" he asked in amazement.

Standing placid as if he were a statue, Paulus finally uttered, "I cursed."

"Yes, I heard. God forgives you. But what did you do to the *bear?*"

"I singed his fur," Paulus answered flatly. He then dropped to his knees and passed out on the ground from the shock.

The old man began to laugh profusely. His laughter echoed across the darkened forest and down into the cave. He sat on his favorite stump still laughing heartily and grabbed the torch that lay next to his unconscious friend. "Well done, brave woodsman," he chuckled once more. "Well done."

The next morning, Paulus awakened on his bed of straw inside the cave. He couldn't remember going back inside after his harrowing experience with the bear, but he was glad to be out of the wet, dewy weather. He listened as the birds called and sang outside in the early morning fog. Crows cawed far off in the distance and as he sat up, noticing the old man was already up and gone.

Paulus stumbled out of the cave to find him sitting over a fire, roasting some food. "Here," the man said, "I have cooked what we had left of the hare yesterday. You must be hungry."

"Yes, thank you," Paulus answered gratefully. He munched on the few bites of rabbit and swallowed it satisfyingly. "I will bring us water."

Before he could get up, they heard a noise coming from the brush farther down the embankment. "The brown bear," the man whispered, "is it back?"

Paulus didn't get the chance to answer. He and the old man were stunned to see four men emerge from the woods, all dressed in brown cloaks. They were all carrying staffs and looked incredibly haggard. Paulus sat nervously on the ground watching their every move. Meanwhile, the old man let out an exasperated sigh and got to his feet.

"Brother Thomas," he exclaimed, "what brings you all the way out here?"

"Your Excellency!" Thomas answered. "Thank the Lord we have found you."

Paulus looked up at his companion with a raised eyebrow at hearing the unexpected greeting. He continued staring at the group of identically dressed strangers with great curiosity.

The old man motioned for them to come forward. "Fear not, Paulus, I know them. Come, come. Sit by the fire and rest. Have you any water? You look like you have been walking all night."

"We have," one of the other men replied. His name was Errol. "We spent days searching for you in the wilderness."

"Paulus, will you fetch these men some water?" the old man asked politely. Paulus immediately got to his feet and grabbed one of traveler's water skins and headed for the stream.

"We did not expect you to have a companion, Your Excellency," Errol said.

"I am so pleased we found you, Your Excellency," Thomas repeated joyfully.

"No need to worry about Paulus," the old man answered them. "He is a wanderer that came upon me months ago. And there is no need to address me in such a manner. I am just a simple monk, the same as you."

Paulus came back very quickly with fresh water. He handed it to the four men, and they thanked him profusely. He sat back down away from the fire and watched the stunning turn of events unfold.

"We have a little fruit as well," the old man said to them, handing them a small sack. "Eat if you are hungry."

"We thank you, Father," Thomas said, passing the berries around. "Father, if I may, we have come to take you back with us upon urgent request."

The old man scoffed and answered, "I have made it clear of my desire to not go back, Brother. This is my home now and I wish for that desire to be respected. I think I have earned it." He thought for a moment as Thomas fretted at his answer. "Exactly *who* is making this urgent request?"

Paulus looked on eagerly awaiting the next response. His mind raced with questions as to who his mysterious companion really was.

Thomas answered as politely as he could, "Your Excellency, er, Father, it is the request of His Majesty King Oswiu's daughter. The Reverend Mother of Whitby."

"Elfleda?" the old man asked befuddled. "What does she want of me?"

"The Reverend Mother wishes to have an audience with you, Your Excellency. We are to make for Coquet Island immediately."

The old man shook his head disapprovingly and said, "This is most unusual even for her. I will think on this matter while you men rest. You are in no condition to make for Coquet right this minute. Neither am I for that matter." He stood from his stump and hobbled over to the cave and Paulus instinctively followed him inside.

The old man plopped down on his bed of straw and mumbled to himself. Paulus gingerly came in and sat across from him, a thousand questions racing through his mind.

Paulus couldn't stand the silence any longer and asked, "You have been hiding out here, have you not? You seem to be a man of great importance."

"Oh, nonsense," the old man shot back. "I am not hiding. I only wished to be left alone in my dying years. It was understood by my superiors. Now it seems they have changed their minds." He raised his eyes toward the ceiling and proclaimed, "Why will they not let me be, oh Lord?" He grumbled some more to himself. "The old crow. She knew it was an invitation I could not refuse."

"I knew there was something about your wisdom, but I could not quite piece together the clues. It seems there is life for you out there too." Paulus smiled at him keenly.

The old man shook his head though, saying, "I am old, Paulus, and my life is at an end. Maybe I have been hiding, but so have you, my friend. God seems intent on reminding us of that."

"I have nowhere else to go," Paulus moped with self-pity.

The old man got to his feet and tapped Paulus on the knee playfully and replied, "Yes, you do."

Paulus began to panic as the man left the cave. "Wait, where are you going?"

The old man emerged and looked upon his eager fellow monks and said, "We will rest today and get a good night's sleep and then we will attend to Elfleda. What does she want anyway?"

Brother Thomas was very relieved to hear him change his mind. "Oh, it is quite exciting, Father. It is said you are to be named Bishop of Hexham."

Paulus re-emerged as well, and at hearing this he was amazed. "A bishop?" he asked.

The old man turned and answered, "See what I mean? God is having His fun with me. Me being made a *bishop*. A hermit, no less, and I was a happy one at that." He grabbed Paulus by the arm and said, "Come on, woodsman. Let us go fishing."

The two wandered down to the stream together quietly. The birds in the trees were chirping happily and the breeze swayed through the long branches of the towering trees. The babbling brook trickled by peacefully as Paulus waded in with his trusty spear. The old man sat down on a nearby rock and watched him fish.

"This is what I do not want to leave behind," the man admitted. "A retired man should be able to enjoy his peacefulness. But I must remember, my vow to God was for life. He has reminded me of that quite well today. I thank thee, oh Lord, for teaching me." He smiled as Paulus stabbed his first catch. "I have enjoyed my time out here though. It especially became provident when you came along. I see now why I came upon that cave just a few days before you arrived."

"What do you mean?" Paulus asked, stashing away his first catch.

"We were meant to cross paths, you and I."

Paulus stopped fishing for a moment and pleaded with hm, "Please, sir. Tell me your name."

The man nodded, knowing it was time. "I am Cuthbert."

Paulus smiled and even laughed loudly. "Ha! I knew as soon as I heard it that I would remember. I *know* this name. *You* are the one who performs miracles."

"Oh, come now, young Paulus," Cuthbert scolded. "I am just a vessel for the Lord's work. I told you once before that miracles are not from man, but of God. Now, enough of this talk and catch a few more. Catch a big fat fish."

Paulus caught enough fish for everyone that night. After supper, the monks decided to sleep outside under the stars. The clouds and the rain stayed away to let them have a long restful sleep before their next journey.

The next morning, the monks and Cuthbert prepared to make their way to Coquet Island to meet the abbess. Paulus sat on the ground, tending the fire outside nervously. He rocked in place anxiously as he knew his friend's departure was imminent.

Brother Thomas approached Cuthbert and asked, "Are you ready, Father?"

"Yes, yes," he answered, sounding annoyed. "Give me a few more minutes."

Paulus got up and approached Cuthbert, looking distraught. "You have enough water and food?"

"Yes, we will be fine." Cuthbert observed him astutely, asking, "Something troubles you, yes?"

Paulus tried to brush his obvious anxiety away and answered, "No, I just do not know what to say at times like this. I will miss your friendship."

"As will I, Paulus."

Paulus gave him a shy but brotherly hug and turned back to his fire. Cuthbert smiled at him warmly.

"Alright, Thomas," he said. "Lead the way."

Paulus watched sadly as the five men headed for the forest when Cuthbert stopped abruptly and turned around. His companions waited patiently for him.

"Woodsman!" Cuthbert called out. "Tell me, why did you come here?"

Paulus stood and courageously answered, "To be!"

Cuthbert smiled broadly and replied, "Then go and continue to be." He then pointed in the direction of the cliffs that overlooked the sea and added, "Your ship awaits."

Paulus looked over his shoulder in a curious manner in the direction Cuthbert was pointing. He didn't understand what he meant and as he turned back the old man and his companions disappeared into the trees. He stood for minutes more staring at the forest, hoping that they might return. When he saw they were indeed not coming back, he sat by the now extinguished fire and hung his head in sadness.

Hours later, he awakened from a deep sleep outside the cave. He thought of the last thing Cuthbert had said to him and with that, he grabbed his walking staff and headed toward the cliffs.

As he walked along the path he and Cuthbert had blazed before, he heard the sound of trotting hooves nearby. From out of nowhere, an enormous stag came bounding up the trail directly at him. Paulus froze and stared wide-eyed at the magnificent animal. In an instant, the deer stopped, pawing his front hoof on the dusty ground and snorting its breath. A large spindly rack sat upon his regal head that he raised proudly, staring defiantly at Paulus.

Paulus in turn breathed in deeply and raised his chest in equal pride and admiration. He nodded with respect and gratitude to have witnessed such a magnificent creature. Paulus remembered what Cuthbert had said about God always being with him on his journey and seeing the mighty stag reassured him and gave him the motivation he needed to move on. He heard a redbird singing in the tree and he paused to spot its bright red plumage high upon the branches. When he turned back to the deer, it was gone.

It would be mid-afternoon by the time he came upon the same spot that he had visited before with Cuthbert. The sun shone brightly over the majestic view and the sea stretched far beyond the horizon.

He noticed an animal trail that lead downward along the rocky shoal of the cliffside. After an hour of steady hiking down the incline, he could hear the waves crashing on the shore. He soon emerged into a clearing on less steep terrain and could see the edges of the water from the few trees scattered about.

It was then he saw it. Far down the shoreline, on a small outcropping of sandy beach, he was astonished to see several men working feverishly to prepare a large ship to head out to sea.

Paulus looked back at the cliffs behind him and saw the spot where he had been not more than an hour before. The cliff where he and Cuthbert had visited towered high above the shoreline. A tear rolled down his face as he waved to his friend who was now miles away, heading back to his life in civilization. Paulus took in a deep breath of fresh sea air and made his way down to his awaiting ship.

Coda

After three days at sea, Paulus arrived on the western shores of Holland. He immediately found employment on river sailing vessels that traversed the various tributaries in the area and eventually found his way down the Rhine River deep into Germania.

His new life found deeper purpose when he met a woman named Greta at the Rhineland village of Koblenz, where they settled. Thus, the Rhys family name and Celtic culture continued to evolve in wondrous and exciting ways in new lands. They would go on to live long lives of happiness and prosperity in the dense forests of the beautiful river valley. Together they reared six children.

Cuthbert was considered a visionary, as legend says he saw a vision of Saint Aidan's soul being carried to Heaven by angels. It was this vision that helped him decide to enter the monastic life as a teenager.

After departing the cave, he met with his old friend, Elfleda on Coquet Island, where it was confirmed he was to be named Bishop of Hexham. He thus returned to his monastic life as leader of a new flock of followers of Christ.

He was named Bishop of Lindisfarne soon after his appointment at Hexham, which he reluctantly accepted. Less than ten years later he was finally granted his retirement due to a painful illness. He returned to his much-desired solitude in a new location on Inner Farne Island but died three months later in March of 687.

After his death, numerous miracles were attributed to his intercession and intercessory prayer near his remains. In particular, the King of Wessex, Alfred the Great was inspired by a dream he had of Cuthbert. The royal house of Wessex made a point of devotion to him, which contributed greatly to the reconciliation between Northumbria and England.

Saint Cuthbert is regarded as the patron saint of Northumbria. His tomb and a shrine bearing his name can be found at Durham Cathedral. He is considered one of the most important medieval saints in northern England.

Part IV

The Year of Our Lord, 1146

In the year of our Lord, 1146, in the German state of Rhineland-Palatinate, there lived a mystic and visionary of the Benedictine order at Disibodenberg. She was cloistered with other nuns along with monks under the guidance of Abbot Kuno. She lived at Disibodenberg for most of her life, being brought there by her parents at the age of six. She was offered as an oblate by her parents to the monastery due to the extraordinary gift of Heavenly visions from God that she experienced as early as age three. She was born in 1098 and the first of her visions began at the dawning of a new century, a time at which many cultists thought the world was coming to an end. The world was just beginning, however, for this young child of God. The child's name was Hildegard.

Hildegard was taken in by the Magistra, a nun called Jutta, who taught her how to read and write. Eight years later, Hildegard took her vows on All Saints Day in 1112.

Volmar, an upstanding man of the cloth and close friend to Jutta, was the prior and father confessor to the nuns at Disibodenberg. He taught Hildegard music and how to play the psaltery and she even learned how to compose her own music. She was also an accomplished student and teacher in the fields of botany and medicine.

Upon the death of Jutta, Hildegard was grief-stricken, but her fellow nuns unanimously voted her the new Magistra of their order. It was then she confided in Volmar of her visions of God's 'Living Light'. Volmar accepted her claims and encouraged her to write them down, knowing that his decision would be met with scrutiny. Clergy from all around were skeptical, even going as far as to say they were of the devil and not from God. She and Volmar would not be swayed however, and in 1147, Pope Eugenius gave his approval for her to document her visions.

News spread of her visions and attracted many followers and visitors to the monastery. It soon attracted one young woman from a small village on the Rhine near Koblenz. A woman enchanted by the writings of Hildegard and completely devoted to God.

Hildegard

"The new postulant has arrived, Venerable Mother," Sieglende announced.

Hildegard looked from what she was reading in the library of the monastery. Several stacks of books lay in front of her filled with writings from philosophers, journals of medicine and even books on plants and animals. "I will be in momentarily," she answered.

A young teen girl, dressed as properly as her family could afford, waited patiently next to her aunt. The girl wore a long beige and white dress with yellow flowers pinned to the hem, something she had done herself only an hour before arriving at the joint cloister of Disibodenberg. She was eager to make the best impression possible on the Magistra. It was the most exciting moment that she had waited for her entire short life. She had always wanted to meet and to study under Mother Hildegard.

The door opened to the waiting room as the young girl twirled around to see who was coming in. Sister Sieglende shuffled in quietly and stood patiently to the side, waiting for Hildegard to come forth. The young girl eagerly awaited her entrance, nervously tapping her shoe on the stone floor.

"*Lisette,*" her aunt hissed under her breath, signaling her to stop her fidgeting. Lisette acknowledged her aunt with a slight frown and when she turned back to the door, she saw Hildegard standing there as if she were a statue. She was dressed the same as Sieglende, covered from head to toe in a long flowing black habit with her hair and shoulders wrapped in white. Adorning her head was a perfectly placed black veil that cascaded to the middle of her back.

"Venerable Mother, thank you for seeing us," Lisette's aunt said cordially. "It is a pleasure seeing you again." She hesitated for a moment as she stepped closer to introduce herself. "You probably do not know me, but I was blessed to attend Mass here from time to time. I am Magnilde."

"Welcome, Magnilde," Hildegard answered respectfully. She turned her gaze to the young lady standing before her and observed her with affirmed interest. The girl stared at the floor as she was instructed to. *Only until she addresses you do you look at her directly,* her aunt had told her before they arrived. Hildegard approached her with a slight smile and asked, "And who do we have here?"

Magnilde stood beside the girl and motioned for her to look up. "May I present to you Lisette, my niece."

"Good morning, child," Hildegard said warmly.

"Good morning, Venerable Mother," Lisette answered politely.

"Please tell me your age."

"I am fifteen."

Hildegard raised one eyebrow and looked at her keenly and said, "You are young. Is it your wish to be placed here?"

"Oh, yes, Venerable Mother," Lisette answered excitedly. She tried not to raise her voice in too much enthusiasm, but she could barely contain herself. "It has been my wish since I was a little girl. I admire you so very much and I have read everything that I can about you. You were far younger than I am when you arrived here."

"You speak correctly," Hildegard answered with a nod. "You say that you can read?"

Magnilde answered for Lisette, saying, "Yes, Mother Hildegard. I have had the good fortune of teaching both her and her brother."

Hildegard nodded once more in approval. "That will place her ahead of many here. This gift will be an asset to you, Lisette." Lisette smiled proudly at her. Hildegard then turned to Magnilde and asked, "Where are their parents?"

"I am sorry to say, Mother, that they have both passed on many years ago," Magnilde said in a sorrowful tone. Lisette's smile vanished as she stared toward the ground again. Hildegard sympathized with her as Magnilde explained what had happened. "Her older brother, Bertold, was four when their mother died giving birth to Lisette. Their father, my husband's brother, raised them until Lisette was six. Unfortunately, he was tragically killed in a logging accident. Johan and I have been their guardians ever since."

"May God give them rest," replied Hildegard. "I am sorry, young Lisette. You have experienced great loss at an early age. God has blessed you with loving guardians, however. But be warned, do not take pity on yourself here. Do not be tempted to use it to gain sympathy or favor. There is no preferential treatment given here and no one is above the other. We are all equal in our devotion. Is this understood?"

"Yes, Venerable Mother," Lisette answered nervously. As she had heard about Hildegard, the cordial pleasantries would be brief, and the strict code of ethical teachings would begin swiftly.

"You may call me Mother," Hildegard offered.

"Yes, Mother."

Magnilde spoke up, saying, "They do not come from a noble family. There is little that their parents could have offered for her, but I come from a family of modest nobility, the house of Stolheim. My husband and I are prepared to gift a small dowry for Lisette." She hesitated as she did her best to step around the delicate matter. "It is not much, but we give all that we can."

Hildegard nodded and said, "It has been explained to me by the Abbot." Hildegard motioned to Sieglende who was standing silently in the corner and instructed, "In that case, she will be assigned to the kitchen and maid duties." Sieglende nodded in understanding. Hildegard turned back to Lisette and said firmly, "You will enter the novitiate assigned to the lower tasks and you will work your way to more desirable ones over time. You will cook and clean, you will wash pots and pans, linens, scrub floors, mend garments and the like. Your body will ache, your arms and legs will tire, but we do these things in service and humility before God. We will attend Mass each morning along with lauds and in the evenings will have vespers and private prayer. You will always be on time as tardiness is not tolerated. All our meals will be held together and taken in silence so we may focus on our thankfulness to God while we nourish our bodies. These are just some of the rules you will follow at this Benedictine Order. Others you will learn in due course. Are you equal to this?"

Lisette's hands trembled as she took in Hildeagrd's firm orders. She felt as if she were about to cry, but she regained her composure, knowing the challenges she would face and answered confidently, "Yes, Mother, I am."

Satisfied for the moment, Hildegard then asked Magnilde, "Tell me your married name."

"My husband is from the house of Rees," she replied.

Hildegard immediately responded, "I have heard this name. It is of Celtic descent, yes? Derived from the ancient Rhys of the Emerald Isle."

Magnilde and Lisette were both impressed. "You are quite knowledgeable, Mother," Magnilde answered. "Legend says they were aided by Saint Patrick himself and freed them from the bondage of slavery. Johan loves to tell his stories."

"Saint Patrick, you say? Who was once a slave himself, was he not, young Lisette?" Hildegard tested.

"Yes, he was, Mother," Lisette confirmed proudly.

"Saint Patrick was enslaved as a young man for six whole years as I recall." Placing her hand on Lisette's shoulder, she said, "You will find a wealth of knowledge to be learned inside these walls, Lisette. We are dedicated to God first and foremost, but we encourage study of those who have gone before us."

"Oh, I am quite eager to do so, Mother," Lisette beamed. "Please, may I see the volumes that you have here? Aristotle? Perhaps even Plinius?"

Hildegard chuckled and marveled at her enthusiasm. "You do indeed thirst for knowledge. There are so many that we can delve into." Her mind wandered as she loved sharing her joy of reading the works of philosophers and the masters of science. She waved her distracted thoughts away and said, "Come, enough talk. You will begin your training as a novice starting now." Lisette's heart leapt from her chest, filled with joy. "It is best to say your goodbyes here."

Magnilde gave Lisette a long and loving hug goodbye. "Thank you, Venerable Mother, for taking her as your novice."

"We will give it a try," Hildegard answered. "Many thanks to you as well. God speed you on your way."

∞

Bertold sat at the table with his uncle Johan and picked at his small meal to start the day. He wasn't looking forward to another day of searching the forest for the choicest wood for his uncle's carpentry shop. He had much more interesting pursuits he wanted to partake in, and his uncle could tell that his mind was wandering.

"Finish up," Johan beckoned him. "I need you to get going. I am needing pine today."

"But Uncle," Bertold complained, "Bruno and I wanted to train and practice sparring."

Johan frowned as he was growing tired of hearing the lofty dreams that Bertold had for himself. "You can spend time with your friends when your work is done. And besides, you are a young man now, Bertold. It is time to put these boyish games aside and foolish dreams of being a warrior. We are not Knights and this is not the Templar. We are farmers, woodworkers and smiths. Leave the noble tasks to the nobility."

"Why should they get all the glory?" Bertold fired back. "I can fight just as well as they. All I need is a chance. That is why I need to keep training."

"We do not work for glory, nor do we fight for it," Johan countered. "We work in the service of the Lord and to aid our neighbors. Now, enough of this foolishness. Go and bring me some wood."

Bertold reluctantly carried his axe over his shoulder as he set out for the forest but made a slight detour near his friend's home. Bruno saw him coming down the path and ran out to greet him.

"Bertold, come look at this," Bruno called out to him. Bertold smiled when he saw him carrying a newly fashioned sword. The blade was broad and flat with an equally large handle and the iron was freshly fired and was tarnished black and gray from the cooling. Bertold nodded with approval as he approached.

"Yes, a fine blade indeed, my friend," he commended.

Bruno handed it to him, saying, "Feel the weight."

Bertold grabbed the handle firmly to feel the hefty iron against his strength. "Nice. Nice, indeed. Not too light, yet not too heavy." He began to parry and thrust with the blade, slicing the air back and forth. "All you need now is a good shield."

"Yes, I may work on that later if father does not get sore at me," Bruno added. "I am supposed to be mending some wagons right now."

"Bruno!" his father called out from their blacksmith shop. "Come back to your chores."

"I have to go," Bruno said as Bertold handed the sword back to him.

Bertold frowned with disappointment but shouted at his friend as he trotted away, "To the Knights Templar!"

Bruno called back, "The Knights Templar!"

Bertold lifted his axe back onto his shoulder and made his way into the forest. The smell of the trees in the soft wind was fresh and birds chirped happily in the branches and the straw underfoot was thick and wet with dew. He wandered around, almost aimlessly, daydreaming and occasionally scanning for the choicest pine. He came into a clearing where the reeds were tall and thick.

In the bright sunshine something caught his eye shimmering on the ground in the thick brush. He held his hand to shade his eyes from the sharp glare that emanated from the grass more than fifty yards away. The light was right on the edge of the clearing near a large oak tree. He approached it curiously, thinking the beam of light would fade as he drew closer, but it did not. When he finally came upon the source, he was stunned to see it was sunlight reflecting off a piece of leg armor. He brushed the reeds away to get a better look and was shocked to see it was a man lying dead in a full set of armor. Bertold jumped back from the grim discovery, his heart beating fast in his chest. The man lay with his helmet still on, but his face shield was open. His eyes were wide in a deathly gaze and his face was pale and cracking with decay. Bertold could not tell how long the man had been dead, but obviously he lay there unnoticed until now.

He put his axe on the ground and knelt beside the fallen knight. He then noticed the knight's shield lying in the tall grass a few feet away, the crest facing upward. The shield had red and black tassels painted on either side with a cross etched in the center. The knight's sword was missing, however.

"I cannot leave him like this," Bertold said to himself. "He must be given a proper burial."

After he dug a shallow grave for the man, he sat down to rest. He gazed at the dead knight and thought respectfully of him but considered his armor as well. He took a deep breath and got back to his feet. "Forgive me, Lord, for doing this. Would be a shame to let a good suit of armor go to waste." He carefully removed the armor from the dead man and then gently placed his body in the grave, crossing his arms over his chest. He then took the shield and placed it over his arms. "Rest in peace, Sir Knight," Bertold lamented.

After filling the grave with dirt, he placed a wooden cross at the head of the plot that he had made from a nearby branch. He stood at the foot of the grave and said one last prayer for the man, then he stared graciously at the set of armor.

∞

Lisette emerged from her room dressed in full habit and she paused for a moment and looked at her attire as a slight grin formed on her face. She wore a veil of white to signify her novice status and she was ecstatic to finally be on her way to becoming a nun.

"Come, Lisette," Hildegard told her. It was only seconds after Lisette had walked out that she was summoned as Hildegard had waited for her purposely. "I walk with all my new novices on their first round of the monastery. It is not so much as a tour, but as a welcoming. You must let these holy walls take you in. Everywhere is the house of God." They continued down dimly lit corridors, outside on covered walkways, past an open garden of trees, shrubs, colorful flowers and then back down another stone corridor. They stopped just outside the entrance to the chapel of the double monastery. "There are no doors to this holy chapel as the House of God is always open to us. Prayer is welcomed at all hours. We are a joint cluster as we share this place with the Benedictine monks. Holy Mass is the only time we will congregate with them, however. No other interaction with the men will be permitted unless myself and the Abbot are present. The only exception to this rule is our prior and confessor, Father Volmar. You will find him most pleasant to be around and he is our primary scribe as well as a noteworthy theologian and scholar. You will learn a great deal from him."

"I have heard many great things about Father Volmar," Lisette beamed once more. "I am very excited to meet him and all that are here." She gazed inside the chapel, her heart swelling with love for her new home. It was not ornate in any way and had wooden chairs lined on either side facing an open aisle in the middle. Behind the plain alter was a painting of the Risen Christ, not on a canvas or framed, but painted directly on the stone wall. She marveled at its simple, yet divine purity. She fell in love with the chapel immediately and turned to Hildegard and asked, "May I go in to offer some prayers of gratitude? Just for a few minutes."

"Of course," Hildegard answered. "I will send Sister Clara in a few moments to show you where you will be assigned. *Guten tag.*"

Lisette was introduced to the other nuns and novices in the convent. There were thirteen others including the Magistra. Three other girls were novices in training as she was, Sisters Clara, Adelita and Frieda. All four worked as maids in the kitchen duties alongside their superior Sister Sieglende.

Clara showed her the rest of their side of the monastery, including the library where they found Volmar sitting at his writing table and two other assistants.

"Father Volmar, this is our new novice, Lisette," Clara said as they both politely bowed to him.

He clumsily rose from his chair and smiled warmly at them. He was short and dumpy looking, and his plain brown tunic looked too large on him. His hair was cut in the traditional manner with hair around the sides and bald on the crown. He smiled broadly as he was always happy to meet new candidates for the novitiate. "A pleasant welcome to you, Lisette."

"Thank you, Father," Lisette answered excitedly. "I am so honored to meet you. I have heard such great things about you and your steadfastness in securing the Holy Father's approval of the Venerable Mother's messages."

"Oh," he chuckled, "then my reputation precedes me. But we must always keep in mind they are God's messages, not the Venerable Mother's."

"Yes, Father."

He motioned his hand toward the volumes lining the few shelves along the walls, saying, "This is our humble library and scribe's room. Helping me today is Sisters Richardis and Petronille."

"Hello, Sisters," Lisette said formally. They both nodded to her quietly and went back to their transcribing.

"We should let Father Volmar get back to his work," Clara insisted. "We will attend to ours."

"Yes, Sister," Lisette obeyed. "Good day to you, Father. Good day to you, Sisters."

"Good day," all three said in unison.

Lisette immediately took to her tasks with joy and enthusiasm. The work was hard and back breaking, and the stone floors ached her feet, but she suffered it all in silence, always carrying herself with a smile and a courteous gesture toward anyone.

She rose early every morning to sit in the garden in the early light to reflect and enjoy its quiet peacefulness. She was always the first to arrive at lauds and always the last to leave the chapel at night after vespers. She had completely immersed herself in the monastic life and she found pure joy in all of it.

One aspect of the Magistra she noticed right away was her incredible singing voice. Hildegard would lead the chants and songs each morning at lauds and Lisette was enchanted by her beautiful voice. She soon learned the songs and chants were compositions by Hildegard herself. The more she learned about her, the more fascinated she was.

As she got more acquainted with her fellow novices and nuns, she began to learn their distinct personalities and character traits. Sister Sieglende was highly outspoken, while Sister Petronille was very quiet and observant. The other three novices were all close as they had entered the convent at the same time. They were always found in the garden studying the herbs and their medicinal purposes as required by Hildegard in their studies. Volmar was always jolly and eager to talk about any subject with them but was devotedly serious when it came to saying Mass and hearing confessions. Lisette admired him greatly.

Then there was Richardis. Everywhere she turned, Lisette noticed that Richardis was always at Hildegard's side, either in Mass, vespers and even when the group was dining. In the short time Richardis had been cloistered with them, she had become Hildegard's closest associate and confidant. Lisette soon learned that she was exceptionally gifted at reading and writing and took personal pride in preparing the Lord's messages to Hildegard along with Volmar. It was Richardis who selected Petronille to assist in the scribe's room due to her gift of illustration. When Richardis was not attending to her tasks, she was with Hildegard.

One evening after vespers, Lisette walked at the foot of the line with Clara as they processed two-by-two from the chapel back to their quarters. Far at the head of the line was Hildegard and Richardis.

"Why is Richardis always at the Magistra's side?" Lisette whispered.

"Is it not obvious?" Clara asked back in whisper. "She is her favorite. And she only arrived here a year before I did with Adelita and Frieda. Sieglende has been here much longer and even knew the Magistra as children. But Richardis, she is her pet."

"We must not say such things," Lisette scolded.

"I have something to show you," Bertold said to Bruno inside the family barn where they practiced sparring.

"What is it?" Bruno asked.

Bertold walked to the far corner of the barn behind the stalls of the milking cows and uncovered a stack of loose straw to reveal something wrapped in an old tunic. "You would not believe what I came across."

"Is this what I think it is?" Bruno asked as the two lifted the heavy object out of the corner. He quickly lifted the flap to confirm his suspicions. "A set of armor, I *knew* it. How did you come by this? It looks to be in perfect condition."

Bertold wasn't going to lie to his friend. "You must not tell anyone, but I literally stumbled upon it yesterday while I was searching for pine. The poor man lay dead in the tall reeds."

"He was dead?" Bruno asked baffled. "What did you do with him?"

"I buried him, of course. Properly. He looked to have been dead for some time. It was quite ghastly."

Bruno looked at him cockeyed and replied, "But you saved the man's armor. Is that moral?"

"It is in my mind," Bertold said bluntly. "I mean I have heard of knights being buried in full battle armor, but most of them are removed of their armor after death save for their shield, or maybe their sword. Armor is very difficult to fashion and hard to come by without a lot of money. Be a shame to waste it in a grave."

"I agree with you there," Bruno responded. "Well, come on then. I know you asked me here to help you try it on. You did, did you not?"

"We have to lift it somehow," Bertold said, scratching his chin whiskers. "Elevate it so I can step into it."

"Look on the back of it, silly. All good armor is fashioned with a hook. Grab that rope over there."

Bertold's eyes lit up when he saw the small ringed hook on the back shoulder of the armor. He quickly retrieved some rope and slipped it through the hole. "We will toss it over the beam," he suggested.

They immediately hoisted the iron suit into the air until it was at shoulder height as Bruno grunted under the weight. "It is heavy, alright. How did you get this thing home by yourself?"

"I dragged it for hours. Come on, hold it steady."

Bruno stopped abruptly and pushed Bertold's shoulder away. "Wait a minute. There was a dead man in this suit. Did you clean this out first?"

"Of course, I did," Bertold answered, rolling his eyes. "I was in here most of the night cleaning it. Now, hold it still."

Bruno tied the rope down and grabbled the metal jacket firmly while Bertold slipped his arms through. "Whoa," Bertold exclaimed. "I can feel the weight already. Fasten it well back there."

The rope pulled taut while Bertold kept his balance. Bruno quickly fastened the armor in the back and then grabbed the rope once more. "Alright, tell me when you are ready. You want the helmet too?"

"Yes," Bertold clamored, feeling the pressure on his shoulders. "Might as well try it all on, right?" Bruno quickly grabbed the helmet and helped place it over Bertold's head. "Alright. We will leave the rope attached. Release it on my signal."

"You look kind of small in there," Bruno laughed.

"Just let go of the rope, will you?"

Bruno let the rope go and stepped away. Bertold grunted under the heavy iron wrapped around his torso and stumbled backward causing his shield to snap shut. "Whoa. Steady. Steady, legs," he mumbled as he quickly planted one leg behind him to keep from falling. "There we go," he gasped. "I can hardly see anything though."

Bruno laughed at how awkwardly his friend was standing and commented, "I can fix the shield so you can see better, but what you need is some stronger legs or else you will roll over like a tortoise."

"Stop laughing. This thing is *really* heavy."

"Try to take a step forward," Bruno suggested.

Bertold steadied himself and attempted to walk forward. "Alright, I will take one step and...*whoa!*" His legs tried to move forward but they could no longer hold the tremendous weight of the iron. He tried desperately to keep his balance, but it was to no avail. He slowly began to tip backward, falling like a downed tree. He landed with a great thud on the straw covered barn floor."*Umpf!*" he belched as he smacked the ground, knocking the wind out of him. The hard metal clanged to the ground and chickens scurried away and the two dairy cows let out a loud moo.

Bruno couldn't help but laugh as hard as he could at his friend. He quickly grabbed the rope and heaved with all his might to lift Bertold back to his feet. He tied the rope down once again to hold Bertold steady. "That was quite entertaining, cousin," he said, still laughing. He quickly slid the face shield up to reveal Bertold's weary eyes, sweat pouring down his face. "But if you are going to be a knight, you had better firm up those skinny legs of yours."

∞

The nuns and novices sat in a circle outside in the garden passing around certain herbs and leaves.

Hildegard waited patiently as they all had a turn at seeing each one. Then she spoke, saying, "God provides us with plants and herbs so we can study to see what uses mankind can make of them," she began. "But before we delve into their uses, we must first strengthen our faith in God who created this nature. To understand nature is to embrace its purity and divinity, but also to heed and respect the parts of nature we are not meant to disturb."

"Like bears," Clara laughed. The rest of the women laughed with her.

"Or poison ivy," Adelita added to more laughter.

Hildegard smiled yet raised her hand to silence them. "There is a time and a place for levity but now is not the time. Who can tell me the herb Adelita is holding?" Richardis raised her hand but Hildegard waved her off, saying, "I want to hear from our novices." Frieda raised her hand. "Yes, Frieda?"

"It is called yarrow, Mother," she answered.

"And what are its uses?"

She thought for a moment and then said, "For wounds on the skin."

"Good," Hildegard commended. "Who can name the long plant Sieglende is holding?" Lisette quickly raised her hand. "Go on," she said acknowledging her.

"It is tetterwort, Mother."

"That is correct," she said again. "And what are its uses?"

Lisette blushed as if the answer were obvious. "Well...it is used to treat warts." The ladies chuckled again.

Hildegard nodded and added, "You laugh, but that is true. Break a piece of the stalk, Sieglende, and show them the inside." Sieglende did as she was told and showed the others the orange sap contained inside the green stalk. "The sap you see is what is applied to skin marks such as warts. It looks colorful and pleasing to the eye and even looks good enough to eat. But that is why we must heed and respect natures gifts and warnings. The sap is good for the skin, but poisonous if ingested."

Sieglende frowned at the little plant and tossed it to the ground. "I will leave it there," she said red-faced. The nuns laughed again in unison.

"And the last herb that Richardis is holding, who can tell me what it is and its uses?" Hildegard asked.

"Parsley," Adelita answered before being called upon. Hildegard frowned at her but allowed her to continue. "We use it in the kitchen to flavor soup."

"That is the easy answer," Hildegard reminded her. "But it also has medicinal uses as well. The roots, leaves and seeds are used for many things, such as insect bites. Or applied to the skin to heal bruises and can even help with issues in our internal organs."

"Oh, it does so indeed," Sieglende sighed. "It does wonders for my stomach aches." The nuns laughed at her again. This time even Hildegard chuckled at her old friend. "That is correct. Mine too." She clapped her hands and stood. "Alright, we will go tend to the patients in the ward now. Novices, pay close attention as this is the first time you will be tending to patients."

The nuns followed Hildegard and Richardis by two's once more, this time to the patient ward at the rear of the monastery. The friars and nuns had taken in the sick whenever possible ever since the monastery was built. It was one of the devotions Hildegard held closest to her heart.

"How does the Magistra know so much about plants and healing?" Lisette quietly asked Clara.

"She has been ill most of her life," Clara answered. "They say she is sometimes wracked with pain and fever for days and bedridden weeks at a time. She has suffered from it since she was a child. That is why she studies the plants and herbs so much and is devoted to the sick. She is one of the most knowledgeable people I have ever met."

"That is so sad for her," Lisette answered with a whisper. "Yet she studies to understand more to help others. And her talent for music is exemplary. Her talents are ceaseless."

"Not to mention being a seer," Clara added.

Adelita turned around, putting her finger to her lips and shushed them. "Quiet."

They arrived in the ward where a few patients lay recovering. Hildegard made a beeline for one man in particular who had just arrived that morning. The elderly thin man lay trembling on his side, clutching the bed linens to his chest, appearing to be in terrible agony.

"This is the man?" Hildegard asked Sieglende.

"Yes, Mother."

"Pull back his cloak, please," she instructed. Sieglende carefully pulled the man's clothing from his shoulders just enough to reveal his badly scarred back. He had rows of jagged lacerations on his skin that covered nearly all his back. They were red and bleeding and some were filled with pus and the man shivered as his head was wracked with fever. Hildegard leaned over him and placed her hand sympathetically on his shoulder. "What have you done to yourself?" The man could not answer but she knew what the cuts and scars were from.

The nuns gathered around the bed and some sobbed quietly at seeing the suffering man. Hildegard scanned over her class and said, "We show compassion for the sick, but we must also be resolute in our care for them. Do not let them see your emotions. They must know we are here to give them the best care that we can. The wounds are from flagellation. It is something I have never condoned but is common with some of the elderly, particularly those who witnessed the end of the last century. Who can tell me the best treatment for this man?"

Adelita raised her hand and Hildegard acknowledged her. "Yarrow," she answered.

"That is correct. It must be boiled and then strained." Hildegard then instructed Sieglende, who was the head nurse of the ward, "Replace the medicinal wrappings three times per day."

"Yes, Mother," Sieglende answered.

Hildegard then addressed the class once more, saying, "Jesus does not ask for sacrifices, but for mercy. We must not scourge our flesh in sacrifice. As John the Baptist said, we must offer the fruits of repentance, but in prayer and in charity to others in need. Our bodies are temples, a gift to our life, fashioned by the hands of God. So, we must take great care of our gift from God."

∞

When Bertold wasn't working in the forest or helping his uncle with the carpentry, he spent all his free time working on his conditioning. Bruno acted as his trainer showing all manner of ways to strengthen his body, particularly his legs. He pushed boulders from one side of a field to the other, he ran countless stretches up and down hillsides. He jumped on top of rock piles and back down again many times in succession until he was breathless.

Bruno even had him wade into a nearby pond up to his waist and said, "Try running in the water from one end to the other."

Sloshing around in the dirty brown water, Bertold smirked and said, "I get stuck in the mud."

"That is why you must not stand around," Bruno hollered from the shore. "Move quickly, keep your momentum going. The water will add strength as it is much harder to move through than the air."

Bertold began to hop and splash through the water until he gained better traction. Soon, he was slicing through the waist-deep water like a gazelle.

He pulled a wagon like a mule, to strengthen his upper body while Bruno rode inside, grinning from ear to ear as he watched his friend work tirelessly. "Heave, Sir Knight!" he called out playfully.

They soon began sparring together with Bertold wearing the suit of armor. His newfound strength made it easy for him to walk and even dance about sparring with a sword. He was becoming the person that he had always intended. He felt at ease moving about and he carried himself with equal ability. They practiced for hours at a time and soon they were both becoming exceptionally skilled with the sword.

After weeks of conditioning, Bertold was becoming a sculpted body of strength. The exercise fueled his enthusiasm, and he was eager to get outside even before the sunrise to do more training.

His aunt and uncle noticed how Bertold was changing as well. Magnilde watched in amusement as Bertold scarfed down his morning meal with a ravishing hunger. "You are becoming quite the manly specimen, young Bertold. And an appetite to match. The young maidens will be following you around like swooning doves before long."

"Let the boy be," Johan scoffed. "I admire what he is doing. But do not forget your chores around here, Bertold."

"I will not, Uncle," he answered, shoveling more food in his mouth.

Later that day Bertold found Bruno outside his home and suggested to him, saying, "I think it is time we crafted a shield."

"I agree," Bruno concurred. "I have been thinking on the matter and I know just how I want to fashion it. My father will let us use the shop in the evenings. Bring some extra torches for light, we will need them."

They worked together for several nights and Bruno used his skill forming the metal and Bertold helped him fire it and pound it flat. They both sweated profusely in the fiery heat. Water was

121

plentiful, and they drank pints at a time to keep up their strength. Finally, after hours of work for many nights the shield was completed. Bruno smiled approvingly as Bertold wrapped his fist around the handle and lifted it to his chest for the first time. The shape of the escutcheon was a seamless, flat edge at the top, with two wedges formed at the top corners. The sides curved perfectly downward to a sharp point at the bottom. The shield was exquisite in every manner and shimmered prominently in the torchlight.

"Now you must adorn it with your own heraldry," Bruno insisted. "It will be as you wish it. That is my gift for your efforts."

Bertold knew exactly how we wanted to adorn his shield. He created black paint formed from ash and mud and then carefully began to set the scene on the face of the shield. In the middle were two perfectly drawn broad, black stripes coming to an angular point directly in the center. He then carefully drew the images of two ravens, one on each top corner. A third raven was added to the remaining field directly centered below the angled stripes.

When it was completed, he proudly displayed it to Bruno. "This is the heraldry that was handed down to me from my father before he died. It has been the mark of our family for centuries. I continue it now on this shield you have created."

"It is superb!" Bruno exclaimed. "What do the ravens symbolize?"

"I have never forgotten what my father told me of the ravens. They symbolize gratitude, wisdom, hope, longevity and fertility."

Bruno laughed and said, "I hope to take part in that last one soon and quite often." Bertold laughed heartily at him, slapping him on the shoulder. Bruno winced and chuckled, "Hey, not so rough, Sir Knight."

∞

Lisette was busy scrubbing some linens in a wash tub when Hildegard approached. "Sister Lisette," she said, "I need to speak with you."

Startled, Lisette stopped her scrubbing and asked, "Should I finish the wash first?"

"No, I will have one of the other novices continue this task. I am in need of you elsewhere." Lisette quickly wiped her hands on her apron and walked with Hildegard. "Come, we will sit in the garden." They walked a short distance and rounded the bend that led to the garden. A stone bench sat on the edge of the beautiful flower garden under the shade of a huge oak tree. Hildegard gestured toward the bench for them to sit. "This is a lovely spot, I think."

"Yes," Lisette answered. "I often come here to listen to the birds sing and to pray."

"I have noticed," Hildegard said. "I do as well. I brought you here to speak of your progress in the novitiate."

"Yes, Mother?"

"You take to your tasks without complaint and you put every effort into all of them," she began. "Your devotion as a novice is commendable."

"Thank you, Mother," Lisette answered, feeling a bit bashful.

Hildegard continued, saying, "It is time, however, to explore your other talents. God has blessed you with an education in reading and writing and now you should put that gift to good use. I have told Volmar that you will report to him in the library on a trial basis."

Lisette dropped to her knees and kissed the Magistra's hand in gratitude. "Oh, *thank you,* Venerable Mother."

"Please, sit next to me, Sister," Hildegard insisted. "You are most welcome. We are in need of you. Work is slow going on the volumes that I have dictated to Volmar and he is needing more help in putting the pages together. The Abbot has allowed two monks to help in the library with you and Richardis. I have agreed to it as well."

"I am most grateful, Mother. It has been my dream to help with your messages from God." She hesitated for a moment before revealing her thoughts on the matter. "I must admit, when I heard of your visions of God's Light, I became envious, as I so wanted that same experience. I was very young though. It was silly of me to be so envious."

"Envy is unsightly and grotesque, it only brings evil to man," Hildegard told her. "Love is above all else."

"Yes, Mother," Lisette answered contritely. Her curiosity was getting the better of her since they were finally speaking on the topic she was most intrigued by. "May I ask you, what was it like to see the 'Living Light' of God? What did He first say to you?"

Without hesitation, Hildegard responded, "I was frozen, as if in a dream, but I was fully awake. The light was beyond anything I could imagine, shining brightly on the horizon, but not so that it blinded. It was warm and inviting and I felt at peace as I gazed upon it. Then I heard His voice. He said to me, 'You are appointed. Write down what you hear and see.'"

"I will be honored to work on these volumes, Venerable Mother. I will do everything you ask."

Lisette entered the library the next morning after Mass, eager to get started. Volmar quietly directed her to a writing table next to Richardis and Petronille. She noticed the two monks at writing tables a few feet behind them but facing the opposite wall.

"You will work here," he instructed, "but in silence. These men are Brother's Vitolius and Hans, who will assist in preparing the parchment paper and binding. They are enjoined to silence as well. Petronille does the illustrations lining the edges first, then Richardis and myself inscribe the text. I will give you the next page to write as a sample." He pointed to her table which already had an ink well and parchment ready for her. "If your handwriting is sufficient, you will be permitted to continue here."

"Yes, Father. Thank you."

"If you need to speak on your work or have a question, come to me first."

"Yes, Father."

Her heart began to beat fast in her chest, and she felt nervous as she sat next to Richardis, who was a seasoned scribe already even at her young age. She glanced over her shoulder at the two monks with their backs turned to them, feeling uneasy about herself knowing her cohorts may be far more talented than she. She was suddenly feeling inadequate and unsure of herself, not knowing how she would perform on her first task.

"Here is the text you will be transcribing to parchment," Volmar said, as he handed her a page from his notes that he had taken during his sessions with Hildegard.

For weeks and months, Hildegard would dictate to Volmar all the messages from God she had received. She knew them all by memory as God intended for her so they could be documented. Once the Holy Father granted his permission, she and Volmar worked tirelessly to get all her visions written down. Now it was time to put them into book format. Hildegard was eager to get God's words out to the masses as soon as possible as it was the last request of God to her: 'Go and spread now all that you have seen and heard.'

Lisette worked diligently on her first writing task. She lettered each word as precisely as she had learned from her aunt. From time to time, Volmar would walk the room, observing the work each of them was doing. He never said a word but slowly walked from table to table.

When she was done, she brought her completed page to Volmar who was sitting at his desk. He held the page up to the light and observed it quietly. Gazing at it for a long while with a contemplative expression, he then picked up another completed page done by Richardis and compared them side by side.

He began to shake his head and Lisette's expression went crestfallen. She was surprised when he uttered, "A complete match. Every detail is the same, as if the two were written by the same hand." He set the pages down and looked at her dumbfounded. "This is exceptional work. This will be your new task."

Johan quietly worked in his woodshop, filing down a long cut of pine that would eventually be fashioned as part of a table. He keenly observed Bertold who was working on another long piece of the same table. He could tell his nephew's thoughts were elsewhere.

"I suppose you will be setting out soon," Johan dolefully offered.

Bertold glanced over his shoulder, wiping the sweat from his brow and answered, "Setting out, Uncle?"

"Well, I would not think you would be doing all this training for nothing. And I know what you have stowed away." Bertold's face reddened with guilt as he glanced toward the back corner of the barn. "You do not have to hide anything from me. I know you want get out on your own."

"Are you angry with me?" Bertold asked worriedly.

Johan chuckled and answered, "No, Son." He stopped what he was doing and leaned the large wooden pillar against the wall. Wiping the dust from his hands, he walked over to Bertold and placed his hand on his shoulder and smiled. "I wanted to get out on my own too when I was your age."

Bertold was relieved that his uncle understood how he felt. It had been gnawing away at his thoughts. He nodded and admitted, "I was wrong to hide it from you, but I do want to set out. I want to see what is out there for me. I just feel it is in me to be in service to God as a defender of the faith." Then he added, "And a defender of the king."

"You do not need me to tell you those are worthy pursuits. You do not have to be noble to defend our faith." Johan smiled at Bertold's fortitude and eagerness to see the rest of the world. "God knows the right place and duty for you. He will guide you. Your aunt, on the other hand, may have a thing or two to say about you leaving."

Bertold laughed and said, "I know. She has reminded me of that for quite some time."

Johan continued, "She knew this day was coming just as I. We want you to find what you are looking for, Son. But remember, this house is always your house. You will always be a Rees no matter where God leads you."

Bertold nodded with pride and a broad smile swept over his face as he set his work down. "Let me show something," he said. Johan watched him curiously as he uncovered a large object, wrapped in cloth. "If I am to be a defender of God, I shall always remember who I am and everyone who faces me." He carefully unwrapped the heavy iron and proudly displayed the shield he and Bruno had fashioned.

Johan marveled at the magnificent, shimmering, shield. He held it in his hands and smiled at the cunning craftsmanship. He glided his palm over the smooth iron surface and over the carefully painted ravens. "This is superb!" he exclaimed. Bertold was exceedingly pleased at his reaction. "And you have rendered the family crest perfectly." His smile slowly faded as he stared at the tool of battle his nephew had created.

"What is it, Uncle?" he asked worriedly.

"You must take care that you do not let your pride get in the way of your aims," Johan warned. "It is one thing to display your heraldry with honor, but it is another to simply show off." He turned the shield and placed the handle into Bertold's hand. "Here, hold it firm to your chest." He looked him straight in the eye and said, "The shield bears our heraldry. The shield is your protection, just as we have been all your life. Let your family always be your protector as you will be for your own family someday. Carry it with your faith in Jesus and you will never falter."

Hildegard circled the table, her hand gliding down the edges as she slowly approached the center. A tear formed in her eye and trickled down her cheek as her fingers delicately touched the finely polished leather cover of the completed text.

Volmar, Lisette, Richardis, and all who had worked so diligently on the project, surrounded the table and waited eagerly for Hildegard's reaction. Their masterpiece sat proudly in the center of the table and it was bound with thick, smooth leather, and the pages were perfectly stacked and aligned several inches high.

Hildegard finally clutched her fingers around both sides and lifted it to her heart. Volmar smiled with joy at seeing her gracious reaction. Hildegard glanced around the room at her companions with sincere gratitude.

"*Scivias*," she told them. "These are the collected volumes of God's message to mankind. It is our duty now to spread these divine words to the masses." She carefully placed the book on the table once more and added with a gleeful smile, "But first, we must celebrate your grand achievement." Volmar and the sisters watched as Hildegard approached the door to the chamber with a sly grin. "I have a surprise for you." She opened the door to reveal Abbot Kuno holding a platter of baked goods, with all the brothers of Disibodenberg quietly and patiently waiting behind him. "Let us welcome Abbot Kuno."

"Greetings to you, Venerable Mother," Kuno said with a smile.

The sisters all cupped their hands and gasped in pleasant surprise. For most of them it was first time any of them had seen, or smelled, the sweet aroma of baked pastries. Kuno happily walked in with the tray and set it on the table next to the newly completed *Scivias.*

"We have baked sweets for everyone," Hildegard announced happily. "The Abbot has blessed us with this wonderful delight, and I am told is the chef as well."

"I am indeed the guilty party," Kuno blushed.

"Come help yourselves, sisters and brothers," Hildegard invited. "The Abbot has lifted the vow of silence and we may indulge in friendly banter with one another."

The sisters were delighted as were the brothers and everyone patiently lined up to get a piece of the sweet baked goodies. Quietly, yet shyly, they took the opportunity to speak to their fellow brethren from the other side of the monastery.

Volmar took a bite of the heavenly sweets and rolled his eyes back in ecstasy, saying, "Worth every effort. Almost...sinful." The group of nuns and brothers standing around him all laughed and giggled as they ate their treats as well.

"You are to be congratulated, Venerable Mother," Kuno told Hildegard. "A monumental achievement."

"Thank you, Abbot," Hildegard said graciously. "It could not have been done without everyone's help and your persistent voice to help sway the Holy Father in Rome."

Kuno smiled deceptively and added, "I have another surprise for you. His Holiness is now wanting to read all your words as is the Archbishop of Mainz. And the biggest surprise is word has come from your friend and mine, the Abbot Bernard of Clairvaux."

"Bernard has written?" Hildegard asked, her voice filled with excitement.

Kuno nodded and said, "He seeks an audience with you to hear the words that you have written."

"Oh, this is wonderful! It is just as the Lord has instructed, 'Bring the Word to the highest in the land and let it flow forth.'"

"Indeed," Kuno said. "I will have Volmar travel with you and two of the brothers."

"Oh, you know how Volmar is afraid of horses."

Kuno chuckled and answered, "He will be fine. He will serve as witness to your testament."

So, Hildegard went forth with Volmar, traveling the countryside and speaking to the highest leaders and dignitaries in the land. She first visited the Archbishop of Mainz, then she made her way into France to visit her old friend Bernard at Clairvaux. After many weeks of arduous travel, they even had an audience with His Holiness, Pope Eugenius.

Word spread far and wide about her visions from God and she taught them wherever she could. Soon, pilgrims from everywhere made the trek to Disibodenberg just to see where the seer resided. They brought food and gifts for the cloistered nuns and brothers and the wealthy and the poor gave monetary donations to them. It was the most wealth Abbot Kuno had ever witnessed in all his time at the monastery. Before long, everyone around knew of the place that housed the visionary of God's 'Living Light'. People came from miles around just to get a glimpse of her or even just to touch the outside walls of the holy site.

After three months of arduous traveling, they finally arrived at Disibodenberg to find the quiet little village had blossomed into something miraculous. Never had they seen so many pilgrims come to visit. People were everywhere and they found it difficult to navigate the narrow cart paths just to get to the gates of the cloister.

Volmar was relieved to dismount his horse and he hobbled over to help Hildegard from hers. "I never want to see that horse again," he moaned. "I must confess, though, the mare had grown on me, but now I must rest my aching body."

"As must I," Hildegard laughed. "I am astounded at all the people gathered outside the gates, though. The Good Lord did not prepare me for such things. I am looking forward to quiet prayer in the chapel and then to prepare the novices for their final vows."

"I am looking forward to my soft bed," Volmar quipped.

∞

Bertold and Bruno hiked northward leading a mule packed with camping supplies and the armor. They walked through the thick forest toward the open fields near Regensburg.

Word had spread throughout the country that the Knights had returned from their crusade that reached as far as Jerusalem and Constantinople. The battles raged for more than two years and ranged all over southern and eastern Europe and the Holy Land. They triumphantly returned with the son of the late Duke of Swabia as their courageous leader. He was known as *Kaiser Rotbart*, or Barbarossa. With his red hair and thick red beard, he was equally intimidating as he was fierce. Yet, he led with a constant and devoted faith in God.

Even before the main armies made their return, word had spread that a third crusade would be mounted on the heels of the second. Bertold had found the moment he had wished for. After three days of traversing the thick forests along the Rhine, Bertold and Bruno came upon the vast green fields that were home to the Knights Templar training grounds.

"Smell that air, Bruno," Bertold sighed as he took in a deep breath of the cool, humid morning air. "It is invigorating. I know we are close."

"Where do you think we will find them?" Bruno asked. "You think they are even here? If I had been at war for two years, I would be taking in a nice holiday by the river. Not preparing to go fight again."

"It is the life of a knight, my good friend. Constantly at the ready."

They walked along the edge of the woods for another hour, the mule whining with every step. Suddenly, Bertold froze in his tracks and yanked the animal to a halt. Immediately, the tired mule took the opportunity to lay down.

"What is it?" Bruno hissed.

"Do you not hear that?" Bertold asked excitedly. "Listen." Indeed, both men could hear the sound of swords and armor clanging in the distance. "We will go no further. I must don my armor."

Bruno motioned to the exhausted mule and said, "I do not think we are going any farther anyway." He side-stepped around the stubborn mule and asked nervously, "You want to go out there now?"

"No time like the present," Bertold answered. "Come on. Let us get these things unloaded."

Bruno heaved the armor off the ground with a rope slung over a high tree branch. He steadied it as Bertold slipped his arms through. In no time he had on the armor and his helmet wedged under his arm. "I will need my sword and shield," he said impatiently.

"Yes, you might need those too," Bruno quipped. "Are you sure about all this? I mean, what are you going to say to them and not get rushed out as soon as we get there?" Bruno was growing increasingly anxious at seeing how frantic a pace Bertold was moving. "Maybe you should sleep on it a night."

"I have had enough sleep," Bertold shot back. "The timing is ripe. I can sense it. It has to be now."

Bruno shook his head and added, "You know this is going to look awfully strange to those men with you just walking up in a suit of armor. They will think you are mad."

"Well, I cannot think of any better ideas. They would not pay any attention otherwise. I have to show up looking the part." Bruno shrugged his shoulders, seeing his point. Bertold donned his helmet and grabbed his shield and sword. "So, how do I look?"

"Like you are looking to pick a fight," Bruno deadpanned.

Bertold lifted his shield and smiled at his friend. "That is an excellent idea, Bruno old boy." He turned and began to march toward the training grounds.

"Oh, no. Forget I said that," Bruno yelped but saw that Bertold could not be stopped. He grabbed the rope and yanked it off the tree branch. "Wait!" he called out. "You will need to stow this at your side. Wait up, will you?"

"Thanks," Bertold said, securing the coiled rope to his hip. "Yes, I may need that." He pointed over the clearing and said, "Look, there they are."

Bertold emerged from the woods and kept a steady march toward dozens of men sparring in helmets and armor. The clanging of metal and the loud crunch of swords on shields grew louder as he continued his march.

On the far side of the field stood two captains, not wearing helmets, quietly observing the training. One was named Alrik and the other his superior, Bartholomew, the head of the Templar guard.

Bartholomew's boredom grew as he watched his men go through yet another required training exercise. As he watched, his gaze was drawn away by a perplexing sight. He noticed a single knight marching toward the field alone with another man unarmed trailing not far behind.

"Who are those men, Alrik?" he asked aloud over the sparring noise. "I do not recognize this knight or the marks on his shield."

"I do not know, sir," Alrik answered, equally puzzled. "I will find out, sir."

Alrik made a beeline toward Bertold and raised his hand for him to stop. "Halt, I say! What are you doing here? What do you want?"

"I am here to fight for the Knights Templar," Bertold bravely answered." Alrik began to chuckle as did Bartholomew, who heard his answer. "I wish to serve the king and be a crusader for Christ. May I inquire who is the captain of the guard?"

"I am the captain of the guard," Bartholomew answered firmly, pushing his way past Alrik. "And I have never seen you before or heard your voice. Reveal your face." Bertold lifted his face shield and stood perfectly at attention with his sword at his side and shield held squarely against his chest. "I do not know who you are, but it looks to me that you have stolen that armor most likely. You do not belong here."

"I can prove myself. I will fight any man here to prove that I belong," Bertold answered defiantly. Bruno stood not far away, watching in amazement as his friend courageously made his case.

"These men are of nobility, born to be knights," Bartholomew continued. "Their fathers were knights and their fathers before them. You, my friend, are not nobility. I can see it in those commoner eyes." Bertold tried not to lose his composure and quietly fumed at the man's insults. "Most of us have just returned fighting alongside Barbarossa in the last crusade. Many never returned. But the knights fought with honor. We fought for Christ."

"I fight for Christ as well," Bertold countered. "I may not be noble, but I am still part of this land and I serve the king."

Bartholomew shook his head and waggled his finger in Bertold's face, saying, "One does not just walk in from the forest and say they are part of the Knights Templar. You are nothing but a wandering vagabond, masquerading as if you were at a ball. Now be gone with you. We have real work here."

"I will fight any man," Bertold pleaded. "I will even fight you."

Bartholomew and Alrik laughed as they turned to walk away when Bertold asked in defiance, "You know what I think? You are afraid to fight me."

The men stopped abruptly, and Bartholomew turned around fuming. "What did you say to me?"

"You heard me."

"So, you wish to fight, do you?" Bertold lifted his sword and clanged it defiantly against his shield. Bartholomew fumed even more. "My, you are a *stubborn* little cuss. Alright then if you think you are *man* enough. I have some time to waste."

"Man enough to crack that thick, noble skull of yours," Bertold shot back, egging him on.

Bartholomew looked over at Alrik and snarled, "Hand me my helmet and sword. It is time to teach this whelp a lesson."

The warrior was a hulking mountain of a man and looked even larger when he donned his helmet. He was easily a half foot taller than Bertold.

Bertold stepped back a few paces and gave a quick smile and a wink at Bruno before closing his face shield. "You are looking mighty confident," Bruno fretted. "You think you could have chosen someone a bit smaller?"

"Have no fear, my friend," Bertold assured him. "I have been waiting for this moment all my life."

"Look out!" Bruno exclaimed.

Bertold whirled around raising his shield instinctively just as Bartholomew came rushing and swirling down his sword. The sword crashed into the shimmering shield, setting off a thunderous boom that echoed across the open field. The shield, emblazoned with the majestic black stripe and equally imperial ravens, fought off every crushing blow with ease.

Bruno was stunned at how well Bertold stood his ground against the mighty Bartholomew. The dozens of men who were sparring stopped their training to watch their captain fight the unknown warrior. They gathered around to watch the spectacle unfold.

Bertold was clearly up to the task, matching the mighty Bartholomew with every thunderous blow. He thrusted and blocked at every turn like a seasoned professional. With every pounding block with the shield, Bartholomew grew increasingly angrier, not believing how well the warrior was fighting against him.

Sweat poured down Bertold's face inside the oven-like helmet and his body wrung with sweat under the armor. His arms ached with every crushing blow, yet he kept up with each parry and thrust, matching him step for step.

The fight escalated and ranged all over. Soon, they found themselves on the edges of the forest with the men cheering on their captain feverishly and Bruno dashing around to stay out of the way. He marveled at the heroic fight Bertold was giving and winced at every thunderous crash Bertold received in return.

The two knights began to tire, and their swords clanged together at a slower pace. Each man grunted with every swipe of the sword and strained to lift their shields to block the next shot.

"You should yield, young warrior," Bartholomew belched in between breaths, finally breaking the silence between them. "You will never outlast me. I can stand the heat inside these iron kettles longer than any man."

"I will never yield," Bertold grunted back. "I do not care how long it takes."

Just then Bartholomew flung another blow and Bertold barely got his shield up in time to deflect it. Almost immediately, Bartholomew seized on the open shot and thrust his sword and clanged directly into Bertold's chest armor. The stunning blow sent Bertold stumbling backward under a large shade tree. Bertold instinctively raised his shield to catch an overhead branch to stop his fall. Bruno let out a sigh of relief as Bertold steadied himself on his feet.

Bartholomew did not stop though as he knew he had an opening and he thrust at Bertold with all his might. Bertold blocked him with his sword and then another with his shield. Bartholomew was relentless in trying to finish him off. With one last effort, he barreled down on Bertold's shield, blow after blow. Bertold dug his boots in hard when suddenly he stepped on a small tree branch. His foot became unsteady on the rolling log, and with blows raining down upon him, he finally lost his balance and went tumbling to the ground.

Bruno looked crestfallen as he watched in horror. Bartholomew raised his sword in victory and his men cheered, echoing across the countryside.

"You are defeated, my little whelp," Bartholomew crowed as he raised his sword and shield once more.

"I do not think so!" Bertold cried. In an instant he rolled to one side and sliced his sword toward the exposed calf of Bartholomew's leg. The blade sunk into his flesh as Bartholomew let out a horrendous screech. Bartholomew reached down to grab his bloodied leg, still yelling in agony when Bertold seized upon the chance and flung his sword from his lying position. The whirling blade sliced through the air and the handle smacked Bartholomew directly on his helmet. Stunned, Bartholomew fell backward and tripped over a stone and went crashing to the ground.

"*Aughh!*" he screamed. "You dirty little cuss, you!"

Alrik and the men stopped cheering and watched in stunned silence as their captain had been felled.

"Move, Bertold," Bruno yelped. "Get *up*." He wanted badly to come to his friend's aid, but he knew the rules. A knight must finish his own battle.

Bertold scrambled around on his back and finally grasped the rope on his side. "Thank God, it is still there," he mumbled. Quickly, he tied one end to his armor behind his neck. He glanced over at his adversary to see if he was attempting to recover as well. Bartholomew was still writhing on the ground, his leg covered in blood, cursing under his breath.

Bertold threw off his helmet to better survey the tree branches overhead. He spotted a good strong one and then took aim with his rope.

"Sir Bart, he is trying to stand!" Alrik shouted toward his fallen captain.

Bertold flung his rope but it missed the branch and fell back to the ground as Bartholomew groaned rolling to his side. Bertold tried again and flung the rope even harder. He was elated to see it fly up and over the branch and fall back down to dangle in front of his face. "Ha!" he cried out. Just then, Bartholomew had rolled over to his knees. Bertold panicked and grabbed the rope and began to heave as hard as he could.

"Pull, Bertold. *Pull*," Bruno exclaimed, urging him on.

"Get *up*, sir," Alrik barked at Bartholomew.

Bartholomew tossed his helmet aside and looked around frantically. "I need something to pull myself up." He clambered with his hands, searching his side, but he had not equipped himself as Bertold had done. His leg continued to bleed profusely, and he knew it would be difficult to put weight on it. He desperately searched for something to grab hold of to push himself up. Then he spotted a boulder several feet away and proceeded to crawl on his knees toward the rock.

Meanwhile, Bertold struggled with his aching arms to pull himself up, armor and all. He winced in pain with each pull. Slowly, but surely, he began to raise himself off the ground. Inch by inch, one heart-pounding grab and pull after another when finally, he triumphantly stood and let the rope go.

"Yes!" Bruno shouted with elation.

Bertold confidently strode over to his sword and picking it up, he headed straight for his fallen adversary. Bartholomew had made it to the rock and had almost got himself to his feet when he felt the cool blade of a sword rest against his neck. He froze in place and waited breathlessly.

"I would not advise you to go any further," Bertold said smartly. He then put his boot to Bartholomew's shoulder and shoved him back to the ground in victory. "Now," he said coolly, pointing the blade at his chest. "Do *you* yield?"

"You little cuss. You have bested me." He rolled to one side and called for his men to help. Bertold put away his sword and helped him up as well. Bartholomew looked down sullenly at his bloody leg and shook his head. "An opportunistic strike, I must admit. Well done. Tell me, Sir Knight, what is your name and what house are you?"

Bruno, smiling happily, came and stood next to his victorious friend. Bertold lifted his shield bearing the three ravens proudly and answered, "I am Bertold from the House of Rees."

"Very well, Bertold of the House of Rees. You have fought gallantly. You are victorious."

∞

The glorious day came when it was time for Lisette to take her vows as a full nun in the Benedictine Order. The chapel was filled with all the brothers and sisters of the monastery, along with local villagers in attendance and Lisette's three family members sitting on the front row. Bertold, dressed in fine clothes, sat and smiled proudly as he watched the proceedings with Bruno and his parents next to him.

Hildegard sat with her long wooden staff in hand on the side of the alter while Volmar, dressed in full ceremonial vestments, stood at the head of the congregation. Standing before Volmar and Hildegard was Lisette, dressed in a fine white gown and veil, grinning from ear to ear.

"In the presence of God," Hildegard began, "and in the presence of those assembled here, I ask you; Do you swear to remain loyal to this cloister and our community through good and bad?"

"I swear it," Lisette answered loudly for all to hear.

"Do you swear under the guidance of the Gospels to seek God, to seek fervently for repentance, and to live your life according to Saint Benedict's rules?"

Lisette repeated, "I swear it."

Hildegard continued, asking, "Will you put Jesus Christ, the only Son of God, before all else, and swear obedience?"

"Yes, I swear it."

"May the Lord who began His work in you complete it," Hildegard concluded.

The entire congregation answered in unison, "Amen."

Hildegard then stood before her and presented her with a freshly pressed black habit and matching veil. Lisette removed her white veil and handed it to her mother. Hildegard then placed the black veil on Lisette, saying, "Wear this veil as a sign that you no longer belong to yourself, but to Christ. With Him, you are joined in God."

Lisette took in a deep breath and said, "Amen."

Hildegard went back to her chair and left Lisette standing before Father Volmar. He raised his hands to the congregation and said, "God has called upon this sister of ours to follow Christ in the monastic life. Let us ask the Almighty to shower mercy upon her and to help her realize the oath she has now taken."

The congregation again answered, "Amen."

After Mass had ended, a reception was held for all who came to witness the glorious ceremony. Lisette fluttered about the room, happy as a butterfly, now dressed in her new habit and matching veil. She was ecstatic to see her family after such a long time, especially her brother.

"I am so proud of you, sister," Bertold said as he embraced her.

Lisette answered graciously, "Thank you. I am so happy to see you. And look at how much you have moved up in the world. You are dressed so royally. Wherever did you get these clothes?" She couldn't help but overhear what people were whispering as they milled about the room, drinking wine and eating sweet breads.

"He is from nobility?" one woman asked her husband.

"Yes, of course. Look at how he carries himself and how he dresses. He is noble indeed."

"What is this I am hearing?" Lisette whispered under her breath. "The people think you are from nobility? From what notion are they saying this?"

Bertold rolled his eyes and answered, "I never said I was from nobility, but everyone thinks that I am. Look at how respectful everyone is."

"Respectful?" Lisette was aghast. "Please tell me how people would get this notion."

"I have become a knight, just like I had always dreamed of becoming," he finally answered. "Well, at least I think I am on my way."

Lisette looked at him flabbergasted. "How on Earth did you become a knight? We never owned a knight's armor. We are not from a noble family. How could you have possibly achieved this?"

He pulled her aside to speak to her in confidence. "I never told you this, but right after you came here, I *found* some armor."

"You *found* some? How?"

He looked around the room so no one would hear and said, "I happened upon this poor dead knight just lying in a field unnoticed. So, I gave him a proper burial and then...borrowed his set of armor."

"You mean *stole* his armor," she answered, raising her voice. Bertold lifted his finger to his lips to quieten her. "From a poor soul lying dead in a field. Bertold, the very idea."

He tried pleading with her and responded, "Yes, but I prayed for forgiveness and for strength to realize my dream, and it happened, dear sister. I fought one of the greatest knights ever and *defeated* him. I have realized my lifelong dream, just as you have today. Is it not wonderful?"

"*Wonderful?*" she blurted out once more. "Living as a lie? I will have no part in this." She grabbed him by the arm and dragged him across the room straight to Volmar. People watched her with amused curiosity, as did Hildegard. "Praying for forgiveness is not going to satisfy me. You must bring this before your confessor."

"Lisette, is this really necessary?" Bertold begged.

Volmar was taken aback when Lisette promptly dropped her brother directly in front of him. He was in mid-bite of another sweet pastry. "Sister," he gulped in between chewing, "how may I help you?"

"Father Volmar, I have your first customer of the day." Volmar looked ever the more puzzled. "Bertold, here is your confessor. May he save your soul from the blazing fires of hell. Volmar, this is my brother, the sinner."

Volmar quickly washed down his pastry with a gulp of wine and stammered, "Um, hello, young man."

"Hello, Father," Bertold said red-faced as his sister stormed off.

"A pleasure to see you again," Volmar said politely.

"Likewise, Father."

∞

Kuno waited patiently for the large oak door to be opened to the vast gathering space on the monk's side of the monastery. Finally, the door opened, and Hildegard walked in.

"Venerable Mother," he said in greeting.

"Good morning to you, Abbot," she said in reply.

"Please, sit down," he offered.

Hildegard paced the floor nervously and answered, "I prefer to stand."

"Very well. I will get straight to the point. There are rumors going around this establishment. Rumors that put the very fabric of our joint cloister in peril. I have asked you here to dispel these rumors once and for all."

"I would like to dispel them, Father Kuno, but I cannot," Hildegard answered bluntly. "The sisters and I have decided to move. That is why I am here to seek your blessing."

"Move?" he asked incredulously. "Meaning what?"

Hildegard didn't hesitate in saying, "It is time that we establish a cloister separate from the brothers. It is time that we have a place of our own."

"And you have made this decision on your own, have you?" Kuno asked, his agitation growing evermore. "This is an impossibility. This monastery has been the home of the Benedictine sisters for ages."

She waved him off and said, "I have already sought permission from the Archbishop of Mainz, and he has granted it."

Kuno became incensed even more and fumed at her, saying, "You dare to go beyond me seeking permission? You have used your friendship with the bishop to undermine me. Well, I forbid it."

"For what reason?" she asked calmly.

"Do you know what it takes to build a fortress such as this?" he blasted. "It took decades of hard, skilled labor to construct these grounds. And where will you get the land and the money? No, your place is here as is all the sisters." He tried to reason with her as she stood stone-faced looking at him. "We are in the midst of the greatest revival the church has ever seen in our time. Our coffers are over-flowing every week. We have visitors from all around the continent coming here now."

"And those coffers would not be so filled if it were not for me," she fired back.

"You watch your tongue, Mother," he warned.

Hildegard ignored him though. "The decision has already been made and so have the arrangements. We cannot focus on our faith and the vows we have sworn to in a place surrounded by men and one that has become an attraction for tourists. We wish only to live in peace and solitude so we may serve the Lord."

"You *created* this attraction," he declared. "What arrangements do you speak of?"

"The land and the monetary funds have been donated by the family Sponheim of my late and dear Sister Jutta. It will be situated on the lands near the Rhine at Rupertsberg. All we need now is your blessing for our cloister to depart."

"And you will never get it, I can assure you," he answered stubbornly. "You build up a frenzy with your *visions* and then you leave us to deal with the ravel left behind you."

Hildegard looked at him with contempt. "You have gone leave of your senses as a priest and a compassionate human being. I shall return when you have calmed yourself as you are acting like a child. The main reason, my dear Abbot, that we ask this of you is that God has asked *me* to lead them there. I *must* do His will!" With that she stormed out of the room.

After her confrontation with the Abbot, Hildegard's health began to deteriorate rapidly. Soon, she was bedridden wracked with pain and fever. The ailments that had ravaged her body since childhood had returned, but this time worse than she had ever experienced. Her body became rigid with paralysis to the point she could not even move, nor speak. All the sisters were distraught and prayed for their mother constantly. Richardis kept a daily and nightly vigil at her bedside, not letting herself sleep.

The sisters asked Volmar to plead on Hildegard's behalf to Kuno, but the Abbot would not listen. "The Mother needs rest and prayers. If it is the Lord's will that she go to the Almighty, then so be it."

Two weeks passed but there was no improvement to Hildegard's condition. She lay awake, her eyes wide open, yet she could not move or speak. She could barely drink water or a spoonful of soup.

As the nuns surrounded her bedside, Richardis, her eyes red from weariness, said to them, "One of us must go on our Mother's behalf. It is not Volmar's task but ours."

"I will go," Lisette volunteered.

Lisette stood before the Abbot pleading for him to show mercy on Hildegard. "The Venerable Mother's condition is not due to me, dear Sister," he explained. "Unfortunately, she has been ill most of her life. We have always known this to be true."

"You of all people show her no mercy. And why? Because she wishes for us to have our own monastery?" Lisette gathered every ounce of courage she had in her. "I know of her past illnesses but let me tell you what else I know about her. It is not illness that makes her bedridden, but the terrible, anguishing distress that has overwhelmed her simply because she is not being allowed to fulfill her duties." She walked closer to Kuno and gently put her hand on his arm and pleaded, "Listen to me, Father. Her purpose is to only obey the Will of God. It has always been this way for her entire life, but you stand in the way of this. Her request of you is not for her own sake but of God's. And now she suffers as she has not obeyed His Will."

Kuno entered the room where Hildegard lay stricken. She had now been bedridden for more than three weeks. The bed was surrounded by her sisters and Volmar was at her side reciting the rosary.

"With all of you here, I will say this," Kuno began, "I have thought on how harshly I reacted to the Venerable Mother's request and I have conferred with the Archbishop. I do not know how long our Mother will be with us, but as for the rest of you, including you Father, I allow you to convene at your new holy site. Volmar will go along with you as your confessor. That is all I have to say." With that, he left the room, and all the sisters wept with joy.

Richardis knelt by Hildegard's bedside and whispered, "Now you may fulfill your duties, Mother."

∞

Miraculously, the next morning Hildegard sat up in her bed and placed her bare feet on the cold stone floor. Her gray hair had fallen from her veil and lay in thin, unkempt strands about her shoulders. "Bring me some water," she said to the stunned Richardis.

As the days passed, her strength slowly returned to her body. Soon, she was walking about the grounds of the monastery, listening to the birds in the trees. Lisette and Volmar walked with her and kept a close eye as they knew she was still weakened from her ordeal.

"Mother," Lisette asked, "may I ask if you remember anything while you were stricken?"

Hildegard thought for a moment, trying to remember anything that she had experienced. "I remember nothing to be honest. It was if I were in a constant state of darkness. The only thing I remember clearly is the morning I awakened three days ago. Before my eyes were opened, I saw a vision of angels, a procession of them too great in number to count. They fought alongside Michael against a fierce dragon and won the victory. Then I heard a voice. One of the angels said to me, 'Eagle! Eagle! Why sleepest thou? Arise! For it is dawn. Eat and drink.'" Lisette and Volmar stood in stunned silence and wonder. "Do you know what this means, my dear Volmar?"

"It means, it is time for us to get back to work," Volmar said with a smile.

"Exactly," Hildegard answered. "Lisette, tell me, would your brother still be at home?"

Lisette nodded and answered, "He said he would stay a month's time before returning to the training grounds. After my encouragement to stay longer, of course."

"Good," Hildegard said. "Let us go visit them."

The next day, Hildegard, Volmar and Lisette arrived at the home of Magnilde and Johan. Lisette was delighted in seeing Bertold outside working with some wood. Magnilde emerged from the house, wiping her hands on her apron and smiling happily.

"Venerable Mother! Father Volmar!" she said exuberantly. "What a pleasant surprise." She gave Lisette a big hug. "Hello, Daughter, you have honored our house. Bertold, go and fetch your uncle." She clasped her hands around Hildegard's and said, "Sister, I am so pleased to hear you are feeling much better now. I have said so many prayers for you."

"You are most kind," Hildegard replied.

Just then Johan came walking up from his woodshop. "Hello, Father and Sisters. How nice to have you here. Please come in for

143

some cool water." He gave Lisette a hug and kiss on her forehead. "Hello, my sweet Lisette."

"Good morning, Uncle Johan," she said cordially.

Hildegard waved off the kind invitation and said, "We will not distract your work for long. I only came to speak to your son."

Bertold put down his axe and walked closer. "Yes, Sister?"

Hildegard got straight to the point and said, "I understand you plan to make for the training grounds soon to continue your quest as a warrior."

"Yes, Sister. God willing, that is my plan."

"I know this is a noble pursuit of yours and I pray for your success in this endeavor, but first, if I may ask..."

Bertold was increasingly curious as to what she wanted. "Yes, Sister Hildegard?"

"I see you have honed your skills as a carpenter just as your uncle has taught you. It would please the Lord, before you take up your warrior pursuits, that you would bring your carpentry skills along with us to Rupertsberg."

"Rupertsberg?" Bertold asked curiously.

Lisette chuckled somewhat, as did Volmar. "It appears you have been called, dear brother," Lisette snickered.

Hildegard placed her hand on Bertold's shoulder and asked, "The sisters at Disibodenberg have been granted permission to start their own cloister at Rupertsberg. Will you lend your skills in building God's house there?"

Johan was so proud and excited he was about to burst with joy. "We will all go, Venerable Mother. We will *all* help you."

"Yes, we will," Magnilde happily echoed.

Volmar clasped his hands together excitedly and said, "God be praised." Hildegard turned back to Bertold and awaited his response.

"Yes, of course. I would be glad to help you, Sister," Bertold answered with a smile.

Lisette jumped for joy and hugged her brother's neck and gave her uncle a big kiss on the cheek. "I knew it! Thank you, brother. Thank you all." Hildegard stood and smiled, knowing she had come to the right place.

Within a few weeks, a caravan of nuns, craftsmen and their families headed through the thick forests along the Rhine River toward Rupertsberg. At the head of the caravan on a wagon with the Count of Sponheim, Stephen III, sat Hildegard. With one hand holding the side of the rickety wagon, she shaded her eyes from the setting sun, straining to see through the thick trees.

"Are we getting close, Stephen?" she asked eagerly. "We have entered Bingen, have we not?"

"Yes, Sister," Stephen answered. "For the last half hour or so. Trust me, I know this land quite well. We will be at the site before sundown."

Hildegard was satisfied for the time being and sat back to relax. "Bingen is an old Celtic name, did you know that?" Stephen shook his head. "It means 'hole in the rock.'" She chuckled a bit thinking about the meaning. "I have no doubt that is what we will find. We will be challenged from the outset. I do not remember this land as well as you, but I was born here. I was taken away at a very early age. I hardly even remember." She sat and contemplated her arrival so many decades before at the monastery at Disibodenberg.

Less than an hour later, they came to a stop. Stephen pointed toward a small clearing just beyond the tall trees before them and said, "We have arrived."

The people began to dismount their horses and wagons and slowly ventured over into the clearing. Brush and tree limbs were scattered everywhere, but Hildegard carefully observed the large plot of land and nodded approvingly. "There is much clearing to be done, but this is the place. May God be with us in our efforts."

The people worked hard every day and camped by night. They lived in conditions most of the nuns had ever experienced before. Coming from well-to-do families and being cloistered all their days at Disibodenberg, some grumbled under the harsh conditions. Yet they all continued to work tirelessly at building their future.

Bertold and the other men worked diligently with the wood in the area, clearing trees and brush. They fashioned furniture and tools for them to use. He even became quite adept as a stone mason, helping to build the foundation and walls of the fortress. Bruno had traveled with them as well, providing much needed assistance with the ironworks as a smith.

After a years-time, the chapel and quarters of the first building were beginning to take shape. Another six months later, all the people were thankful to God when they were finally able to sleep with a roof over their heads. There was still much work to be done, but the abbey was finally taking shape.

By the fall of 1151, the chapel and their quarters, and even the beginnings of a courtyard, were now complete. Throughout all this time Hildegard continued her music compositions as well as dictating even more of her visions to Volmar.

One day, he was reading through her compositions and curiously asked, "What is that you have written, *Ordo Virtutum*?"

Hildegard smiled as she was glad he asked. "It is a play with music to accompany it. I wish for all of us to produce this play and have parts in it. It is about the morality of life and how we have confrontations between our virtues and vices."

"Very interesting," Volmar answered, nodding his head. "You want us to sing? You know, dear Mother, I have a terrible singing voice." Hildegard laughed at him. "And what is this? You even have a part for the devil? Who would you have in that role?"

"I had you in mind," she chuckled. "The devil is without song, remember?"

"Ha," he laughed. "You old crow."

∞

Lisette stood outside the walls of the newly completed abbey with her brother and aunt and uncle.

"I cannot thank you enough for all that you have done for us. I know you are missing our old home though. And I know you are anxious to resume your training, Bertold. I pray God will always guide you."

Magnilde gave her a long hug, saying, "We will miss you, Lisette."

Just then, Hildegard emerged to say goodbye to them as well. "I thank you with all my heart for what you have done here. God is pleased with the house you have built for Him. As am I."

"God be with all of you, Venerable Mother," Johan said from the wagon.

Hildegard gazed at Bertold and said, "It will please me immensely to see you again, young Bertold. I see great things for you."

"Thank you, Sister," Bertold answered warmly. "I hope to see you again one day as well."

As the visions continued for Hildegard, the scribes worked diligently in recording them just as they had done for the book *Scivias*. The beginning of a new volume began to take form, and Hildegard declared it would be called, *Liber Vitae Meritorum*.

In between her dictations and musical compositions, she was routinely summoned to have audiences with various dignitaries and heads of state. Upon returning to the monastery at Rupertsberg in the spring, she was devastated to hear some shocking news about her closest companion, Richardis.

Lisette and Clara watched as Hildegard ran to the garden and wept. "What has our Mother so distraught?" asked Clara.

"Something terrible has happened," Lisette answered, a tear rolling down her cheek. "Sister Richardis is being called away."

"What?" Clara asked, shocked. "No one has ever left the order before. This is horrible news. We must comfort our Mother." She began to fret and asked, "Why is she being called away?"

Lisette shook her head, holding back her tears. "The Archbishop has assigned her to Bassum and to be made abbess there."

"This is unheard of," Clara complained. "What will Mother do?"

"I do not know, perhaps file a petition on Richardis' behalf. But does Richardis really want that?"

Clara looked at her perplexed, "What do you mean? You think she *wants* to leave?"

"It is just a feeling I have. We must pray for them both, Sister."

Hildegard did file a petition with the Archbishop and even with the Holy Father in Rome, but in the end, the new assignment for Richardis was upheld.

The news became even more devastating for Hildegard less than a year later when word came that Richardis had unexpectedly passed away. Hildegard locked herself in her room for days mourning her death. A letter arrived several days later that was by Richardis herself, written on her deathbed. She expressed how saddened she was about leaving her sisters at Rupertsberg and how she regretted it every day. This sent Hildegard into an even deeper depression that lasted months.

The years slowly passed, and life returned to normal at the abbey. Construction continued at the monastery with more additions and covered walkways and Hildegard was pleased with the progress. She was teaching a class on botany one morning in the garden when word arrived from a courier on horseback.

She abruptly stopped her lesson after reading the note and said to her students, "I am needed by the king." She rushed inside the convent and went straight to the scribe's room where she found Lisette and Volmar diligently working on a new text.

"Lisette," she said breathlessly, "I have been summoned once more to see Barbarossa. This time, I would very much like it if you came with me."

"But we have our work here, Mother," Lisette complained.

Hildegard nodded in understanding, but said, "Yes, I know. It will be here when we return. This matter is far too important though. You shall see."

As they neared the castle of King Frederick, also known as Barbarossa, they stopped their horses at a soldier's barracks. "Why are we stopping here," Lisette asked.

"I want to inquire about your brother," Hildegard said pointedly.

Lisette went flush as she had not seen Bertold in years. "He is here? How would you know?"

"We shall ask to make certain," Hildegard answered. She approached the sentry posted at the gate and asked, "We would like to speak to one of your men. His name is Bertold."

The sentry looked at her calmly and asked in return, "Bertold from the House of Rees?"

"Yes, that is he. May we see him?"

The sentry turned to his companion and ordered, "Go and find the stableman called Bertold. These nuns wish to see him."

"Stableman?" Lisette asked aloud. Looking at Hildegard, she asked, "And how did you know he was here?"

"God told me he would be here," Hildegard whispered.

Lisette looked at her with a shocked expression. After all the visions she had recorded over the years, she was still amazed that such minute details were disclosed to her by the Almighty. The miracle was confirmed when Bertold emerged from the barracks and walked out to the gate.

"Lisette!" he cried as he ran out to them and hugged her tightly. "Greetings to you, too, Venerable Mother. How did you find me here?"

"The Lord works in mysterious ways," Hildegard said with a smile. "I was wondering if you would like to take a ride with us. We are on our way to see the king."

His face went pale and asked, "To see the king? Um, alright. Yes, if you wish. Let me retrieve one of the horses."

He came back almost immediately riding a fine black stallion and found Lisette and Hildegard waiting on their horses. "I am so pleased to see you again, Lisette."

"As am I, Bertold. You look well. But why is it they call you a stableman?"

Bertold shook his head and answered, "They will only let me train and take care of the horses. They still will not let me formally join their ranks."

"Then why do you stay?" Lisette pleaded. "Johan could surely use your help at home."

He persisted though and said, "I just feel there is something more for me here. That is all."

They soon arrived at the palace and they were escorted to the throne room of the king. It was also where the king preferred to hold his private meetings as he preferred not the formal setting of a traditional throne room but instead a more relaxed meeting place for himself and his guests.

Hildegard instructed Bertold to wait outside the chamber for the time being. A guard opened the door and said to her, "The king will see you now."

She and Lisette walked into the large, elaborate room. Instead of a throne, there was a writing table filled with business letters and ink wells. Another table was neatly adorned with fruits and breads and decanters filled with wine with fresh goblets for the guests. Paintings and tapestries adorned every wall and musicians played soft music in the corner. In the middle of the room stood Barbarossa.

He was an imposing figure with broad shoulders and dressed in long tailored garments of royal gold, white and maroon. He had a full head of dusty red hair with a matching, carefully trimmed, beard and mustache.

"Ah!" he said in a booming, yet friendly voice. "The seer has returned." He crossed the floor and knelt before her to kiss her hand. "I am honored by your presence once more, Venerable Mother."

"It is pleasing to see you again, Your Majesty," Hildegard answered. "I thank you for the invitation to the games that you have graciously told me about over the years. I find them quite fascinating."

"Games?" Lisette blurted out.

"Yet, you have never seen them. Thus, my invitation to you," the king said cordially.

Hildegard stood with her staff as she addressed him. "I am pleased of your progress as sovereign of this land."

Barbarossa bowed in thanks, saying, "I am honored to hear of your satisfaction. How may I make your stay more comfortable?"

"If I may," Hildegard began, "I am eager to attend this event of yours, but I am also here at the behest of a friend. I have come with a warrior who wishes to serve you."

"And who do we have here?" he asked, gazing at Lisette, ignoring Hildegard's business for the time being.

She tried not to get impatient with him and answered, "This is Sister Lisette, one of my chief scribes. She knows of all the words I hear and the visions I see."

"You are most fortunate, Sister Lisette. You are the protégé of one of the most influential voices of our time. I am envious, but most of all, happy for your sake." He returned his gaze upon Hildegard and asked, "What is it that you seek?"

She went straight to the point and stated, "There is a young man who is not of noble blood who wishes to serve as one of your warriors."

Barbarossa stroked his red beard for a moment and walked over to the refreshment table. "May I pour you some wine?"

"No, thank you, Your Majesty."

"Such a strange request of a nun, to ask a king about a potential protector of the throne."

"His aims are much like yours, Your Majesty," Hildegard explained. "His only wish is to serve God as a protector of the faith under your authority."

"But he is not of noble descent? You would not be here asking for my permission if he were."

"He is a commoner, Your Majesty."

"A commoner?" Barbarossa asked curiously. "One of which who has never had an elder to serve in the Templar. What you ask is an impossibility."

"But all things are possible with God, Your Highness," Hildegard said with a wink and a smile. "As you know very well."

Barbarossa smiled with a hint of delight in knowing of her prowess in foresight. "What makes you so certain I would entertain such an impossible request?" He turned to take one last swallow of his wine goblet and set it down on the table.

"It is simple," Hildegard said confidently. " I have seen it."

Barbarossa whirled around with a wide grin on his face. "Ah! So, the seer has seen something more!" He sauntered over to Lisette and proclaimed, "My dear, Sister. Let me tell you about your mentor. She told me of how I would be crowned at Aachen, and she spoke truly. She then told me how I would be made emperor by His Holiness in Rome, and she spoke truly once more. And now she tells me of a peasant who would join my knights. My dear Sister, when the Venerable Mother has something to proclaim to me, I am all ears." He carefully thought of what Hildegard was asking and the implications that came with it. He gazed at Lisette once more and asked, "And how do you fit into all of this?"

"The warrior she speaks of, Your Highness, is my brother."

"Ah, the plot thickens. Your mentor is wise as she is insightful with political matters. Tell me of your brother."

Lisette cleared her throat and answered, "He works as a stableman at the soldiers training grounds. His name is Bertold."

"From what house?"

"Bertold from the House of Rees, Your Majesty," Lisette answered.

He began to stroke his beard in deep thought once more. "I have heard this name." Hildegard and Lisette were both surprised at hearing this. "I have heard this name amongst the men in their quarters during times of leisure. It is attached to a rather amusing story regarding one of my finest warriors." He motioned to one of his aides and commanded, "Send for Bartholomew. I wish to see him."

"Yes, Your Majesty."

He then looked over at Hildegard and asked, "I take it the young lad is here with you today?"

"Yes, he is. He is outside the door."

Barbarossa motioned to his other aide and said, "Send for Bertold."

"Yes, Your Majesty."

The large wooden door opened and in walked Bertold. He rushed to his sister's side and embraced her once more, still very happy to see her. For a moment, he forgot all about proper greetings for the king. "Forgive me, sire." Flustered, Bertold regained his composure and knelt before him. "Your Majesty," he said politely.

"This reunion warms my heart," Barbarossa said. "It is obvious you have not seen each other for some time. Rise, young warrior."

Standing, Bertold replied, "Thank you for seeing me today, Your Majesty. It is an honor."

"It seems our meeting has already been foretold amongst the stars and the Heavens. You are welcome. Tell me of your family. Who are your mother and father?"

Lisette answered for him, saying, "Our parents died when we were both very young. Our mother while giving birth to me and our father a few years later in an accident. We were raised by our aunt and uncle, Johan and Magnilde Rees."

"A noble task, indeed," Barbarossa said with a nod, "taking on the role of patriarch in the wake of a brother's passing. I admire this greatly."

Just then, Bartholomew entered, frowning just a bit when he saw Bertold was in the king's throne room as well. "How may I be of service, Your Majesty?"

"Ah! The mighty Sir Bart. Thank you for coming on such short notice. Tell me, great knight," Barbarossa mused, "is this the 'whelp' I so often hear about that bested you that one summer day in the fields?"

Bartholomew answered sheepishly, "Yes, Your Majesty. It is the same man."

"Very well, that is all I need of you. You may go," he said chuckling.

"Yes, Your Majesty," Bartholomew said, feeling humiliated as he slunk out of the chamber.

Barbarossa returned his attention to Bertold and said, "Young warrior, your reputation has preceded you. And I am told by the upmost authority that I should consider doing what no other sovereign has done before. And that is let you prove yourself. Are you equal to that?"

"Oh, yes, Your Majesty," Bertold answered excitedly. "It has always been my dream to serve you and to fight for the Lord God."

"Then it is settled. In three day's-time I will be holding a tournament as you well know. Defeat any of my men in the arena, in the event of my choosing, and I shall grant your wish." He raised his finger to emphasize the importance of what he was granting, however. Bertold stood quietly and breathlessly for the king to continue. "But be certain, not to be a member of the Templar, but to be a part of the next best thing; a member of the palace guard. Is that satisfactory?"

Bertold could barely contain himself. He noticed that the king was smiling, almost laughing, as was Hildegard and Lisette. "Oh, yes, Your Majesty. But…what is everyone laughing at? Forgive me for asking."

"All in good time, young Rees. All in good time."

The day arrived for the knight's tournament and Hildegard and Lisette sat alongside the king and his wife, Empress Beatrice. The arena was filled with hundreds of spectators that surrounded a carefully manicured field of brown pitch.

Hildegard watched with amusement and curiosity as the soldiers battled in sports such as fencing and sword and shield combat in full knight armor. There were battles on horseback and feats of strength including the javelin throw and the iron toss. Then they watched skill competitions in archery and spear throwing.

After each event, the crowd cheered with enthusiasm and Hildegard smiled approvingly. "Exhilarating," she mused. "I quite enjoy the spirited competition."

"I am glad to hear that," the king agreed. "So do I."

"It can become quite violent at times, though," Lisette added.

The time came for the final event and the crowd waited breathlessly as the king stood and addressed the crowd, saying in a loud voice, "We now come to the crowning event of the day. Two warriors will meet on the field of battle in the event of my choosing." He motioned to the field below and announced, "To my right is the honorable knight, Sir Bartholomew!"

Bartholomew emerged from under the tiltyard dressed in full shining silver armor. He carried the shield bearing the red cross of the Templar and the crowd cheered wildly.

"To my left is the challenger from the House of Rees, Bertold!"

They clapped politely as the unknown knight emerged in the same gray armor that he wore years before when they first fought. He carried his shield bearing the black stripe and three ravens, that was newly polished and shimmering in the sun.

"Look at him!" Lisette marveled. She could not believe it was her brother. He walked and stood bravely next to Bartholomew before the king.

Hildegard smiled and added, "Magnificent."

The king continued, "Sir Bart and Bertold, welcome to the arena." He gazed at Bertold first and said, "It appears your adversary has asked for a rematch. I have granted his wish." He then looked at Bartholomew and said, "Sir Bart, I grant you this challenge in Bertold. You will face each other in the joust."

A hush fell over the crowd as it was the event they had all been expecting to see. Suddenly, they began to cheer wildly in anticipation.

"Oh, my," Lisette worried aloud. "He has never jousted before."

Bertold looked dejected and increasingly nervous and said to himself under the roar of the crowd, "I have never jousted before."

Bartholomew smiled and wisecracked at him, "Do not worry, stableman. It will be over quickly."

Barbarossa continued, "The first man to score three strikes in five or the first to knock his opponent off his steed shall win!" The crowd roared once more. "Knights, take your places."

Men brought out the horses with Bartholomew to ride a white and brown stallion and Bertold a solid black stallion. They brought out wooden platforms for them to walk to mount their respective horses. Both knights gave up their shield, and then were directed to their horses. Once mounted, they were handed their helmets, and then finally, their lance. Each lance was easily over twelve feet long with a blunted tip.

Bertold felt its weight and was awkward in his hand. It felt like nothing he had held before. "This is impossible," he muttered to himself. "He is going to split me in half."

"He does not know what he is doing," Lisette complained aloud once more.

"Sit still, Sister," Hildegard scolded. "He will be fine."

"How can you be so sure?"

Barbarossa stood and called out to the quieting crowd, "Let the joust begin!" They roared once more in delight.

Bertold stared down the jousting rail that stretched for thirty yards. His horse was antsy, jostling from side to side, anticipating the impending charge. "Steady, boy. Let us just make a successful pass, shall we? We will learn as we go. Well, I will learn. You probably know more about this than I do."

The starter came out to the center of the railing carrying a red pennant. The crowd grew quiet as he raised it high and Bertold quickly closed his face shield, remembering it in the nick of time. Both riders watched intently, ready to make the charge at the falling of the pennant. The starter snapped it down and the knights kicked their horses, aiming their lance down the line. Bertold raced like thunder toward him and in a flash, Bartholomew tore past him with the tip of his lance aimed directly at his chest. *Clang!* The piercing noise shocked Bertold out of coherence as his own lance never came close to striking his opponent. Bartholomew was precise, however, and served a crushing blow to Bertold's chest armor. The crowd erupted in jubilation as Bartholomew triumphantly circled back to his starting point.

"Oh, my Lord! Help him!" Lisette cried.

Bertold clung to his mount as best he could while listing to one side, barely keeping hold of his lance. The shock of the blow nearly knocked him unconscious, but his horse kept galloping back to the starting point as he was trained. Soon, Bertold snapped back into coherence and his chest ached like never before. "Oh, dear Lord," he coughed and wheezed. "Give me strength." He tried his best to focus on his task. "Think of what you are doing. It is not a sword, but an extension of your arm. Steady yourself."

The starter came out once more with the red pennant. "One strike to Sir Bart!" he called out loudly. The crowd approved boisterously. He raised the pennant as the crowd hushed and with a zip of the red flag the riders were off in a flash.

Lisette held her hands tightly to her chin as she watched Bertold perilously charge Bartholomew. Bertold aimed his lance as the two came together in a thunder of hooves like shots from a cannon. To his amazement, Bertold was able to graze the side of Bartholomew's arm and at the same moment, Bartholomew's lance pounded Bertold directly in the shoulder. The crowd went wild with excitement once more as the two riders rounded the arena.

Hildegard leaned over to Lisette and said, "See, he is getting better already."

"He is getting *pummeled*," Lisette cried. "I cannot bear to watch."

"Oh, my shoulder," Bertold groaned. "Thank God for this armor." He ached more than ever, and his head was dizzy, and his stomach grew nauseous. He tried to shake the dizziness from his head, but he felt like the world was spinning.

"Knight, are you set?" his aide inquired as he steadied Bertold's horse.

Bertold regained himself and answered, "Yes, I am set."

The starter once again marched to the center of the arena. "Two strikes to zero for Sir Bart!" The crowd went into a frenzy anticipating the final blow. He raised the red pennant and checked both riders to see if they were ready. The red pennant came flashing to the dirt and the knights charged one another at full speed once more. Bertold steadied his lance, his stallion charging like a beast on fire and extended his arm and tightened his muscles and braced for the crushing impact. To his shock, he delivered an incredible blow to the center of Bartholomew's chest, sending him flailing wildly on his horse. Expecting the worst, Bertold was stunned to see he had passed through untouched.

The crowd was equally stunned as they saw their hero doing his best to stay on his mount. They soon began to cheer wildly, seeing the match had become much more interesting.

"*This* is what they came to see," Barbarossa commended. Hildegard sat and smiled proudly, and Lisette was too stunned to say anything.

Bertold and his horse trotted back to their place and the handler gave him an approving smile. "Well done."

"Thank you," Bertold answered, feeling much more confident.

"Do not get too brash. He is as mad as they come now, boy. He will want to finish you right here and now. I can assure you, there will not be a fifth go-round."

Bertold knew his aide was serious and nodded in understanding, saying, "Then I will have to finish him right now."

Barbarossa looked over at his guests and said, "It will end here as I can sense it. Sir Bart is fuming. I can see the steam rising from his helmet."

"God be with him," Lisette prayed for her brother. "Please just do not let him die."

"He will not die," Hildegard said confidently. "He is only just beginning."

The starter shouted to the crowd, "Two strikes to one in favor of Sir Bart!" He raised his pennant and the crowd fell deathly silent.

Bertold lowered his face shield and whispered to his mount, "Steady, boy. Follow my lead."

The red flag sliced the air and the knights set out in full charge. The roar of thundering hooves could be heard for miles as they raced at top speed at one another with each second charging harder. Amazingly, yet deceptively, Bertold dipped quickly to his left and his horse responded with equal grace. The unexpected move distracted Bartholomew just enough to create the opening Bertold was hoping for. In a dramatic flash, Bertold popped back up straight on his horse and delivered a decisive strike to the center of Bartholomew's chest. The sound was deafening, and the crowd watched in awe as the wooden lance splintered into thousands of shards. Bartholomew was sent sailing off his mount and bouncing hard to the ground with a terrible thud. Bertold was stunned and shocked, as was the crowd and the king.

The people roared at the thunderous and decisive blow. The king stood and clapped his approval as Bertold circled the arena in triumph. The cheering would not stop as Bartholomew was helped

157

to his feet in agony. He removed his helmet and winced terribly as the crowed continued their celebration. Shaking his head, he slowly hobbled off the field of battle.

As Bertold dismounted, he removed his helmet to the joy of the crowd and ascended the steps to his elated sister, Hildegard and King Frederick. Lisette ran to her brother and hugged him tightly. She was overjoyed at his success and admired him greatly for his bravery and courage. "Thank God you are alright, brother."

"Trust me," he said relieved. "No one is thanking Him more than I."

"A heroic triumph," the king commended. "I see great things in your future, Sir Bertold. Great things indeed."

"As do I," Hildegard said with a wink and a smile.

Coda

Bertold earned his way into the palace guard, just as Hildegard had foreseen. He became a respected leader amongst the men and one of the closest associates and advisers to the king. He met a young maiden a year later, named Hanna, whom he married soon after. Together they had three sons and two daughters. Nearly forty years later, Captain Bertold set out alongside Barbarossa on the Third Crusade. After three arduous years of battle, that ranged all over the Earth, Barbarossa met his demise in a drowning accident in Armenia in the River Saleph. Bertold and his men took the king's remains to Antioch where they were interred at the Church of Saint Peter. Disease soon swept through the area and claimed the lives of hundreds of soldiers, including Bertold himself.

Sister Lisette remained at Rupertsberg the rest of her life. She followed in her mentor's footsteps and became the chief scribe at the monastery. She never stopped yearning for knowledge, as she understood its significance as it pertained to her deeply devoted faith. She died just after the turn of the century in 1201.

Hildegard's visions from God continued until her death in 1179 at the age of eighty-one. In 1174, just five years before her passing, her greatest achievement in writing was completed. *The Book of Divine Works*, or *Liber Divinorum Operum*, was completed with the aid of Sister Lisette and other dedicated nuns at Rupertsberg and Eibingen, the second abbey founded by Hildegard. It is considered one of the finest works in visionary documentation.

Throughout history, Hildegard has been viewed as a saint by many branches of the Roman Catholic Church. However, she was not formally recognized by the Vatican until 2012 when Pope Benedict XVI proclaimed that the 'liturgical cult' of Saint Hildegard was to be extended to the entire Catholic Church in a process called 'equivalent canonization'. He named her a Doctor of the Church for "her holiness of life and the originality of her teaching." She is the fourth woman in history to have this honor bestowed out of only thirty-six Doctors of the Church. The Pope called her "perennially relevant" and "an authentic teacher of theology and a profound scholar of natural science and music." Her feast day is celebrated on September 17th.

Part V

The Year of Our Lord, 1260

In the year of our Lord, 1260, the German empire had seen itself splinter as a result of the numerous crusades around the known world. Unlike England, France, and Spain which had developed strong centralized monarchs, Germany moved in the opposite direction. After the death of Frederick II in 1250, attention was forced upon regions they had previously conquered, such as Italy, Sicily and Jerusalem. All the while, people in the German homeland were left to fend for themselves and were thus scattered through various areas north of the Rhine and Frankfurt and southward into Switzerland and Austria.

As a result of decades of wars, many families were left without fathers and sons who died serving the kings. Many children were left orphaned and the burden fell upon the goodness of charity that was mostly found in the religious orders and monasteries. Mothers left alone who could not care for their children were sometimes forced to offer some, if not all, as oblates to the church in order for them to be educated or simply to survive.

Those lucky enough to still have their families intact sought highly coveted positions within the numerous monasteries that dotted the German countryside. It was not uncommon for families to be hired as caretakers of the property as well as to assist with the numerous orphanages that they housed. Their assistance allowed the friars and nuns to dedicate their time in other areas of charity, such as teaching and tending to the poor and sick.

However, such positions for needy families were scarce as each monastery only had one vacancy. Once established, a family could be in possession of these prized appointments for generations. However, on rare occasions, these vacancies would come available.

Such was the case at the Benedictine convent called Saint Mary at Helfta. Only established two years prior in the quaint town of Eisleben, the nuns of Saint Mary were in desperate need of new caretakers as they themselves had cared for the grounds since its inception. It wasn't until the arrival of a little orphan girl were their prayers answered. The little girl's name was Gertrude.

Gertrude

The man hobbled into the office of the prior at Saint Mary's convent and limped noticeably with every step favoring his right leg. Gunther Rees sat down with his wife, Odelia, and their two children. On the other side of the large oak desk was Father Edgar, the prior at Saint Mary. The Rees' had waited anxiously for weeks to finally have their interview with him.

"Please make yourselves comfortable," Edgar said cordially. "Thank you all for coming."

"Oh, thank you, Father," Gunther answered nervously leaning forward, clutching his cap tightly between his hands. Odelia lightly tapped his leg for him to sit back and relax. Gunther grinned at her slightly and slowly slid back on his chair. "We are very happy to be here." He motioned to his wife and said, "This is Odelia and our two children, Klaus and Annamarie."

Edgar smiled at the children who stood quietly behind their mother and said, "A pleasure to meet you Frau Rees. How old are your children?"

"My pleasure as well, Father," Odelia answered. "Klaus is ten and Annamarie is seven."

"Wonderful. It is a lovely age. There are a dozen or so other children here at the orphanage. There is ample time for them to play together in between their studies." The two children smiled at the notion but remained quiet as they were instructed. "You are capable in washing duties as well as the kitchen, I take it?"

Odelia readily nodded, saying, "Yes, quite capable. I have cooked and cleaned since I was little. I even help cook at my sister and brother's homes. They have many children."

"I see. That is very good. The sisters will welcome an experienced cook in the kitchen. We have some barnyard animals that will need tending to such as poultry and goats for milk."

Odelia immediately responded, "The children would be very good with them, fetching eggs, milking. They know this very well."

Edgar nodded approvingly and then turned his attention to the understandably anxious Gunther. "So, Herr Rees. Please tell me why we should select you and your family for this post."

"Oh, please," he stuttered, his hands trembling. "Please call me Gunther."

"Very well, Gunther. What makes the Rees family the right choice for Saint Mary priory?"

"Well," Gunther began, motioning to Odelia, "she is quite skilled in the kitchen. She is the best cook I have ever known. And the children, they will do their chores without question. Sweeping, helping their mother. The boy is a learned apprentice, he will do anything you ask. He has learned many of the skills I have; carpentry, stonecutting and masonry."

"And how about gardening?" Edgar asked.

Gunther glanced at his wife, knowing full well she had done most of the vegetable gardening throughout their marriage. "Gardening? Yes, yes. We all know gardening. We grew many things."

"Before the accident," Edgar reminded him.

Gunther clutched his cap even tighter and stared at the floor for a moment as it was the topic he was dreading. "Y-yes, Father. That is true."

While the adults talked, the children couldn't help but notice the goings on outside the office window. It was springtime and the wooden shutters to the abbey were open to welcome the cool breeze and Annamarie grew curious when she heard the laughter of children outside. She then saw the blonde hair of a little girl running around happily just below the window. Annamarie smiled, knowing the girl must be close to her age.

"May I ask how it happened?" Edgar inquired. "If you do not mind."

Gunther shook his head fervently, and answered, "No, I do not mind. I was doing some patch work on the roof one day and lost my balance and fell. It was not far and had I landed softly I would have been fine. Unfortunately, I landed on my side and my leg hit a large rock on the ground."

"And your leg was broken in two places," Edgar finished his thought.

Gunther bowed his head sadly and said, "Yes."

"You were not able to work for months until you healed enough to walk. And in the meantime, the land you resided upon…"

162

"Was lost," Gunther admitted. "Her sister and brothers have been kind to us during that time, but now I am fully capable of working. There is no need to worry, Father. I will not let you down."

"I know your intentions are sincere, Herr Rees," Edgar continued, "and your desire to work is strong. I can see that, and I admire you for it. But the job of caretaker of these grounds is a demanding one. As you know, construction is still being done on the expansion wings, but they are nearly complete. That being said, I am now focusing on the grounds themselves. They are in poor shape after the initial construction. We would like to build walkways, plant gardens and trees. We would like these grounds to become a peaceful place for our religious to go and reflect and have ample spaces for the orphans to play in the summers. And being spring, there is little time to waste before winter arrives once more." Gunther nodded at all the tasks he listed, knowing each one would be difficult. "Do you feel your leg is up to such hard work?"

Sweat beaded on Gunther's forehead, not wanting the opportunity to slip away just because of his bad leg. He was about to answer when suddenly the door flew open and in ran the little girl that Annamarie had seen outside. She looked to be no more than four years old and she danced and twirled and trotted around the room. The children were delighted at seeing her and giggled at her antics.

"Hello! Hello!" the little girl said cheerfully as she skipped around the chamber. She stopped directly in front of Annamarie and said sweetly to her, "I like you. We will be friends." She smiled at Klaus and said, "You too." The children giggled even more.

"Sister?" Edgar called from behind his desk. "You must excuse the interruption," he said to the Rees'. "She is one of the orphans who just arrived this morning."

The little girl danced over to Odelia and said happily, "Hello, what is your name?"

"Hello, young lady," Odelia answered politely. "I am Frau Rees."

"I like you, Frau Rees."

"Um, Sister?" Edgar called out again.

Just then, Sister Irma came dashing in frantically. "I am so sorry, Father. She is too fast for me. Come along, Gertrude."

Before she could grab her arm, Gertrude hopped over to Gunther and smiled at him broadly. "I like you the most." Then she whispered in his ear, "I will help you." Gunther smiled at her quizzically.

Edgar waited impatiently for Sister Irma to escort Gertrude out and when the door was closed, he turned his attention back to the family. "I do apologize. You see a little already of what it is like here. We love our children dearly, but they can be a handful."

"She was delightful," Odelia beamed.

"Mother, I want to play with her. She was nice," Annamarie spoke up.

"Shh," her mother scolded.

"Well," Edgar continued, "where were we? Ah, yes. You were telling me about your unfortunate accident. I am sorry, Gunther, but I do not think this is a job you will be physically up to. I know the rest of your family are quite capable and qualified, but I am mostly worried about you and your leg."

Gunther hesitated in trying to persuade him, saying, "I know, Father, I understand. But I will work hard, I can move about even without a walking stick. Please, for our sake, let us have one chance."

Edgar sat back in his chair and thought for a moment, staring outside. "There is a large tree on the grounds in the far corner," he began. He stood and pointed out the window and Gunther got to his feet to see the tree he was referring to. "That is a place the sisters and I would very much like to start a rose garden. There are some wild ones growing near that tree. Do you know much about rose bushes?"

Gunther gulped and looked back at his wife. Neither of them knew much of anything about rose bushes. "Yes," he stammered, "rose bushes are…are quite lovely."

"No matter what I do," Edgar complained, "I cannot do a thing with those wild bushes. The flowers can be so breathtaking, but the thorny branches are such a nuisance." He went back to his desk and sat down again. "I will offer you this; I will arrange for you a trial period of one month where you learn the grounds and get to know everyone and about life in general here at the priory. After a month's time I will review your family's progress and decide then if this post will be a permanent one. Is that agreeable?"

"Yes! Yes, Father," Gunther said excitedly.

"The one thing that I ask of you, Gunther, is to see what you can do with the rose garden by the large maple tree. Other tasks will be given to you, but this particular area is where I would like to begin in beautifying these grounds. Are you equal to that?"

"Yes, Father. I will begin right away. All of us will."

Odelia stood and hugged her husband graciously and then hugged her children as well. "Thank you, Father."

"You are quite welcome. Sister Mechtilde will be here shortly to show you around."

Sister Mechtilde was young, not even twenty years old when the Rees' arrived at Saint Mary. She had come from a devoted and pious family and was always enchanted with the life her older sister had chosen. Her sister was now the abbess of the cloister and shared the same name as their newest orphan, Gertrude.

As soon as she was of age, Abbess Gertrude took her vows as a Benedictine nun and because of her family's wealth, she was well educated and quickly ascended to the head of the tiny school at the abbey. She also had exceptional talent for playing music and was gifted with an exquisite voice. She was polite and soft-spoken and always had a warming smile for everyone.

"Greetings to you, Rees'," Mechtilde said as she entered the prior's meeting room. "I am Sister Mechtilde, one of the teachers here at the school. I would be happy to show you our lovely home."

"Thank you, Sister," Gunther said graciously. "Come children, let us follow Sister Mechtilde."

They walked out into a stone corridor that was lined with large, open-air windows. Gunther could see right away the large tree Edgar had pointed out and the fact that most of the grounds was brown and barren. Mechtilde could see the dismayed look upon his face immediately.

"As you can see," she began, "due to the newness of our beautiful abbey, all the activity over the years has stripped away the vegetation surrounding us. We are in great need for a handyman such as yourself."

"Yes, Sister. You may count on me. We will all do our best here," Gunther assured her.

She crouched down and smiled at the children. "Please, tell me your names."

"I am Annamarie," she answered sweetly. "This is Klaus. He does not say much."

Mechtilde laughed and said, "I am so happy to meet you both. You will love it here."

Just then, little Gertrude came scampering by with Sister Irma not far behind. "Hello!" she said again, still very chipper. "These are my new friends. Can I come with you?"

Irma sighed in relief and pleaded with her cohort, "Please, can she go on the tour with you? I am exhausted."

Mechtilde chuckled, "Yes, Gertrude can come along too." She looked at the spry young girl and said, "Did you know my sister's name is Gertrude also? Wait until you meet her. She is the abbess here and she is very friendly."

"I like her name," Gertrude answered with a wide grin. "She is named like me."

Satisfied the little girl was busy for the time being, Irma leaned toward Mechtilde and said, "I am going to sit down."

"Follow me everyone," Mechtilde said.

Gunther struggled as he walked, limping badly on his left leg. Mechtilde appeared oblivious or pretended not to notice. They came upon the chapel which was just down a dirt walkway from where they taught the children.

"The doors are always open to offer up prayers to God and for daily Mass each morning at sunrise," she said, continuing the tour.

There were other nuns milling about doing their daily chores, sweeping, hanging linens out to dry and tending to the orphans. Klaus and Annamarie took notice of the other children and how they ranged in age. Some were toddlers, some were close to their own ages and others were nearly grown.

"Before I show you to your quarters and the kitchen, we will walk out to the garden so Herr Rees can get a closer look at our grounds."

"Gunther, please," he insisted.

"Of course," Mechtilde replied.

As they walked behind the sister out into the garden, Gertrude skipped over to Gunther and immediately took his hand. He looked at her puzzled once more while she returned his curious gaze with a broad smile. He looked over at Odelia as if he did not know what to do. She just laughed and shook her head.

When they stopped, Mechtilde hesitated before she admitted, "These, I am afraid, are the rose bushes. Father seems determined to rescue them."

Gunther took off his cap and scratched his balding head a bit as he stared at the ghastly sight. They were lined up one after the other but were covered in dead leaves and branches. The bushes themselves were almost indistinguishable due to the incredible number of thick weeds on the ground and multitudes of spindly vines climbing anywhere and everywhere.

"Well, boy," he deadpanned, "let us get to work. Go fetch the tools that we brought with us." Immediately Klaus ran to get his father's tools.

"We will leave you to it," Mechtilde said with a smile. "I will take the rest of us to the kitchen and your living quarters."

"I want to stay," Gertrude said, still skipping around on the dirt. She stopped for a moment and asked politely, "May I stay with them for a while, Sister?"

Mechtilde gave her a stern look and replied, "Only for a little while. I need to introduce you to the other children. And do not get in Herr Rees' way."

"It is no burden," Gunther assured her. He turned back to survey his seemingly impossible task. "I do not know where to begin," he muttered to himself. Soon, Klaus came running back with a rolled-up leather pouch that contained some basic tools. Gunther nodded at him and said, "Find me the good cutting blade. We will start with that." He looked down at Gertrude who was still happily skipping around and said, "Well, young lady, where do you think we should start?"

Gertrude jumped for joy and clapped her hands excitedly after getting her first task. She went directly to the end of the bushes and reached her hand in between all the weeds and vines and found a perfectly green leaf on the rose bush.

Gunther cautioned her and called out, "Careful. There are thorns."

"I am not afraid," she said calmly, still feeling the soft, newly formed leaf in between her fingers. She smiled and then pulled her arm back unscathed. "This is where we start," she said gleefully.

Gunther glanced at Klaus who had a placid expression due to the daunting task, then he nodded in agreement, saying, "The lady says to start there, so we will start right there. Hand me that blade, Son." He hobbled over to the spot where Gertrude stood and then he said, "Stand back."

Bit by bit, and piece by piece, he started to cut away the vines and discarded them on a pile a short distance from the bushes. While he worked on the vines and dead wood, Klaus turned his attention to the weeds and started pulling them by hand.

Gertrude danced and played while they worked and before long, she heard Sister Irma calling her to the classroom. "Goodbye!" she called out with a smile and ran toward the abbey.

Klaus and his father worked at clearing the rose bushes the rest of the day and as the sun started to set, they had a huge pile of rubbish smoldering and the smoke rose high into the air. Their hands and arms were scarred and cut from thorns and spindly weeds. Gunther's leg ached terribly, and he barely could make the short trip to the brush pile with another handful without grimacing badly.

The sun was setting when Father Edgar meandered out to see how they were doing. In the twilight, he could see actual shrubs that lined near the tree, free of all the clutter. There were seven bushes in all. "My, what work you have accomplished!" he said in amazement. "I can almost make them out now. Well done, men."

Gunther did his best to disguise the great agony he was in and nodded appreciatively. "Thank you, Father."

Edgar looked over at the brush pile and said, "You can let that smolder and burn the rest tomorrow. You must be famished. There is a water basin in your quarters where you can refresh yourself. Annamarie can show you where we will eat supper tonight."

"Thank you, Father. Thank you."

Mechtilde stood at the head of the dining table. Each side of the long table was lined with sisters clad in their black habits and veils that were trimmed in white. At the opposite end was the small group of children and then the Rees family standing next to Father Edgar. The whole assembly stood behind their chairs waiting to hear the blessing sung by Mechtilde.

"*Gratias tibi ago*," she began in Latin, with a heavenly voice.

The rest of the people answered with, "*Domine Iesu*."

"*Gratias quia in diem*."

"*Domine Iesu*."

"*Gratias quia quod cibo.*"

"*Domine Iesu.*"

Then the assembly concluded together, saying, "Amen." Everyone sat down and began their meal together.

"How did you enjoy your first day, children?" Edgar asked them as they ate.

Klaus smiled sheepishly, his arms and hands scarred with cuts, and said, "Very good, Father."

"I like it here," Annamarie added. "The soup is very good."

"It certainly is," Edgar commented, taking another spoonful. "It is true, your mother is a fine chef."

"Thank you kindly, Father," Odelia said, blushing.

Edgar then noticed Gunther's hands as well as Klaus'. "Goodness, I had no idea the vines and thorns were so treacherous. You are both covered in lacerations. Please let one of the sisters tend to your wounds after supper."

Gunther was shy and didn't want to be a bother, saying, "No, no. They are just scratches. The boy and I will be fine." Odelia nudged his leg under the table, knowing how painful the cuts must be, especially for their young son. "They will heal, Father. It is no trouble."

Later that night, the family doused all but one candle to get ready for bed. The four of them stayed in a small room that was equipped with one bed and thick linens on the stone floor for the children. The children appeared to be fast asleep when Gunther plopped down in exhaustion next to Odelia. He groaned appreciatively, easing the pressure off his sore leg. He then noticed how painful his arms and hands really were. As he observed the cuts in the faint candlelight, he glanced down at his son who was tossing restlessly on his makeshift bed.

"You should have had the nuns tend to Klaus," Odelia scolded. "Look at him. He cannot fall asleep. You keep him out of those thorns tomorrow and let him go to school. You can handle the garden on your own for a while."

"I will need the boy's help from time to time," Gunther moaned back.

"His studies are important too. He spends any more time in that jungle out there, he will not live to see twenty."

Gunther adjusted himself and moaned some more, "Stop your kidding. He will be fine."

She looked down at his right arm and saw it still had fresh blood coming from the cuts. "And what about you? Here, let me put a wrap on this." She carefully bandaged his arm for him as she worried under her breath, "Do we really need the position this badly? To come home battered and bruised? It has only been one day, and you can barely stand. I can manage in the kitchen and washhouse just fine, but it is you they have their watchful eye upon."

"We must pray for strength, Odelia," he said, lifting his tired eyes toward her. "And yes, we do need the position this badly. Pray that God will guide us."

The next morning after attending Mass and lauds with the nuns, the family sat down with the rest of the convent for breakfast. After the blessing that was sung by the abbess, she came down to introduce herself formally to them.

"Good morning to you all," she said cordially. "I trust your first night was restful?"

"Yes, thank you, Reverend Mother," Odelia answered.

"The biscuits you baked are just divine," she said chuckling. Abbess Gertrude was a short, stocky woman and was known to have a hearty appetite. She was older than her sister Mechtilde, but her face had very similar features. It was easy to see that they were related.

"Thank you, again," Odelia said graciously.

Little Gertrude, sitting between her and Annamarie, yanked on her sleeve and said, "I love them too but now I am full." She slid back in her chair and nonchalantly brought her extra biscuit to Gunther. "Here, you can have my last one. You need your strength."

"How kind of you," Gunther said with a smile. He noticed Klaus licking his lips as he was still quite hungry. "I will split it with Klaus if that is alright with you, young lady."

"*Oui, monsieur*," Gertrude said with a curtsy.

Odelia looked surprised as Klaus eagerly grabbed the other half of the biscuit and scarfed it down. "My," she said, "now you are speaking French."

After breakfast, the children went off to the classroom and Odelia returned to the kitchen to clean up and prepare for the noon meal. Meanwhile, Gunther grabbed his set of tools and limped his way toward the garden. Before he knew it, a little hand scooped up his and held on gently as she sauntered happily next to him.

"Hello, again," he said to Gertrude. "Will you not be late for your studies this morning?"

"I wanted to see God's flower first," she responded innocently.

Gunther stared at her blankly with a thin smile, and asked, "His flower?"

"Gertrude?" Sister Irma called out. "Come now to the classroom, please."

"Yes, Sister," she said with a pouting look.

Gunther let her hand go and turned back toward the garden when she tugged at his sleeve. He looked at her and she motioned for him to bend down. "Do you want to whisper something more?" he asked. As he turned his ear to her, she gently kissed him on the cheek instead. He stood with a perplexed and dumbfounded expression on his face. She giggled and twirled and skipped her way back to the abbey. Gunther just shook his head and chuckled at her. "I have never seen such a child," he muttered.

He made his way to the garden to find Father Edgar standing before the rose bushes in awe with his hands clasped on top of his head. "It is unbelievable!" he exclaimed.

Gunther limped as fast as he could to catch up to him and asked, "What is it, Father?"

"I thought maybe in a few weeks or months we might see some improvement, but...but look!"

Gunther turned his focus from the priest to the rose bushes and his mouth fell open. Growing on the last bush at the end, was a single, yet stunning yellow rose in full bloom. "Good Lord," he gasped. Just then he heard the soft laughter of a child in the distance. He looked over his shoulder to see Gertrude still giggling and playing in circles around Sister Irma.

"Do come inside now, young lady," he heard the sister say. A few seconds later they both disappeared into the classroom.

He returned his gaze to the spectacular flower that proudly displayed its majestic color and form at the very spot where Gertrude had him begin his pruning the day before. He looked back at the classroom door and laughed in disbelief. "You are right, Father, it is truly unbelievable. These shrubs must have been in better shape than you had thought."

"I imagine so!" Edgar exclaimed once more. "It is the first one we have ever seen." He looked over at Gunther and commended him, saying, "Well done, sir." He stammered around in a flustered manner as he walked over to smell the scent of the rose. He inhaled and leaned back closing his eyes with a dreamy look on his face. "Oh, my," he cooed, "what a Heavenly scent." He nodded with approval and said again, "Well done, indeed."

Gunther stood and marveled at the single rose for a few moments more when he remembered the brush pile. He hobbled over to see what was left of it, so he could start another fire. However, when he saw it, he looked all around, thinking it had been smoldering in another place. He found nothing though until he finally came across a small pile of blackened soot. It was no more than a couple feet in diameter and his jaw dropped again, knowing there was a very large pile of debris still left the day before. "Fire was hotter than I remember," he contemplated out loud.

In the classroom, Sister Mechtilde was teaching the language lesson for the day. They were learning basic prayers in Latin. "We will learn to recite them from memory and learn how to read and write them as well," she explained. She glanced over at Gertrude who was sitting on a wooden bench on the front row next to Annamarie. She was amazed at how attentive she was. There was no fidgeting, no laughing or giggling as the little girl was completely fixated on the lesson at hand.

After about thirty minutes of going over each of the prayers, Mechtilde then asked for volunteers to see if any could stand and recite each one. One of the older children raised her hand and said, "I will try, Sister."

"Alright, Haisel. Come to the head of the class." Haisel began to recite the *Our Father*, but then hesitated in the middle. "That is alright. See if you can finish the *Hail Mary*." Again, Haisel started out beautifully but then stuttered and her face went flush.

"I thought I knew them, Sister," Haisel admitted sadly.

"You may sit down. Would anyone else like to try?"

Klaus and Annamarie both looked at each other with anxious expressions, hoping and praying they would not be called upon. To their surprise, Gertrude shot her hand in the air and said enthusiastically, "I would like to try."

"On your first day learning Latin?" Mechtilde asked curiously. Gertrude nodded excitedly. "Alright, you may give it a try."

Gertrude immediately stood in front of the class and began to recite the *Our Father* in perfect Latin. Each student looked at each other in amazement and as soon as she finished the Lord's Prayer, she went right into the *Hail Mary* and the *Hail Holy Queen.* Mechtilde stood with her mouth agape. As the little girl continued rattling one prayer after another, she ran outside and grabbed Edgar by the arm and dragged him into the classroom.

"*Listen* to this child," she exclaimed. "She has recited all the prayers I have taught them today and now she is reciting the *Creed*!"

Gertrude continued reciting the prayers in Latin and ran straight through the *Apostles Creed* without missing a single line.

Edgar stood dumbfounded as he listened to her speak the exquisite prayers in the ancient language. "Is the Creed part of the basic plan you teach?" Mechtilde shook her head. After Gertrude finished, she stood before the stunned group of children and adults alike. "Child," he asked, "when did you learn your prayers in Latin?"

"When Sister taught us just a little while ago," she answered.

Edgar and Mechtilde were both astonished. "And just now you were reciting the *Apostles Creed.* Did you know this prayer before?"

"Oh, yes," she replied with a huge smile.

"When did you learn to recite such a long prayer in perfect Latin?" he asked again.

Gertrude didn't hesitate and answered, "This morning when we were at Mass." Mechtilde's jaw dropped once more.

"The child is a prodigy," Edgar blurted out. "That is *two* incredible things in one morning. I need to sit down."

Mechtilde looked at him curiously and asked, "What was the other incredible thing?"

Just then, Irma stuck her head into the doorway and exclaimed, "Everyone, we have a little miracle out in the garden. Come see!"

173

The children cheered and dashed out into the courtyard past the weary Edgar and Mechtilde. Mechtilde side-stepped her way out of the classroom, leaving Edgar to plop down on one of the benches with a stunned looked upon his face. "I think I want to see this, Father," she said. "Please excuse me."

Everyone had stopped what they were doing when they heard about the beautiful rose in the garden. Nuns smiled happily as they observed the bright yellow bloom and others lined up to smell its delightful fragrance.

Even Odelia came out to get a look at it. She found her husband who stood nearby with a humbled expression and asked, "Did you really do this?"

He shrugged and answered, "You know I do not know much about flowers. All I knew was the weeds and vines had to go."

"You must have seen the bud yesterday, no?" she asked.

He looked over at Klaus who came up beside them and said, "We were so busy, I had not even noticed. Did you, boy?"

He shook his head and said, "I do not remember, Father. It must have been there."

"It must have," Gunther said nodding.

All the while, Gertrude ran and laughed and played with the other children, paying little attention to the small crowd marveling at the beautiful rose.

The next morning, Gunther and Klaus made their way out to the large tree and were surprised to find Edgar there again, this time sitting on the ground in a stunned trance.

"I do not believe it," he uttered under his breath. He knew the two were standing next to him, but he couldn't stop staring at the row of bushes.

Gunther dropped his tools to the ground and landed with a clanging thud. He was speechless as was Klaus. All seven bushes were covered with dazzling roses in various stages of bloom. Some were fully open including the yellow flower from the day before. It was the most amazing sight any of them had ever seen. The two shrubs on either end were yellow, with the two next to them on either side blooming in light pink. In the center was the largest of the seven and it was adorned with a multitude of stunning deep red roses.

"Fascinating!" Edgar bellowed again. "I have no words for this." He rolled over to one knee and looked up at Gunther and asked bewildered, "What did you *do* with these shrubs?"

"I…I do not know," Gunther stammered. "All we did was clear away the chaff and weeds."

Edgar got to his feet and nodded, saying, "Just as it says in Matthew, chapter thirteen: 'Heaven is like a good man who soweth good seed in his field.'" He patted him on the shoulder and said, "You are indeed a good man for this garden."

Gunther felt embarrassed and answered, "I cannot take much credit, Father. The shrubs have been here for a long time."

"You are modest, but that is alright. You did well, too, young Klaus. Well done." He gazed at the stunning sight and said again, "I am still breath-taken by this. The sisters will be in a frenzy when they see it." He called out to the nuns that were outside hanging linens to air, saying, "Sisters! Sisters! Tell the others to come this way!"

As they stood and watched the activity at the abbey begin to stir, Klaus noticed something else on the ground. He tugged on his father's sleeve and whispered, "Father, look." Gunther looked down at the spot he was pointing and saw several sprouts of another plant coming up as well as some wildflowers that were orange and light blue. "Is this not where we burned the weeds and branches?"

"Incredible," Gunther answered. "The ashes and scalding of the ground have made the soil fertile. But so quickly?"

Before they knew it, the entire convent had emptied out into the garden to see the latest stunning display. The nuns were speechless and some even crossed themselves while clutching their rosaries.

The abbess approached Edgar and proclaimed, "This is surely a sign from God. I have known roses since I was a child, but never have seen such a transformation."

"All things are possible with God, my dear sister," he added. "We will say a special prayer of thanks tonight for this wonderous gift." As the sisters marveled and smelled the inviting scents of all the flowers, Edgar noticed what had averted Gunther's and Klaus' attention. "Ah, what else have you found?"

Gunther smiled sheepishly and said, "We have some wildflowers coming up. Maybe it was the nice rain we had a few days ago."

"Yes, quite so." Edgar's mind was churning now. "Do you know what would be very nice as an addition to these lovely roses? Some wild plants to attract butterflies. We could make this into a serene place to come and reflect and to admire the beauty of butterflies, hummingbirds and the like."

Gunther looked at Klaus and shrugged. "Yes, that would be very nice indeed."

Suddenly, Gertrude and the other children came running past, calling out happily, "Butterflies! Butterflies and hummingbirds!"

He had no idea where to start, but Gunther nodded and said, "Yes, I think we can manage that, given some time. After the boy is done with his studies, we will get some garden tools and start tilling the soil all around. That should do some good I think."

"Yes," Edgar agreed. "That is an excellent idea." He clapped his hands and announced, "Alright sisters and children, let us return to our tasks. There will be plenty more time to enjoy the roses."

Everyone moaned in protest, especially the children, but Gertrude kept running and giggling everywhere she went. She covered every inch of the open space with her friends trailing close behind and Gunther chuckled as he watched them play.

He and Klaus went to work every morning tilling up the soil around the entire garden area. As the days went by, the sun became hotter and Gunther's leg ached more and more. After another long, hard day's work, he gingerly lay down on the small bed next to his wife. She could tell he was wracked with fever as he closed his eyes and moaned softly to himself. She noticed dark splotches on his pant leg, so she slowly slid the pants up to his knee. She gasped at the sight, seeing the grotesque scar on his leg. It had become infected and was filled with blood and pus. She knew he was in agony and tears filled her eyes with worry. He was so exhausted he didn't even notice her treating and dressing the wound for him.

He woke up the next morning feeling dreadful. Odelia had barely slept the night before as she had stayed up caring for his leg. "We need to get up," he said wearily. "It is almost time for Mass. We must not be late."

Odelia sat up and looked down at the children who were fast asleep. "You cannot go like this. You cannot even stand. Let the children and I go, and we will tell them you have fallen ill."

He strained to sit up, easing his feet to the floor. "They must not think I am ill, or we will never be placed here permanently. They would send us away immediately. Look, we have less than three weeks left until he decides on our fate. I can do this."

"Is it worth dying for?" she asked with tears in her eyes.

He took her hand in his and said, "Let us go to Mass as a family. We will pray for guidance. Get the children up."

Odelia held him steady as they slowly walked to Mass with Klaus and Annamarie following behind them. No one in the chapel said a word and after Mass, Odelia went to the kitchen to help prepare breakfast.

As he picked at his breakfast, Gunther was feeling nauseous. He didn't have much of an appetite at all.

"Good morning, Herr Rees," Abbess Gertrude said to him. "Are we feeling alright today?"

He cleared his throat and managed to make a smile at her, saying, "Good morning, Reverend Mother. Yes, I am doing well. Ready to get the day started." She looked a bit concerned at him but smiled politely and continued to her seat at the head of the table.

Breakfast was over and the nuns left one by one as did the children. Gunther was left alone, still trying to muster the strength to stand on his own. Little Gertrude lingered about at the foot of the line as the children slowly walked single file to their classroom. She stopped suddenly behind Gunther and put her hand on his shoulder and whispered, "God will lift you."

He looked wearily over his shoulder at the little girl and as she walked away, he could see for the first time a look of sadness in her eyes. He took a deep breath and closed his eyes and said to himself, *God give me strength*. He placed his palms on the table and pushed as hard as he could to lift himself up. Slowly, he got his feet underneath him and stood. He took in another heavy sigh and slowly put one foot in front of the other. His limp was worse than ever, but he was finally able to move on his own.

When he reached the garden, he was surprised to see the children playing and the nuns were raising their hands to the sky and praising Jesus aloud. Father Edgar was off to the side near his office observing all that was going on.

Why are the people doing this? Gunther wondered to himself. He hobbled some more up the gradual slope to the main garden area and then he saw it. Everywhere he looked was greenery. Butterfly bushes with white buds, tiny shrubs with red tubular flowers and pink, purple and orange wildflowers were growing everywhere. In the center of it all was a brilliant display of fluttering butterflies.

Gunther's heart quickened in his chest as he steadied his gait. Soon, he was standing in the middle of all the natural beauty and had forgotten all about the pain in his lame leg. The stunning beauty had taken his breath away. What was once a barren landscape was now a vibrant, thriving habitat. At the head of the incredible scene were the brilliant rose bushes, still bursting with color.

He closed his eyes and thanked God for what He had created. He couldn't help but smile and laugh as he looked all around at the fresh vegetation. Butterflies were everywhere and even hummingbirds zipped about quickly, yet gracefully from flower to flower. In the middle of it all was Gertrude and she stood with her arms outstretched and butterflies seemed to gravitate to her. They landed on her fingertips, her arms and shoulders, even on her head. She just stood and giggled at the fun of it all.

Gunther limped over and knelt on his good knee in front of her. A butterfly landed on his nose and he laughed before it flew away. He shook his head and asked, "Who *are* you?"

She looked at him and asked in return, "Has God lifted you?"

He nodded and whispered, "Yes, He has."

"I do not know how you did it, Herr Gunther," Father Edgar said as he came up behind him, "but this place is nothing like when you arrived here. It is like Heaven here on Earth."

Gunther got to his feet and placed his hand on Gertrude's shoulder, saying, "A little prayer and a lot of Mother Nature's good help, Father. I cannot take much credit at all."

"Again, you are being modest. But tell me, how is the leg if you do not mind me asking?"

Gunther nodded and admitted, "I was tired yesterday, but some good rest and the delicious breakfast, and of course this newest surprise, I am feeling much better."

Edgar nodded and added, "That is good to hear. You know, now that we have this pleasant garden to enjoy and pray and reflect, what it needs most now is some benches to sit upon."

"That it does," Gunther agreed.

"The builders left some decent cutting blades and tools behind after the abbey was completed. I preserved the little area as a makeshift woodshop. Would be a good chance for you to practice your carpentry skills. After all, Jesus was a carpenter too."

Gunther sighed heavily and answered, "Indeed, He was, Father."

He was reluctant at first, but the change of pace was welcoming to Gunther and it also gave a chance for he and his son to get out into the woods for a while. The prior allowed them to take two horses and a wagon to select some good trees in which to build garden benches. Riding on the wagon was a welcome rest to Gunther's leg.

"We will look for a tall cypress tree," he instructed. "The wood is durable and mostly free of insects."

Klaus sat quietly as he looked around for cypress trees. He finally broke his silence and asked, "Do you think they will let us stay, Father?"

"I do not know, Klaus. All we can do is the best we can and pray."

The sway of the slow-moving wagon rocked them back and forth as Klaus asked another question. "Do you think the garden was some kind of miracle?"

Gunther laughed a bit, and said, "It is a miracle anything grew at all, knowing how little experience I have. I certainly do, Son. I certainly do." He stopped the wagon and pointed. "Look. That is fine cypress tree right there."

They took turns chopping at the base of the trunk, with Gunther firmly planted on his good leg with each swing of the axe. Within no time they had felled the massive tree. "We will need four good equal lengths cut from the center," Gunther instructed. They spent the rest of the morning clearing away the smaller branches and cutting the girth of the tree into four equal parts. Using the horses

179

and a harness, they guided each length onto the wagon and by mid-afternoon, they had all four logs loaded. They reached the abbey by sundown and Edgar was pleased to see they had returned with a select choice of wood.

"Excellent wood, Herr Gunther," he commended. "You can smell the fresh scent of it."

Some of the children and the nuns came out to greet them and the large haul of wood. "Come inside and quench your thirsts," Odelia said to them. "We have food for you."

After washing up, Gunther and Klaus ate hungrily at the long table with all the other inhabitants of Saint Mary. As they ate, Odelia leaned over and whispered, "How is the bandage on your leg?"

"It needs looking at," he answered in a tired voice.

After vespers, Gunther and the family made their way back to their quarters to retire for the evening. As they walked down the corridor, they were surprised to see Gertrude walking behind them. She was soon walking in between Annamarie and Klaus holding their hands.

"Is it not time for you to get on to bed?" Odelia asked.

"I wanted to say goodnight to my big brother and sister," Gertrude answered sweetly. Then she grabbed Gunther's hand and asked, "Will you take me to the chapel?"

Gunther looked at his wife with a blank expression. "We have just come from the chapel, little Gertrude."

"But we did not say goodnight to Saint Joseph," she pleaded.

"Saint Joseph?" he asked curiously. She nodded with a wide grin.

Odelia tried to hide her smile and motioned that he should go with her. "Very well, then," Gunther answered. "I think we should go and visit with Saint Joseph."

"Goodnight, brother and sister," Gertrude said to them happily. "Goodnight, Mother Rees."

Odelia's face lit up and she smiled warmly at the child and hardly knew what to say. "Sleep well, little one."

Gertrude dragged Gunther back to the chapel and he limped to the corner where a statue of Saint Joseph stood. Flickering in the candlelight, the statue was displayed with a cut of wood and an axe.

Gertrude stared at the statue with a cheerful expression, saying, "Saint Joseph was a carpenter too. He taught Jesus. He was the best father ever. I love him so much."

"I love him too," Gunther answered. "I always look to him whenever I am unsure of myself as a father. You know, he is the best example of all fathers. Knowing Jesus was God's Son, he never hesitated in raising Jesus as his own."

"I think you are just like him," Gertrude asserted.

Gunther laughed and said, "I do not know about that. He is far above me. I just do the best I can to follow his example." He gazed upon her, wondering what had really happened with her family. He decided it was time to ask. "Gertrude, what became of your parents?"

She kept staring at the statue and answered plainly, "I do not know. I never knew them, but I did know my grandfather. He was very kind to me. People brought me here after he died. Did you have a grandfather?"

"Well, yes. Like everyone I had two, but I never knew either of them as I only heard stories. You know, one of them was an extraordinary man."

"Oh, please. Tell me about him," she said excitedly.

Gunther smiled and continued, "He was a great warrior who served the king as a brave knight until he died one tragic year. Not in battle but from a terrible illness."

Gertrude became silent and appeared sad at hearing of his grandfather's tragic death. "I want to serve a king," she said softly.

It was then Gunther realized she was no longer looking at the statue but at the crucifix of Jesus hanging behind the altar. He patted her on the head and said, "For such a young girl, you are certainly wise. Now, you should get to bed."

As they turned to walk out, she turned and said, "Goodnight, Saint Joseph."

For seven days, Gunther and Klaus worked diligently at carving down the wood. Soon, he had the pieces he needed to assemble two benches. They carefully sanded and smoothed the surfaces of each section, then began the delicate work of piecing them together. First, they took the thickest cut and made that the foundation of the sitting area. Then they fastened the legs to the bottom. Next, they carefully attached the backrest and finally some ornately cut armrests. Under the armrests were delicate carvings of leaves and flowers, each precisely cut as if they had been taken from a real tree. Then the crowning touch to each bench, at the center of the backrests, Gunther carved a perfectly etched image of a rosebud on one bench, and a single redbird on the other.

He and Klaus stepped back from their masterpieces and admired them with a smile. "Well done, Son. Well done," he said.

The next morning Gunther emerged to find Edgar staring at both benches that were now placed in the garden facing the large tree. "Superb!" he exclaimed. "You truly have a gift from God, sir. These are simply stunning. Now I see your true calling."

"Thank you, Father."

Edgar came to the point rather suddenly though. "We will share your wonderful creation with the sisters soon, but I would like to speak to you about the *real* need here at the convent."

"Yes, of course, Father," Gunther responded, feeling nervous all the sudden.

"My first concern, though, is about your obvious handicap. You have done marvelous things for us here without question. But I have noticed the great toll it has taken on you in such a short time. I worry about your well-being and that is why I hesitate to ask of you this next task before your trial period ends."

Gunther took a deep breath and answered, "Father, I will respect any decision you make about our family. I am prepared for anything. I just wanted to thank you for letting me have this chance. It has been my honor to have served you and the sisters here. My family loves and appreciates everyone but I know my leg does not fit into your long-term goals. I am just grateful for simply having the opportunity. As far as your next request, I will gladly do my best to fulfill it."

Edgar nodded and said, "I appreciate your honesty. Your heart is a good one, Herr Rees." He cleared his throat and began. "What the sisters really need is a water well. For now, we have relied on a peasant from Eisleben bringing water from the river on a mule cart each morning. You have seen him before. He goes by the name Timmons."

"Yes, we have met, Father."

"Timmons is getting on in years, though, and we cannot rely on him forever." He looked straight at Gunther and asked him honestly, "Do you think this is something you could do?"

Gunther thought for a moment and said, "I remember digging a well with my father when I was a boy. We were not very successful in finding water, but I do remember the lessons he taught me."

"An honest answer, and an honest attempt is all I am looking for," Edgar responded. "We should place it somewhere here in the garden area, accessible to the kitchen."

"Yes, Father."

"Like I say, it is a tough task to ask of any man, let alone someone with a weak leg. I leave it up to you."

Gunther nodded with confidence, saying, "I will do my best, Father."

That afternoon, the sisters and the children came out to admire the latest addition to the charming gardens. As people tried out the new benches and commended its artistry, Gunther found Odelia and stood next to her.

"He wants me to dig a well now," he whispered to her.

"*What?*" she hissed at him. "That will require tons of stones and back-breaking labor. How does he think you will manage that?"

"I do not think he does," Gunther answered solemnly.

Odelia shook her head as a tear formed in her eye. "He has given you a task that makes it easy for him to decide our fate. The shame of it. After all that you have accomplished."

Klaus sat on the wagon with his father and fretted about their newest chore. "How are we going to do this, Father? We have never dug for water before. We have always gone to the river."

Gunther tried to remain upbeat and answered, "Well, we have the digging tools, but we will need stones to shore up the water if we strike any." He could see how sullen his son was and tried to cheer him up. "Do not worry, Klaus. If we are not needed here anymore, the Lord will guide us to new work. Keep hope and never lose faith."

They spent the rest of the day gathering stones to build a wall for the well. When they had all the wagon could hold, they set out for the abbey once more. When they arrived, they stopped at the

183

crest of the incline as the weight was too heavy to go any farther down. It was still at least an hour before sundown when they noticed one side of the wagon sinking in the mud. Gunther looked at his son worriedly. "Let us unload as much as we can on the outer edges of the garden, so they are out of the way," he instructed. "We must not let the wagon sink any farther, lest we lose the wheel."

Mechtilde and Edgar stood in the corridor watching as Gunther and Klaus struggled with the stones in the early evening darkness. "Why did you ask this of him?" she asked. "He can barely stand."

"I left the chore up to him to decide," Edgar said in his defense. "I know he is just trying to impress me, but it is clear that we must continue our search for another family with a strong caretaker, not a feeble one."

"I do not believe my ears," she retorted. "From a man of the cloth. Has he not impressed you enough with his beautiful garden and the greenery and now the miraculous benches he created? And look how the children have gravitated to the entire family. It is as if they have adopted them all. If you ask me, he is the strongest man I have ever known. "

They worked past darkness until the cart was fully unloaded and Klaus was thoroughly exhausted while Gunther could barely speak, much less walk. Klaus did his best to support his father as he helped him inside.

"Where have you been?" Odelia cried. "You have been working yourselves to death. And for what?"

"Please, wife," Gunther pleaded. "Just let us sit and rest for now."

She held back her tears and said, "I have some food waiting for you in the kitchen. Everyone has already eaten and finished with vespers. Come."

They made it inside the kitchen and sat at a small table to eat their supper and Gunther could see how terribly tired his son was. "Go wash up, Klaus, and get some rest. Mother will clean up here."

Gunther slowly finished his meal as well, while his wife paced worriedly behind him. She stopped and placed her hands on his shoulders. "Please do not move the stones anymore," she begged him. "Let the well be for someone else. Let us just go and find work elsewhere." He squeezed her hand as she wept.

"Why are you crying?" a young voice said from the doorway.

They both looked to see Gertrude standing there with her usual smile on her face. "Child," Odelia said to her, "it is quite late. Let me take you back to bed. We will say a prayer to Holy Mary for rest."

She took her by the hand, but Gertrude resisted momentarily. "She does not need rest like we do," she said plainly. "She will wait for us at the dawn. Goodnight, Father Rees."

"Goodnight, Gertrude," he answered tiredly.

Gunther sat awake before dawn as he had only slept a few hours. He didn't know why after such hard work the day before, but he was eager to start the new day. He remembered it was Sunday, however, so he waited patiently for the time to go to Mass.

After their morning meal, he set out from the dining room. "You are going back out there? On a Sunday?" Odelia asked with a frown on her face. "Even God rested on the Sabbath."

"It will be alright, my wife," he assured her. "I just want to go see something."

Annamarie and Klaus both looked at each other and at little Gertrude still sitting at the table. "Let us hurry and finish and go with him," Klaus said excitedly.

Gunther strained on his aching leg as he hobbled outside. The cool morning air was refreshing to him after a nice hot meal. The children quickly caught up to him and asked, "What are you going to look at, Father?"

He looked around the vast and beautiful garden he had helped create and said to them, "I do not know. I just want to come out here."

They helped him up to the top of the incline and made their way over to the benches. He plopped down on one of them and the children squeezed next to him. "It sure is lovely out here, is it not? We did a good thing here." They listened to the birds chirping in the trees and they could smell the inviting scent of the rose bushes. "We only have a couple days left here. We might as well make the most of it and stretch our legs a bit, shall we? Go run and play."

He watched as the children ran together and laughed and played and before long the rest of the orphans came out to join them. Gunther just sat and watched all the children play in the early morning sun and smiled. "If I do not live another day," he said to himself, "I will be happy because of this moment."

185

He decided to stretch his legs as well and got to his feet. He lightly stomped his foot on his bad side, and it felt firm as the aches had subsided with the rest he had gotten. He slightly limped around the bushes and shrubs and took time to smell the rosebuds. He then noticed the small rut the wagon wheel had made the night before. He meandered over to it and noticed it had filled with water. "Had some rain last night," he muttered aloud. He glanced over at the pile of stones he and Klaus had unloaded and just shook his head.

Klaus ran over to him and asked, "Where will we try to dig the well, Father?"

Gunther shook his head again and answered, "I do not know. I suppose somewhere near the bottom of this incline. But I may just let it go, Son."

"Should we at least try? We will have one more day."

Gunther smiled back at him, saying, "Let us just enjoy this day." They walked down the slight hill a short way to go back inside the abbey when they heard Gertrude calling out to them. "What is it, child?" he asked. As she ran toward them, he noticed a stream of water pooling around his feet. "Goodness," he said, "must have rained more last night than I thought." Gertrude came skidding to a halt before them. "What is it?" he asked again.

"Where are you going? We need to get started."

"Get started with what?" Gunther asked curiously.

"The well, silly," Gertrude laughed. "Mother Mary is waiting for us."

She ran to the top of the incline and pointed to the wagon rut. "Dig here, Father."

Gunther hobbled back up the hill and said to her, "But that is just rainwater in the hole from last night. Plus, it is at the top of the hill."

"Dig here. Dig here," she insisted again.

"We should rest today, child. It is the Sabbath."

Gertrude shook her head feverishly though. She would not take no for an answer. "It is alright, Father, God will not mind."

Gunther scratched his head and said to Klaus, "Go get my shovel."

Klaus immediately came running back with a shovel and handed it to his father. Gunther set his feet and started poking at the muddy hole. Satisfied, he began to dig a few shovelfuls of mud.

186

Then, a few more. The more he dug, the more the water filled the hole. "Would you look at that?" he muttered as he kept digging. His energy became stronger as he dug, and his smile became broader and broader with every stroke. Gertrude stood and watched with a gigantic grin on her face. "*Look* at that?" he said again, almost in hysterics. With one last plunge of his shovel, suddenly the ground began to gurgle and spurt trickles of water nearly a foot in the air. "Look! It...it..."

"It is *water*," Klaus finished for him, laughing.

"A spring!" Gunther shouted. "It is a *spring*." He threw down the shovel and laughed and cried and hugged the children with glee. Annamarie and the other children came running up to see what all the commotion was about. "Look, children," he said, "we have water!"

He stepped back for a moment as the children laughed and giggled in the water as he thought of what he must do next. "We have to contain it somehow," he said to himself. "Channel it to one area."

One of the children scooped some of the water into his hands and took a drink. "It is so cool!" he exclaimed. "It tastes wonderful. Please, Herr Rees, come and try it."

"Alright, I will," he said with a smile.

"But first, say a prayer of thanks," Gertrude suggested.

He picked her up and hugged her tightly. "You are so right, young lady. Let us recite the *Hail Mary* together. Pray with us children." Everyone stopped and recited the prayer in Latin just as they had been taught. When they were done, he set Gertrude down and knelt by the spring and cupped his hands and let the cool water fall into them. He slowly lifted his hands to his lips and drank the water closing his eyes and smiling toward the Heavens. "Now *that* is refreshing," he laughed out loud. He looked over at Klaus and instructed, "Gather up as many digging tools as you can. Annamarie, go fetch the Abbess and the Prior. We need to summon as many mason workers and diggers from the town as possible. We must move quickly. Go children, go!"

Gunther was left alone with Gertrude who stayed by his side. He got to his feet and started toward the pile of stones when he noticed something. He looked down at his leg and stopped. Then he began to walk a few more steps and stopped and started again.

He was no longer limping! "I do not believe it," he uttered. Gertrude just stood and watched with a smile as he walked even farther up the hill and in perfect stride. Then he began to jog with an expression that was nothing short of ecstatic. He stopped in place and said to her, "The pain is gone, and my leg feels as strong as an ox! It is a miracle!"

He ran back down the hill and snatched her up in his arms and twirled her around. She laughed and giggled as her legs whirled in the air. "You feel better now?" she asked.

"Do I feel *better*? I am a new man!" He held her in his arms and said, "You did it. I do not know how, but you did it. *All* of this."

"No, silly," Gertrude laughed. "Mother Mary did it. And a little help from God."

He lifted her high into the air, laughing, and cried out, "Lord Jesus, be praised!"

Stunned once again, Father Edgar did as Gunther had asked and had people from all over summoned to the abbey to help. Before the days end, they had dug a deep well for the water and surrounded it with stone and masonry. They built a stone wall all the way up the incline to the spring to channel the flow. They then surrounded the spring itself with another wall with a small opening on one side to let the water flow downward.

Edgar was shocked to see how quickly it all had come together. Just as he had hoped, the well was situated just outside the kitchen door. As the sun set, the entire garden had been completely transformed and Edgar stood admiring it all, not knowing what to say.

That night, Odelia examined Gunther's leg and said in wonder, "The scar is still there."

"Yet I can walk as strongly as the day I married you," he said beaming. He hugged her neck tightly and they both wept with joy. "Tomorrow, we must go and speak with the Prior. There is something we must do."

"Yes, we must," she agreed.

The next morning the two of them sat with Edgar in his office. "God has taught me a valuable lesson in humility," he admitted. "I ask for your forgiveness in doubting you."

"There is nothing to forgive, Father," Gunther assured him. "All these things have been of God. We are just His humble servants, just as you."

Edgar smiled in agreement. "But on the other matter. It is obvious that we find good homes for all the children whenever possible. In your case, however, as I am hoping you will stay on as our permanent caretakers, I do not feel it necessary for you to formally apply for adoption of little Gertrude. Quite honestly, I think she has adopted *you* already."

Tears streamed down Odelia's face as she replied, "We want to be parents to *all* of them. Now and for the rest of our lives."

Gunther put his arm around her and held her tight and said, "You can count on us, Father."

Coda

The Rees' did indeed stay on as caretakers of Saint Mary the rest of their lives. Their own children grew up at the abbey until they were of age to decide what they wanted to do.

Klaus settled with a young maiden from Eisleben, named Greta. They lived nearby the abbey and raised five children of their own. Gunther and Odelia became the proud grandparents of nineteen grandchildren and countless other great-grandchildren from their 'adopted' children that grew up at the abbey.

Annamarie became inspired by her closest friend and adopted sister, Gertrude. They both dove into their studies head-on. Gertrude had an insatiable appetite for knowledge and Annamarie, although older, followed closely in her footsteps. Gertrude became fluent in other languages, including Latin, and received an education in a variety of subjects. She then began studying the works of the Fathers of the Church, including Saint Augustine. She formally joined the monastic community at Saint Mary at the age of ten and Annamarie did the same at age thirteen. Five years later, they both became members of the Benedictine Order of nuns.

At the age of twenty-five, Gertrude experienced the first of her Heavenly visions that would continue until her passing at the young age of thirty-six. Her visions altered her life and she saw it as a new beginning for herself. Her priorities turned from secular learning to primarily Scripture and theology. She was always an exceptional teacher and scribe and soon began writing for the sake of her students.

Some of her most notable works include *The Herald of Divine Love* and *The Herald of God's Loving Kindness*. There is also a collection of her works called *Spiritual Exercises*, many of which are still used today. She contributed to the works of her beloved teacher and mentor, Mechtilde, who is also known as a saint and mystic of the church. This collection was called the *Book of Special Grace*.

Gertrude of Helfta, or Saint Gertrude the Great, was canonized by Pope Clement XII in 1677. She is known throughout the world and most notably in Latin countries. She is called the Patroness of the West Indies and in Peru her feast day of November 16th is celebrated with great splendor and enthusiastic revelry.

Part VI

The Year of Our Lord, 1660

In the year of our Lord, 1660, central Europe had only been twelve years removed from the devastating and costly Thirty Years War. The long and deadly campaign raged throughout most of Europe but none more severe than in the central lands that flanked both sides of the Rhine River. From Koblenz to Basel, villages were ravaged, churches were burned, and entire families were displaced.

With the Peace at Westphalia in 1648, the long and seemingly endless war had finally come to an end. Some sense of normalcy returned to the German areas along the river, but rebuilding took decades. The small convents and priories that were laid waste to during the war began to put their communities back together bit by bit, year after year.

As they worked tirelessly to re-establish their churches and monastic communities, they relied heavily on the teachings of a certain pastor located in Paris. The pastor was a highly influential scholar of the day and was instrumental in the ways of educating young men studying for the priesthood. Letters from the pastor were of great importance and served as tools in each place of study. However, correspondence was seldom as the territory between the Rhine River valley and Paris was often occupied by resistant Spanish forces. The road to Paris was fraught with peril and only the bravest and most daring could successfully traverse the various outposts, as well as mountains and rugged forests.

With the news of the declining health of their beloved Pastor Vincent, and an injury to the Pope's official courier from Rome, the brothers called upon a master rider to deliver a letter from the Pope of upmost importance to the pastor before it was too late.

From a tiny hamlet called Herbolzheim, there came a volunteer. A young man who was dedicated to family and his Catholic faith, but also a devoted follower and admirer of the teachings of Pastor Vincent. Since childhood, his greatest desire was to meet the fabled teacher in person, and this was his chance to realize his dream. The challenge would be highly dangerous, but the reward would last a lifetime. His name was Michael.

Vincent

A rider rode along briskly on his mount heading northward from Rome. He was an official courier of the Vatican specially selected by His Holiness the Pope. He rode across the open highlands keeping a watchful eye out for hostiles that could be waiting to spring an ambush. As the rider neared the heavily wooded terrain of the Rhine River valley, he slowed the horse's pace in search of water. Soon, they came upon a trickling brook in which to drink.

The middle-aged man dismounted the horse and patted its back as they stood by the water's edge. He knelt by the stream to refill his pouch and to splash some fresh water on his face. The horse settled and began to drink from the stream as well. Quickly, the man stood and darted his eyes around, checking for any sign of followers. Seeing that the horse had drank its fill, he patted the animal once more before leaping on its back.

Before he could flick the horse into a trot, a water snake came wriggling by swiftly in the current startling the horse. The spooked animal neighed with fright and reared on its hind legs before dashing across the shallow stream. The crazed horse quickly darted out of the water and turned sharply throwing the rider who yelped in agony as his leg smashed against jagged rocks as he thumped to the ground. He watched helplessly, moaning in the dirt, as his horse trotted away.

The man lay in torturous pain, trying desperately to roll to his side with his shattered leg doubled under his knee awkwardly. He gritted his teeth, panting breathlessly due to the shock and pain. With great determination, he was able to plant his good leg in the dirt and push himself head-first up the incline. He looked about for a stick or branch that he could reach and with luck, was able to grab a small one just behind him. Quickly, he snapped it in half and shoved the wet wood between his teeth. His chest lifted and fell as he nervously gathered his strength and in one swift action, pushed as hard as he could farther up the slope. His broken leg dragged under his knee and suddenly snapped straight; he moaned loudly, doubling over in excruciating pain, until he passed out from the shock.

When he awakened, his leg was numb. He pushed himself up with his hands and dragged his battered body to a nearby tree and leaned against it. He was thirsty and he looked all around for his water skin, but it was nowhere to be seen. He began to whistle hoping the horse was not far and still had the water secured to its back. Miraculously the horse came trotting up to the injured man, neighing appreciatively to his call. With great relief he noticed immediately that the water skin was still secured to the animal.

"Got your fright out of you, did you?" he asked the horse with a nervous laugh. "At least you still have my water. But we are not out of this yet, boy."

Attached to his belt was a length of rope and he quickly unwound it and then surveyed the branches overhead. He spotted a thick one about ten feet high and taking a deep breath, tossed one end of the rope perfectly over the branch and falling directly back into his awaiting arms. He looked over at his patient horse and said, "That was the easy part."

He then proceeded to tie the other end around his torso just under his armpits. He pulled on it tightly to secure the knot and then took another deep breath. Wrapping his fingers tightly on the rope, he began to pull. The movement shot pain through his entire body and with every inch, the numbness in his leg receded and the horrifying pain returned. His face turned red and his eyes watered with every excruciating pull. Soon, he dangled high in the air with his legs swaying lifelessly underneath him. He did not know how much longer he could hold on before he went tumbling back to the ground. His arms became numb and trembled with each painstaking second. He mustered up the strength to call his horse one more time to step underneath him. The horse did exactly as he wanted and as soon as he could, he quickly lowered himself onto its back.

The man let out a tremendous and grateful sigh of relief as he settled on his mount. He nodded in appreciation and patted him gently on the neck. "Good horse," he muttered. "Good horse." He secured the rope to his side and then took a long, satisfying gulp from his water skin.

∞

Brother Adel came rushing into the small chamber belonging to his superior, Pastor Jakob. "Father," he gasped breathlessly, "a rider has just arrived from Saint Peter's in Rome. He is badly injured."

Jakob looked up from his reading and asked, "From Rome? This far north?"

"Apparently he had to traverse around large swaths of Spanish garrisons."

"He is injured? Please attend to him immediately."

Adel nodded nervously but hesitated. "Yes, Father. He is being looked after as we speak. But..."

"But what?" Jakob asked impatiently. "Speak up, man."

Handing him a leather parcel, Adel answered, "The courier brought you this. It is from His Holiness himself."

"His Holiness?" Jakob asked dumbfounded. "We normally hear from a spokesperson like Cardinal DeAngelo." He carefully unwrapped the parcel and examined the initial post inside. "Wait, it is from the Cardinal. He writes this parcel contains a letter of the upmost importance from His Holiness and is addressed to..." He paused for a moment as he quickly re-read the letter to make certain he saw it clearly.

"Addressed to?" Adel asked curiously.

Jakob looked at his cohort and answered, "Pastor Vincent." He sat down at his desk and thought on what must be done. "The courier obviously could not penetrate the enemy territory to get to Paris and came straight to us instead. After the dreadful news we received yesterday, this is quite profound, even prophetic. We must act quickly. When is our next courier from Paris due?"

"Not for another three weeks, sir," Adel said glumly.

"And the poor man from Rome, is the injury serious?"

Adel nodded, saying, "I am afraid so, Father. His leg appears...mangled. He claims to have been thrown after his mount was spooked by a serpent. Miraculously he was able to climb on once more and ride the rest of the way here."

Jakob looked quite impressed and responded, "That is a miracle. The poor lad, we will say a Mass for him. But first, we must act. Have Elias assemble the villagers immediately."

Later that morning, the people of the small town of Herbolzheim gathered at the temporary chapel of Saint Margaret Church. The people talked quietly amongst themselves about what the matter could possibly be about. Many were still saddened by the news that was brought to their town the day before and most of them now expected the worst.

Pastor Jakob came and stood before them and asked for quiet. "We have an urgent matter," he began. "I have in my possession a letter from His Holiness in Rome addressed directly to our beloved Pastor Vincent DePaul in Paris." The people began to murmur and some even wept. Jakob cleared his throat and continued, saying, "I am told it regards a matter of dire importance. As everyone heard yesterday, our dear friend and teacher Pastor Vincent is in failing health and near death. We need to get this message from His Holiness to Pastor Vincent as soon as possible." The crowd assembled was relieved to hear that Pastor Vincent was still alive and began debating to themselves what must be done. Jakob raised his hands and urged them to be patient. "The courier to Paris left long ago and is surely days out now and the next is at least three weeks from returning. And I am told the courier from Rome who carried this important letter is suffering with a badly broken leg. In short, we need a volunteer."

The murmuring stopped and people either stared at the floor or looked anywhere else but at the pastor. Jakob stood defeated in angst, hoping that someone would raise their hand. He knew he had to admit to the dangers of such a task and the great distance one would have to travel.

"I know the route has many perils, and only the most experienced riders can evade capture in the Spanish-held grounds. But we must rise to the aid of our beloved friend and theologian before it is too late. All of us are called by the papacy at this moment." He desperately scanned the chapel for hope in anyone's eyes. "If I were younger, I would go myself. And I need Brother Adel here. Plus, he is not so adept at horse riding." The gathering chuckled a bit at him. "But if I may add…"

"I will volunteer," a voice suddenly called out. A man sitting in the middle of the congregation stood and repeated. "I will volunteer, Father."

"Michael," Jakob answered in relief, "we all thank you for this brave acceptance."

Michael sat down again to a look of appreciation from all that were gathered. All except his wife, Anna, who stared at him with consternation.

Michael Rees was a tailor by trade but during the years following the war, was forced into learning other duties. Since he was good with his hands, he learned the art of cutting stone and soon became foreman of reconstruction of the town church at Saint Margaret. Everyone knew him as quiet and soft spoken, but a hard worker and steadfastly dedicated to the church. He and his wife shared a son, Matheus, who was only three.

The villagers had all returned and Michael approached the pastor afterward. "The church thanks you for your service in our time of need, Michael," Jakob said in private. "Come with me and I will give you the letter in question. I suppose Saint Margaret will have to wait a little while longer."

"Yes, Father," Michael answered. "You need not worry though. The church will be completed."

"I have all the faith in you, but are you sure you are up to this? I know the path is dangerous and unknowns are everywhere. But I must know, why did you volunteer? You are a young father."

Michael assured him, "I will be prepared for the danger, Father. I am an accomplished rider, and I will return to young Matheus. My faith in God is strong."

"I know it is, my son. I am most grateful to you."

Michael took the leather parcel into his hands and said, "I have admired Pastor Vincent since I was a boy. His letters have always inspired me, and it has been one of the things I enjoyed most when you would teach us from them. My dream has always been to meet him someday."

Jakob nodded in understanding and added, "Let us hope you still can by the time you arrive."

Later that afternoon, Michael stopped at the stables that were maintained by his closest friend, Elias.

"I need the fastest horse you have," Michael said bluntly.

"I was wondering when you would stop by," Elias said with a smile. "I have five strong horses to choose from. You do know what you are getting into, right?"

Michael shrugged his shoulders and answered, "It is a long ride through the wilderness. You and I have done it many times."

Elias nodded and replied, "Yes, but this is not a week's long hunt for wild game. And we never rode all the way to Paris just to hunt." He looked at him firmly and warned, "Michael, there are going to be garrisons between here and Paris. Men who are not happy about their situation. If they catch a rider near any of their camps, they will not hesitate to kill him. You must be careful and steer clear of them."

"That is why I need the fastest horse," Michael agreed.

"Let me show you what I have."

They walked to the side of the barn to see the five horses in the pen. There were three brown mares and two black and brown stallions. Elias pointed to one of the stallions and said, "The male on the left, he is a bit feisty, but he can be ridden. Any of the rest will have the endurance you need to get to Paris and back. Choose any you like."

Michael considered each horse carefully as he scratched the stubble on his chin. Out of the corner of his eye, he noticed another horse in a separate pen behind the stable. The solid black stallion paced around restlessly back and forth. "What about the black one on its own over there?" he asked.

"Oh," Elias answered, "let me show you. Three days ago, I tracked that magnificent fellow for an entire day before I finally corralled him. He is something is he not?"

"An entire day?" Michael asked astounded. "Impressive. *He* is the one that should carry me."

Elias laughed and said, "Michael, that stallion is wild. He has not been broken."

"Then I must break him. I knew it the moment I set eyes on him that he is the one."

"You do not have time for this," Elias protested. "What if he throws you and you get injured? The reverend will surely be calling on me then. You know I cannot be gone for a month."

Michael scoffed and said, "Get him into the mounting pen, he is not throwing me. Not this day."

"You must be crazy," Elias said, shaking his head.

Michael lowered himself onto the anxious stallion and the horse kicked and bucked furiously in the confined pen. "Easy, boy.

Easy!" he cried. The horse continued to thrash about wildly as Michael barely hung on while clinging to a fistful of mane. "Let him go," Michael insisted.

"Have you lost your senses, man?" Elias belched. "He will start snorting fire before long."

"Let him go, I say!" Elias shook his head and lifted the gate and bolted out of the way.

Immediately the black stallion leapt from the pen in a fury, neighing, snorting, kicking, and jumping everywhere. Michael bounced around like a ragdoll, hanging on for dear life. In a matter of seconds, the animal darted for the perimeter and cleared the six-foot fence easily. Elias' eyes bulged in amazement as he watched his friend get taken for a maddening ride. He ran around the pen and dashed closer to watch the ensuing battle. The mad stallion kept up its ferocious dance while Michael stayed with him on every leap. The horse tried every which way to throw him, snorting and kicking in a frantic display. Again, the animal raced around the countryside, then headed for a steep embankment.

"Oh, no," Elias fretted. "The animal is *deranged*." Startled, Elias ran toward the cliff only to see the horse carry Michael over the edge in a terrifying leap. Both man and beast disappeared over the side in a horrific scene. "Dear God!" Elias cried. He skidded to a stop to look down the steep hill only to be shocked as the horse, with Michael still on its back, came racing back up the hill, leaping over the shrubbery and pounded the dirt with a fury.

Darting around in circles with better control, Michael let out a fiery yell. Elias was bewildered and exclaimed, "My Lord, they are *both* mad."

The mighty black stallion began to ease its pace and relented control to his rider. Michael's hair was a ragged mess, but he sat proudly although sweating profusely. He tested left and right turns and taught the animal quickly to slow and stop. Elias shook his head in astonishment and stood with his arms crossed with a silly grin on his face. "I think you two were made for one another," he finally said.

"Ah!" Michael bellowed. "He is fine animal. The best I have ever ridden. He patted the horse on the back appreciatively. "You put up a strong fight." Elias produced a rope to secure the animal as Michael held it steady. "Easy now." He slipped the rope over its head delicately and handed it to Michael. He brought the horse to a stop and he dismounted. Hanging onto the rope, he walked around to face the snorting, exhausted horse. "Let me get a good look at you. And you get a good look at me. We will work well together, yes? Yes, we will," he said as he stroked the animal's cheeks. The horse began to calm, still stomping its hooves. "I promise I will take good care of you. Together we will go see the Pastor."

Anna stood in the yard with her hands on her hips as Michael approached on the fine black stallion. Her cheeks were streaked with dried tears as she had been waiting patiently for him all afternoon.

"I see you are finally home," she said in a worried tone. "You had to go and see Elias even before coming home to talk to me, did you? Your own wife. When were you going to talk to me about this?"

Michael got off the horse and secured it to their fence and came over to hug his wife. "You knew I did not have a horse for such a ride. I am here now. Let us go inside, my love."

A small fire was burning with a kettle suspended just above the smoldering flames. On the wall above the fireplace hung a small, embroidered tapestry of the family heraldry. In the center was a faded, angled black stripe and two ravens near each top corner and the third standing below the stripe. Just above the heads of the top two birds was the family name etched in gothic lettering. Matheus was playing quietly next to his mother while she stirred the soup in the kettle as her husband sat down behind her.

Anna was short with dark hair and a few freckles scattered on her thin, pale cheekbones. She was a plain and simple farm girl, but she was also very beautiful and smart as a whip. At twenty-five she was just two years younger than Michael. She grew up the daughter of a sheepherder and milk maid on the flowing hillsides of Rheinhausen. Although one of eight daughters, the moment she and Michael set eyes on one another, they knew they were destined to marry. She loved him from the very start, and he loved her.

He sat looking at her lovingly, knowing how upset she was. "Something smells good, my love," he said sweetly.

"It is almost ready," she answered without turning around. She let the vegetable soup simmer a bit more and she sat with him at the table. Matheus climbed onto his father's lap at the same time.

"Why should you be the one to go?" she finally asked. "There are other men."

He shook his head, curling his lip. "No one else was stepping forward and I could see the reverend was looking desperate." He thought for a moment on how to word his thoughts. "I do not know. I just felt something inside telling me to stand up. Knowing Pastor Vincent is ill and possibly near death, I felt it my duty."

"Your duty is here, Michael, with me and Matty. I know we will get along fine, but I do not want to do that, not for an entire month. And then the thought of you getting hurt, or worse. My mind has been a mess all day."

"I know, and I am sorry, Anna," he said, putting Matheus down. He took her hand into his and assured her as best he could, "I just feel it is something I must do. Pastor Jakob was right when he said we serve the Pope as well as the parish. This could be my only chance to meet a man I so admire. You admire him too. It is right that we come to his aid."

She shook her head and began to cry a few tears. "I know it is right," she admitted. "I will miss you too much, though. We have never been apart like this. Matty will look for you too and wonder where you have gone. And what of the church and the garments? Johannes was here today asking about his son's wedding coat."

"The church can wait. It will rise when I return. As for Johannes, his son will not be wed for another five months. I will have plenty of time to work on it." He pulled her over to sit on his lap and he kissed her softly on her forehead. "You and Matheus are my only worry. I will miss you both tremendously."

She caressed his cheek and asked, "You are not worried about the soldiers you might encounter? I am. I cannot hide my worry on this."

"I must be cautious and follow the marked trails the couriers use." He nodded confidently as he thought about the task ahead. "God will be with me on my journey. I have no fear."

Later that night after dinner, they lay next to each other in the dim firelight. Matheus was fast asleep on his bed across the small room.

Michael whispered softly to her as he brushed her dark hair away from her eyes, "Elias and Louisa will come by from time to time to see if you need anything."

"I know they will," she answered softly. "I am not worried about that. It is what you face that I am anxious. It is not just the soldiers, but the wilderness as well. There are many dangers in the wild. It is a trial like no other, Michael."

"And there is much beauty to be seen too, though. I enjoy getting out into the country," he said with a smile. "All that will be missing will be my wife and son, who I will yearn to share it with." He sat up on his elbow and recalled his lessons from the church. "Do you remember one of the passages Pastor Vincent wrote? 'Do not be surprised by your trials, as the Son of God has chosen them for our salvation.'"

"Yes, it is one of my favorite passages," she answered. "I know how you admire him so, my love. I will pray you get to meet him, and he has recovered by the time you arrive." She looked away from him and fretted once more. "A month is so long, Michael. How I will miss you so. It is our last night for a long time."

He looked over at the fire and his son to assure he was still fast asleep. He gently pulled her to him and kissed her lips lightly and lovingly, saying, "Then we had better not waste it sleeping."

The next morning Michael and Anna emerged from their home to find Pastor Jakob waiting for them on a horse. A colorful sunrise shone behind the priest as he waited patiently.

"Jakob!" Michael exclaimed unexpectedly. "Did not expect to see you here this early in the morning."

"Good morning, Michael. Hello, Frau Rees. And good morning to you too, young man," he said to little Matheus. The little boy smiled shyly and hid behind his mother's legs. "Just came to see you off, Michael. Heard you had an interesting time breaking in the stallion."

Anna looked at him curiously and asked, "You had to break him first? You did not tell me this."

Michael laughed as he walked over to his horse and said, "We had to get to know one another."

"Have you the letter?" Jakob asked.

Michael motioned to the leather satchel strapped across the horses back, saying, "Have it here, Father. No need to worry."

"Splendid. May the wind be at your back and God bless your journey."

"Thank you, Father." Michael squatted down to give Matheus a big hug. "Mind your mother now. I will be back before you know it." He then jumped onto the waiting stallion and Anna handed him his bow and made sure his quiver was filled with arrows as she secured it to the other side of the saddle bag. Steadying the horse, he stopped next to his wife. He leaned over to kiss her one last time and to hold her hand.

"Next time you ride to Paris, you are taking me with you," she said with a sly grin. She opened the saddle bag and stuffed in a large bundle of food and then handed him a water skin.

He flung the strap across his shoulders and smiled at her, saying, "I love you."

"And I you."

Jakob, still on his horse, stood next to Anna and Matheus as they watched him ride away. "Be cautious, my son," he called out. "And give our blessings to the Pastor from everyone here in Herbolzheim."

"I will!" he called back as he trotted away. "Goodbye my cherished!"

So, he set out westward toward the Rhine River sitting upon his magnificent stallion as they trotted at a steady gait. They traveled across vast fields of green, scattering small herds of sheep and goats. The view of the river valley was spectacular as the morning sun spilled over the hillside, filling the shadows with fresh, vibrant light.

By mid-morning, he had reached the river and knew from his hunting trips with Elias there was a stone bridge crossing the Rhine near the hills of Schonau. He only worried that the bridge might be guarded. They walked at a steady pace along the fast-moving water and when he spotted the long, narrow stone crossing, he slowed to a stop. He stepped cautiously to the water's edge under the cover of a large tree to let his horse drink. As the horse quenched its thirst, Michael looked all around for any sign of troops.

There was no one around on either side of the bridge as they crept closer. When they reached the foot of the narrow bridge, he patted the horse and asked, "What do you think?" The horse snorted nervously as it could sense Michael's trepidation. "I think it is clear. Step up." The horse trotted onto the cobbled bridge and Michael urged him to up the tempo. "The sooner we cross, the better," Michael mumbled.

They made it across safely to French soil and continued into the dense trees. All was quiet on the other side, save for the steady breeze in the high swaying branches. He knew they had reached France, but he also knew there were pockets of Spanish troops still scattered about the entire eastern countryside. "Now we must really keep our eyes sharp," he whispered to his mount.

The terrain became more rugged as they pressed onward into the mountains. When the path became more navigable, he decided to hunt for small game to have for his supper that night. The horse instinctively trotted around trees and through thickets to flush out game or pheasants. With luck, a hare scampered from the thick brush and Michael cut it down with one swift arrow. With the hare dangling at his side, they settled into a small grove to stop for the night. The sun had fallen behind the mountain peaks and darkness was coming on quickly.

Michael sat by the fire, roasting the hare while the horse grazed in the ample grasses nearby. "I sense some rain coming on, boy," he called out. As soon as he spoke, he heard the thunder in the distance. "I will get busy on a lean-to." A gentle rain began to fall in the darkness just as he had finished setting up a small lean-to made of branches and thick brush. It wasn't perfect but it was enough to keep his head dry and get some decent sleep.

The next morning, he awoke to the sound of the stallion snorting around the grass near his head. He felt the hot, smelly breath emitting from its nostrils right on his face. Michael rolled over with a groan. "What a way to wake up," he moaned. "Are you trying to tell me something? Alright, I am getting up."

The ground was wet from the rain but the fresh smell in the air was invigorating. He had wrapped the remaining cooked meat from the hare in dried goat skin the night before and found it untouched and still fresh for his breakfast. As he finished his meal, he noticed the horse had stopped its grazing and had his ears pinned back as it stared into the trees. He could tell the horse sensed something, so Michael gathered up his gear and quietly walked over to the anxious animal.

The light was still faint as the sun had not risen and he whispered to the horse, "Is it deer? It is a good idea, but we have little time for large game." He patted the horse and said, "Have no fear. We will let them pass."

Just then, Michael saw what the horse was sensing, and it was not deer. Immediately Michael fell to the ground out of sight. Fifty yards into the thick trees, he could see firelight and several soldiers gathered around it. *How did we not see them the night before?* his mind raced. *It must have been the rain.* He thought quickly on what he must do. *We must escape undetected before the sun rises.* His heart pounded in his chest as he slowly reached for the rope on his horse and untied it as they crept away as quietly as they could. He did his best not to alarm the horse or cause it to make any sudden noises. Hiding behind a large oak he scanned the area and planned his best route to safety. His journey had only begun, but he knew he could not afford to fail this soon. He had to find a way around them.

He spotted a good opening between some trees that led to the pass, so he slowly walked alongside his horse as stealthily as possible until he felt it safe to climb on. They had only walked about twenty paces when they surprised a Spanish soldier behind some shrubs relieving himself. Michael froze as did the horse.

Momentarily shocked, the soldier gathered his trousers and yelled as loud as he could, "*Intruso! Intruso!*" He clumsily ran toward his garrison still holding his pants as Michael quickly threw himself on his mount and took off in a flash. "*Esta huyendo!*" the soldier called out again, pointing in Michael's direction.

A dozen soldiers poured out of the forest clambering to their horses in pursuit. With his horse fresh from a long night of rest, Michael raced far out ahead of the soldiers. The trail to the pass was a lengthy switchback with rocks and pebbles strewn in their path. As Michael tore up the mountain well above the soldiers on the trail, the trampling horse kicked and pawed its way up, sending a shower of stones raining down upon them.

At long last, he reached the summit and stopped momentarily to see how far behind they were. He saw they were only minutes away, so he kicked his horse into fast motion. "Come on, boy!" he yelped and quickly descended the switchback trail on the western side of the peaks. Eventually he heard the yells of the soldiers as they reached the summit. "We have not lost them yet, my friend," he called to his steady mount.

They picked up speed as the trail became more manageable and it was then Michael noticed the astonishing view below. As they raced along, a smile crept over his face as he took in the spectacular natural beauty. The rolling mountains stretched to the horizon to the north and south. Westward, the slopes cascaded in a sumptuous blend of green and brown embroiled in a tapestry of vibrant spring wildflowers. He could even catch glimpses of a flowing river meandering through the valley. *Simply amazing,* he thought to himself. *If Anna could see this.* He smiled even more when he realized he and his mighty stallion had pulled farther ahead of the pursuing Spanish soldiers. He could still hear their shouts, but they fell farther and farther behind.

The horse quickly rounded another sharp turn that banked around a large wall of boulders. Michael was stunned to see two dozen more soldiers blocking their path. His heart jumped into his throat with fright and instinctively jerked the horse left to run headfirst down the treacherous slope. Shocked, the soldiers cursed and yelled with their swords drawn, saying, "*Seguir en la búsqueda!*"

Michael's command of French was much better than his Spanish, but he clearly understood what the soldier had commanded: *Follow in pursuit!* As he and his crazed mount charged straight down the mountainside, his only thought was, *They are just as crazy as we are.*

Soon, he had three dozen soldiers on his tail. As they quickly approached the next trail crossing, he yanked the reins to the right to get back on the path. He darted his head to one side to check for the pursuers and noticed right away how far they themselves had descended in their maddening dash. It was a harrowing stretch that even Michael couldn't believe they had traversed unscathed.

The mighty chase entered another swath of mountainous climbs and quick descents as the trail became even more rugged. The soldiers were gaining on his tiring horse as the thunder of hooves raged behind them. "We *must* go faster," Michael shrieked out loud.

The trail narrowed as they entered a stretch along a vast mountain wall of rock. Far below the trampling horses was the first signs of the whitewater rapids of the churning river. The spring thaw had brought about the melting snow that was now flowing quickly downward in a breathtaking display. The water deluged any open space with magnificent waterfalls dotting the landscape.

As the footing became more treacherous, Michael had no choice but to slow their pace. "If we have to slow down, so will they," he said confidently. He looked over his shoulder and sure as he said it, the soldiers had slowed down as well. The trail was so narrow, they had no choice but to run single file.

As he rounded another bend, he heard the commander yell to the man in front to make another charge. Michael's eyes widened in horror when suddenly the lead pursuer drew his sword, frantically kicking his mount. The trail was barely wide enough for two horses, but the soldier just kept coming, screaming and cursing the whole way. The man caught up to Michael quickly and soon as he did, he slashed at his head. Michael ducked in the nick of time and popped back up to punch the soldier in the eye. Temporarily stunned, the soldier kept up stride for stride. The two horses bucked, kicked and snorted nose to nose down the dusty, rocky trail. Again, the soldier swiped at him a second time and then a third with Michael dodging every blow.

The two raced down the trail, leaving a calamitous cloud of dust and debris behind. They continued their bitter fight not knowing they were headed straight for the harrowing edge of the cliffs. As Michael fought off another slash and punch from the rampaging soldier, his eyes widened in terror as the edge of the trail was seconds away. Neither man had time to react when both horses soared over the trail's edge in a terrifying, bloodcurdling fall toward the river below. Both man and beast separated in mid-air in the horrific drop, with the soldier bouncing perilously off a tree branch. His body flipped end over end until it landed with a crushing thud on the jagged rocks. All the while Michael and the two horses fell like stones, narrowly missing the deadly branches and plunging into the swirling river with three tremendous splashes.

Seconds seemed like minutes as Michael thrashed about underwater. The impact stunned him momentarily and he lost all sense of where to turn. Miraculously, he soon popped to the surface like a cork. He coughed up water and cleared his eyes only to find himself in a churning, swirling mass of whitewater. He was a natural swimmer, but after the shock of the fall, even he found it difficult to stay afloat. The current was intensely swift and all he could do was try his best to hold his head above the raging fury.

Boulders were everywhere in the maddening river and before he could swim out of the way, he was slammed into a giant rock, crushing his arm. He wailed out in pain as the water threw him around the rock and back into the flowing current. The pain seized his entire body, and he could barely keep his nose above the water. Holding his arm, he kicked as hard as he could, looking for anything to grab onto. He spotted a clump of tree branches several yards in front of him and kicked and thrashed about with all his might trying to reach them. The nearest branch was just out of reach when a sudden rush of current lifted his body, throwing him down onto a cluster of floating logs. He luckily fell on his good shoulder as he hit the logs with a *whump!* His legs quickly fell back into the water between the narrow branches, but he was able to cling to one of them with his good arm.

Soon, the river entered the valley floor and the current calmed. Clinging to the small branch, he kicked his way to shore and then collapsed on the rocky banks. After catching his breath, he rolled to his back in exhaustion and extreme pain. Observing his badly broken arm, he knew he had to act quickly. He tried to snap the soggy branch that saved him but couldn't with one arm. Gritting his teeth, he grabbed his arm, took a deep breath, and with one yank, snapped his arm back into place. He wailed in excruciating agony, even coughing up blood after biting his tongue. His body shook and convulsed due to the searing shock until he finally passed out.

When he awakened, he had no idea how long he was unconscious. The sun had begun setting and the sky was a brilliant mass of color. The river continued to flow lazily by, but there was no one around but him. His arm ached tremendously but he was able to get to his feet. He tore at the hem of his shirt sleeve that was still wet but managed to rip enough free to make a sling.

After securing his arm, he spotted something several hundred yards down the riverbank that made his heart sink. He jogged and stumbled his way over the rocks and mud until he came upon the stallion. The poor animal lay in the mud, still breathing but his two front legs were badly broken.

Michael fell to his knees and cried bitterly, stroking the animal's mane. "I am so sorry," he wept. "If only I could put you out of your misery." Tears streamed down his face as he tried his best to comfort the horse. "I shall not leave your side. I will suffer with you."

Michael stayed with the horse all through the night eventually drifting off to sleep just before sunrise. When he felt the warmth of the sun on his face, he opened his eyes. He sat up and looked down at his faithful friend to see that the stallion had died during the night. He mournfully hugged the animal's neck and whispered, "You will never be forgotten, as you ran like the mighty wind."

He sat on the rocks, feeling fatigued and very hungry. It was then he heard a noise nearby and his heart began to race as he could only think it to be soldiers who had caught up with him. To his pleasant surprise, he heard a hoof pawing the dirt and a low snuffle of a horse. Michael got to his feet and walked around a large tree to find the other horse, standing alone and unharmed.

Michael looked to the Heavens and said a prayer of thanks. He slowly approached the beige horse that snorted softly at his presence. The horse was not alarmed in any way and almost seemed glad to see a person. "How did you possibly survive that fall?" Michael asked aloud. "You are one lucky horse." He just stood there chuckling at his good fortune and then started thinking of his mission. "We must still go to the Pastor."

He walked back to his stricken horse and saw that the bundle was still strapped to its back. He unclasped it and carried it to the other horse and grabbing its mane, he climbed on with his one good arm. He winced in pain as he swung his leg over but landed firmly on its back. "There is nothing we can do for our friend now, but we must pick up the torch and finish what we came to do. And find us something to eat." With that, he flicked his heel and they set out together.

He rode through the flatlands and sparsely populated forests and was happy to find of grove of apple trees. Michael jumped down from the horse and observed the ripening red fruit hanging from the branches. "I bet you would not mind some of these," he mused to the animal. He fed some to the horse who eagerly devoured them and then took a few bites himself but made a face due to the sourness. "Not quite ripe yet but I am not caring too much. You probably arc not either." He took another bite from a different apple and commented, "This one is not bad." He fed some more to the horse and before long their appetites were satisfied.

Michael noticed a stream nearby and walked with the horse over to quench his thirst. He knelt by the stream and eagerly scooped up handfuls of water, one after the other. Wiping his mouth with his sleeve, he stared at the horse and said, "I lost my water pouch. I do not know how far I can go without one. I hope we keep finding these streams." He got to his feet and said, "Come over here and drink. You need it too." The horse just stood motionless ignoring him. "What is the matter?" The horse looked away as if he were not interested. "What? Are you afraid now? Well, you have to drink something." He tried pulling on the reins, but the horse wouldn't budge. "Look, it barely goes to your knees. I think you will be fine." Shaking his head, he finally said, "Let me try this." He climbed on the horse and then slowly led him to the stream. Feeling safe, the animal drooped its head to drink some of the water. Michael was relieved and laughed, saying, "I guess you were a bit spooked back there."

After days of riding, they came upon a small village that had a narrow river running through the middle. Without his bow and arrows and his water skin, Michael had grown quite hungry and his horse was exhausted as well.

He stopped to speak to one of the locals who was passing by with a load of hay. He spoke in French, asking, "Hello, there. Might I ask if there is a local merchant selling food and supplies?"

The man looked at him suspiciously and answered, "Just up the road a bit. What do you want?"

"I have been stranded for days without food or water. And my horse is needing some hay."

The man could tell Michael was telling the truth as he looked quite disheveled. He nodded and pointed up the path, "They will have fresh straw. Tell the shopkeeper Francis sent you."

"Thank you," Michael answered appreciatively. "I am quite grateful."

He soon came upon the only shack that stood along the path in the heavily wooded area. He found fresh straw and tied his horse next to it to let him eat. Then he walked around to the entrance and before he could enter, an old woman opened the door and blocked his way.

"What are you doing here?" she asked with a bluster. "We do not want any outsiders."

Michael hesitated, "Um…Francis sent me here. He said you have some food and perhaps a water pouch. I would be very grateful."

"Oh, he did, did he?" she answered sarcastically. "Well, tell me this, stranger. Is Francis still alive or did you kill him? You did not kill him, did you?"

Michael looked aghast and answered, "No, madame. Francis is alive and well. I can assure you."

She wrinkled her nose and curled her lip as the answer seemed to satisfy her. "Wait here," she ordered and came back momentarily with a bundle of food. "Here. If Francis says you are good people, then that is enough for me." She stopped short of handing him the food and asked once more, "You sure you did not kill him?"

"Yes, I am quite certain."

"Fine then. Here is some fresh loaves and some rabbit. I roasted it myself this morning, you can have what is left. You can have this too if you like," she said, handing over an old water skin.

Michael was amazed and said, "I cannot thank you enough, madame. Tell me, what is this place called?"

"Bar-le-Duc," she answered gruffly. "And where might you be headed on a soldier's horse? I know a royal mount when I see one. You either found it wandering about or you have stolen it. My guess it might be the latter."

Michael rolled his eyes and he munched on one of the loaves of bread. "No, I did not steal it. But I can assure you the poor fellow who used to ride it will not be needing it any longer."

The old lady laughed and asked, "What? Did you kill him? You can tell me."

"No, he died in a fall. A rather nasty one too. It was not my fault. He was the one who chased me off the cliff in the first place. I lost my horse and his horse lost him. So, here we are. It just sort of worked out that way."

"That explains the arm in a sling. Here let me fix you another. That one looks wretched." She magically produced some cloth from under her apron and quickly replaced the sling around his neck. "I like you. You keep me entertained," she said chuckling.

Michael then noticed another old woman just inside the house, singing to herself. The lady saw him staring with an odd expression and said, "Oh, do not mind her. That is just Francis' wife, Claire. If you killed him, she probably would not notice anyway. She just sings all day, but she cannot help it. A bit of a sapling fell on her head years ago during the war." Michael just laughed and shook his head. "Where are you headed?"

Michael gulped down some water and said, "To Paris. I have an urgent letter addressed to Pastor Vincent."

"Pastor Vincent?" she asked, sounding astonished. "Well, why did you not say so in the first place?" She slapped him on the shoulder playfully. "We love Pastor Vincent. He is always sending his missionaries here to bring food for the poor. He is a wonderful man."

Michael was intrigued. "You have actually met him?"

"No, but the young priests that come here are most friendly. They always speak very highly of him." She laughed heartily once more. "You should have told me before. Here, I will bring you some more rabbit and bread, all that you need."

She quickly returned with more food for him and gladly handed it over. "You are most kind as this is more than enough. How far am I from Paris?"

"About three days, love, but do not feel you need to rush off. You can stay a while longer if you need some company." She smiled with a wink of her eye and said, "And by the way, its mademoiselle, if you get my meaning."

He rolled his eyes and answered, "That is quite alright. I should be on my way as it is. Thank you for your kindness."

Two days passed and he knew he was drawing closer to Paris as the terrain had changed, and the forests were behind him. He rode across prairies and rolling hills of green and the spring rains would come and go as they sojourned on. They came to a large tree out in the open of the vast country and decided to stop for the night. He built a fire and ate the last of the bread he had with him.

He looked over at his horse, who was quietly grazing, and said, "We had better make Paris by tomorrow because this is the last of the food." He leaned against the tree and poked at the fire. "Just think of it. Tomorrow I could be sitting and talking with the Pastor himself. I cannot believe it." He started to fall asleep imagining what it would be like in his presence. "Such an inspiring man..." he mumbled and fell asleep.

The next morning the air was crisp, and the birds chirped loudly in the tree above. Michael rubbed his eyes and rolled to one side and as soon as he did, he spotted a small bird on a branch just feet from his head. The little bird was yellow with black wings and it chirped softly, seemingly unaware of Michael.

"Hello, little fellow," he said. "You have an inviting song for this day. Much happier than the other squawking I awakened to." As Michael sat up and leaned against the tree, the little bird was not frightened away. "What a brave fellow you are." He even got to his feet and the bird didn't move. "We will have a good day, will we not? I believe that we will."

He gathered his things and climbed onto his horse with his one good arm. The yellow bird stayed put on the branch, still singing away. "I wish you joy of it, my feathered friend. Thank you for your greeting."

He rode onward until he came into a shallow valley that was flanked on either side by two small hills. As he continued, he sensed something and brought his horse to a stop and looked about curiously. "Something is not right," he whispered to his horse.

Suddenly, at the crest of each hill, a long line of regiments appeared out of nowhere facing one another. Michael gulped and said to himself, "Oh, dear. I am caught right in the middle."

Each soldier was dressed identically on both sides. On one side they wore gray coats and black trousers and on the other side, the same gray coats but red trousers. What Michael found the most curious was he did not see any weapons save for a single bugler and two flag bearers on either side.

Michael panicked as he nervously surveyed the line of troops on either side. "We need to get out of here."

Just as he said it, the bugler sounded his horn and a soldier to his right stood high on his horse and yelled, "*Charge!*" With that, all the men called out raucously and spilled down the hillsides toward each other.

"Yes," Michael yelped, "it is *definitely* time to go. You better *run*, horse." He dug his heels in and the horse let out a frantic neigh and took off running.

As the armies came together at the center, they veered in the same direction in the valley right behind Michael. Before long, the entire French regiment was on his heels.

"*Hyah!*" Michael yelled as he urged his horse as much as he could.

Over a hundred horses and men poured into the plains in a roar of thunder, all barreling down on Michael and his stallion. As they tore toward the western horizon a huge cloud of dust followed and Michael was frantic as he rode the horse hard and swiftly. The thundering herd inched closer with each pounding stride.

Men shouted with battle cries, horses snorted and bucked and bounced off one another in a calamitous pack of pandemonium. As they bore down on him, Michael feared the worst, hoping and praying he would not be yanked from his mount and trampled to death.

Soon, the gang of soldiers, horses and sweat caught up to him and to his surprise, they did not challenge him. They continued speeding across the prairie with reckless abandonment and it was then he realized the soldiers weren't chasing him. They were *racing* him. They were racing each other, and he was caught helplessly in the middle. His only choice was to race along with them or get trampled underfoot.

The roar of the rumbling hooves could be heard for miles. Peasants stopped what they were doing to watch the incredible sight and boys climbed trees to get a better look at the awesome race. They yelled with their fists in the air, urging the rampaging riders on.

In the middle of the madness was Michael and his trusted steed. As the riders set a steady gate amidst the chaos, two soldiers from the red team were running stride for stride with Michael.

One of them called out to him, yelling, "What are you *doing* out here?"

Michael gave him a crazed look and fired back, "The same thing *you* are doing. *Running!*"

Horses bounced off one another like fruit rolling in a basket. In a flash, a few riders were tripped mid-stride and went smashing to the ground in a cloud of dust. "*Whoa!*" was the cry from all around who skillfully danced around the fallen and kept running.

Michael went racing back to the same soldier who spoke to him and shouted over the deafening roar, "What is going on here?"

The soldier happily shook his fist in the air and yelled, "The first to the River Seine is the victor!"

The magnificent spectacle flashed across the prairie, racing up and down slopes, across streams and dodging fences and trees. The leaders of the pack were both from the red and black teams and men challenged each other with ferocious tenacity.

As his fear subsided, Michael became engrossed in the competition and smiled as he knew his horse was up to the challenge. So, he kicked his mount even harder and charged toward the front of the thundering pack.

The outskirts of the city were in sight as they raced on and the hand-fighting and raucous shouting subsided when they headed into the final stretch. Men pushed their horses with everything they had, and dozens were neck and neck as they tore a path to the city's southern gates.

Michael weaved in and around his fierce competitors, forcing his way to the lead. Riders from the red and black flanked his sides, leaning hard into every pounding stride.

They sliced over the final ridge that overlooked Paris and the River Seine was in clear view a thousand yards in front of them. It was a clear and sunny day, but everyone around heard the tumultuous roar of thunder. By the river Michael could see the banners fluttering in the air that represented all the various regiments. He could also see many spectators had gathered at the line to see the frantic finish.

The riders made their final desperate push and the heat from the ground, the rumbling of beasts and the malodor of sinew and sweat emanated from all around. Michael leaned with all his might and though his broken arm ached with horrendous pain, he held on with both hands for dear life with every ounce of strength he had left. In a cloud of breathtaking drama, the riders exploded across the finish line to the jubilation of the adoring crowd. The finish was such pandemonium, no one clearly saw who the victor was.

One by one, the riders pulled their mounts to a stop to the cheers of the boisterous spectators. It was a triumphant finish and in the middle of the celebration was Michael, who was thoroughly exhausted. Soldiers ran their horses around him, patting him on the back and shaking his hand.

Then a man from the black team, who appeared to be a captain, stopped his horse alongside Michael's. "You made a fine run, lad," he said respectfully. "You did not know what you found yourself in, did you?"

Michael nodded, still catching his breath, and said, "Admittedly, I did not. I was only making my way to Paris."

"Well, you arrived here just a little sooner than you expected," the captain joked with him.

Michael then asked, "Sir, can you tell me which way to the convent Saint Mary of Angels? I have an important message to deliver."

The captain smiled with confidence and called out to the regiment, "Did you hear that, men? We were challenged by a courier!" The group of soldiers laughed and kidded Michael just a bit. The captain turned to Michael with a grin and said, "For a man who rides with your skill, it is my honor to escort you there."

Michael's heart filled with pride and he leaned over to whisper to his horse, "Did you hear that, old boy? We are getting an escort."

The soldiers proceeded to line either side of the southern gate to Paris and with the captain at the head, Michael followed him into the city.

The city of Paris was grander that anything he had ever seen before. They trotted past rows and rows of living quarters for the commoners, green parks dotted with fountains and freshly groomed paths and even fabulous palaces for the wealthy. Magnificent stone bridges crossed the Seine in a number of places and carriages and horses and pedestrians alike were everywhere. It was the busiest place he had ever seen.

Soon, they arrived at a modest building adjacent to a small chapel. The captain stopped and pointed to the building, saying, "Sir, this is Saint Mary of the Angels. It has been an honor riding with you. I bid you *adieu*." With that he quickly whirled his horse around and trotted away.

Michael watched him disappear around a corner as he dismounted his horse and secured it to a hitching post. Standing before the abbey, he observed one small window in the front and a single door that led to the living quarters and another for the chapel. He gazed at the faded white spire that stretched high into the air, topped by a single cross. He grew nervous as he pulled the leather bundle from his horse. Climbing the short staircase to the abbey, he knocked on the door. He looked about but the streets around the area were deserted and all that he could hear was the distant sound of trotting horses and rickety carriages. No one else was around but him.

Michael waited for someone to answer the door, but no one came. So, he took a deep breath and decided to push the door open. Stepping into a small corridor, he was alone except for one small candle burning on the far wall. "Hello?" he called out. His voice echoed throughout the chamber but to no answer. He proceeded down the hallway with the bundle tucked under his sling.

"Hello?" he said again as he reached the end of the hallway.

Suddenly, he heard a feeble voice respond, "I am in here, my son."

He looked to his right and saw there was a single door slightly ajar down a narrow passage. Michael walked slowly to the door and pushed it open. A short, peculiar man dressed in a black tunic with a white collar and black cap on his head, shuffled across the floor carrying a water kettle from a nearby fireplace. "Come in, my son. Come, come," the man said in a joyful tone. "Sit down. Rest your weary legs."

Michael smiled at his light-hearted welcome and entered the room. "Thank you," he answered politely and sat at the only chair opposite the man's desk.

The old man poured two cups of hot water and stirred in some fresh tea leaves. "Even in the spring I find it difficult to stay warm," he grumbled. "Will you share some tea with me?"

"Yes, of course," Michael responded. "Thank you. You are most kind."

He shuffled over and set one cup on the desk for Michael, then proceeded around the other side to his chair. He sat down and took a long drink from the hot cup of tea. "Ah!" he exhaled gratefully. "That hits the spot."

When he saw his face clearly, Michael couldn't contain his joy as he realized who the man was. "Sir, are you Pastor Vincent?"

"I am he," the man answered with a smile. "You have come a long way, have you not?"

"Yes, Father, I have." Michael squirmed in his chair as he was overjoyed to be speaking with him. "I am so pleased you have recovered. This is joyous news. I cannot tell you enough what an honor it is to meet you, Father. I have studied and learned from your letters since I was a boy."

Vincent laughed as he sipped on his tea and answered, "It warms the heart to hear that, my son. Almost as much as my tea."

Michael loved his playfulness and jolly spirit and hardly knew where to begin. "There are so many things I have wanted to discuss with you. I so admire your constant work with the poor and your education of the clergy. It is truly inspirational." He clumsily took a sip of his tea and continued, "I even ran into some very friendly people at Bar-le-Duc. They had nothing but fond things to say of you."

"You are very kind," Vincent chuckled.

"Oh," Michael stammered, setting his cup down with a clank. "I almost forgot. The reason I came all this way." He took out the leather bundle and unfolded it. He reached inside and produced the letter from Rome. "I came to give you this, Father. I am afraid it got a bit wet over a week ago, but I was able to preserve it. It is a letter from His Holiness in Rome and said to be quite urgent."

He extended the letter across the desk, but Vincent just kept sipping his tea and said, "You can set it there. Thank you, my son." Michael hesitated as he knew the importance of him reading it, but he reluctantly did as he was told. "Tell me your name and where you are from."

Michael relaxed in his chair and picked up his tea and smiling, he answered, "My name is Michael Rees. I came all the way from Herbolzheim. Pastor Jakob sends his warm regards from our church, Saint Margaret."

"A wonderful little village. I visited your town as a young man in my return to France."

Michael was surprised. "Is that so? The people will be most excited to hear that story. I suppose you have traveled a great deal in your mission."

Vincent nodded and said, "Far and wide, yes. Tell me of your family."

Michael beamed with pride and said, "I have a beautiful wife named Anna and together we have a son, Matheus."

"And you shall have more blessings on your house," Vincent said joyfully. "God bless them all." He set his tea down and said, "Michael of Herbolzheim, the man who courageously crossed the frontier." He glanced at Michael's broken arm and said, "You were injured out there too."

Michael shook it off and said, "It will be fine. Tell me, Father. Did you grow up in Paris?"

Vincent leaned forward and asked, "Do you know why they call me Vincent DePaul?"

"No, Father. Please, tell me."

"My father chose that name when I was a boy. My parents were simple peasants from a village called Moras. But when they were married, he worked on a farm near Pouy and we took on the name *'de Paul'* since there was a tiny stream nearby called the Paul. Father grumbled and said it sounded too much like nobility, so he instructed me to write our name as *'DePaul'* instead of *'de Paul'*. Silly as I look back on it now."

"That is an amazing story," Michael concurred. "I have often wondered as you are such a prolific writer with great wisdom, what are some of the people that inspired you as a writer?"

Vincent thought for a moment and then answered, "Some very inspiring work was done by the good Bishop of Geneva, Francis de Sales. His views in the *Devout Life* always inspired me. And let us not forget the apostle Matthew. He was a simple, yet cantankerous old tax collector," he said, chuckling as Michael smiled at his humor. "But he is a wonderful example of how the Sacred Heart of Jesus transformed him. To me, his gospel is one of the most exquisite. Such a gifted scribe he was."

"I wish I could sit and listen to you all day," Michael said. "This is truly fascinating." Vincent laughed out loud at him. "Well, I know your time is precious though. I must not impose on you any longer." He got to his feet and beamed with happiness. "I am so pleased at having met you Pastor Vincent."

Vincent got up from his chair and answered, "And I am pleased to have met you, Michael Rees. Thank you for what you have done for me in service to His Holiness."

"It is my pleasure, Father." He hesitated for a moment and finally asked, "Would it be too informal if I ask to embrace you?"

Vincent laughed even louder and said, "Do not be silly, come and give me a great big hug. Just like a bear." The men laughed and embraced with hearty pats on the back. Vincent glanced at his arm in the sling and said, "And take care of that arm."

Michael reached for the door and turned back around and said, "I will. And thank you, Pastor Vincent. I shall never forget this. May God be with you always." With that, he turned and walked back down the corridor and turned the corner. As he walked outside, he turned to look back at the window once more and Vincent was there giving him one last smile and a wave. Michael grinned broadly and waved back to him.

He noticed as he approached his horse that a large gathering of people had assembled along the cobbled street that ran alongside the chapel. Everyone was dressed in black and he heard some women sobbing. He walked over to the crowd curiously to see what was happening and soon a black carriage with a single horse slowly walked down the street before the people.

Michael looked at a woman who was wiping tears from her eyes and asked, "What has happened?"

Through her sobs, she answered, "It is our beloved Pastor Vincent. He passed away suddenly last night."

Michael's blood ran cold with shock as he took in the words, feeling like he had been hit by a strike of lightning. 'No," he said. "That cannot *be*. It is not possible!" A tear ran down his face as he turned to look back at the window where Vincent had been standing, but he was no longer there. His hands began to tremble, and his body shook with uneasiness.

As the carriage slowly passed, Michael noticed the body inside was made visible for the people. He quickly shuffled between the mourners to get a closer look as the carriage passed by. Inside was the placid face of Vincent DePaul, the very person he was speaking to only moments before. Michael fell to his knees and wept. *How could this be, Lord?* he asked himself.

A passer-by helped him to his feet and motioned for him to follow the congregation behind the carriage in procession. Michael stopped and looked back at the window of the abbey as he clasped his hands around his head in disbelief. His arm no longer felt any pain as he stared at the vacant window one last time. Tears of joy rolled down his cheeks, knowing he had been given a precious gift from God. He did not know why he was gifted with a Heavenly visit from the Pastor, but he would cherish the sacred moment for the rest of his days.

Coda

Saint Vincent de Paul is known throughout the world and is credited with starting one of the most well-known charities in the Catholic church that provides aid to the poor and still thrives today. Part of the *'Vincentian Family'* of charities, the Society of Saint Vincent de Paul was established in 1833 and is present today in over one hundred and fifty countries.

He wrote countless letters to dignitaries throughout Europe that are studied and revered to this day. He is also credited with being the architect of the standard that is used in seminaries around the world to educate young men entering the priesthood.

Similar to Saint Patrick of Ireland, Saint Vincent was also enslaved for a short time as a young man. While at sea on a missionary voyage, he was captured by pirates and was held as a slave in Tunis as well as Istanbul. After two years, he earned his release and returned to France to continue his Christian mission.

Michael Rees returned to Herbolzheim by a northern route to avoid the Spanish troops. He fulfilled his promise to help rebuild the sanctuary of Saint Margaret church and after its completion, he carried on with his first trade as a tailor.

Less than a year after he returned, Anna gave birth to their son named Johannes. Like his father, Johannes became quite adept working as a tailor. Matheus grew up to be a farmer and craftsmen, learning the art of stonecutting and masonry. Michael and Anna Marie had eight children in all.

The three trades would be handed down from generation to generation as the town slowly transformed into modern times. The Rees family remained in Herbolzheim for another two hundred years, during which time Germany itself would undergo many more of its own transformations.

A pivotal time in history was fast approaching, however. A time at which horrific battles would be waged in Europe as well as the young nation of America. It was a time of great strife, but also a time of great wonder and Heavenly inspiration. No one saw the significance coming from out of nowhere in the form of a simple peasant girl that lived at the foot of the Pyrenees in southern France.

Part VII

The Year of Our Lord, 1865

In the year of our Lord, 1865, while civil war raged in America into its fourth year, the German Confederation was inching perilously closer to its own civil war. The German Confederation was made up of large swaths of territory with the Kingdom of Prussia and the Austrian Empire being the largest and strongest members. The rest of the Confederation consisted of various smaller kingdoms, duchies and grand duchies, and principalities. The Kingdom of Bavaria, as well as the Kingdom of Hannover and Saxony, were smaller and less powerful cogs in the system.

It was the time of Otto van Bismarck of Prussia and Emperor Franz Joseph of Austria. Caught in the middle were the smaller and more vulnerable areas such as Grand Duchy of Baden, where the tiny village of Herbolzheim rested. As the tensions rose between the two powers, the lower classes in between had little choice other than to choose a side or get out of the way. Those who were fortunate enough to immigrate to a new life of hope in America did so but with the outbreak of civil war there, that choice became less attractive as time wore on. Those who did not want to be involved militarily here or there stayed in their beloved homeland at the risk of famine or certain death.

Herbolzheim was primarily made up of farmers and engineers of various trades that worked in creating modern roads and water systems as well as railroads. Like most of Europe, the innovation of the railway system was well underway, linking every large city and some smaller areas. The only thing that stood in the way of the steel revolution was war.

At the same time in southern France, local authorities and priests in the tiny village of Lourdes, as well as the Vatican in Rome, were debating the occurrence of possible miraculous visions of the Virgin Mary as witnessed by a simple peasant girl seven years before. It was a series of events that would rock the very foundation of the Catholic church and inspire millions of pilgrims all over the continent. In particular, it caught the attention of a woman in Herbolzheim who yearned to know more. Her name was Barbara.

Bernadette

A clock ticked on the wall in a steady unnoticed rhythm. It was a cuckoo clock in the form of a Bavarian chalet and hung just to the side of a fireplace. The faintest of light peaked around the dusty-beige curtains of the small one-room cottage, while the remains of a fire smoldered and glowed amongst the ashes. Above the fireplace, resting on a small mantelpiece was a frame containing an old, faded, and torn parchment adorned with three ravens and an angled black stripe. At the top of the parchment were the barely legible letters of the family name.

At half-past five in the morning, the clockworks came to life ringing one chime as a tiny door simultaneously opened at the top of the chalet. As quick as one could catch a glimpse, a charming wooden cuckoo bird sprang forth and announced a single 'cuckoo'. The tiny bird retreated into the chalet and the door snapped shut.

A woman stirred on her bed and rolled over to shake her husband awake. "Casper," she whispered, "wake up or you will be late for work."

Casper sat up and put his feet to the cold stone floor and reached over to grab his pipe resting on a bedside table. He lightly tapped it on the table to discard the old ashes.

His wife, Barbara, rolled over to the other side with a frown on her face. "Tell me you are not going to start smoking this early."

"I am cleaning it out," Casper yawned.

"You are scattering filth everywhere. Just more for me to sweep," she complained. "Quiet or you will wake Bertie."

Casper walked over to the fire and stirred the hot coals and threw on a couple small logs. Soon, flames popped up around the wood and he smiled with satisfaction as he sat in a nearby rocking chair to put on his shoes.

Barbara came over, tying her apron as she rounded the table and opened the door to a narrow iron stove. She took a small shovel and scooped some hot coals from the fire and threw them into the bottom container. Quickly, she shut the door that made a loud clank.

"Quiet or you will wake Bertie," Casper chuckled.

"Oh, quiet yourself," she hissed back. "I will fry you an egg and a strip of pork belly."

As she cooked the food in an iron pan atop the stove, a small toddler began to squirm in her bed. Casper got to his feet and walked over to her. "Ah, Bertie, Bertie, Bertie," he cooed softly.

The child rolled over, pretending she didn't hear him. "Rise and shine, little Bertha," he said softly again.

"No, Papa," Bertha protested.

Barbara frowned with her hands on her hips, saying, "Let her sleep some more, Casper."

He pulled down the covers to see his little girl pouting at him. "No, it is time to get up and start helping your mother."

Bertha rolled over and put her arms around his waist. He cradled her head in his arms and she closed her eyes. "Back to sleep, Papa. You be my pillow."

"Come eat your breakfast," Barbara told him. "Or you will be late. Time to get up, Bertie."

"No. No, Mama," she whined.

"Yes, yes."

Casper came and sat at the table to eat his eggs and bacon and Bertha came and plopped down next to him and promptly laid her head on the table.

"Head off the table, young lady," Casper scolded. He quickly scarfed down the food and took a sip of his hot tea. "I must be going. Get dressed and help your mother."

Barbara helped him put on his coat and asked, "Where are you working today?" He put his arm into the other sleeve as she handed him a bundle for his lunch.

"We are putting down the final foundation today for the new road at Rheinhausen. I will be back by sundown."

She kissed his cheek before he headed for the door and said, "Do not stay long at Helmut's tonight or I will come looking for you."

He leaned over and kissed Bertha on the top of her head who had laid her head back down, saying, "Mind your mother today. And wake up." Smiling at his wife, he said, "Stop by Helmut's later. We will share a pint before supper."

Just then the clock chimed again, and the cuckoo popped out chirping six times. She patted his leg with a flirtatious grin and said, "The cuckoo tolls for thee, Herr Rees. Get going."

It was mid-March, and the air was still very cold and crisp, and Casper could see his breath as he exhaled, walking toward the work site wearing his dusty-brown bowler hat. Drifts of melting snow were scattered about the dirt streets and alleyways. As he walked along, he happened upon his two brothers-in-law, Franz and Viktor Doerle.

"Hello, boys," Casper called out.

"Ah, good morning, Casper," Franz answered. "Ready for another warm day?"

Casper nodded as the three men walked briskly together. "Spring is coming in like a lion. How are the boys at home?"

"Just fine. Augustus woke up with a bit of a runny nose though."

"Ah, but Josepha knows just what to do for that," Casper commented. He glanced at Viktor and said, "You are awfully quiet this morning."

"Did you boys hear the latest from Austria?" Viktor asked worriedly. Both men shook their heads. "There are growing protests against the unification and now it seems the Italians are siding with Bismarck on the issue."

"Always with the politics, eh Viktor?" Casper asked with raised eyebrow.

Viktor scoffed and answered, "What do you think would happen if the Austrians refuse unification? I think they are being setup if you ask me. And with the Italians and French getting involved, it is getting too close for comfort. The grumbling will be right on our doorstep."

"It is none of my concern," Casper answered, knowing it was not what Viktor wanted to here. "We have a road to finish and soon it will be time to plant the crops."

"Ah, the ground is too hard," Franz said, munching on a piece of bread.

"It may not be your concern now, brother," Viktor warned, "but soon you may not have a choice but to pay attention."

The sun peeked in and out of the clouds for most of the day, warming the men only somewhat as they worked. The crew of twenty men made good progress on the new thoroughfare that would lead from the center of town to the river and nearest bridge.

Casper gave last minute instructions as the sun began to set, saying, "We will need your mules and plow tomorrow, Franz. We need to dig a deeper gutter on both sides of the road for proper drainage."

Franz nodded as if it were understood, saying, "I will have it arranged in the morning. Are we going over to Helmut's?"

"Of course, I need to rest my feet for certain," Casper said in a tired voice. "Barbara will come by with the baby. Will not Josepha come with the boys?"

Franz shook his head with a disgruntled look and said, "She will not like me hanging out there too long. The boys are getting to be a handful now. Viktor will go though, as long as Anna will be there, right?"

Viktor rolled his eyes and answered, "She would not give me the time of day, boys. You think I am the first man to flirt with her in that tavern?"

Casper laughed and said, "Come along, then. Maybe tonight is your lucky night."

At Helmut's Tavern it was the same crowd from the village as it was every evening. Helmut was in his usual place behind the bar filling pint after pint of beer while his wife's niece, Anna, waited on tables as she did each night. It was a place where everyone came after a hard day, including the children. It was especially popular on Saturdays when Helmut and his wife Bruna would cook their signature schnitzel and spaetzle. In the warmer months, they would open the back yard of their home and tavern and turn it into a biergarten for dancing and fellowship.

Casper sat at a long table with his cousin Joachim and his good friend Karl Winter, who both worked with him on the road crew. "Well, Joachim," he began, "in a few months we will be here for your wedding reception."

Joachim tipped back his mug of beer and said, "Do not try to frighten me, cousin. June is still a long way off. I still have plenty of single life left."

Casper laughed and said, "It will be here before you know it."

"Do not do it I keep telling you," Karl chimed in. "You will never see me getting tied down like that. Look at Casper."

"Do I look tied down?" Casper laughed. "You are too much. Do not listen to him, Joachim."

Just then Barbara came striding up with Bertha in-tow. "There you boys are. Getting started without me, are you?"

Casper stood and gave her a quick hug and a kiss. "I will have Anna bring you over a pint." Bertha came and jumped on his lap. "How is my little girl?"

"I am hot, Papa," the toddler said.

"Oh, have a sip of this cold ale," he laughed as she wrinkled her nose.

"Do not dare to give her that, Casper Rees," Barbara scolded him.

"It smells funny, Papa. Can I have sarsaparilla, please?"

Anna came by the table just as Viktor sat down. She handed Barbara her usual and already had a sarsaparilla for Bertha. "Oh, Anna," Viktor drawled, "I will marry you if you only bring me a pint."

"You will get your pint, old boy, but I will not be marrying a pig farmer," Anna answered promptly. It was a routine she and everyone else in the tavern was familiar with.

"I keep telling you, woman. I am an engineer, not a pig farmer," Viktor said in his defense.

She playfully tapped the side of his cheek and asked, "Then why do you always smell like one?" She promptly headed back to the bar leaving the table in laughter.

Viktor sat red-faced and mumbled, "They are not my pigs. They are the village's pigs."

"You should have just asked her for the time," Casper said as the table erupted once more. He put his arm around his wife and said to her, "I have a surprise for you."

"Oh, a surprise. Do tell," she said with a curious smile.

Casper had a wide grin on his face and said, "I have arranged for us to see the opera in Freiburg this Saturday at the theater."

Barbara leapt for joy and hugged his neck. "We are going by train?"

"Yes," he said with a smile.

"Oh, and I can wear my best Sunday dress!"

"Yes, you can."

She was so excited she could barely contain herself. "What music are we going to hear?"

"I have bought tickets to hear music from your favorite composer, Rossini. They will be performing his final opera, *William Tell*."

She hugged his neck once more and said, "Oh, Casper, he is my favorite. I just love his music. What a lovely surprise."

"We will not return until Sunday, so Franz and Josepha will watch little Bertie," he continued.

"Hooray!" Bertha yelled.

Barbara fretted for a moment and said, "Those boys can be so rough though. I suppose she will be alright."

"Josepha will look after her. She will be fine."

Karl had been sitting quietly, sipping his beer, and overheard them talking of their plans. "Casper, if you are going to Freiburg, see if you can find a newspaper and bring it back. We can all read it. I want to know the latest of what is happening in America."

"America?" Barbara asked curiously.

Karl nodded, saying, "It is said their Union troops have gained the upper hand. That Lincoln will follow through with freeing the African slaves."

"Lincoln," Casper nodded in agreement, "such an intriguing fellow. I still have the transcript of his address two years ago after their battle at Gettysburg. It was an article from one of their newspapers. Such an inspiring man."

Barbara shook her head and added, "Casper loves to read about President Lincoln."

"He started out as a lawyer you know," Casper added.

Viktor slid over and chimed in, asking, "Where did you get the article?"

"His cousin sent it to him in the mail," Barbara answered. "He emigrated one year before their civil war began."

"I am curious if they recruited him into their army," Viktor wondered aloud. "I hear they hand men rifles and force them into military service as soon as they step off the ships."

"Do not be silly," Casper chastised him. "They would not do that to an emigrant who risked life and limb traveling thousands of miles."

"Oh, yes they would," Viktor fired back.

Karl tapped Casper on the shoulder and said, "I want to see this article. Is it in English?"

Casper nodded, saying, "Yes, but he married an American girl who helped him translate it. I have both the English article and the translation. Come by the place one evening and I will share it with you." Casper pulled his pipe from his coat pocket and tapped it on the side of the table. He quickly stuffed the pipe with tobacco and lit it.

"Ugh," Barbara protested. "You have started puffing on that thing. That must mean you are done with your beer." She grabbed Bertha by the arm and said, "And time for us to get home and wash up for supper."

"Oh, Mama," Bertha protested.

"Come along. That goes for you too, Casper."

He walked over to the hat rack and grabbed his brown bowler. Tipping it to the table, he said, "I will see you in the morning, boys. A good night to you all." Then he called out to the bar and said, "Helmut, Anna, God bless!"

"See you next time, Casper," Helmut called back.

Karl jabbed Joachim in the shoulder and said, "See, that will be you in three months. Mark my words."

Saturday arrived and Barbara and Casper stood at the depot, waiting on the next train to Freiburg. Barbara was dressed in her finest and only dress of royal blue with gray shawl and Casper was looking dapper in a black suit and top hat. There were many people milling about the station at Herbolzheim, also waiting on the train. A conductor paced impatiently up and down the platform, glancing at his pocket watch at every turn.

Barbara stood smiling with her arm in Casper's as they waited on the train. "The suit still looks wonderful on you," she said sweetly.

"The same suit I wore when I walked down the aisle with you," he answered with a chuckle. "Fits perfectly, does it not?"

She blushed and said, "Maybe a little snug in the middle, but I can live with that."

He kissed her and said, "You are looking as radiant as the day I met you."

Just then the steam of the train was seen puffing above the trees as it rounded the bend into the station and finally came to rest. Passengers filed off quickly and then the Rees' were able to climb aboard.

"This is so exciting," Barbara cooed as she took her seat. Casper stowed a small cloth overnight bag on the rack above their heads along with his top hat. He sat down next to her and she said, "It has been so long since we took a ride on the train. This is a real treat." He reached for his coat pocket and froze when she added, "But do not start puffing on that pipe of yours." He shook his head and laughed and held her hand instead.

They arrived at the station in Freiburg to bustling activity and throngs of pedestrians. Carriages and horses were everywhere with conductors and patrolmen guiding people through the proper gates to the streets.

It was only a short walk to the theater at the town center and they made it just in time for the performance. People waited in a long line to get into the theater, all dressed in splendid attire. Barbara relished every moment of this rare night out for just the two of them. Within minutes they were entering the grand hall of the theater; mirrors on both sides of the gallery space made it seem endless with people. A tremendous chandelier hung in the center of the hall ornately decorated with flowers and birds and eight large candles burning brightly above the bustling chatter.

Ushers stood at the top of a large staircase, politely motioning for patrons to take their seats in the auditorium. Casper and Barbara had wonderful seats in the fifth row and Barbara couldn't help but looking all around the finely decorated theater. The walls were light pink and lined with candelabras on both sides. Gold etchings adorned the ceilings edge as well as the mezzanine and private balconies that lined either side.

"It is beautiful in here, is it not?" she asked him.

"Indeed," he answered as the orchestra conductor made his entrance. The musicians all stood in his honor and the crowd applauded graciously.

Barbara couldn't take her eyes off the performers on the stage, but she was also equally mesmerized by the orchestra itself. At times the music of *William Tell* became riveting and powerful, then would transition to melancholy and romance. She was enthralled by the whole experience as was Casper.

During intermission, they adjourned to the gallery space for refreshments and cigars and pipes. Casper refrained from joining the men with a hearty smoke as the room was filled as it was.

230

The second act was even more enchanting than the first. As the maestro led the orchestra to the final thunderous conclusion, the entire theater stood and cheered raucously. The performance was a dazzling, yet crowning achievement and the crowd was so appreciative they called on the performers and the maestro seven times to applaud and cheer them once more.

Finally, the audience began to slowly trickle out of the theater. It was well past eleven in the evening, but the streets of Freiburg were still vibrant with activity.

Casper and Barbara stood on the street corner amidst all the people, he in his top hat and she in her blue dress and gray shawl. The air had turned chilly after the sun had set and Casper looked over at her and asked, "How about a nightcap in the café near the hotel before we retire?"

Before she could answer, a loud boisterous crowd came marching around the corner, chanting and calling out demands. All the chatter of the theater patrons subsided to whispers as the young men came clambering by, shouting and clapping.

"What is going on, Casper?" Barbara asked worriedly.

"I do not know," he answered. "Looks to be some kind of demonstration."

The protesters numbered over fifty people and soon they stopped in the heart of the square just outside the theater and shouted even louder, shaking their fists in the air. *'Wir sind gegen die Vereinigung!'* they shouted over and over.

"What are they shouting? I do not like this," Barbara said, ducking behind her husband.

Casper looked on dumbfounded as it was something neither of them had ever witnessed before. "It seems they are loyalists to the Austrian emperor."

Barbara became increasingly worried and fretted, "Why are they here? Please, let us leave, Casper."

Suddenly, someone in the middle of the crowd fired a pistol straight into the air and the entire square erupted into screams and pandemonium.

Casper immediately grabbed his wife and led her away from the chaos. Barbara was sobbing as they tried their best to weave through the hysterical people. Eventually, they found their way to quieter streets and they walked briskly until they reached the small hotel near the railway station.

"Let us just go to our room and we can leave on the first train to Herbolzheim," Barbara suggested. "I have never been so frightened."

They sat in their second-floor hotel room, still hearing the shouts and anarchy several blocks away. Occasionally they would hear more gunshots and screams. Neither of them could sleep at all and Barbara trembled in his arms and wondered aloud, "Why cannot the authorities put a stop to this?"

"There are too many of them," he responded. "We will get out of here first thing. Try to sleep, my love."

As they lay quietly, neither of them able to sleep, she whispered, "The opera was an absolute triumph, dear. Thank you for taking me. The overture alone was worth the trip."

"I enjoyed that part too, love. At least that was unspoiled."

The next morning, the weary travelers waited patiently to board the earliest train for Herbolzheim. They climbed the steps and walked down the car to their seats and collapsed in them as neither of them had slept more than a couple hours. They hadn't been sitting there long when conductors came rushing through the cars telling passengers to disembark.

Casper got to his feet and demanded, "What the devil is going on now? What is the meaning of this?"

The conductor answered firmly, saying, "The train is being commandeered by a military authority of high personage. They are needing it to travel to Heidelberg. Everyone off, please."

"I must protest," Casper prodded. "Our stop is along the way to Heidelberg."

The conductor only repeated himself, "Everyone off."

"This is outrageous!" He grabbed Barbara by the hand and led her off the train.

"What will we do?" she asked, bewildered. "Josepha will not know what has happened to us."

Casper shook his head in exasperation. "I will try to find us a carriage going north."

In less than twelve hours, the city of Freiburg had turned into chaos and no one really knew what was going on. As they stood in the station, Casper noticed a newsstand and decided to buy a copy.

"Maybe this will give us an idea of this madness. Karl had asked for a newspaper anyhow."

After an hour of negotiating, Casper was able to secure two spots on a carriage headed to Herbolzheim. The ride was long and arduous, but they finally reached their home just before sunset. They were both exhausted and sore from the bumpy ride. Franz and Josepha were shocked to see how distraught and tired they were and that they had not arrived by train. Bertha was ecstatic to see them and she ran to her mother and hugged her legs.

"Mama! Papa!" she cried.

Franz was stunned to hear of the calamity in Freiburg. "The military is taking over trains? So, it has started. This is not what our country needs again."

Casper handed him the newspaper and discreetly said, "You will want to read this. Give it to Karl when you are done."

The next evening after the day's work was done, Karl and Franz went over to Casper and Barbara's instead of their usual stop at Helmut's. Barbara gave them all something to drink while they sat around the small table in the firelight. The newspaper sat in the middle of the table.

"The loyalists are demanding control of the whole confederation?" Karl asked perplexed.

"Or total independence if the Prussians refuse," Casper added.

Franz shook his head and said, "That will cause certain war and we are caught in the middle. The confederation is meant to be as one. Without Austria to balance the power, we are nothing but pawns."

Karl then said, "We were pawns already."

"The Grand Duke has always been favorable to the Austrians," Casper said. "I do not understand their actions in Freiburg."

"Bismarck will not stand for any of this. I have heard rumors of the armies gathering every capable man," Karl warned.

Franz looked at him curiously and asked, "Gathering them for what?"

"What do you think? Military service. We will be forced to choose a side."

Barbara pleaded with them and said, "Enough of this talk. I do not want my child hearing this."

Karl nodded and agreed, "She is right. My apologies. It is just a rumor." He turned to Casper and asked, "Could we see the article you spoke about?"

Casper thought for a moment, he was still conflicted about the political fall-out they were discussing. "Oh, you mean about Lincoln?"

"Yes."

"One moment. I always keep it right here on top of my desk." He got up and crossed the floor and found the article on the desk near the fireplace.

Karl chuckled as the cuckoo clock struck eight and asked, "I had forgotten you had one of these clocks. Where did you get it?"

Casper gave the clock a glance and said, "A peddler was in town the same year Bertie was born. He had come from a village in the Black Forest called Schonach."

"Ah," Karl recalled, "I am familiar with that village."

Casper came back to the table and carefully unfolded the American article and the German translation. "The address was not lengthy but straight to the point. They say Lincoln spoke directly from the battlefield where thousands died. Listen to this. Lincoln said, 'Our fathers brought forth to this continent, a new nation, conceived in liberty, and dedicated to the proposition that all men are created equal.' That is quite profound, do you not think?"

Karl was fascinated and answered, "It most certainly is. Do you think Bismarck would ever say such a thing to his people?"

"No," Franz piped up.

Casper continued. "And look at this part. Here he talks about dedicating a portion of the field to the fallen men, but then goes on to say, '…that we here highly resolve that these dead shall not have died in vain. That this nation, under God, shall have a new birth of freedom, and that government of the people, by the people, for the people, shall not perish from the Earth.'" Casper looked around the table to see if they were paying attention. "Did you hear that? A new birth of *freedom*."

Franz looked curiously at the article and asked, "What does that mean 'by the people and for the people'?"

Casper sat down and answered, "Well, it means just what the Americans have been doing since 1776. The people decide who the government leaders are."

Barbara nodded and added, "We certainly do not do that here."
Karl shook his head and added, "They are still embroiled in civil war."

"Yes, but look here," Casper pointed toward the newspaper he bought in Freiburg. "Lee's troops are said to be surrounded after Sherman's march last winter. I get the feeling their war may be close to an end."

Franz scanned over the article he was referring to and agreed. "You may be on to something. It appears we could have war almost at any time here. What would we do? We are on the fringes in our village, but what could stop them from coming here and doing what they want?"

"Nothing," Karl answered. "We are not military people. We are farmers, laborers."

Barbara became irritated and repeated, "Do not talk about this, I say. You are beginning to frighten me and Bertha."

Casper waved his hand and said, "Let us talk outside, gentlemen."

As they were walking out, Karl casually asked, "What was the name of your cousin who emigrated to America?"

Immediately, Casper could see the dismay on his wife's face. "Come, let us step outside." The three left Barbara sitting at the table staring at the newspaper mournfully.

The men stepped out into the chilly evening and Karl asked again, "Your cousin who emigrated, what was his name?"

"His name is Heinrich, my great uncle's son." Casper looked distraught however at mentioning the name. He looked sorrowfully at his friends and said, "Just do not mention him around Barbara. He was the godfather to our boy. We even named him after Heinrich."

"God rest him," Franz said sadly. "We are sorry, Casper. We did not want to dredge up those awful memories."

"It is alright. We have Bertie now, but Barbara still gets quite sad at times."

Karl nodded and added, "Yes, I apologize old friend. I just wanted to know where he settled."

"It has been over a year since he last wrote, but he said it just so happened to be in the same land where Lincoln was a boy."

"The same land as Lincoln? Astounding."

"Yes," Casper continued, "he spoke about how many Germans were already settled in the area adjacent to the grand river called *Mississippi*."

"Yes, yes. But what was the land called?" Karl asked impatiently.

Casper scratched his chin whiskers and said, "Hmm, let me see if I remember. The land is called, *Illinois*."

Barbara sat at the table glancing through the newspaper while Bertha climbed on the chair next to her. She flipped through the pages until something caught her attention. She stared wide-eyed at the article headline that read, *More Cures Attributed To Waters At Massabielle*. "This is amazing!" she blurted out loud.

Bertha looked at her with a happy smile and echoed, "Amazing, Mama!"

Later that night after the men had gone home, Casper and Barbara lay awake in bed. Casper noticed how she was in deep thought with an expression that conveyed a sense of wonder. He looked at her and asked, "What has you so awe-inspired this evening?"

She kept staring at the ceiling until she finally answered, "Do you remember that little girl from Lourdes a few years back? The one who claimed visons of the Holy Mother?"

Casper nodded and said, "Ah, yes. The Soubirous girl. Yes, her story was quite profound. Did you hear something new?"

"Oh, come now," she laughed. "You have been carrying around that paper for days and you did not even notice? They are reporting more miraculous cures from the spring there in Lourdes in the little grotto where the visions occurred. The spring itself was one of the first miracles."

He laughed at himself, saying, "Oh, how silly of me. I must have overlooked it. More miracles, you say? That is fascinating."

"I wish we could have taken little Heinrich there," she sniffed. "Maybe things could have been different."

"Oh, you must not think that. No one really knew at that time if the waters were miraculous or not. Everything happens for a reason, my love. Our child was needed more by God in Heaven. Please, do not upset yourself."

She tried to hold back her tears. "I know he looks down from Heaven upon us and his baby sister. But it is so inspiring to hear after all these years that miracles are still happening there." She sat up in bed and leaned against her pillow. "They put that girl through so many trials. For four years they questioned her repeatedly about the 'lady' in the grotto. It was amazing how she stood up to them each time, never once changing her explanation. I remember praying so much for her to let the Holy Father in Rome side with her."

"And finally, he did," Casper added.

"Can you imagine being told by an apparition that they are the 'Immaculate Conception'? I cannot even fathom such an experience. God bless her."

Casper nodded and said, "She is truly blessed indeed."

She looked at her husband lovingly and said, "I wish we could travel to Lourdes and see the grotto. Wash in the waters of the spring."

"It is a great distance from here. It would take many days. I would like to see it too, but not with Bertie being so young."

"Yes, you are right," she relented sadly. "The article mentioned that arrangements were being made for her to leave Lourdes, away from the spotlight of curious people."

"That is a good thing, I think," Casper said. "If there is one person who needs rest away from the authorities, it is Bernadette Soubirous."

From then on, Barbara couldn't stop thinking about the visionary from France. The thought of what the young girl from Lourdes had experienced consumed her. She had avidly followed for years the news of how Bernadette was interrogated relentlessly about the 'lady' in the grotto. She sympathized with how she was cast as a liar and a prankster. Her faith was never swayed however, she knew deep in her heart that Bernadette was being honest. She felt a deep need to know more about her, not just see the miraculous spring and the grotto, but to know more about Bernadette herself.

A few weeks later she visited the local church of Saint Alexius and Father Georg was out in the garden tending the rose bushes. From the corner of his eye, he saw her opening the gate.

"Ah, Frau Rees, how nice to see you," he called out. "I am so used to seeing you with the little one."

"Hello, Father," she said. "She is with Casper if you can believe that. Hopefully not spending the entire day at Helmut's."

Georg put down his plowing tool and asked, "Here to discuss the upcoming activities for Holy Week?"

Barbara shook her head and answered, "No, I was hoping to talk to you about something else. But we can discuss Holy Week too."

"Oh, let us go inside where it is cooler," he suggested. They sat in the office of the rectory while Georg wiped the sweat from his forehead. "How can I help you today?"

Barbara got straight to the point and said, "I wanted to ask you about Bernadette Soubirous."

"Oh, yes. How could I forget the young girl from Lourdes? It is quite extraordinary, is it not? Having the Holy Father's blessing has done such great things for the church."

"Yes, her visions confounded me the first time I read about them. I have always wanted to visit Lourdes ever since." Barbara hesitated though. She didn't want to get too far off topic.

"Something else is bothering you though," he answered.

She didn't know how to put it into words, but he waited patiently. Then she said, "I want to know more about her. If it were seven years ago, she could not have been more than fourteen. I remember being that age. Having such a thing as the Virgin Mother speaking to me, I just do not know how I could have managed."

"God chooses His messengers wisely," Georg said. "It is not for us to understand nor for Bernadette. But the important thing was that she accepted it. And do not forget, she maintained all this time that it was not the Virgin Mother, but a 'beautiful lady' that spoke to her. It was not until the lady spoke the words 'Immaculate Conception' did the church take formal notice."

Barbara finally revealed what was truly on her mind. "I would so much like to meet her. I know people from all over wish to have the same thing, but the reason I have inside me I just cannot explain. I feel something is drawing me to her. I can barely sleep at night."

Georg smiled sympathetically. "Your love for God is exceptional. I can see that. A human being actually conversing with a member of the Holy Family is beyond our comprehension. Those who do not believe, no explanation will suffice. But those of us who do believe, no explanation is necessary. Still we are human. We want to be close to these rare beings."

"Yes!" Barbara cried. "I want to be near her. I want to talk with her and tell her that I love and appreciate her."

"There, there now. These things we must pray on. Bernadette Soubirous is a rare being, but she has also been hounded by ecclesiastical authorities for years. And probably will be until her passing. My prayer is that she be left alone."

"Tell me, Father," Barbara persisted, "I read that she is to leave Lourdes. Do you know where she will go?"

Georg thought for a moment and said, "The bishop once told me he had met Peyramale, the Dean of Lourdes, who was the child's confessor at the time of the visions. For years he had advocated for her entry into the religious life."

Barbara nodded and said, "Yes, that would make perfect sense."

"Yes, she was not destined for the common life. Peyramale argued that since the Virgin Mother condescended her, a peasant girl, that she should not hide away as a servant but to embrace her calling to God." He thought for a moment more before saying, "The school that she attended was run by the Sisters of Charity. It is quite possible that if she were to take religious orders, it would be with them at their convent."

"Where is the Sisters of Charity convent?" she asked curiously.

"That is the only puzzling part of the equation. It is quite a long distance north of Lourdes. A hard journey by carriage. I am not certain if Lourdes has been connected by railway now or not. Regardless, the convent is located in Nevers."

"Nevers?" Barbara gasped. "I know where that is! It is not far from Paris or from here."

Georg shook his head though and said, "But my dear child, a cloister is not for the general public unless invited. Especially for one Bernadette Soubirous. If taken there, she would be well protected from the public eye. Obtaining access would be virtually impossible."

"I know," Barbara said sadly, "but knowing she could possibly be that much closer gives me hope."

"One thing else you must consider," Georg said, raising his finger to make a point. "Once she becomes a postulant, she would not enter the convent with her given name. All the sisters would know her by a new name and only the sisters would know this name."

Barbara stared at her feet with dejection. "If God wishes it, then that is something I will have to find out."

It was the end of another hard day at work. In the morning, the road crew had put the final touches on the new thoroughfare at Rheinhausen and in the afternoon, they shifted their work to the large croplands to till and weed the soil.

Casper sat at a corner table at the tavern with Karl and Joachim. Instead of their usual beer, they decided to have a glass of absinthe instead. Anna brought them three fresh glasses of the clear green liquor with a decanter of fresh water, a small tin tray of sugar cubes and the requisite pouring spoon. She gave them all a smirk as she set the drinks down and said, "Living a bit on the fancier side tonight, are we boys?"

Karl shrugged his shoulders, saying, "It has been a hard day, love. We needed something a bit stronger this evening."

"Careful who you are calling love," she teased.

"Come back after I have had one of these," he countered. "It will loosen my tongue even more." The three at the table laughed heartily as Anna just smiled and sauntered away.

Casper took the holed spoon and placed it across his glass of absinthe. Then he placed one sugar cube on the spoon, then proceeded to pour the water over the sugar. The cube gradually melted as the water trickled through the spoon and into the waiting, sparkling clear-green absinthe. Immediately the cloudy louche appeared and Casper quickly stirred the rest of the sugar into the liquor. "Here you are," he said to Karl, handing him the spoon, who proceeded to do the same. Casper raised the glass to his nostrils and took in a long whiff of the intoxicating aroma. "Ah!" he exhaled satisfyingly. "The anise brings out such a wonderful bouquet. Reminds me of sweet licorice." He finally took a sip and smiled happily. "That is what I needed after such a hard day."

As the men sat around the table relaxing and enjoying their absinthe, Karl leaned over to Casper and said, "I have been thinking about your cousin in America."

"Have you now?" Casper said, sipping his drink.

Joachim looked up from his glass and asked, "You mean cousin, Heinrich?"

Karl continued, "Yes, I was wondering where he set sail from."

Casper looked at him directly and answered, "He set sail from Hamburg."

"Hamburg? He traveled that far just to get on a ship?"

Joachim shook his head and said, "It is the only port in Germany for cross-Atlantic ships. At least for passengers. It does not make it easy, that is for certain. I often wondered why he left in the first place."

"Heinrich was always different, always a maverick," Casper answered. "I believe his father was quite harsh with him, but I always admired his skills as an engineer."

"I will tell you why," Karl interjected. "His father may have been harsh, but my guess is he was tired of working for the greater good of the Grand Duchy. In America, you can work for yourself. You said he was married now. I am certain he has started work on his own accord. Can you imagine being an independent worker? No superiors to answer to?"

Casper nodded and concurred, "Yes, having your own business does sound appealing."

Anna brought them another round of absinthe and snickered, "I could not help but overhearing you boys. I would say this stuff does loosen your tongues a bit. I hear you speaking a lot about America. What are you boys cooking up? Thinking of getting out before the kettle boils over?"

Joachim looked at her and answered, "Who me? Emigrate? I cannot think of doing such a thing. I am about to be married."

She looked suspiciously at Karl and Casper and asked, "But what about you two. What is going on here?"

Casper waved her off and said, "We are only speaking of my cousin in America, nothing more."

Just then, Barbara and Bertha came walking up to join them as usual, but she rolled her eyes when she saw them drinking absinthe. "Anna," she drawled, "you know these boys start talking too carefree when you bring them absinthe. No telling what they are up to."

She smiled sheepishly and answered as she returned to the bar, "It sounds to me they are up to a lot. I will bring your usual."

"What does she mean by that?" she asked Casper.

"We are just sitting here chatting, dear." He kissed her and asked as she sat beside him, "How was your day, my sweet?"

"It was fine." She quickly changed the subject to what was really on her mind. "I have been trying to learn more about the Soubirous girl. I just cannot get her off my mind."

"The girl with the visions?" Joachim asked.

Barbara nodded anxiously and said, "Yes, that is her. I went to speak to Father Georg, and he suggested she might be living now in Nevers with the Sisters of Charity."

Anna overheard the conversation when she came back with a glass of beer for Barbara and some milk for Bertha. Bertha wrinkled her nose and said, "I wanted sarsaparilla, not milk."

Casper chimed in and said, "Milk will be just fine for you tonight." He turned back to his wife and asked, "Nevers, you say? It is between here and Paris if I am not mistaken."

"Yes," she continued, "but he said if she is there, she mostly likely would have changed her name when becoming a postulant. I have done some research. Nevers is accessible by train, but only from Paris."

"Are you saying you want to travel there?" he asked confounded. He looked around the table with amusement, saying, "She wants to go to Nevers now." The men chuckled and Barbara fumed.

"I am only saying that is how one gets there by train. I think you have had enough of the 'poet's third eye' for one evening." The men laughed even louder.

Bertha looked at them quizzically and asked, "What is a poets third eye? Is it a scary monster?"

"A green one, apparently," Karl teased, as Bertha recoiled in her chair.

Barbara was getting agitated by the minute. "Seriously now. The one thing that plagues me the most is what name she could have taken if she did indeed join the convent."

Anna circled around the table once more, picking up empty glasses and leaned over toward Barbara. "I may have some ideas on the subject. I will come and see you tomorrow. I too am quite taken by Bernadette and her visions." Barbara appreciatively smiled at her and felt more at ease. She was greatly curious as to what Anna might know.

Just then, Viktor came rushing to their table with a pained expression on his face. "What is it, Viktor?" Casper asked. "You look like you have just seen a ghost."

Viktor slapped a recent newspaper down on the table and said, "I came across this at the depot as I was cleaning the station. The news from America is both wonderful and terribly upsetting at the same time."

Casper looked around the table with a perplexed expression. Everyone else quieted down and stared at the newspaper in shock. Their faces fell when they saw the glaring and horrific headline stating Abraham Lincoln had been assassinated.

Casper picked up the paper in disbelief, asking, "*Assassinated?*" He dropped the paper on the table and collapsed in his chair with a stunned look. Barbara looked at him sympathetically, she could tell the news had ripped right through his heart.

Karl anxiously twirled the newspaper around and examined it. "It says here that General Lee surrendered two weeks ago." He looked around the table with surprise. "The American war is over." He then returned to the unspeakable headline and read the article below. "Only a week later after the war was declared over, Lincoln was shot by an assailant while attending the theater. He died the next morning." He put the paper down and bowed his head into his hand silently. The entire tavern went deafly quiet.

Bertha looked quite worried and asked, "What is wrong with everyone? Someone died, Mama?"

She pushed back from the table and answered, "Yes, honey. I think we should go home now. Go get Papa's hat for him."

Casper was numb as he got to his feet and clumsily put on his bowler hat and stumbled his way back home with his wife and child, leaving the tavern in deathly silence.

As they got home, Casper quietly walked over to the cuckoo clock and slowly wound the chain back to the top. Barbara silently warmed their supper while Bertha played at the table. They ate a quiet dinner together and then put Bertha to bed. Casper just sat in his rocking chair, staring at the smoldering fire and after putting her apron away, Barbara slid her chair next to his and sat down.

"I am sorry, Casper. I know you are upset," she said, breaking the awful silence.

"No," he said. "I am the one who should apologize. I was just so stunned I knew not what to say."

"He was a great man," she said. "And God let him live to see his goal be accomplished in freeing the American slaves. He ended a long and terrible war."

"Yes," he agreed. "Thank God for that."

She looked at him thoughtfully, knowing how hurt he was. She knew how much he admired the American president and his wisdom, but she had a feeling something more was on his mind. "You have been thinking more about America have you not?" she finally asked. "About your cousin there?" He nodded as he rocked in his chair. "Are you considering what I think you are?"

Casper looked at her and said, "Karl has been speaking about it frequently lately. I think Franz is concerned too. Particularly after what we saw in Freiburg."

"Oh, it was horrible."

"To tell you the truth, I had contemplated emigrating once before. After we lost little Heinrich, my soul was lost. Neither of us could console one another. I did feel at one time of just taking us both and leaving the pain behind. It was too much to bear." He tried holding back his emotions as he knew his wife had already begun to cry. "I am so sorry for speaking of this. But it consumed me as I know it did you. But then the war broke out in America, so I decided just to forget about it. It was too dangerous."

She took a deep breath and dried her face and said, "The tide may turn yet here in our own country and perhaps war can be avoided. We must at least give it a chance. I love our home too much, even if there is sadness in our past."

"I know, love. I know," he said, squeezing her hand.

The next morning while Barbara cleaned the house, she heard a knock on the door. She opened it and smiled at her expected guest. "Anna, thank you for coming by," she said warmly.

Anna stepped inside and patted Bertha on the head, saying, "Hey, little Bertie."

"Hi!" Bertha answered cheerfully.

Anna turned to Barbara and said, "I am sorry for my eavesdropping yesterday, but it is hard not to hear in my position."

"It is quite alright," Barbara said.

"I have always been fascinated with the visions at Massabielle," Anna continued. "I would love to go there myself to the grotto, but I could never afford the trip. When the news of all that was happening started coming out, I read as much as I possibly could about it. It was not often when I could read a newspaper but when I did, I saved everything." She produced a small pouch and set it on the table.

"Here, sit down," Barbara suggested. "I will heat some water for tea."

The two of them sat down and Bertha squirmed in between them to see all the news articles Anna had saved about Bernadette Soubirous. "The authorities in Lourdes just hounded her and her family," Anna pointed out. "They did not believe her claims and tried their best to ridicule her. Even the church and the school. But look here, her biggest supporter before the church gradually came around, was her aunt Bernarde Casterot, her mother's sister. You were asking about her name, right? If she ever became a nun?" Barbara nodded anxiously as she listened. "Well, I know from my own sister who became a nun that when you first become a postulant, they ask you to choose a name. The Sisters of Charity all go by the name 'Sister Marie' in honor of the Virgin Mother. But to distinguish each nun, they choose a second name that is often related to their family. And in most cases, they choose from their godmother's name."

Barbara put her hand to her mouth in amazement. "This is so fascinating. Please, go on."

"Well, I learned from this one small article from 1862, right before the Vatican officially agreed to her visions as genuine, her aunt is referred to as her 'godmother'. I think if she is at the Sisters of Charity in Nevers, then she probably calls herself Sister Marie Bernarde." Anna smiled at her with a triumphant expression.

"That is extraordinary, Anna! I think you are right too. I do not see how it could be wrong. Oh, my. Just think if we could somehow go and visit with her." Barbara's mind was racing a mile a minute. "I know it sounds impossible and maybe absurd too. But I just cannot stop thinking about it." She held Anna's hands and thanked her. "Let us get some tea; I want to hear everything you know."

On Sunday after Mass, it was a beautiful sunny morning outside Saint Alexius Church. As they did often in the warmer months, the people gathered in the courtyard of the church to visit and watch the children play. The men often sat in their top hats and coats discussing politics while the women gathered in the shade of the trees. The children laughed and played with a German shepherd dog that barked and yipped amongst them.

As the men sat, the topic of Lincoln's assassination had not gone away. "I cannot understand a country," Viktor began, "that would fight and die for their leader only to let him be shot in the end. It was not worth fighting for in my opinion. One would not dare shoot a Prime Minister or even an emperor."

Karl dismissed it and said, "Would they not? That is rubbish. If the opposition were strong enough, they could certainly do it."

Viktor shook his head and added, "Just their presence would leave people in awe and incapable of doing them harm. That is the difference between a great leader and just a man chosen by the peasantry."

Casper became agitated with his brother-in-law's ignorance and spoke up. "The American people voted for Lincoln in a democratic process. It is something completely foreign to us. We do not get to decide who our leaders are. Lincoln was a man of great courage and sacrifice who believed in the freedom of all men black, brown or white. Bismarck and Franz Joseph obtained their posts by the elites who selected them for their status or for the so-called 'birthright'. They fight to obtain power and control. Lincoln fought for liberty and justice and to grant freedom to *all* men and women, not just some of them. There is a clear difference there. It was a gift that he obtained for his people, a gift that he gave his life for. That, to me gentlemen, is the sign of a true leader worth fighting for."

A few days later, word arrived that more protests and riots had occurred to the north in Stuttgart. The news spread quickly that two men had been shot in the midst of the chaos. Casper sat at the bar alone talking with Bruna and Helmut.

"The violence and unrest are growing all around us," he fretted.

Bruna just laughed it off, saying, "Just a bunch of hot-heads making noise in the summer months. Once the cold winter returns, they will cool off."

"I wish it were that simple," Casper lamented.

Helmut shook his head and said, "Do not worry yourself so much, friend. We have seen these uprisings before. The authorities will knock them down. Be certain of it."

Casper disagreed though and said, "I am afraid our friends in Austria may push the Prussians too far this time. We here in the countryside will have little power to stop any of it. What will we say if they come asking for volunteers?"

Helmut joked, "They can ask me all they want, but then who will serve them a pint when they get thirsty?" He became serious again and added, "Listen, I have heard you and some others talk more and more about America. You are not thinking of leaving, are you?"

"No one has decided anything, Helmut. Calm yourself."

Helmut shook his head and added, "You cannot do this. This is our home. This is our village. We all must stay here and remain strong. We might be farmers and peasants, but Herbolzheim is nothing without its people. What can America provide that we cannot?"

Casper got up from his stool and answered, "Right now, my good friend, nothing. But if war were to break out here, then America has everything to offer. A chance to live without it."

Spring slowly turned to summer and by mid-June the time had come for the wedding of Joachim and his betrothed, Imelda. The entire village attended the wedding Mass at Saint Alexius and the crowd spilled out into the courtyard. After the nuptials were exchanged and the Mass was celebrated, the large gathering migrated to Helmut's biergarten for a grand celebration.

They first toasted to the bride and groom and allowed them the first dance to the traditional German folk songs. As the band played, the crowd clapped as the happy couple danced together for the first time as man and wife.

Then the crowd became even more raucous as it was the men's turn to dance. Several of the men, all dressed in lederhosen and Tryolean hats, marched onto the wooden dance floor. They were followed by an equal number of ladies dressed splendidly in long traditional and colorful dresses. Casper, Franz, Viktor, Karl, Helmut and even Father Georg joined them in the circle. In the middle was Joachim leading them all in the Schuhplattler. With delicate precision, the men tapped their heels and stomped their feet to the delight of the crowd. Then they danced in a circle weaving in and out with the ladies before returning to the middle for another round of tapping and stomping.

It was a rowdy and joyous time while the beer flowed with abundant food for everyone. Children danced their own versions of the folk dances and polkas and laughed and giggled as they did. The partying went on into the evening and well past midnight.

The next morning, Casper sat in his rocking chair, nursing his sore head. Bertha sleepily walked across the room and climbed onto his lap. "Where is your mother?" he muttered, his head pounding.

"She is still sleeping," Bertha answered with a yawn.

"Well, why are you not sleeping?" he asked.

She nestled her head against his chest and said, "You woke me."

Hours later, Barbara stood by the chair smiling at the two snoring away on the rocking chair. She looked over her shoulder at the clock that was about to strike seven. Suddenly, it sprang to life and chimed and cuckooed seven times.

"Ugh," Casper moaned as he awakened. "That noise. What is laying all over me?"

Barbara laughed and said, "She is called our daughter. Come on Bertie, rise and shine." She picked the little girl off his lap and held her in her arms.

Casper shook the cobwebs from his head and said, "She is so hot. I am burning up. We need some snow on the ground."

"Not likely in late June," she answered. "Get up or we will be late for Mass."

Bertie opened her eyes and lifted her head off her shoulder and said, "We went to Mass yesterday."

"That was for the wedding. Today is Sunday. Come on, get dressed."

The congregation stood half asleep in the church, many yawning and others barely able to keep their eyes open. As Father Georg gave the final blessing, a commotion could be heard outside. A few people turned around to stare at the back door and others tried to look through the stained-glass windows. Shouts were heard and horses trotted by neighing loudly and anxiously.

The people dismissed without even singing a closing hymn and quickly exited to see what was happening. They stood in horror as the streets had filled with loyalists dressed in beige clothes and berets. Amongst the throng were a smaller contingent of soldiers and policemen. The shouts and yells grew louder as pushing and shoving began, and no one knew where the crowd had come from. They didn't recognize anyone that was clambering in their streets.

"What is happening here?" Franz asked out loud. "Who are these people?"

Viktor answered matter-of-factly, "They go from village to village trying to intimidate people. Scaring people." He put his hands to his mouth and yelled, "Get out of our town!"

Josepha scolded him, saying, "Stop it! They will rush at us next. The children are frightened to death."

Franz then said, "Maybe we should go back inside the church."

Father Georg quickly directed the people back inside, trying not to arouse the ire of the mob. He hoped and prayed the local authorities could keep them at bay.

Casper worried aloud as they sat nervously in the pews, "What of our homes?"

"What about my tavern?" Helmut echoed. "I have not cleaned up from yesterday. I cannot just sit here. I need to get to my home and my tavern." He and Bruna got up immediately and left.

"God be with you," Father Georg told them.

The yelling and shouts grew louder outside and soon, gunfire was heard. The crowd inside the church gasped as they heard screaming in hysterics.

"Dear God, what is happening here?" Barbara said with her eyes closed.

Casper stood and said to the priest, "We need to go, Father, or there will be nothing left of our homes. This is the same thing as we saw in Freiburg."

"Let them pass, please," Father Georg pleaded with them.

Bertha grabbed Casper's hand and said, "Papa, sit." He relented and sat down again.

Barbara looked relieved and said to him, "Think about it. We do not have much to steal anyway."

They waited close to mid-day when they decided it was time to go outside. The noise had subsided, and people had grown weary of sitting in the tight confines. One by one they cautiously exited and began going back to their homes.

Casper and his family stopped to check on Helmut at his tavern and he stuck his head out and said, "They trampled the grounds out back pretty badly but luckily we kept them out of here."

As they walked the streets back to their home, the evidence of the riots was surreal. Many places were ransacked and trampled but the most sobering sight was the dead bodies of three young men. Two were dressed in beige trousers and one was a member of the local police. Barbara tried to shield their daughter from the horrors that lie in the street, but her efforts did little. Bertha sobbed and soon Casper picked her up and carried her the rest of the way home.

Casper was discouraged to see the door to their cottage was left hanging on one hinge. They walked into their small home to see some chairs toppled and the iron stove tilted against a column. The cuckoo clock had been knocked from the wall and lay partially cracked open and what few papers he had on the small desk, were strewn about everywhere.

Casper shook his head, taking in all the destruction. The only thing left undisturbed was the priceless family heraldry still standing above the fireplace on the mantle. "You were right," he finally said. "We really did not have much to take. They damaged the clock and a few other things that can be fixed. But the one thing that did mean something to me still stands above the fireplace." He stood pointing at the three ravens on the two-hundred-year-old parchment. "It is still here."

Barbara walked over holding Bertha's hand and embraced him. "It means something to us too." They walked outside once more to observe their town that had been vandalized. She took a deep breath and finally said, "If you are still thinking about leaving, then I am with you. Let us go before it is too late."

A week later Casper sat with Karl at Helmut's having a beer. "What do you know about passenger ships?" Casper asked him directly.

Karl looked at him with a guilty grin and said, "I thought you would never ask. I am my own man here, Casper. I have no family. I am an easy target for these militias, and I do not care one way or the other about their cause."

"You are preaching to the hymnists, Karl," Casper laughed. "What do you know about the ships?"

He looked around the tavern to make sure no one was overhearing, then he produced a flyer that advertised passage to America. "I picked this up in Heidelberg a month ago," he explained. "From what I can see, getting a space on one of these ships is the easy part. It is relatively inexpensive. The hard part is getting to Hamburg, and of course, the actual sailing across the Atlantic."

"Well, what do you mean by inexpensive?" Casper continued asking.

Karl leaned in closer and explained, "Most of the ships are British, so they deal in pounds. The cheapest fare is just over three pounds each. We can easily raise that on our pay. I will help you in any way if you need."

"And they sail to New York?"

Karl nodded, saying, "Right to Manhattan island."

Casper thought for a moment and then said, "We agree then that we go and find Heinrich in Illinois, yes?"

Karl nodded once more. "It is quite possible we can travel by train from there after we arrive. What is the village he settled in?"

Casper answered, "Quincy, Illinois. He told me there are many Germans settled there already."

Just then, Franz came and joined them with a worried look on his face. "Anna, a beer please," he called out as he sat down.

"How is everything, Franz?" Karl asked casually.

He went straight to the point and said, "I do not know about you two, but Josepha is getting very nervous about all this nonsense going on. I am too, quite frankly. I have four young boys and one who is an infant still. I cannot be snatched by some rebel group for military service." He leaned in closer and said, "Be honest now, boys. You know the wives all talk just as we do, and they are all frightened to death. If you are thinking of emigrating, you have to include me in the conversation."

Karl patted him on the shoulder, saying, "Do not worry, you are in the conversation. What of your other siblings and Joachim?"

"Viktor is being stubborn. You know how he is. He would rather stay and fight with the rebels. Johanna will not leave either. And Joachim…" He trailed off and just shook his head.

Casper nodded and said, "As much as we love them, everyone has to make their own choice."

Anna came striding over with another round of beers for them and said abruptly, "Whatever you boys are discussing, I can tell you right now I want in."

Casper gave her a coy grin and said, "You are brave as you are beautiful, young lady. Will not Helmut miss you here?"

She sat down in the middle of them and replied, "I am not as young as you think." She looked over her shoulder and then back at her friends. "And I just work for Helmut, I do not sleep with the man."

The three men erupted in laughter and Karl added, "I think he has Bruna for that."

Anna grew serious and whispered, "If I get a chance to go to America, I am going. But I do not wish to go alone."

"Well," Casper said, "I believe we have a quorum here. But let us keep it to ourselves for now. Franz and I will talk things over with the families. We will not be able to keep this quiet for long though. We must be fair to our other family and friends."

All were in agreement as they adjourned from the table and went home while Anna went back to work.

That night Casper told his wife what he had learned from Karl about the ships and cost of the passage. He also told her that her brother Franz was interested in going too.

"Yes, I know," she answered. "Josepha already told me. It is the right thing to do with their four boys. I am worried about Viktor and Johanna though. She has no one here and Viktor is so hot-headed at times."

"Perhaps we can still talk your sister into coming with us. Viktor will decide on his own I am certain. Anna and Karl would like to come as well."

Barbara shrugged with a slight grin and said, "I think she secretly loves Karl, if you ask me. Helmut would be upset but I am actually happy for Anna's decision."

Casper could tell something else was on her mind though. "What is it, my wife?"

"We do not know yet when the time will come, but I do have one request."

"Go on," he urged her.

She shuffled in place before she could get the words out. "I want you to take me on another trip before we leave for Hamburg. I would like to go to Nevers."

He took in a deep breath and thought of what she was asking. "You want to see Bernadette."

"Yes, I do."

He sat down at the table and Bertha immediately jumped in his lap. "Hello, little Bertie." He kissed her cheek and then asked, "Say we make it to Nevers. Then what?"

Barbara sat next to him and said, "Well, we go and look for the Sisters of Charity. All we can do is ask if we can visit with her."

"And if they say no?"

She started to cry as she could no longer hold in her emotions. "Please do not try to discourage me. Please, do not. You want me to follow you to America and I will. I will leave the rest of my family here, our friends, our whole life we have made here, as I know war could happen anytime. But I must do this. Just let me do this for myself. Even if I do not see her, I at least want to try."

He looked at his daughter who waited patiently for his answer, then he looked at his loving wife. "Let me see about the arrangements. Then we will go and find Bernadette Soubirous."

A week later, their plans were no longer secret as the entire town knew of the families and individuals who decided to emigrate to America. Emotions were mixed and bittersweet, but no fingers were pointed, and no blame was put at their feet. The realization that their friends and family would be leaving soon became evident. The only thing that wasn't known yet was when it would be.

It was late in the day when Casper was walking home from the fields. The harvest had begun, and the men were aching from the backbreaking work. As he meandered home, he spotted a familiar, yet peculiar man peddling his wares near the train depot and stopped and smiled at the man and said, "I remember you."

The old man spun around. His back was covered with a makeshift display of cuckoo clocks attached to his shoulders. Nearly a dozen clocks were hanging across the funny looking man's back with leather straps. He walked back and forth wearing a Tyrolean cap asking any passers-by if they would like to buy a clock. "Hello, old chap," the man said cheerfully. He stood with a smile as if nothing looked oddly about himself.

"Hello, to you," Casper said with a laugh. "You are the man from Schonach. I bought one of your clocks a few years ago."

"I am indeed," he said. "Ah, yes. I remember you quite well."

"Welcome back to Herbolzheim."

"Why, thank you. It is good to be back. Tough business these days though."

Casper nodded and said, "Yes, these times are strange indeed, even harsh on delicate things like your wonderful clocks. I would be happy to give you some business if you think you could help me."

The old man was happy to oblige and asked, "What can I do for you?"

"Well, in the midst of the calamity that charged through our town last month, they managed to damage my clock. I was wondering if you could repair it for me."

"The buggers," the man huffed. "They tried to come through Schonach, but we ran them back into the hills. They should know to leave a man's clock out of political matters. Bring it to me and I will repair it right away."

Casper came clambering into the cottage and headed straight for his damaged, beloved clock. "What is the matter?" Barbara asked.

"The peddler from Schonach is here," he blurted. "Can you imagine that? I have not seen the man since I bought the thing from him years ago, and now he is back just after it was damaged."

"Unbelievable," she gasped. "If he can repair that clock, it is definitely going with us."

He grabbed the clock and all the chains and quickly kissed her cheek. "You are right about that. I will be back!"

The peddler was able to repair the clock in less than a day, restoring it to full working order. Casper had it back on their wall the very next day. They also learned of the arrangements Karl had been making for all the people going to America. The next ship from Hamburg that could take them would be leaving on the fifth of August. They all decided that would be the date they would attempt to leave, giving them enough time to travel to Hamburg.

Casper sat with Barbara at their table as the clock ticked in the background. "If we are to go to Nevers, we will have to leave sooner than the others. We would then have to meet them at the port in Hamburg."

Barbara thought for a moment of how soon they could leave. She looked at him and asked, "You are done with the harvest?"

"Almost. Nothing others cannot finish."

"And your wages?"

Casper answered casually, "I plan to collect them at day's end tomorrow."

Barbara shrugged her shoulders and said, "Well, today is the second. Why not head to Paris on the train on the fourth. We may as well start our journey sometime."

"The fourth of July?" he asked with a smile. "You do know what that date signifies, do you not?"

"No. What does it mean?"

He laughed even louder. "That is the day of independence for America. That is the day we will start our journey."

Word spread quickly that the Rees' were leaving the next morning, so at the end of the workday, all manner of people gathered at Helmut's tavern. When Casper and Barbara walked in, they were overwhelmed. Everyone they knew was there to send them off with a grand celebration.

Helmut gave him a large pint of beer and said, "Herbolzheim will not be the same without you folks. May God be with you. I just wish you were not taking my waitress with you."

"Thank you, old friend. We will look after her, I promise."

The music played and the beer flowed, and people danced into the night. At three years old, Bertha never quite understood the meaning behind the wonderful gathering, but she would years later, even though she would remember very little of her hometown.

Well into the early morning hours, Casper stood outside Helmut's with Franz and Josepha, Viktor and Karl. Viktor stood shaking his hand, saying, "I wish you were not leaving, Casper, but I understand why you are doing it. Take care of my sister."

"I will, Viktor. If you ever change your mind or your sister Johanna's, please follow us. The more we are the better we are as a family. I have only one wish for you, Viktor. And that is to do

your best to stay away from the fight. The town needs you here."
He turned to Karl and Franz and said, "Make sure you look after
Anna. We will meet you in Hamburg no later than the fourth of
August."

Josepha gave Barbara a hug. "Say hello to Paris for me. I hope
you find what you are searching for in Nevers."

"Thank you," she said graciously. "So do I."

Casper had the only piece of luggage they owned sitting on the
table in their cottage. They had put everything they had of value
into the small footlocker. The clock was carefully wrapped and
stowed at the bottom along with other personal items and
valuables. He left one narrow space at the top for one more item.
He walked over to the fireplace and carefully took down the
framed parchment and Barbara wrapped it delicately in a cloth and
then they slid it into the specially made slot in the locker and shut
the lid.

"Everything we have is in this small case," Barbara fretted. "As
if our whole life were stuffed into one insignificant box."

Casper put his hands on her shoulders and smiled, "Even if it
sinks to the bottom of the Atlantic, we are still the Rees family.
This is not the end, my dear, but the beginning."

They climbed aboard the train to Paris and took their seats and
it was then they noticed all their friends and relatives had gathered
around the train on the platform. It seemed they had come from out
of nowhere and Casper pulled open the window and said to them,
"We did not know all of you were coming down here. Wait, we
will come out to you and say goodbye properly."

Father Georg interjected as the train whistle blew. "There is no
time, Casper. We only came down to see you off once more, and
to share a bit of a hangover with you."

Casper and Barbara began to laugh along with their tears. "I
have a bit of a sore head myself, Father," he said, still laughing.
"God bless you all. Thank you for coming down."

The train began to pull away and the crowd waved to them with
well wishes and tears. "God bless you on your journey!" Father
Georg called out.

The train slowly made its way to Paris through the rolling
Vosges mountains. Bertha was glued to the window as the train
chugged its way through the various mountain passes. The views

were breathtaking and the three of them sat excitedly as their adventure had begun and Casper opened the window to let in the cool mountain air. They were in awe of the vast ranges of green and the endless array of trees that stood like sentinels guarding the frontier.

After riding for nearly half a day, the terrain began to level on the valley floor. They rolled through thick forests, seeing birds of all kinds and wild animals galloping in and out of the thick brush. Bertha would giggle and smile with each deer she saw and especially loved seeing the hares scampering away from the clickety-clack of the train.

Day turned to evening and the sunset over the vast open spaces was spectacular. As darkness overtook the train car, the three family members rattled off to sleep with Bertha snuggled in between them.

The sound of the whistle awakened them as the train jolted to a stop. It was mid-morning the next day when they had arrived in Paris and the station was abuzz with activity as it was in the heart of the city.

They disembarked and searched for information about the departing trains and to get something to eat. When Barbara saw that he was looking to buy some food, she put her hand on his arm, saying, "We still have plenty that I wrapped for us before we left home."

"I know," he explained, "I just thought we may need to add to it. We do not know when we can depart for Nevers or what we will find in accommodations once we arrive."

They soon learned that the next train to the small village of Nevers was not until the next morning. Casper checked his money and then looked for a way out of the train station.

"Do we have enough to stay overnight and still be able to make the fare for the steam ship?" Barbara asked worriedly.

"Not to worry," he answered. "I planned for these contingencies for this side trip. We will be fine." He held out his arm to escort her and said, "Come, how often will we get a chance to explore Paris?" She smiled and grabbed Bertha's hand and they set off to explore the wonderous city.

They spent the day walking the lush gardens near the Seine River and the Champs-Élysées. They then took a carriage ride down the river to view the massive cathedral of Notre Dame. Casper marveled at the tremendous, yet ornate building and they walked inside and were in awe of the towering, decorative ceilings. They prayed together in the astonishing cathedral and then continued walking slowly down each side, observing all manner of sculptures and stained-glass windows.

"Have you ever imagined such a glorious church?" Casper asked in wonder.

"There are no words," Barbara gasped.

Their feet were tired after the long, glorious day of touring Paris and they found an inexpensive hotel near the station to stay the night. The next morning, they were at the depot bright and early awaiting the only train to Nevers and Barbara was on pins and needles as they waited on the platform.

"I am so nervous. I cannot believe we are doing this," she said, her voice filled with anxiety. "What will we find when we arrive there?"

"God will reveal it to us, my wife. I am excited too."

Bertha yanked on her sleeve and asked, "We will see the lady, Mama?"

"I do not know, Bertie. We will certainly try."

Soon, the train arrived, and they boarded and took their seats. They weren't expected to arrive in Nevers until mid-afternoon. The sky was overcast and drops of rain fell on the windows of the car as they slowly traveled southeast from Paris. Barbara sat somberly and patiently as the train rattled along and the clouds grew thicker and before long thunder and lightning could be heard and seen in the distance. She wrung her hands nervously together while Bertha and Casper fell asleep to the swaying of the train.

While they slept, the train drew closer to the small village of Nevers and Barbara couldn't sleep at all watching everything pass them by. The rain subsided and soon the sun began to peak around the gray and white clouds and before long, a rainbow formed amidst the light rain and sun rays. She shook her daughter awake and exclaimed, "Look, Bertie, a rainbow!"

Bertha's eyes widened in awe and she gasped, "Wow!"

They finally arrived in the charming village of Nevers and the skies were clear with a fresh smell of rain in the air as they stepped off the train.

Casper looked at his wife and asked, "Should we try to find the convent today?"

"Yes, yes," Barbara answered nervously.

"How is your French?"

She shook her head with a grin and said, "Better than yours. I could see that when we were in Paris. I will go and ask someone for directions." She approached a conductor and asked in French, "Pardon me, monsieur. Could you tell me which way to the Sisters of Charity convent?"

"Three blocks in that direction, madame," he answered politely.

Barbara gulped hard and answered, "Thank you, monsieur." She walked nervously back to her waiting husband and daughter and said, "Follow me."

They walked down the quiet streets of Nevers. There were a few people around, but it was quite the contrast to the bustling city of Paris. The small buildings and chalets were well-kept and summer vegetation and flowers were everywhere to see. They could tell the village was not large and Casper noticed but one hotel on the quiet main street.

They had walked the requisite three blocks when they came upon the largest building in the town. It was surrounded by a high beige stone wall that traversed another two blocks and around a bend. There was a small gate at the first corner and a simple lamppost adjacent to it.

Barbara walked across the street and approached the gate ahead of them. Etched in a cornerstone by the gate was the name *Couvent des Soeurs de la Charité*. Her heart pounded in her chest knowing they had finally found it.

Casper and Bertha came up behind her and he said, "This is it. Looks very impressive."

"Yes," she gulped once more. "I should ring the bell." She found the rope attached to a small bell on the side wall and gave it hard yank. Bertha covered her ears at the sound of the loud bell and Barbara stood nervously as they waited for someone to come out.

It seemed like an eternity to her, but only a minute had passed when a wooden door opened that stood more than fifty yards from the gate. A nun walked out dressed in a black habit and veil with her head wrapped in white that cascaded over her shoulders. With her hands clasped and her head bowed, she approached the large iron gate.

"Yes, madame?" she said in French. "Are you here to donate food for the poor?"

The question had stopped Barbara's entire train of thought for a split-second and she stammered, "Well...I..."

Casper stepped forward and quickly answered, "*Oui*, Sister. We have some food for the poor." He produced the pouch of food they had bought in Paris and offered it to the nun. "It is not much, but please, if it will help." Barbara watched stunned, still unable to get the words out.

"Thank you," the nun replied. "God bless you and your child."

She turned to walk back inside when Barbara snapped out of her trance. "Excuse me, please. I beg your pardon." The nun smiled and returned to the gate. "Might I ask, could it be possible to visit with one of your postulants, Bernadette Soubirous?"

"Are you a relative?" the nun asked.

Barbara looked at her husband and both shook their heads. "No, we are not," she answered.

The nun shook her head and said, "I am sorry. We do not allow visitors here at the abbey. God bless you." She turned and walked back inside and closed the door.

Barbara stood, clutching the gate and staring at the door, her eyes filling with tears as she trembled. She looked about helplessly, not able to control her emotions. Casper came and put his hands on her shoulders, trying to console her.

"Let us go and find a place to rest. Perhaps we can try again tomorrow."

She said nothing and continued to weep as they walked back down the street toward the hotel. She didn't sleep at all that night and just stared out the window of their room toward the convent. "She is there," she whispered to herself. "I can feel it."

The next morning, before Casper and Bertha had even gotten out of bed, Barbara was dressed and had already gone to buy some more food at an open-air market.

Casper was surprised when he saw the extra fruit and vegetables and said, "I thought we still had plenty from Herbolzheim. Why are you up so early?"

"I want to go back to the convent. If anything, we can bring more food for the needy. And all I can do is keep asking if we can see Bernadette. Maybe one of them will have a change of heart."

Casper looked over at Bertha who was still yawning and trying to wake up. "It is worth a try. Let us get up."

As they walked together toward the convent, birds were chirping and fluttering from tree to tree to Bertha's delight. She stopped every now and then to smell the flowers and roses that were in nearly every yard.

"It is a lovely town, is it not?" Casper asked. "If the young lady is here, I am happy she can be in such a peaceful village."

"She must be in there, Casper," Barbara answered. "I just know it. Yesterday when I asked for her by name, the sister did not say there was no one inside with that name. She just said they did not take visitors."

"She asked if we were relatives as well," Casper added.

"Exactly." Barbara made the sign of the cross as they approached the gate a second time. "God help us."

Again, she took a deep breath, and rang the small bell that hung on the outside wall. After a few moments, the wooden door opened, and the same nun slowly walked to the gate.

"Are you here to bring food for the poor?" she asked as she did the day before.

"Yes," Barbara replied with a smile. "I have brought many fresh vegetables and fruit, straight from the market."

The nun opened the gate and took the large bundle from her and said politely, "Bless you, child."

"Sister," Barbara pleaded, "I know visitors are not allowed, but we have traveled a great distance to be here. Could we possibly visit with Bernadette Soubirous? Just for a moment?"

"I am sorry," the nun repeated. "We do not allow visitors here at the abbey. God bless you." She slowly closed the gate and then proceeded back to the convent and closed the large wooden door.

Barbara stood at the gate, clutching the bars in terrible dismay. "What must I do, Lord?" she whined to herself.

Casper sympathized with her, knowing the result would be the same. "Let us walk around and see more of this lovely town, shall we? It will help brighten our mood."

They walked down the street that flowed along the side wall of the convent and found a small café at the corner opposite of where the wall rounded a bend. An iron fence about ten feet across stood between the breaks in the wall as it curved around and lined the convent grounds. A small park bench sat alongside the short stretch of iron fence, with rose bushes on either side of it.

"What a lovely setting," Barbara said to herself as they sat at a sidewalk table in front of the café.

"Some hot tea and cold milk will do us good," Casper said. "And perhaps a warm pastry." Bertha was delighted at the thought. Then Casper noticed a small shop next door that sold religious items and trinkets. "Maybe I will step inside and have a quick browse while you finish your tea."

Barbara sat with Bertha as they had their pastries, and she couldn't keep her eyes off the beautiful roses that lined the small iron fence on either side of the park bench across the street. There were three shrubs on either side of the bench, all with pink or yellow roses. Just on the other side of the fence was a single bush with stunning red roses. Barbara smiled at the simplistic splendor and beauty of the small scene.

Casper emerged from the tiny store with a curious smile on his face. "Look at what I found in this delightful little shop," he said. "I thought this would be something we could read on the train and on the ship."

"What is it?" she asked curiously.

Casper displayed a small book that was written in German. "It is a book about particular Catholic saints throughout history. It must be in relation to the young Soubirous girl."

"Oh, my," Barbara exclaimed. "Related in what way?"

"It is collection of writings from various saints who were visionaries. Those who heard the voice of God and were sent as His messengers."

Barbara gasped again and responded, "Goodness in Heaven."

"Look," Casper continued joyfully, "these are just some of the people mentioned: Saint Gertrude of Helfta, Saint Hildegard of Bingen, and it even has a chapter pertaining to Saint Patrick."

"How wonderful. I know how you adore Saint Patrick."

Casper shrugged with a smile, saying, "Well, my mother was part Irish as you know, and father was a bit Irish too. Welsh and English as I recall."

"Is there anything about Bernadette's visions?" she asked.

Casper shook his head and replied, "I am afraid not. What she witnessed must still be in the process of being documented. But is it not fascinating?" He set the book down and immediately Bertha scooped it up. "You know, dear, we should not stay much longer than tomorrow. We need to give ourselves as much time as possible to reach Hamburg on time. The first train back to Paris tomorrow is at ten in the morning."

Barbara nodded sorrowfully, staring at the book in Bertha's hands. "I know."

Bertha looked up from the book and said, "I like the pictures of the saints, Papa."

The next morning, Barbara was already dressed again long before her family had awakened. She again had hardly slept the night before and her red, bloodshot eyes had dark, sagging circles under them. Casper awakened and looked at her sympathetically as he could tell she hadn't slept much again.

"We should leave as soon as you are ready," she said softly.

He nodded and said, "Of course."

They walked down together and stood outside the hotel and Casper looked at his pocket watch and said, "We still have a couple hours before the train departs. Would you like to walk down there one last time?"

Barbara nodded tiredly and said, "I suppose."

They walked down the quiet street while Bertha again skipped along, smelling the flowers and waving to the birds in the air. Barbara looked sadly at the convent as they approached it a third time. "We have nothing to give any longer," she lamented. She reached up and gave the bell one hard pull.

Moments later, the wooden door opened, and the now familiar nun came out to greet them. "Yes, madame? Are you here to bring food for the poor?"

Barbara shook her head sadly and answered, "No, Sister. I do apologize. We have no extra funds to buy more food for them. We only wished to come and give our best to you and to the postulant Bernadette Soubirous. I know we cannot visit, but I just wanted to tell you that. Please tell her we are praying for her and all the Sisters of Charity."

The nun nodded and said in reply, "God bless you, child." She quietly turned and walked back inside and closed the door.

Casper glanced at Barbara, thinking she might be crying but she wasn't. "I think we both know the young lady does reside here. Maybe it is enough that at least we have seen her new home."

Barbara became very distraught as she stepped away from the gate. "Why should it be enough? Why am I forbidden to look upon the child? She stood in *front* of the Virgin Mother. On the same ground she conversed with Her. Does not anyone see what a miracle that is?"

"Of course, we do, my love," Casper answered. "But that is why she is here. She was brought here for a reason. Closed off from the world, from gawkers and curious people. She was brought here because the whole world sought her out. We should honor her wishes and let her be at peace."

"What about *my* peace?" Barbara cried. "I do not wish to disturb her or raise her upon a pedestal. But my soul will not rest until I know that she *is*. To actually see a child who has spoken to and *seen* our Virgin Mother. Why can *I* not be at peace?" She walked quickly down the street along the wall and fretted and stammered. "This idea of America has overwhelmed me. I know it is I who raised the notion of leaving, but I am *tormented* still. And I must find what I am searching for before I can go on. I *must*. I know my answer lies here." She raised her voice to the Heavens and said, "God, please *help* me find it."

She cried and tears rolled down her cheeks as she continued walking until she came upon the park bench at the corner surrounded by rose bushes. Casper and Bertha came and stood by her and letting out a deep sigh, he said, "We will let you calm down and go over to the café. We will wait as long as you need, love." She sniffed and nodded yes to them.

She sat on the bench and could smell the fragrant scent of the flowers all around her. She closed her eyes and took in a deep breath, trying to calm herself.

While she sat, she heard a voice nearby, saying, "The golden roses are so beautiful."

Startled, Barbara opened her eyes, and she was surprised to see a young girl, no more than twenty, sitting on the other side of the iron fence. She was dressed in a black habit and plain white veil. Barbara turned around on the bench to face her and said, "I am sorry, I did not see you there, Sister. Yes, they are quite beautiful."

"I so admire their beauty and the colorfulness of God's nature," said the young lady.

Barbara smiled at the young girl's polite demeanor and she felt at ease speaking to her. "I enjoy it outside too," Barbara said. "It is where I like to go if I am sad or need uplifting. You have such a lovely garden here."

The young girl replied, "God gives us the birds and the trees and flowers to uplift us. To bring us joy amongst sorrow." Before Barbara could say anything, the young girl reached through the fence and placed her hand on hers, saying, "Do not be afraid for your journey. God will be with you and deliver you safely. And many blessings there will be on your house."

Barbara tried not to cry as she squeezed her hand in return. "Thank you, Sister. That means so much to me."

Just then, an older nun came out and said to the young woman, "Come along now, Marie Bernarde." The nun helped her to her feet as they walked slowly back to the abbey.

The young woman turned with a slight smile and said to Barbara, "Goodbye." She stumbled along the way as she turned, with one leg appearing to be hobbled, as the other nun held her steady.

At hearing the girl's name, Barbara's eyes widened as she caught her breath in a stunned gasp. Her jaw fell open with her hand to her mouth in disbelief, her face flushed red with shock. Tears streamed down her face as she watched the young lady being helped back inside. She composed herself, trying not to cry as she watched them take every step. Before they reached the door, she saw Bernadette turn and smile back at her one last time. As the door closed, Barbara buried her face into her arms and wept profusely.

Casper emerged from the café carrying two coffees and Bertha with her milk and pastries. They sat down to see Barbara sauntering up with a huge smile on her face. "Is one of those coffees for me?" she asked in a bubbly voice.

"Indeed, it is," Casper answered with an odd grin. "You seem more cheerful now."

"Yes, I am, my dear husband. Yes, I am." She smiled at him and then she caressed Bertha's cheek and said, "You may not believe this, but I just saw her. I even spoke with her."

Casper was dumbfounded. "You *did*?" Where?"

"Right across the street. I did not even realize there was another bench beside the red roses. Yet, there she was. Sitting there, smiling and enjoying the garden. Another Sister came along and called her Marie Bernarde."

"And you are certain that is her religious name?"

"As certain as the day is long, my love." She grabbed Bertha and lifted her up, spinning her around. "Oh, I am so happy! I love you so much, little Bertie!"

"I love you too, Mama!" the little girl giggled as she twirled around.

Casper sat and smiled in happiness and total awe. "Astounding," he said. "Simply astounding."

It took them the better part of three weeks to get back to Paris and then make their way to the northern coast of Germany. On the third of August, they arrived in Hamburg and were lucky enough to find the Doerle family and Karl and Anna. They had only arrived in Hamburg the day before. Together, the eight of them were able to secure passage on the steamer, *SS Borussia.*

The morning of the fifth, everyone in the anxious group rose early from their modest confines at the Hamburg Boardinghouse, which was situated near the port specifically for cross-Atlantic passengers. Between the Rees' and Doerle's and Karl and Anna, they had only three steamer trunks to carry. Casper and Franz handled two of them while Karl and Anna carried the other. Barbara and Josepha looked after the children as the group slowly made its way to the boarding area.

The streets were crowded with workers and travelers alike, so they stayed as close together as possible. After rounding the corner of the lengthy customs house, they finally were able to see their ship for the first time. They all stopped and stared at the long, yet narrow steamer ship that was lined with three towering sailing masts. The ship had a muddy brown and black appearance and clearly showed its age and ocean wear. The *Borussia* was one of a dozen or more steamer ships that routinely made the passage to New York, and it was easy to see that she had seen many voyages.

"It is big," Casper blurted.

Karl stood shaking his head in awe and said, "I have never seen a ship so large."

"And we will be aboard at least two weeks," Anna added, looking on in disbelief.

They slowly made their way to a large tent that fronted the gangway to the *Zwischendeck*, or steerage compartment. Casper went to the head of the line when their turn came.

"Name?" asked the immigration official. He sat waiting to jot down all the passenger's names and ages.

"Rees," Casper answered.

"How many in your party and their names and age and occupation?"

"Three. Casper, thirty-four, farmer. Barbara, twenty-eight, housewife and our child Bertha, age three."

The man quickly jotted down their information on a ledger for the manifest and quickly waved them along. "Next!"

Karl and Anna stepped forward and did the same, then Franz followed with his family of six.

As Barbara carried Bertha up the rickety gangway, she looked over her shoulder at Casper and asked worriedly, "We are really doing this?"

"Yes," he answered, grappling with the trunk. "We are doing it. Do not worry."

The group made it onboard and found their bunks in the massive steerage compartment that comprised of a single room almost the entire length of the bowels of the ship. There were no windows and only two narrow staircases on either end that led to the outside promenade deck. The steerage passengers were only allowed outside on deck during certain hours and only in small, assigned groups, and only if weather permitted.

Barbara stared at the cramped bunks and mumbled, "This is it for a long time."

The eight travelers set sail from Hamburg later that morning, August 5, 1865. They traveled up the picturesque river Elbe and into the North Sea. The *Borussia* then sailed through the English

Channel and out into the northern Atlantic and the next day they sailed past the last piece of land before heading to open waters.

Casper stood with his wife and daughter as the seas were calm and their group of steerage passengers could mingle about on deck.

"What do you think that land is there?" Barbara asked.

"It is Ireland, I am certain of it," Casper answered.

"Ah, the Emerald Isle. How wonderful!"

Casper added, "And the home of the Bishop of Ireland, Saint Patrick."

Seventeen days later, the weary travelers arrived in New York at the Castle Garden depot that was situated on the tip of Manhattan. After two weeks at sea, the ground was wobbly under their feet, but they soon adjusted. The throng of activity at the customs house was more than enough distraction as they filed slowly through the process.

After hours of waiting to get through, they finally emerged into the American metropolis of New York. With little command of English, they were able to find the railway station and secured passage to Chicago.

As they waited, tired and beleaguered at the railway station, they took notice of the huge throng of people passing by. People of all manner of cultures and occupations, going from one place to another. Others were railway attendants who were daily fixtures in the organized chaos.

Casper shook his head in amazement, saying, "After four long years of war, everyone is so incredibly busy. It is as if the activity never stops in America. Fascinating."

"And they do not even notice us," Barbara added. "We do not speak a word of English and we still just blend right in."

"We are like everyone else here, my love," Casper said, holding her hand as they sat. "Other than the natives out west, everyone else is an emigrant just as we are. Here for different reasons but with the same goal in mind. Freedom."

Four days passed when they arrived on the banks of Lake Michigan in Chicago and tiredly waited for the next train that would bring them south to Springfield.

One day later, they arrived in the small station in the heart of Illinois and Casper looked desperately around for a place to get some food for his hungry family. He and Franz were walking everywhere when they came upon a regiment of Union soldiers in blue uniforms marching down the street in unison. As they stood and watched the small parade, they spotted a flier on the wall of a shop. "What does it say?" Casper asked.

"I do not know," Franz admitted.

Suddenly a young man came waltzing up and asked in a cheerful tone, "Wanna see where honest Abe lived right here in Springfield?" Casper and Franz both politely smiled with confused expressions. "Yep, old honest Abe lived and worked here as a lawyer and then became a state legislator long before he was ever president." He handed them a copy of the same flier they had seen on the wall. "Be sure to tour the home of 'ol honest Abe. Enjoy the sights folks and welcome to the land of Lincoln!"

Casper looked at Franz crazily and asked, "What did he say about Lincoln?"

"Beats me."

The train to Quincy would not leave until the next morning. It would make one stop at Quincy and then head across the Mississippi to Saint Joseph, Missouri which was the end of the line.

The eight travelers sat at a tavern just outside the station the night before they boarded what they hoped would be their last train. As Karl jogged up with his ticket, he leaned over to Casper and said, "Should be there by noon tomorrow."

Casper smiled tiredly and clinked his beer mug to Karl's and said, "I will drink to that."

The next morning, the air was full of anticipation and excitement as Casper looked at his wife and daughter and said, "Tonight we will sleep in our new homeland, God willing."

The whole troop boarded the train and set out and after five long hours, the train steamed into the small station at Quincy just after twelve in the afternoon. They slowly disembarked and stretched their tired legs and immediately began checking out their new surroundings.

Casper noticed large fir trees and abundant groves of birch. As they walked through the depot and emerged on the other side, he took in a long breath of fresh air. "Feels very similar to Germany," he said to himself.

As they got their bearings, they looked around the small, town square that seemed to be situated near some high bluffs. He had momentarily lost track of Bertha when he whirled around looking for her.

Out of nowhere, Bertha came racing up to him and his wife and exclaimed, "Papa, come see this!"

They staggered to keep up with her until she came to the edge of a dirt path and pointed out over the bluffs at a tremendous view of the Mississippi River. Then he noticed the incredible railway bridge that expanded across the mighty river.

"Incredible!" Casper bellowed.

"Oh, my goodness," Barbara exclaimed. "It is beautiful!"

Just then, they heard a voice speaking to them in German. "I helped build that bridge, you know?"

Casper spun around to see his cousin, Heinrich, grinning from ear to ear. Standing next to him was a young woman and three children.

"Heinrich!" Casper exclaimed. "How did you know we would be here?"

"I received a telegram not long ago from Father Georg. We have been checking every train since then."

Casper was astounded and answered, "A telegram, how about that? Old Father Georg!" He motioned to his fellow travelers and said, "You remember Barbara's brother Franz and wife Josepha. And these young men are their boys." He put his hand on Karl's shoulder and said, "This is Karl Winter, and this young lady is Miss Anna Ilg. The best waitress Helmut ever had."

Heinrich laughed and said, "I am so happy you finally arrived." He looked over at his wife and said, "Meet the family. This is my wife, Sarah, and these are our boys, Michael and John and our daughter Connie."

Casper tipped his hat and said, "A pleasure to meet all of you. Barbara you know, and this little lady is Bertha, or Bertie as we call her. Bertie, this is your Uncle Heinrich and Aunt Sarah."

"Hello!" she said cheerfully. She ran up to Connie and gave her a nice hug. "I love your home."

Barbara looked at Casper and took off his cap and gave him a huge bear hug. Then she lovingly kissed him on the cheek, saying, "I love our new home too."

Coda

Casper and Barbara Rees settled in nicely in the close-knit German community of Quincy, Illinois. Together, they had three more children in Quincy; Heinrich, who was named in memory of their first son, and Edward and Josephine.

Casper continued his work as an engineer and stone mason and began his own business that specialized in Earth-moving necessary for digging basements, filling hollows, grading streets, and putting in sewer and water lines. He not only helped build the modern roads in Quincy, but in many surrounding communities. The business of Rees Construction is still in operation today.

In 1866, the tensions between Prussia and Austria reached a boiling point and resulted in a horrific conflict called the Seven Weeks War or the Austro-Prussian War. Men were recruited far and wide for this bloody conflict that resulted in the deaths of over 150,000 men and countless scores of injured.

At the same time in France, Bernadette Soubirous took her vows on July 29, 1866 at the Sisters of Charity convent. Unfortunately, since childhood, she had suffered from such diseases as cholera and chronic asthma. Later in life she developed a painful tumor on her knee due to tuberculosis. She was never able to return to Lourdes to see the dedication of the Basilica of the Immaculate Conception in 1876, a church the 'lady' had asked to be built during one of Bernadette's many visions. She died at the young age of thirty-five on April 16, 1879.

The city of Lourdes attracts millions of pilgrims to the grotto at Massabielle each year. Replicas of the sight have been built in numerous places around the world, including the campus of Notre Dame in South Bend, Indiana. Her visions of the Virgin Mary are well-documented and are an important part of Catholic doctrine. To this day, miraculous cures continue to be attributed to the waters at Massabielle.

She was declared Saint Bernadette of Lourdes by Pope Pius XI in June 1925. Miraculously, her body lies incorrupt in a glass coffin that is displayed at the Sisters of Charity Convent in Nevers, France.

Epilogue

Michael and Anna Rees were the earliest ancestors directly linked to my family. In his genealogical research, my father was able to trace them all the way to Casper Rees, who was my great-great grandfather.

The travelers aboard the *SS Borussia* arrived seventeen days later in New York on August 22, 1865, four months after the Civil War had ended. Casper and Barbara would have three more children after their historic voyage across the Atlantic.

Casper was still relatively young when he passed away in 1890 at the age of fifty-nine. Barbara passed away four years later one day after her fifty-seventh birthday. That same year of 1894, my grandfather, Frank Henry Rees, was born. He lived to the ripe old age of ninety-five.

My parents, Richard and Claudia, are still going strong and have been married now for an incredible sixty-three years at the time of this writing.

The rest of my siblings and cousins are scattered across the United States, including Illinois, Missouri, Maryland, Washington D.C., Louisiana, Mississippi and Texas, just to name a few. Not to mention the many Rees descendants that still reside in Quincy.

Quincy has held onto its strong German roots throughout the centuries and still plays a pivotal role in commerce with its central location along the Mississippi River in the heart of the Midwest.

As I stated earlier, it was not an easy task selecting the historical holy figures depicted in these stories. I chose them due to the inspiring stories they themselves had and the great impact they had on their communities, the Celtic culture and the world. Some are more obscure than others but still the importance of each saint is no less than the other. It is just seven examples of how ordinary people throughout the centuries can have a profound impact on one family or even an entire melting pot of cultures.

This book is not just dedicated to the Rees family, but to all my family, especially those who were gone too soon: My grandmother Helen Lennert Rees, my maternal grandparents Claudia and James Henry, Uncle Tom and his daughter Susan, Aunt Madeline and Uncle Tony, Uncle Bud and my brother John. In my life, these were just some of the people who showed that you don't have to be in the history books to live beatific lives.

As I said before, there are saints among us and all we need is God's grace to shine a little light for us to see them. Then we may see that there is a bit of sanctity in all of us. *God bless*.

Foreground: Casper Rees (right) and his eldest son, Heinrich (left), standing with the work crew of Rees Construction in downtown Quincy, Illinois, paving the corner of 12th and Locust Street – circa 1880's.

Made in the USA
Monee, IL
30 September 2021